Blooming Time

A Where is Now Story

Mary S. Sheppard

ISBN13: 978-0-9860575-1-9
ISBN10: 0986057517

Cover art by David Campbell
Photo licensed through Depositphotos images.

Visit my website: www.maryssheppard.com

Dedication

*I have been fortunate to have many supporters to allow
me to write and to encourage me and I dedicate my first
book to them. I'd like to thank first and foremost, my
husband, Greg, who not only helped with "like" and "dislike"
opinions, but also in helping me distill the future. Thanks
also to my sisters and friends who didn't mind being the
guinea pigs and read the first versions of this book,
especially Najoo, Rosa, Kacie and Carol. And finally to my
parents, who never questioned my dreams.*

Table of Contents

Temporal Transporter Travel Rules and Processes
– Amended for BIOTIME LABS - version 1.0

1. The Temporal Transporter, or TT, can only be used to go back in time, for time regression.
2. The lab set all the target dates to pre-2000. This will ensure that travelers will not have contact with themselves. There is no need to use any target dates after the year 2000 to meet their goals.
3. Time travel process –
   a. Time and space are carefully calculated to ensure the traveler arrives to a good location in the past.
   b. The TT pushes travelers to the past and pulls them back to the present. It is the main driver.
   c. The transport markers help with the return. The transport marker provides additional energy and also encapsulates the traveler for safety during transport.
   d. Once the transport marker is set in a location and time, it can be used immediately to transport the traveler back to the lab.
   e. If further regression is required, the time travel setter returns to the marker, retrieves it and goes back another year from there. This can be done as many times as needed.
   f. Transport markers are not set in every year. They are currently limited in number and their reuse allows further time regression.
   g. Initially transport markers are moved back one year each day. Regressions of a year in one day have been confirmed to have no ill effects on the time traveler. (See Notes).
   h. To return to 2066 and the lab, you must be in physical contact with the transport marker. Two people can travel together.
4. Influencing the present with actions while in the past is illegal. The Time Travel Committee will determine the gravity of the infraction and the appropriate punishment will be applied.
5. Keep contact with the locals to a minimum. The lab will check the people's lifeline to see if any changes have

occurred once the traveler has contact with them. Not knowing whom you will encounter ahead of time, the first meeting might have some influence, but from then on it is monitored.

6. Lifelines are the plot of a person's life and can only be plotted for the past.
7. Hours in the past match the hours in the present.
   a. If the location is the same, i.e. Pacific Time for both the lab and the travelers, the time of day is the same.
   b. This lab will also match the day of the week to simplify things, especially in communicating with one another.
8. The transport marker provides a transport radius of 800 kilometers. Arrival location can be anywhere within that radius.
9. The transport marker should be moved from a location after a certain number of uses (to be determined on a case by case basis).
10. All time travel setters will have a location chip implanted subdermally to help in locating them if lost or injured.

Notes: The calculations take almost a day to complete, but larger regressions are being considered. Currently regressions of three years in one day are the norm and up to five year regressions are being considered.

Chapter 1
BioTime Labs

Amy looked up from her work and realized it was time. "They should be here soon. Do you want to go?"

Her assistant Susan nodded. "This trip was longer than any other, so it will be nice to see them back."

Both walked out of the lab and took the metal stairs down. BioTime Laboratory occupied a large warehouse. Several smaller labs, just like Amy's, hugged one wall along the first and second floors, while along the opposite wall, management, medical and human resources had their offices To the far right was the cafeteria, and the giant electric generators were to the left. And out in the middle of the warehouse stood a raised platform with a large spherical cage on top: the Temporal Transporter. Next to it was a smaller structure that looked like the scanner in an airport and this was used for the transport of objects.

A group of people had already gathered around the platform with the spherical shaped object. The size of the group was smaller than the first times, but it still numbered in the dozens.

"This is still exciting," said Susan.

"Yes, it is hard to imagine when it will become routine."

"Well, I hope I get selected to go before that happens. I am ready to drop everything with a moment's notice."

Amy doubted Susan would have a chance to go anytime soon as she was just an assistant. She didn't want to burst her bubble, but many others, including herself, would go before. Currently there were twenty-eight candidates on the approved list and almost all were more qualified than Susan.

"I do understand why they are sending people like Gustav and Anthony right now," Susan continued. "They need men to set things up in the past, but soon they will include women, and your project is so valuable I am sure it will be among the first selected."

Yes, history seemed to favor men, thought Amy. Men were able to travel freely and they were allowed access to many places closed to women, so it was natural men were the first travelers. These first travelers left the time transport markers in the years they visited. They were called time travel setters, or time setters for short.

Her project was one of eight currently being evaluated. Each was dedicated to a different period in time and to a different place around the world. The scientists were aware of the work the others were doing and each competed with the others, vying to be the first to be selected.

Of course she thought hers was one of the most important, but she also knew she was biased. She told Susan so.

"No, I know the corydalis curvisiliqua is considered a top priority."

Amy was going to ask her how she knew, but they had arrived at the structure and Susan left her to move near the front.

"Did you hear?" whispered a fellow scientist next to her.

"Hi, George. Hear what?" asked Amy.

"They placed a marker near Durango."

"Durango?" she repeated with amazement. It had to be her project, she thought. There were no other projects that required that location. "Durango, 1895?"

George smiled at her. "Of course."

"You really think my project will be next, George?" she asked, trying not to be too hopeful.

"It looks that way. I guess congratulations may be in order."

"I would wait for the formal announcement before you do that."

Suddenly the lights flickered briefly and through the curved metal piping and wiring, two human forms appeared. The group clapped in excitement and self-congratulations. This trip had involved staying in the past for many days, and it had been completed successfully. The travelers had now returned to 2066.

As Anthony and Gustav stepped down from the platform, Dr. Holbrook greeted them. Together they headed to his office to be debriefed. With as many trips as they had done, Amy knew that BioTime should be getting closer to launching an actual mission.

Susan rejoined Amy and they returned to the lab together.

"Susan, how could you know that my project is at the top of the list?"

"Are you blind?"

That didn't answer her question, so Amy just looked at Susan.

"I know," Susan rolled her eyes. "If it does not concern your project, you barely notice, but Danny and I are dating, and he tells me things."

Danny, thought Amy, as in Dr. Daniel Holbrook? It was strange to hear him referred by his first name, much less Danny. Many scientists on the project, including her, had the title of doctor, but few used their titles. Dr. Daniel Holbrook, head of BioTime Laboratory, was the exception, insisting everyone use the title when addressing him. Many even used the title when talking about him, although the adjectives that followed in those cases were not as nice.

"You really didn't know that we have been going out seriously for several months? Didn't you see us at lunch together?'

"I don't think so," she said. She would have remembered.

"Well, open your eyes, Amy. I know work is important, but it is not everything."

Yeah, sure, she thought, returning to the data that was projected around her. The data was coming together nicely and soon the conversation with Susan was out of her mind.

Amy was positive the flower she was studying, the corydalis curvisiliqua, would prove to be the cure for depression. After running hundreds of tests, she had found that, based on the chemical content, the plant was the solution. Almost equally exciting was finding it had no discernable side effects. Of course, without having the real plant, she had to assume some of the chemical characteristics, and that is why it was important to get an actual specimen. Nature usually offered the best way of assembling chemicals so that they worked well together. She was even hoping that once she had the plant she could test it to cure other nervous diseases.

"Susan, can you set up the centrifuge again? I am ready to run another test."

"Oh," said Susan looking at the clock. "I have a lunch date with Danny at noon."

There was still twenty minutes before then, thought Amy. "Can you at least set it up? I will finish."

"I'm sorry about that," said Susan starting the preparations. "I didn't know you were planning to work through lunch."

Amy rarely stopped working at noon. Susan should have known this after the two months they had worked together. Susan had been not been at BioTime much before that. In fact, now that Amy remembered, it was Dr. Holbrook's strong recommendation that had gotten Susan the job as her assistant. It made sense now. Susan was his type; 5'6", blonde, slim and willing to be devoted to him.

Luckily, it turned out she was not a bad assistant, and Amy would give her a B, maybe B + for effort when she was in the lab. She had good research qualities, learned quickly and was smart when motivated, but she lacked focus, had no confidence and constantly belittled her work. If you did that too often, everyone would start to believe that what you did was trivial.

After Susan left for lunch, she started to graph the results in a projection in the space in front of her. She changed parameters, re-plotting the results and moved the elements until she could see all of them clearly in three dimensions. She liked to add colors and patterns to the graphs feeling it made her see things more intuitively. Suddenly Susan walked in and Amy realized that two hours had gone by.

"Amy, did you eat lunch?"

"No, I was in the middle of this. It is interesting to see how the chemicals interaction with each other."

"I think the cafeteria closed."

"That's all right, I think I have a nutrition bar in my desk."

"I could have brought you something," said Susan returning to her stool. "I realize now that you didn't know about Danny and me because you skip lunch so often."

It may be true, thought Amy. She found a nutrition bar and munched on it as she thought of how to set up the next experiment.

Soon she had filled the lab with multiple projections. Together, they started processing the chemical signatures, graphing the results, and then reprocessing for different characteristics. Susan was at her best here, and they went through the variations quickly. Hours later they took a break.

"I think it is time to go home. I'll see you tomorrow?" Susan started to pack her things.

"Wow," said Amy noticing it was close to seven. She smiled. "Time flies when you are having fun. Isn't this late for you?"

"It looked like you needed the help," said Susan

"I appreciate it." Amy stretched and turned away from the projections. "Do you have a date with Dr. Holbrook?" She would never be able to call him 'Danny'.

"No, he said he was busy tonight."

"He is probably debriefing Anthony and Gustav."

"No, that was done earlier," said Susan a bit distracted. "You want to get some dinner with me?"

"Sorry, maybe another day. I really want to try to finish a couple more graphs and then call it a night. I also want to get in early to talk to Dr. Holbrook about some of my ideas."

"I understand. Well, good night," said Susan leaving.

It was past nine when Amy reached her apartment. Even though she was forty kilometers from work, up in the Hayward hills, it took less than ten minutes on the fast train. Proximity to the lab was one of the reasons she had picked that location. She also liked the fact there were several regional open spaces nearby and she had hoped to enjoy them at some point. Of course that was the plan, but her usual late working hours did not help.

She opened her fridge and found milk, a couple eggs, some suspect raviolis and a bunch of dried up green onions. The freezer had frozen chicken and pizza. She had had pizza yesterday, she thought. Maybe she could make an omelet, but without vegetables or cheese it didn't seem appetizing. The chicken? It was too much effort, so that was out. Tomorrow, after work, she would leave a bit earlier and stop at the grocery store. She started heating the pizza. At least it has onions and tomatoes, she thought.

She called her aunt while she waited. Aunt Betty had raised her after her parents had died so she was much more than just an aunt. She tried to call at least once a week.

"Amy, how are you?" Aunt Betty answered right away.

"Fine, sorry it's kind of late Aunt Betty."

"You must be working late again."

"Yeah."

"Did you eat something?"

"I'm heating it up right now."

"I'm glad you can make your own meals. Isn't your domestic aide on the blink?"

"Yeah, I just sent him in; it's just a software upgrade."

"It seems 'he' has not been too helpful so far. I haven't seen a reason to buy a newer aide."

Her aunt's aide was very primitive. It didn't shop or prepare meals; it only cleaned. "He will be good as new."

"I hope so, my dear. Luckily, I like to cook, so I don't need something else doing that for me. Speaking of that, you should come over to dinner this weekend."

"I'll try Aunt Betty, but we're working seven days a week."

"Are you still working on that yellow flower project?"

"Yes, it is coming along quite nicely."

"And is Susan, your new assistant, working out?"

"Yeah, Susan is doing all right. She is a fast learner."

"I ran into Ryan's mother the other day. She says he also works at BioTime."

"I think I have seen him."

"He was a nice boy in high school. I remember you went out with him."

"Not exactly, I went out in a group and he happened to be there."

"Oh? This could be an opportunity to go out with him. His mother said he is not in a relationship."

Oh great, thought Amy. Her aunt was going into the matchmaking mode. "I don't see him much. He works in a different part of the lab and he has different interests."

"You mean interests other than work? Amy, you can't just have one thing in your life. You have to try to get out more."

"Sure, Aunt Betty. I'll try." She had learned that it was easier to promise than to disagree.

Chapter 2
The time is now

Dr. Holbrook stood at the front of the auditorium as the large group of employees of BioTime filed in.

Amy had not had a chance to talk to Dr. Holbrook in the morning. His assistant, Beebe Chavez, told her he was busy. "He has asked me to make sure he is not interrupted, since he is getting ready for an important meeting."

Amy saw two silhouettes through the frosted glass of his office door. "Someone is with him?"

"Yes, Francine from the government agency, you know, one of our sponsors."

Amy knew about the sponsors. The government, through the agency called GovTime, had been first to travel through time. That had been about a year ago. Since then, the government had started to license the technology to others.

BioTime was the first company to be awarded the license, due to their altruistic objective of curing diseases. She also knew that bringing plants from the past was thought to be easy.

She saw the shadows move and they appeared to merge, but she knew it could be a trick of perspective.

"Isn't that funny," said Beebe, pointing out the same thing, "I always wonder about that."

Yes, quite funny, thought Amy.

Later that morning all employees were invited to a meeting. Everyone was quite eager to attend, as the subject line was 'Decision Time'.

Dr. Holbrook took the stage as the last stragglers took their seat. "I have called this meeting for an important announcement. We have made a decision on what the first project will be."

The buzzing of the crowd intensified and several people looked towards Amy. George waved and signaled thumbs up. Amy's heart stopped.

"But first I would like to thank our intrepid time travel setters," started Dr. Holbrook. "As all of you know, this group have been at it for several months, and due to their dedication and effort, we now have several transport markers placed in key destinations. Please, if you could stand as I call your name, Anthony Kane, Gustav Jones, Ryan Campbell, Don Gillespie," he continued as all twelve men stood up.

Most of these men had traveled in quick bursts. They went back in time, one year, set a transport marker and then returned to 2066. The following day they would return to the transport marker, wherever it was, retrieve it, and move back another year before returning to the lab again. It was a painstaking process, but it had been determined to be the safest.

Everyone had concerns on how fast one could move through time, so they were doing it cautiously. Of course, safety was always balanced with impatience and faster returns, and Amy knew that was a constant struggle. She also knew that in the last month they had successfully tested going back three years in one day. Three times faster, she thought, was three times better.

The transport marker was the key to everything. Without it, one could not get back home. While the laboratory machine did most of the work, pushing and pulling the traveler through time, the transport marker created a gas encapsulant that would protect the traveler when he returned. It also provided an extra boost of energy to ensure the traveler made it back.

"There they are," said Dr. Holbrook interrupting her daydreaming. "Here are our time travelers, our heroes. Thank you for your work." He led the group in clapping their appreciation.

"And now for the announcement you have been waiting for. Our first project is," Dr. Holbrook took a dramatic pause, "the search for the corydalis curvisiliqua."

A huge smile broke on Amy's face. Some of the scientists nearby mumbled their congratulations and she acknowledged happily.

Susan, sitting next to her, squeezed her hand and whispered, "Congrats."

Dr. Holbrook outlined the reasoning for the choice. They had just planted the transport markers in 1895 successfully, and the area around it was quite desolate, meaning minimum local interaction. The mission itself was straightforward and preparations for it were further along than others. Most of the components, including clothing, money and implements of the era, were ready to go. In addition, the return on investment would be quick, as there was a high degree of confidence that the particular plant could be used to cure depression.

"The corydalis curvisiliqua has been extinct for over a hundred years, but it was quite ubiquitous in 1895. Of course, we will continue to place transport markers in the other sites and times and the next mission will depend..."

Amy stopped listening for a moment wondering who would travel with her. Having a man there would be helpful, and she looked around the room analyzing the options. One of the twelve time setters would not be a bad choice.

"We have also decided on the team that will be sent."

This is it, she thought, getting ready to stand up.

"Anthony and Gustav, please come up."

Amy blinked hard. She must have misheard, but she could see Anthony and Gustav walking up to Dr. Holbrook.

"Oh, I am sorry," whispered Susan. "He should have picked you instead of that bozo Anthony."

Amy didn't understand. She was the expert. Her training had emphasized that particular time and that particular location. Those guys were not as prepared as she was. It was her project!

"As you all know, Dr. Amy Waterman has done a wonderful job in getting this project is ready," Dr. Holbrook signaled in her direction and people turned to look at her. She tried to remove the look of shock from her face.

"Well," he continued. "Anthony and Gustav will need all our help in getting ready, and I want everyone to make themselves available. All right then, now it's time to bring back the blooming past."

He loved to end his talks with that phrase in reference to their work with plants, but today Amy was not amused. How could this be, she wondered as she stood up slowly and followed the crowd out of the auditorium. Dr. Holbrook caught up to her.

"Amy, can I have a word?"

She followed him silently to his office.

"I am sure you are excited about your project being picked."

"Yes." She did not sound excited.

"You might be wondering why you were not selected to travel."

"Yes, I wondered," she said containing herself from saying anything more.

"These two men have been to 1895 several times. They are familiar with the people and the way things work. In fact, after my talks with them I realize that men may be better equipped for this trip. I know it sounds horrible, but that is the reality."

"If you apply that criteria, Dr. Holbrook, women will never go."

"I don't know if that is true."

"Of course it is. Do you think England in late Renaissance times was better for women than Durango in 1895? Or how about Peru in the Inca times?" These were the times and locations of other projects. "You have twenty-eight candidates that have been vetted and fifteen of them are women. Are you prepared to tell them they will never go?"

"I will not tell them anything that preposterous. Each mission is separate and I will determine the best team in each case."

"I am the best person for this team. I know the language and culture like the back of my hand. I have excelled in all the simulations we ran of the time."

"I know that, Amy. I have your test results right here, but the decision has been made. There are others involved in making that decision and I cannot change it." Dr. Holbrook lifted his shoulders as if saying it wasn't his fault.

She knew the government had a say in the operations of the lab and maybe they had pressured him. In any case, he wasn't going to change anything. "Will that be all, Dr. Holbrook?"

"Yes."

She stood up.

"Actually, there is one more thing. You should show Anthony and Gustav how to recognize the plant and where the best places are to find it. As you know they are scheduled to leave next week."

"Sure," she said. What else, she thought.

"I am so sorry," said Susan when she got back to the lab.

Amy sat down and closed her eyes. She had been working so hard and had done everything so well she had been certain she would be the one selected for this trip. The fact her project was first didn't mean as much. Second or third with her going would have been much better.

"Knock, knock. I hope I am not interrupting," said a voice from the doorway.

She opened her eyes to find Gustav Jones.

"I hear you are the expert on this yellow flower, and I thought you could tell me everything I need to know about it," he said.

"Sure, Gustav, come in." Amy noticed that Susan was not in the lab.

"I know you are one of the candidates for time travel, so I hope you are not too upset you were not selected this time."

"I am extremely disappointed, Gustav," she said. What did he expect?

"Oh," he smiled nervously as if she were joking. "You will probably go the next time."

"It is all right, I know it is not your fault. Let me show you what you should look for. Is Anthony going to join us?"

"No. I will be in charge of this project and there is no reason to involve Anthony. You know, he is slowing down a bit. It could be age," he grinned.

"I didn't think he was that old," said Amy thinking that he was in his early forties.

"Maybe it is all relative. How old are you?"

"Twenty-six."

He nodded. "I remember that age well."

It was hours later that Susan appeared. Gustav had left a while before. Her eyes looked puffy and red.

"Are you all right Susan?"

"I'm surprised you noticed."

"Excuse me?"

"You are usually so focused in your work."

"Well, as you know, today is not a stellar day for me."

"It is all about you, isn't it? What about me? You don't have a clue."

It was true, thought Amy. She really didn't know what Susan was talking about.

"Well, I am going home," continued Susan.

"But you haven't finished here."

"Oh yes I have," said Susan and walked out the door.

It was later she found out what Susan was referring to. Apparently she had gone to see Dr. Holbrook and found him with another woman. The silhouettes that Amy had seen merge, well, it was not perspective, and it seemed Francine was the Doctor's new paramour.

Poor Susan, thought Amy. She had been so happy with 'Danny'. It really was not a good day for either of them. It was only five o'clock, but she was not motivated to start anything at work and she packed her things to leave.

Then she had a thought. She called Susan and waited for an answer. She left a message.

"Hi Susan, it's me, Amy. I was just wondering if you wanted to catch dinner tonight. I'm heading home, so call me." She then headed to the grocery store.

That evening, with her freezer filled with frozen vegetables, a semi-baked bread finishing baking, a frittata on the stovetop, and a glass of red wine in her hand, her phone rang. It was Susan.

"How are you?" asked Amy.

"You must have heard about Danny."

"Yes, I am sorry."

"I went to talk to him about how unfair it was what he had done to you, and I found them together."

"I'm sorry," repeated Amy.

"How embarrassing. I always embarrass myself."

"That's not true."

"Of course, it is embarrassing. I thought he loved me. It might be because he told me he loved me, so I flaunted it whenever I could. I spent all my free time with him, but it was obviously not enough for him. I am just a failure and now everyone in the lab knows it."

"I don't think people will think that," said Amy racking her brain for something that would prove her statement. "You are smart, nice and a very competent person."

"Thanks Amy, but everybody knew about us. They knew about our relationship. How am I going to go to work tomorrow?"

That is the problem of having an affair with someone at work, thought Amy, but saying that would not help. "You can't give up your career for him. Just come to work and we will avoid him as much as possible. I am not eager to see him either."

"You know he promised I would be one of the first time travelers."

How could he have promised that, thought Amy. What an idiot.

"It wasn't such a far fetched promise," she said. "I scored 425 on the test."

"That is good," said Amy, a bit surprised. That was just 70 points less than her own score and she had studied that period for quite a while.

"We have both been misled by that man. My life is ruined because of him and your life, seeing that your life is your work, is also ruined."

Amy had not thought of it so bleakly. "There are other men and other projects," she said, but it did not sound convincing.

Chapter 3
Tuning the transport

Susan did not come to work the next day. Amy felt a bit disappointed that her speech had not inspired her to show up.

She started to work on the crates that were going to be shipped to 1895. They would contain all the equipment needed by Gustav and Anthony, and they needed to be transported before the travelers. She and Susan had run many scenarios so she knew what was needed.

Transporting objects had proven quite successful. They had confirmed they could send a box anywhere, in any time, with high precision. The transport of people, on the other hand, was proving to have some problems. A meeting was called that afternoon to discuss that.

Dr. Holbrook arrived to the meeting with Francine. "I think most of you have met our GovTime liaison, Francine Hunt."

Everyone nodded.

"Well, go ahead, Anthony and Gustav, tell the group what you told me."

Gustav started talking about the transport process. "So everything was pretty much as expected except when I arrived, Anthony was not next to me."

"I was about thirteen kilometers away," said Anthony.

"I don't understand," said George. "Isn't the transport set to deliver both travelers together at a certain distance from the marker?"

"There is an eight hundred kilometer limit on the markers, and that is why we need several markers in each time, but that is not the problem. We now have a marker set in San Francisco, and this new one is next to the cabin in Durango. This will allow us to go to those places directly. The problem seems to be that one person is sent to where we want, but the person sitting next to them is sent somewhere else," said Dr. Holbrook.

"Does it have to do with the distance between the seats? Maybe that distance is amplified as we got back through time," said George.

"I don't think it is the distance between the seats," said Gustav. "The seats have not moved and yet it seems the problem is getting worse. Isn't that right?"

"I agree," said Anthony. "On the first trips, when we were setting the markers, we traveled alone and that was not a problem. Recently, when we have traveled together, the distance between the two travelers has grown. On my second trip, I was several thousand feet away from my fellow traveler. On the third trip, the distance between the travelers was about two kilometers, the fourth trip was over three kilometers and on this last trip, like I said, it was thirteen kilometers away."

"How are we going to fix this?" asked Gustav.

"I don't think it is much of a problem," said Dr. Holbrook. "Thirteen kilometers from each other is not that much."

"I agree," said Francine, nodding to emphasize her agreement.

"It could be more than thirteen kilometers, Dr. Holbrook," said Amy.

"Why do you say that?" asked Dr. Holbrook.

"Well, the distance between the travelers seems to increase with each trip."

Dr. Holbrook looked at her crossly. "Even if it was twenty kilometers, my statement is still valid. In the context of time and space, twenty kilometers is trivial. At least you both arrive at the same time in the general location, correct?'

"It is the same time," agreed Anthony.

"So we have a problem, but it is not going to stop our launch day. Any questions?" he looked around and no one said anything. "Well, moving on. Francine would like to inform you of an exciting development. Please."

She smiled at him and stood up. "Several very important representatives from the government will be here for the launch day. It will be very exciting to have them and I can't stress how important this is for us. It could help secure the future funding of the lab. Security will be high that day, so we are asking non-essential personnel not to come for the launch."

"What does that mean?" asked George.

"I am making a list of who can attend and I will let you know," said Dr. Holbrook. "You understand that it only affects this launch, because of the visitors and the security. All of you have already seen the transport functioning, so you will not miss much. And you will be here for other launches. I am sorry if it interferes with your work, George."

"So I am on the non-essential list," said George.

Dr. Holbrook lifted his shoulders as if saying it wasn't his fault.

Amy had seen that response before and her opinion of her boss went down another notch.

The next day she was at work alone again. She had left another message on Susan's phone asking if she was planning to show. How could she be so inconsiderate? Relationships come and go, but a project such as this was once in a lifetime, and they had to get everything right. It was especially true since this was the first project and everyone will be watching and judging.

As she went through the checklist one last time, Dr. Holbrook walked into her lab.

"I'm glad I caught you here, Amy. I just wanted to let you know you are welcome to come to the launch on Tuesday."

"That's nice," said Amy, "since it is my project."

"Yes, I thought you would be pleased," he said missing her sarcastic tone.

"Dr. Holbrook, do you really think there is no problem when the time travelers are sent together but arrive in different places?"

"Were you not at the meeting?'

"Yes."

"I believe like I said. There is no problem." He looked at her. "Look, Amy, I know what this is about. You had your heart set on going, but you are not the best person for this job. I am sending the people that will ensure the success of this trip and I would think you would support that."

She didn't say anything.

"Well, I hope you can put this past you and realize that there are other opportunities for you here."

She nodded. Even if she was disappointed, about not traveling, she did love her work at the lab. But he had not answered her question.

"I'm glad you agree," he said. "Well, I see you are packing the boxes. How is that going?"

"I am almost done."

"I know I can count on you to do the best job."

"Of course, Dr. Holbrook."

"All the work we've done will pay off. The world will be a better place because of us. We'll be able to correct the mistakes that our ancestors made by allowing species to vanish into extinction. We will bring those back and develop natural medicines. It is the start of a new future and just think, you are here at the beginning."

With a bit more rehearsal it could be a great speech, thought Amy as she watched him walked away.

Chapter 4
Susan

Amy arrived at work early the next day, and Susan was already there. It was a pleasant surprise. Even if it was Saturday, with the upcoming trip, a lot of people were at work.

"Good morning, Susan," she said.

Susan turned and gave her a small smile.

"I was a bit worried when you did not come in the last couple days," said Amy.

"I was reassessing my life. I don't know how you can put up with the bullshit from this place."

"I really don't have much else," said Amy, thinking that was not so inspirational.

"I don't have anything else either. I sometimes wonder if that was a requirement to get this job," she said thoughtfully.

"I don't think so. There are people here with interests other than work. Look at George; he is happily married," said Amy, opening a box to put the final items in.

"Yeah, but he is an exception. By the way," said Susan. "I just finished checking that box," she pointed. "Should I seal it?"

Amy nodded. "Yeah, I needed to add a couple of items into this one."

"Well, I hope we got everything."

"We should have. That's why we script the missions and run the scenarios. Gustav and Anthony told me they are not great cooks, so I am adding some extra nutrition bars."

"I don't think they will starve in the ten days they will be gone. In the worst case, they can always go to a restaurant; 1895 is not so backwards."

"Yes, that is true, but it's better we send everything they need. It will limit their interactions with the locals." She finished sealing the second box. "Okay, let's finish this last box and take them to the transport. They have to go today."

"We can't send anything while the travelers are there, can we?"

"That's right. I'm not sure why, since it is a different transport system, but I have heard that the transport causes some time fluctuations that may affect the travelers so we don't do it."

"I heard that too. At least if there is a problem in sending the boxes, nothing serious happens. You can resend objects. Humans, on the other hand, are so frail."

"Yes, that is why we extra cautious." Amy was half listening Susan as she looked over the checklist. "Hand me that metal piece other there." Amy pointed to it as she made room in the crate.

"It is a piece of a water pump, isn't it? It looks very worn," said Susan, handing it to Amy.

"It is supposed to. Everything should look of the period."

"How did Gustav and Anthony do this before? I don't think we sent boxes ahead of time for them."

"They didn't need extra equipment. On the previous trip they were on the road every day. They arrived to San Francisco and immediately took the train and then the stagecoach to Durango. They did it the fastest possible way with the least amount of contact with the locals. This trip is different. In the worst case, they could stay ten days looking for the flower. We don't want them to depend on the locals."

"And they should survive with this stuff," said Susan.

Amy thought that was a bit strange to say.

"I heard the transport has already been calibrated for the trip tomorrow."

"Yeah, everything should be ready," Amy nodded. "Hey, Susan, even if we are not going, you have to admit it is an exciting day. It is our project and the flower will bring cure to many."

"Yes, Amy."

They loaded the boxes onto a maglev cart and directed it out of the lab and towards the smaller transport. This was a few meters away from the platform where Gustav and Anthony would sit tomorrow.

"Right on time," said the technician. "Do you have the inventory?"

Susan gave the technician the inventory and started to go through the list. Amy noticed George standing nearby and went to talk to him.

"Hi, George."

"What a travesty that they are not sending you."

"It happens."

"You know I am a candidate on that list, and now I am doubtful I will ever go."

"You should not worry; after all, you are male," she smiled.

"I worry. My physique is not like Anthony's or Gustav's."

"I don't think that is a reason to prevent your going." George was quite rotund, but there were people like him in the past.

"They are also younger than me."

She didn't say anything, as that could be a limiting factor. Life expectancy in the late 1750s, which was George's project era, was in the mid-thirties, and George was older than that.

"Well, I came to see the preparations today," said George, "since I have been barred from coming tomorrow."

"I think that's a shame. Why not let all employees come?"

"Well, you heard the doctor."

"Yeah, you'll catch the next one."

"The next one better be my project," said George as he walked away.

"Hey, be careful," someone shouted.

Amy looked in the direction and saw the warning was not meant for her. A couple of technicians were working on the platform.

"Don't get too close to that," shouted the same man. "Damn, you know how sensitive these senso-static controls are."

"I was not that close. If they are so sensitive, you better set them right before they travel."

"Of course I will," said the other angrily, "but I had them set right before you came along."

Maybe it was good thing she wasn't going on this trip she thought as she returned to the lab. Everyone was very much on edge.

Susan returned to the lab shortly afterwards. "Hey, did you mean to put this in one of the boxes?" She picked up a large envelope that was on her desk.

"No, it's cash and Gustav and Anthony will carry that with them. It has bills and coins of the time."

"Have you put enough in there?'

"We have information about what things cost in 1895. Remember you helped me make the budget?" Amy didn't wait for a reply and turned to continued the work on the chemical compositions.

Hours later, Amy happened to glance at the clock and it was past seven. The lab was still buzzing with people. The boxes had been transported and all indication showed they had arrived close to the marker near Durango. The level of excitement in the lab was almost as high as the first time they sent anyone to the past. That had been almost six months ago.

"You want to go out for dinner?" she asked Susan. She still felt bad having rejected her the first time she had been asked.

"No. That is very nice of you, but I am going straight home," said Susan. "Will you be much longer?"

"No, I will go home soon."

Susan left after that, but Amy started to resolve one of her puzzles and her estimate soon turned to three hours. By then, the lab was very quiet.

"Dr. Waterman," the security man making his rounds was at her door. "Working late?"

"Hello, Evan, yes. Tomorrow is a big day."

"Congrats on getting your project on first."

"Thanks," she said and the lights flickered.

"What was that?" she asked. It was as if someone was getting the transport ready. "Nothing is scheduled to transport at this time."

"I better check it out," said Evan, leaving the lab.

Amy followed him, curious to see what it could be.

As she reached the ground floor she could see that the platform was lit with the usual spotlights, but she could not see anyone. Then the noise intensified. Someone must be inside the cage, she thought.

"The transport is getting ready to go," shouted Amy, running past the security guard. He picked up his pace and together they ran towards the structure, but Amy knew they were not going to make it.

She was right. By the time they reached the structure, no one was sitting inside.

"Do you think someone transported?" asked Evan.

"Maybe even two people could have gone."

"Well, the camera caught them," he pointed to the security camera watching them.

The camera would have sounded an alarm if it did not recognize the person, so it had to be someone from the lab and someone who was had clearance to be in this area.

"I've called my boss and he is on his way," said Evan. "I'm sorry, Dr. Waterman, you will have to stay longer. No one is allowed to leave until this is cleared up."

"Sure," said Amy, but it didn't matter; someone had already left.

Later that night an emergency meeting was convened. Seeing that it was close to midnight, a surprising number of people were there. Dr. Holbrook had arrived, of course, and not surprisingly, Francine had arrived with him.

"How can this have happened?" asked Dr. Holbrook shaking his head.

No one answered wondering what part of 'this' he referring to.

"Wasn't there security in place?" asked Francine.

"Yes, there was," said Evan's boss, the head of security. "But we worry more about outsiders breaking in, and we do not focus on the scientists that have been cleared to work here. They have been well scrutinized already."

"I still cannot believe Susan did this," said Dr. Holbrook.

The camera had shown her quite clearly starting the machine and quickly strapping herself in the structure. She had taken a risk by not getting into place before the launch, but it looked like she had managed it.

"Dr. Waterman, can you add anything?" asked the security chief.

As soon as she had found out it was Susan, she knew she would be asked. Susan was her assistant, and they may feel she was responsible for her.

"Susan was quite upset on Wednesday," she looked at Dr. Holbrook. He was to blame for that, and a couple of other people threw him a glance as well. "She did not come to work the next two days, but she came in today and she was fine. She helped me get the boxes ready for transport this morning, and she worked late tonight on some analysis. At no time did she mention anything that would hint at something like this."

"Nothing?" asked Dr. Holbrook.

"Nothing. As soon as I found out it was she that was gone, I looked through her things in the lab. I found a note." She put it on the table. "It says she has gone to Durango to complete the mission."

"Well, we have to bring her back," said Dr. Holbrook. "There is nothing else to be done. The corydalis curvisiliqua project is put on hold, and this takes precedence."

"But Dr. Holbrook," said Francine softly. "A lot of money has been invested in this project. Are you sure you want to throw all that away? What harm can she do by herself?"

"We have started running the lifeline simulations, but without knowing whom she is contacting, it will be harder to catch changes in the time line."

"Why can't we do both?" asked Gustav. "We can find Susan and the flower and bring them both back."

"I think that is a wonderful idea," said Francine.

Dr. Holbrook looked interested. "Do you think that is possible?"

"Sure," said Gustav. "Only thing is. I don't think Anthony is the best person to bring back Susan."

They all looked at Anthony.

"I went on one date with her," said Anthony rolling his eyes. "It was not a big deal."

Susan had called him a bozo, remembered Amy. "I have to agree with Gustav," she said. "Even if it was one date, you made an impression Anthony."

"It's best I go by myself," said Gustav. "It actually makes sense since Susan and I can transport back together."

It did make sense, thought Amy. The transport could only handle two people at a time.

"No," said Dr. Holbrook. "You will not go by yourself. There has to be someone else who is acquainted with this period as well as both of you." He seemed to think about it for a while and then he said, "Amy, you might you fit the bill."

Of course she was the best and obvious choice based on her knowledge and ability, she thought. She should have been the first choice.

"I believe you are a friend of Susan's?" asked Dr. Holbrook.

So the friendship was the swaying factor, she thought. Well, she wasn't going to quibble. "Yes, I am," she said much more confidently than she really felt.

"It also looks like you are current on all your vaccinations," said the Dr. Knobby, as he looked at his screen. He was the on-site doctor and was familiar with the medical history of all the employees.

She nodded. She had been ready to go.

"I want you to leave as early as possible," said Dr. Holbrook. "We can fine-tune the transport so you will arrive at the time of day when you can catch the stagecoach into town. You might even run into Susan waiting for the same stagecoach."

"That will make it too easy," said Gustav, "but are you sure it is necessary for both of us to go?"

"Yes," said Dr. Holbrook. "I think Susan will need some persuasion, and I think Amy will be a better choice for that."

Gustav looked resigned.

"Now, both of you should go home, pick up what you need and meet back here in two hours. Amy, we have your measurements on file and we will outfit you with period clothing when you get back. Make sure you do not take any of the modern clothing."

Amy knew he meant she could not take her underwear. That would not be invented under early 1900s. It could be worse, at least drawers and camisoles were common in 1895 and a one-piece combination of both was widely used.

"At least it looks like Susan dressed appropriately," said Dr. Holbrook.

"And whatever she didn't take she will be able to buy," said Amy. "Susan took the cash meant for Gustav and Anthony. We will have to print more money before we go."

Chapter 5
Durango by stagecoach

Amy closed her eyes. When she opened them the sun was beating down on her. She felt all right, she thought, as she started to breath normally. The transport had been flawless. She had arrived exactly at the spot she was supposed to. She didn't know the date, but at least the location was good. She should clarify, the location was correct; good was the wrong adjective, she thought, as she looked at the rickety wooden lean-to that was used as a stagecoach stop.

Regardless, here she was in 1895. A smile came to her lips, but it did not last. Gustav was not with her.

She spun around looking in all directions. She could see quite far in the mostly flat and desert-y landscape. There were plenty of cacti and shrubs, but no sign of Gustav. In fact, there was no sign of Susan either, although she had not really expected that. Then she saw a cloud of dust near the horizon and it was moving.

What was it, she wondered. She would kill for sunglasses, but those wouldn't come along for another 40 years, so she squinted, trying to make out the reason for the dust. Then she figured it out. It was the stagecoach, and it was coming fast.

She took deep calming breaths. She would have to take it. She did not know when the next stagecoach would come this way. She was about to meet real people of the era. She hoped her language was not too different from theirs and that her clothes were appropriate. She could see the stagecoach getting larger as it made its way towards her, and she gave it a little wave hoping that would make it stop.

The driver pulled the reins, and the stagecoach stopped just past her. He jumped off and shouted, "Five minutes, everyone, five minutes." He opened the coach door. Two male passengers stepped out of the coach in a hurry and headed behind the lean-to.

The driver turned to her, "Good morning, Miss. Where are you heading?"

"Good morning. To Durango."

He looked her over. "Is this the only bag you have?"

She nodded. It was mostly clothes, as everything else should be at the cabin. He picked it up easily and threw it on top of the coach. "Step right on inside. There's plenty of room."

Amy peeked inside and saw a lady sitting against the opposite door. Luckily, there was no third bench. She had read how some stagecoaches put a third bench in the middle. The people sitting there would have no backrest and they had to interleave their knees with passengers sitting on the other bench. She stepped into the dark interior.

"I wouldn't sit there."

Her head swung around towards the voice. She had not seen the well-dressed man in the shadows. "Both gentlemen that stepped out were sitting there," he continued. "You'll have more room sitting next to me."

Sounded like some sort of pick-up line, she thought, but she could handle him. She said, "Thank you," and sat down between the woman and the man. It was going to be cozy, but thankfully the lady next to her was quite small.

The two men got back in and the driver closed the door. Immediately she noticed the smell. It was sweat mingled with dust, with a slight undertone of whiskey. It was going to be a long trip. She tried to cover her nose casually, but it was hard to pull that off. The lady next to her had a handkerchief, and she wished she had brought one like her. Leaving in a hurry, she had not packed as carefully as she would have liked.

The reason for taking the stagecoach was so people would see her arrive and not question how she had gotten to Durango, but there had to be a better way, she thought.

"I couldn't help overhearing that you're going to Durango?" asked the man next to her.

"Yes."

"I live there."

"How nice."

"Have you been there before?"

"No."

"Then how do you know it's nice?" The man smiled at her.

She had to smile back. He had caught her attempt at trivial conversation.

"But, you're correct in assuming it is nice," he continued. "It is a good place to live. What takes you to Durango?"

"I am meeting a friend." She tried to keep her answers short and simple. She would probably have to repeat them and she wanted to be consistent.

"By the way, my name is Rick LaForce; nice to make your acquaintance."

"Amy Waterman," she said as she tried to shake his hand. The others in the coach didn't seem eager to meet and it was better to leave it that way, she thought.

The stagecoach followed some sort of dusty trail, and it was not long it went over a ridge and started down into a valley. Through the window, she caught glimpses of an approaching town.

"Farmington," said her new friend.

Farmington was over eighty kilometers or fifty miles from Durango. She should think in miles in this era, she thought. It would take another six hours to get to her destination. The ride was taking an interminably long time.

The scientists at BioTime had agreed that appearing close to Durango out of nowhere would cause too much suspicion; so taking a stagecoach from a distance was the best course. Maybe next time, they could choose a closer town, thought Amy, adjusting herself on the hard seat.

"You picked an interesting place to catch the stagecoach," said Rick.

The comment was along the lines of what she was thinking, and she wanted to hear a local's opinion. "Why would that be?"

"It is remote from almost everything."

"A friend was heading east so he dropped me off at the stagecoach stop. Where are you coming from?" It was best to deflect any more questions with some of her own.

"Silver City," he said. "I was looking to invest in a mine down there."

"A silver mine?" she grinned.

"It is a silver mine," he smiled slightly, "but I don't think there is much ore left in it. I don't think it would be a good investment."

Amy smiled. He was downplaying the mine too much. If she was a betting person, and she was sure he was, she would bet he was going to invest in the mine.

After six more hours of bone rattling, she stepped out of the carriage. Her muscles were sore and cramped, but she was relieved that the first phase of her trip was over. She stretched and took a deep breath. The air was clean and fresh and she smiled, feeling reenergized. She felt positive that this was indeed the beginning of a wonderful future for everyone.

As soon as she found the little flower, she could return to the future and they would start the testing. Everyone would forgive Susan, and together they would work on unlocking the healing power of the flower. Everything was going to work out fine.

As she waited for her luggage, she noticed a man across the street watching the carriage intently. He started to smile at her and then his smile quickly vanished. The man wore a star on his vest. She wondered if he had seen something wrong with her.

"How long did you say you were staying?" asked Rick, coming up to her.

"I didn't say, but it should not be more than ten days, maybe less."

"In and out as fast as you can," he said.

"I am expected in San Francisco by the end of the month." It was an excuse to account for their hurry. They would actually be using the transport marker at the cabin to go back.

"You don't need to have an excuse. I don't blame you. It is obvious you are a cultured lady, and this town probably does not have enough to offer someone like you. I hope someday it will be different."

The man had pride in his town, she thought, wondering what she could say. If she said she would come another time, it implied the town was not good enough right now. "I just have a schedule to keep."

He smiled. "Nicely avoiding my culture reference. Do you need help with your bag?" he asked as she was handed her bag.

She knew that men in this era thought that women were weaker and she expected they would offer their help often. "No, thank you," she said, "it is not heavy."

"In that case, I will be on my way," said Rick. "I don't feel like talking to the sheriff right now." He glanced at the man with the star. "Have a pleasant stay in Durango."

The sheriff had started making his way towards them and, as Rick walked away, she thought he might follow him, but he continued towards her. She decided she didn't want a confrontation with the law out in the open either. She looked around and saw she was near to the General Store. They needed some supplies for the cabin, and she had been assigned to get them, so she picked up her bag and walked into the store.

The interior was dark, and it took a moment for her eyes to adjust. The store sold a large variety of items, including hardware items, as well as foodstuff and clothing. Some items were displayed on shelves near her, but beyond the counter she could see a room lined with more shelves, and there were big sacks piled on top. Two men were standing behind the counter and both looked at her as she walked in.

"Good afternoon. May I help you?" asked one of them.

"Good afternoon," she walked towards the man. "I have a list of items I need and wondered if you could supply them?"

"May I see the list?"

She handed him the list just as someone entered the store behind her.

"Oh, good afternoon, sheriff," said the store clerk to the person behind her.

"Good afternoon, Mr. Grayson."

Mr. Grayson looked back to her. "I will see what I can do." He turned and walked into the back room.

She could feel his eyes boring into her the back of her head. She finally turned to him.

"Good afternoon," he said.

"Good afternoon," she said and remembered to bow her head slightly. It was the custom. He was over six feet tall, at least four inches taller than her.

"Sheriff Lindsey at your service," he walked over and shook her hand.

"Amy Waterman."

"I saw you arrive on the midday carriage, Miss Waterman."

"Yes, I did."

"And as you are here buying supplies, you must be planning to stay for a while?"

She smiled at his powers of observation and nodded slightly.

"If you don't mind me asking, how long are you staying in town?"

"No more than ten days and probably less," she said.

He nodded taking the information in. "I guess you are not staying at the hotel?"

"You guess correctly." She shouldn't be so facetious, she realized as soon as she said it, but luckily he smiled. She looked up at his face and was surprised to see that he had all his teeth and even more astonishing they were white. He also had the clearest green eyes she had ever seen.

"I have most of the items on your list," said Mr. Grayson, causing her to look away from the sheriff.

"Can you have the items delivered?" she asked.

"Where would you like them delivered to?"

She paused thinking about the answer. It was something they had talked about before coming. In this era, addresses were not so exact. Saying things like the house next to the post office was acceptable, and the green house next to the railroad would mean something. She hoped so. "The house is four miles east of here; it is close to a ridge that runs..."

"You mean old McCabe's house?" interrupted the sheriff.

"Yes, that is it," she said, relieved they had understood.

"Delivering there will not be a problem," said the clerk. "Tomorrow afternoon all right?"

"Tomorrow afternoon is fine," she said.

He handed her the list back. "This is what is what I don't have. You might want to check the apothecary down the street."

"Thank you." She took out a five-dollar bill and paid as the sheriff continued to watch. It was a bit unnerving. The bill had been made to the best specifications and aged carefully, but she would not want the sheriff to study it too carefully. The clerk took the money without hesitation.

She turned to walk out and the sheriff held the door for her.

She bid the clerk and the sheriff a good day and headed to the apothecary with a slight spring in her step. That seemed to have gone quite well.

After the apothecary she would get the horse that Gustav and Anthony had purchased previously, and soon she would be at the cabin.

Hopefully she would get to the house before sunset and she hoped Susan would be there by then. That would be the best possible scenario and then they could find ...

"Excuse me, Miss Waterman," a voice interrupted her thoughts.

She turned to find the sheriff. "Sheriff?"

"It just occurred to me that you are heading in the same direction I was going and I could accompany you."

"To the apothecary?"

"No. I meant to McCabe's house."

"Oh, I couldn't impose on you that way." She didn't want him to accompany her. She did not know if Susan was there and in what mental state she would find her. The boxes that had been shipped from the future might also arouse suspicion. It was easier if he did not come with her.

"It is no imposition; like I said, I am already heading that way."

He sounded determined and if she continued to say 'no' it would make him suspicious. She thanked him for his offer and told him she needed to get the horse from the stable near the outskirts of town. "I can get the apothecary supplies tomorrow."

Chapter 6
The cabin in desolation

They rode in silence for a while. The stable had shown her the two horses Gustav had purchased and she picked the charcoal colored one. They were soon on their way. She had to admit having the company and someone who knew the way was not a bad thing.

She was glad she was wearing clothing that allowed her to ride a horse normally and not sidesaddle. By now a lot of women were riding this way, especially in the West.

She just couldn't believe how dry the air was out here, and even though it was late afternoon, the sun was still hot. And everything was dusty.

"Have you been here before?' asked the sheriff.

"No. It is my first time in Durango."

"Why would someone like you stay at an isolated cabin like McCabe's?"

She laughed. "Someone like me?" I don't think you know someone like me, she almost said. "Mr. McCabe was a friend of the family's, and he said we could stay at his cabin any time we liked."

"I didn't mean to imply that you were trespassing, only that it is a very rustic place and you might have been more comfortable at the Strater Hotel."

"Hmm," she said. He obviously didn't think that women could hack it in a "rustic" place.

They continued in silence for a moment.

"You ride quite well," he said trying to appease.

"Yes, even at this slow pace."

"Oh?'

"I think this horse should be able to go a bit faster," she said as she jabbed her heels into the horse's side. The horse leaped forward and she crouched low. This was better, she thought as the horse moved smoothly though the wide-open landscape. The wind rushed through her hair and she finally felt free. It had been a long time that she had felt that way. Smiling, she turned and saw the sheriff following close behind.

They reached the cabin quickly, and she realized the word "rustic" was really an upgrade to describe the house. The place was falling apart. She jumped off the horse and studied the cabin while she pinned her hair back in its place.

"Is it as you expected?" asked the sheriff joining her.

"I guess the good thing is no one will try to rob this place."

"Yes, there is that," he laughed. "I do remember a barn in the back. I'll take your horse."

"Thank you, I am going to look inside." She walked onto the rickety front porch and noticed that at least the flooring and supports looked solid even though the porch railing had gapping holes in it. She turned the doorknob and the front door swung open. Amazing, she thought; no one had locked the place. Of course, what would have been the purpose of locking it? There was nothing to steal and anyone who wanted to come in could break one of those thin glass windows. Amazing, she thought again; the glass was so thin you could feel the temperature outside.

"It does not look so bad on the inside," said the sheriff as he came in, "but the barn might be in better shape."

"Are you joking?"

"Are you ready to go back to the hotel?"

"No. I will stay here. My friends are coming, and I have to get this place somewhat presentable."

"So you will be by yourself tonight?"

She suddenly became aware she was alone with this man. She realized that even though he was a sheriff, history was full of stories of bad sheriffs. Her hand casually moved into her pocket and to the stun gun. "I will not be alone. My friends will arrive before sunset."

"Good. Well then, I will be on my way."

"So you really have something to do this way?"

"Yes, I do," he looked surprised at her.

"Good," she nodded. He had not made up the excuse to accompany her.

She followed him out the door and watched him get on the horse. "Sheriff?"

He turned to her.

"Thank you."

He touched the brim of his hat and trotted away.

Hours later she sat on the recently dusted kitchen chair. She had found the boxes. They had been sent to the barn and even if the sheriff had seen them, their look was of the period. She was just thankful that the boxes were with her and not somewhere else. The transport of equipment had proven once again to be more reliable than the transport of humans.

She had also found the transport marker that had been placed next to the barn. It looked like an old stump. It could be moved, but it was partially buried and it was heavy enough that any movement would not be by accident. She was relieved she had found it. It was the key to returning home.

The first box she opened was the one with the perimeter monitoring system, and she set it up immediately. It worked almost like radar with the cabin at the center. If any human crossed the set perimeter, she would be notified. She would also be able to see the person using a small projector she set in the bedroom.

Next, she setup the communication link, or ComLink, as they called it. There was an old cupboard in the kitchen and it would provide an ideal place to store it. At two by three inches, the device could be carried, but it felt bulky compared to what she was used to using in the future. She turned the device on. "Hello. Can anyone hear me?"

Dr. Holbrook's voice came through clearly. "Hello Amy, I was waiting to hear from you."

"Hello, Dr. Holbrook. I am at the cabin, but Gustav and Susan are not here."

"Oh, that is unfortunate. We have not heard from Gustav yet. Did the boxes arrive?"

"Yes. I have not finished unpacking them, but so far so good. I set up the perimeter monitor."

"All right. We will try to get in touch with Gustav. He has his own ComLink. We'll let you know if there is any news; otherwise, we will talk tomorrow. There is probably a lot to be done to get the place ready, so we'll say goodbye."

She said goodbye. He was right. She tackled the water supply next and, as suspected, the water pump needed parts. She used some of the tools she had brought with her and replaced the rusted pieces. Finally, she was able to fill a bucket with fresh water. It would save her a trip to the river, wherever that was.

The sun was close to the horizon as she finished cleaning the kitchen. For warmth the first night, since she did not have firewood, she would use the insta-warm blanket. In the morning she would have to find another source of heat. She was exhausted and went to bed without eating.

Chapter 7
Domesticity

The bright light of the morning sun woke her up early. There were no shades on the windows, and she mentally added curtains to the shopping list the next time she was in town. She pushed herself out of bed feeling cold, dirty and hungry. Maybe she should have stayed at the Strater Hotel in Durango for the first night. But it was wishful thinking. She could not risk all that contact with the people of Durango.

She walked into the cold kitchen and looked outside. It was a clear, frosty morning and icicles had formed on the mouth of water pump. In 1895, plumbing was available only in large towns, so even Durango would not have any. That meant that even if she went to that nice hotel, she wouldn't have running water in her room.

She decided to get the stove working first. Once she did that, she would go outside to get that cold water, heat it up and then finally she could wash her face and brush her teeth. Luckily, the toothbrush and toothpaste had already been invented. Afterwards, she would have a cup of tea. It was a long process to achieve something so simple.

Hours later she munched on a nutrition bar and sipped on tea, feeling a tinge of resentment. Everything was not as ready to go as promised. She should be looking for the corydalis curvisiliqua and not wasting time on trivial things like setting up house. And where were the others?

She spent the rest of the morning unpacking the boxes. She found the packets of prepared food that only needed heating to be ready. Funny, she had thought of Gustav and Anthony when packing the packets and now she was the one that was thankful to have them.

She was not a chef, but friends had told her that her Mediterranean cuisine was good. She smiled thinking about trying to make Mediterranean food out here in this desolate place.

It was at the bottom of the last box that she found a solar shower. What a wonderful surprise, thought Amy. It was not on her list of items, but Susan must have thought to include it.

"Hello, Amy? Hello." She heard the voice of Dr. Holbrook calling her from the cupboard.

"Hello, Dr. Holbrook."

"How are you today?"

"Fine, but there is still no sign of Susan or Gustav."

"We spoke to Gustav, and he appeared just outside of Grand Junction. That is over 270 kilometers or about 170 miles from you."

"Grand Junction? 170 miles? So when is he arriving?'

"It will take him three days on the stagecoach, we think," Dr. Holbrook paused for a moment. "I hope you are all right staying alone."

"Alone is not a problem. It's the people I worry about. Even though the ones I have met seemed all right, they do question outsiders."

"Yes, that is why it is better you stay away from the town. On that topic, you need to give us the names of everyone you have come into contact with."

It was standard procedure. They were going to track the lifeline of each person to see if the contact with her had changed their future. Only the people that had had some meaningful exchange with her needed to be included.

"I met Rick LaForce on the stagecoach and Sheriff Lindsey in the town. There was also a store clerk, Mr. Grayson, but the only conversation I had with him was about the items I purchased. Those items will be delivered this afternoon, so I will see him again."

"The sheriff. Did you have any problems?"

"No, he accompanied me to the cabin since he was heading this way, but it was just that, nothing else."

"He was not overly curious?" asked Dr. Holbrook.

"No. I told him our cover story, and once he saw I was staying at the cabin, he seemed to accept it."

"Okay, well, we are going to run these names through the computer. Two is not a bad number of contacts." Dr. Holbrook had obviously discounted Mr. Grayson and that was all right. The computers would be busy enough with the contacts that Gustav and especially Susan were making.

"What about Susan? Any ideas?" she asked.

"We now know there was a problem with her trip."

"Is she all right?" she said fearing something awful might have happened.

"The transport went all right. She was sent east of Denver, but she knows where the cabin is and is probably making her way there. She is smart and should be able to do it."

"I know she knows where the cabin is, but Denver is over three hundred miles away," said Amy. It would take her more than five days by stagecoach.

"Her money has probably run out," said another voice from the future.

"Why do you think that?" asked Amy. "She took all the cash we had."

"Well, it looks like she has been there four weeks already," said the voice.

"Four weeks!" Amy was astonished. "How did that happen?"

"The senso-static controls had been set correctly earlier, but during the day they drifted. We checked the logs and the cameras confirmed it. In the morning, right before you and Gustav left, the senso-static controls were adjusted correctly. Her place and time of transport were very different from yours," said Dr. Holbrook.

"She does not have enough money for four weeks," said Amy.

"We know."

No one wanted to add what else might have happened.

The general store delivery arrived that afternoon, and Sheriff Lindsey accompanied the cart.

Mr. Grayson brought in the items she had purchased and then he left. The sheriff stayed.

"Did you accompany Mr. Grayson because he was going your way?" she asked.

"No, I came to see you."

She smiled, delighted at his straightforward manner.

"I wanted to see if you were all right," he explained himself. "I did not see your friends arrive on the stagecoach and wondered if they had arrived some other way."

"They did not arrive. I was hoping they would be here last night, but apparently they have been delayed."

"Are you going to spend another night alone out here?" He seemed genuinely concerned.

"It is fine. I am all right here." And the less contact with you will be for the best, she thought.

"The cabin does look much better now." He stepped around the kitchen and looked towards the bedroom. "You will need curtains in the bedroom."

"I came to that realization this morning when the sun woke me up."

"Yes, the bedroom window faces east." He turned to look at her. "Do you have a gun and do you know how to use it?"

She was surprised by the question and didn't answer.

"A gun, with bullets," he suggested.

"Bullets?" She realized as soon as she said it that it had come out wrong. She was accustomed to a stun gun that would incapacitate, but not injure or kill.

"All right, I think that you will be needing some instruction. Come outside with me." He led the way to his horse. He took his rifle off the horse and handed it to her. It was heavy and immediately the barrel fell into the ground. She tried to keep the end from hitting the ground.

"I am going to lend you this rifle. Mind you I am only lending it to you for it is a favorite of mine. You will return it to me when you leave in ten days or sooner."

She smiled. "It is nine days or less."

"Fine. Now let me show you how to shoot, and then we can do some target practice."

She knew how to shoot. Many of the time travel candidates had been taught to use the various weapons of the era, but the only weapon they had been given for the trip was the stun gun. When someone was stunned, they stayed incapacitated for fifteen minutes. In addition, a chemical was pricked into the stunned subject and that would ensure they did not remember what had happened minutes before. With that, a plausible story could be suggested to them, and they wouldn't remember the stun gun. No other weapon had been deemed necessary.

She pulled the rifle up on her shoulder and reluctantly followed the sheriff.

39

For the next minutes, she let him show her how to load a gun and how to shoot. Then he asked her to practice. The rifle was heavier than what she was used to, so her bullets were off target at first. Then she got the hang of it and started to hit the target.

"You are a fast learner," complemented the sheriff.

"It must be the teacher," she said, trying to be serious.

Then it struck him. "You know how to shoot, don't you?"

"Yes."

"But you don't have a rifle or hand gun with you?"

"No," she said. Nothing that would shoot bullets, she thought.

"All right. I shouldn't have assumed you needed lessons, but you could have told me."

"I thought a refresher lesson would not hurt."

"Okay," he nodded. "I will still lend you my rifle."

"Thank you, sheriff. I appreciate that."

"You can call me Jeff."

That night was better than the one before. With the stove working, the cabin was cozier and she was able to heat one of those instant food packets. It made a decent meal. She briefly thought of inviting the sheriff to supper, but knew it was a dumb thing to do.

She had enjoyed their conversation and more. She thought about the target practice and how his hand had rested on hers and she had not pulled away. She should have, she knew. Any more contact with him might ruin his lifeline. She just had to avoid him from now on.

Chapter 8
Angry men

The following morning Amy took her horse out toward the hills. She found several fields of flowers, but the special corydalis curvisiliqua was not to be found. Towards midday, she reached a field of flowers near the top of a ridge. This was the most promising location based on soil conditions, she thought. There was a yellow flower among the others, and she dismounted to study it closer.

That is when she heard the men arguing. It sounded as if they were just on the other side of the ridge. At first she could barely hear what they were saying, but soon, as their voices got louder, she heard everything. The insults between them escalated and then one said, "Don't push me, I will kill you."

"Try it. Just try it and see what happens." It was said with such deliberation it sent a shiver up her spine.

She didn't even peer over the ridge to see who they were. She retreated carefully to her horse and led him away quietly. She soon arrived back at the cabin. It did not feel far enough from the ridge, she thought. Locking the flimsy door did nothing to dispel the vulnerable feeling.

Come on, she chided herself. She couldn't get scared of a couple of men. She had her stun gun and the sheriff's rifle, and she could also see anyone coming way before anyone got there. She decided to bake biscuits to get her mind off things.

At first she did it to pass the time, but soon she was enjoying the process. As she put the biscuits in the oven, she had a sense of accomplishment. She had never baked before, even from a mix. Soon the smell coming from the oven was quite good.

Sheriff Lindsey showed up soon after that.

"You are beginning to be predictable," she told him, trying not to show how glad she was to see him.

"Is that good or bad?"

"Good. If you become too predictable, it is not so good, but right now it is very good."

"I'll keep that in mind."

She offered him tea and the biscuits that were just coming out of the oven.

"The biscuits smell wonderful."

"I hope they taste as good as they smell," she said. There was no need to tell him about the mix.

He sat down at the kitchen table while she prepared the tea.

"This is not exactly a social visit," he said.

"Oh," she sounded disappointed and then she mentally scolded herself for sounding that way.

"Yesterday, there was a murder nearby."

"Was it by the ridge a couple miles east of here?"

He looked at her surprised. "Yes, how did you know?"

"I was up on the ridge this morning, and I heard a couple of men arguing. They were threatening to kill each other, so I left as quietly as I could. I did not actually see them."

"You did the right thing. There is silver mine half way down that ridge, and there have been rumors about it. Some say there is silver in there, and others say it is just a ploy so the owners will get investors. I don't know who is right, but the man who was killed was found there."

"Was he the owner of the mine?"

"No. Jeb was a small time miner who lived in town and who probably had no reason to be there. I am still trying to determine the facts. This happened yesterday, so you could not have heard it, unless you were there?"

"No. I was there this morning."

"I am heading there now."

"By yourself?"

He grinned. "Are you concerned?"

"I would think you would go with a group, or at least with a couple of deputies." Wasn't that standard practice? There was only one of him and there were two of them.

"No, a sheriff usually goes places by himself."

She nodded. She shouldn't care.

"Would you like me to come back this way?"

No, part of her said, warning of the interaction with this local. "Yes," she said, it would make her feel better.

Later that afternoon, Dr. Holbrook called as scheduled. "Amy, today I am accompanied by some of your fellow coworkers who are curious to hear about your surroundings."

"Hello, everyone," she said and a chorus of voices answered.

"Were you able to search for corydalis curvisiliqua?" asked Dr. Holbrook.

"Yes, I spent the morning looking in various locations and I think I found it, but I was not able to verify if it was."

"Why was that?" asked someone who sounded like Francine.

"I heard a couple of men arguing nearby and thought it best to leave." It sounded silly now that she said it.

"Oh," said Dr. Holbrook. It was a quiet 'oh' implying all sorts of faults with her.

"A man was shot to death near the ridge yesterday." She had not known about that when she was there, but she wanted them to know how dangerous this place was. She wasn't being frightened of just anything.

"How terrible," someone from the future said. "Are you in danger?"

It sounded like George. "No. I am all right. The sheriff came by to inform me about it."

"I am worried about the interest that sheriff is taking with you," said Dr. Holbrook.

"There was a murder nearby and he is investigating. He thought I should know."

"I guess you have a point," said Dr. Holbrook.

Of course, she wasn't going to tell them she had asked him to return. "Any news of Gustav?"

"No, but he should be in Durango tomorrow."

"Well, thank goodness. I will try the ridge again tomorrow morning, and hopefully the men are no longer there."

"I think you should return to us tomorrow with the specimen." It sounded like Francine.

"What do you mean?" Amy knew what was implied, but she wanted it spelled out.

"Go get the flower and come back. You don't have to wait for Gustav or for Susan," said Francine.

"But Susan does not know where the transport marker is," said Amy. She wouldn't be able to get back. And who was in charge anyway, she wondered.

"We will have Gustav wait for her," said Francine.

"We do have news on Susan," said Dr. Holbrook.

"Where is she?"

"She is in Grand Junction."

"Wow, that's impressive she got that far," said Amy. "So she be will be arriving with Gustav?"

"She should be," said Dr. Holbrook.

"Amy, this is George. How is it? What is the feeling of the place?"

Amy wanted to tell him things in detail, but wasn't sure the others would appreciate it. "It is huge," she ended up saying. "Nature is huge here. All the colors seem brighter and different from the Bay Area. The sky seems bigger and bluer and the colors of the soil and the hills are filled with shades of browns, reds and yellows. It is both beautiful and overwhelming. Of course, part of that is just being in Durango."

"Yeah," said George.

"It is also very primitive. It takes a very long time to get anywhere, and I really miss indoor plumbing. You can imagine. There's also a lot of dust, and it coats everything. The wind blows constantly, and it seems to go right through the cabin."

"There may be a fix for that," said Dr. Holbrook, "but we don't want the cabin to appear too fixed up."

"Don't worry, it does not looked fixed up, although structurally it is sound," she quickly added. "I know Gustav and Anthony worked on that, and they did a good job. By the way, I was thinking of going into town to get curtains. The bedroom window faces east and the sun shines in very early. It may also help with blocking the wind, as well."

"No, Amy, I don't think you go should go. Remember, we're trying to keep contact with the locals at a minimum. Maybe Gustav can buy the curtains on his way in. The stagecoach does stop in Durango," said Dr. Holbrook.

"Okay, that will work, as well."

"All right then, we will talk tomorrow. Let's make it later in the day to give you time to get the flower."

"Oh, Dr. Holbrook? What about the lifelines of the people I have met?"

"The store clerk and the fellow on the stagecoach show no change. The sheriff's lifeline is blank."

"Blank?"

"Yes, there was some sort of error, so we are running the lifeline again."

A couple of hours later, the sheriff returned. She saw his image projected on the bedroom wall and fixed her hair unconsciously. Then she caught herself; what was happening? His lifeline was blank, but what did that mean? Had she already caused some problem for his future?

She stepped out onto the porch as he rode up.

"Good afternoon, again. Were you expecting me?" He smiled.

"No. I was just going to get water from the pump," she lied.

He jumped off his horse. "Give me the bucket; I will get the water for you."

Oh yes, she had forgotten the bucket. She went back inside and came out with the bucket. As she gave it to him, he didn't say anything, but he grinned.

She went back inside and surveyed the food situation. By the time he returned with the water, she had made a decision. "Would you like to stay for supper?"

"Supper?"

"Yes, the meal people have in the evening?"

"Of course I know what supper is, but," he paused.

"Oh, I am sorry," she realized what she had done. "You must have someone who is waiting for you at home."

"No," he said slowly. "There is no one at home, but I did not want to impose."

"It is not an imposition, and I would welcome the company."

"All right," he said as he sat down at the kitchen table. "Your friends have not arrived."

"Not yet," she said as she poured water into a big pot. She was going to make pasta with tomato sauce, from a can. She had cheese and dried herbs to spice up the sauce. She also had the biscuits. It was not the greatest meal, a bit heavy on carbs, but it should be all right.

"Are your friends really coming?" asked Jeff.

"Yes, they gave me a range of dates and tomorrow is the last day. One of them will definitely be here tomorrow." She couldn't tell him how she knew.

"If you like I could send a telegraph to inquire."

"If they don't show up tomorrow, I will take you up on your offer. Thank you."

The pasta took about twenty minutes, and by then everything else was ready. Jeff opened a couple of beers and helped her set the table. With the lantern and candles, there was enough light.

They started to eat, and she had to admit it was not bad.

"This is good spaghetti," said Jeff.

"So do you eat spaghetti often?" She knew the first pasta factory had been established in Brooklyn in 1848, but wondered if it was a common food out here.

"No. They do not serve it at the hotel where I go out for meals."

"So you don't cook?"

He looked at her strangely. "Of course I cook when I am traveling, and even when I am in Durango I cook often, but sometimes I go to the restaurant."

Of course he would have to cook when he was on the road, she realized. He would starve otherwise.

"You are quite different," he said.

She smiled. "I probably speak my mind more often than you are accustomed to. Women from the city are like that."

"No, that's not it. I have been to New York and San Francisco and I have never met someone like you."

She didn't know what to say. After the intensive studies of the customs and the language, and scoring high on the tests, she thought she would have fit well. "How am I different?"

"The questions you ask are phrased a bit differently, and there are other things. You are obviously a woman of means, yet you travel without a servant or a companion. You decide to

46

stay in this," he waved his hand, "this cabin instead of the more comfortable hotel. You know how to shoot, but do not have a gun, you see the list goes on."

"I am not a criminal," she joked.

"I have no doubt that is true. Most criminals would carry a gun, and most would not invite a sheriff for dinner. Maybe you should tell me more about yourself?"

"Okay, but first tell me about yourself."

"All right, but there is not much to tell. I was born in Denver; my mother came from New York and my father was born and raised in Denver. I went to college there and then decided to become a lawman soon after I finished my studies. I have been doing this since."

"What did you study in college?"

"Geology."

"Geology," repeated Amy wondering how a geology major became a lawman. "Okay, I was born in San Francisco. My parents," she paused. "They both died in an accident when I was twelve so my aunt raised me."

"I'm sorry."

"Yeah, I still miss them," she said. "Like you, I also went to college, but at the University of California in Berkley, and I studied biology." It was all true, except the biology part. She knew women had been allowed in Berkley in 1870, so that could be true, but her degree in biochemistry would not be taught until at least 130 years later. Biology was the closest to what she was doing.

"So you live in San Francisco?"

"Near to San Francisco."

"So why are you here for ten days or less?"

She smiled, thinking he was not going to let that go. "It is eight days or less now, and we thought Durango was a good place for the three of us to meet before we continued our trip west."

"You and your two lady friends."

She realized having a man stay with them might be misconstrued in this era. "One is my lady friend and the other is her brother, Gustav."

"Ah, and it is he that arrives tomorrow?"

"Yes."

47

He looked at her as if searching for meaning to his arrival. "Good. I am glad you will have a man here with you."

There is nothing between Gustav and me she wanted to say. But then, why should she? She left it unsaid.

"Meanwhile, I want you to come into town with me tonight."

"Why?"

"I don't want you alone here after what has happened. I still don't know if Jeb was killed for a reason or randomly. If it was for a reason, you might be safer, but since I don't know, I prefer you out of harm's way."

"I don't want to go to town, and Gustav will be here tomorrow."

"I am not inviting you to my home," stressed Jeff. "I will take you to the hotel. It is quite respectable."

She looked at him not budging.

"Do you have money to pay for a room? I can lend you the money," he offered.

"I have the money."

"I don't understand why you are so obstinate about this. Are you not a tiny bit scared being alone out here?"

"I am afraid."

"Then?"

"Why don't you stay?"

"You want me to stay here?" he exclaimed.

"Well, I want to stay here, and I would feel much better if you stayed with me."

"I am not a baby sitter for rent," said Jeff, a bit annoyed.

"Well fine, then. Go, but I cannot go with you."

"You will not go is more like it." He studied her. "You are an obstinate lady, but I will stay. The cabin is close to the ridge, and I have to be there early tomorrow morning."

She had extra pillows and sheets, and she pulled the two overstuffed chairs together to make a bed. He helped, but it was obvious he was not pleased, and there was little conversation between them. Afterwards, she picked up the bucket to get water to make hot tea and he intercepted her.

"I can get that."

"It's all right. I don't want to get used to having you here."

"For the next eight or less days?"

48

She laughed and gave him the bucket, but then walked outside with him. The night was crisp and clear and there were hundreds of stars lighting the black skies. She gave an involuntary gasp, and Jeff looked at her.

"What is wrong?"

"The stars. They look amazing tonight."

He looked up, "They usually look this way."

"There are so many it is hard to distinguish the constellations."

"Well, there is Orion," he pointed, "and there is the North Star."

"Yes I see them now. And Cassiopeia, the 'W'."

"That's right," he said.

He continued to the pump and filled the bucket. As they walked back she said, "I notice you don't smoke."

"It is a smelly, expensive habit."

"You are quite correct on that. Please never start. And don't chew tobacco either."

"See, that is exactly what I mean. You say things very differently."

That night, as she lay in bed, she found it hard to sleep as she thought of Jeff on the other side of the thin bedroom door. He was handsome and considerate, quite different from what she had expected in an 1895 man. Then she realized what she was thinking. What was she doing?

Having the sheriff there was safer, her mind reasoned. Safer in one way, more dangerous in another, replied her mind. It wouldn't happen, she told herself; she had control of her feelings.

Chapter 9
The sheriff

The next morning Amy awoke with the rising sun again and dressed quickly. When she stepped in the other room, she did not see Jeff. The sheets had been folded neatly. Maybe he left, she thought, remembering he wanted to go back to the ridge early, but then she noticed the water boiling. He could not be far.

She started making breakfast.

Almost immediately, Jeff walked in, "Good morning."

"Good morning. Would you like some eggs for breakfast?"

"That would be wonderful," he said.

"Did you sleep well last night?"

"Yes. Did you?"

"All right," she said. Once she had finally fallen asleep, she had slept well.

They sat down to have the eggs and biscuits with a strong cup of black tea.

"I am sorry I don't have coffee," she said.

"This tea is fine. I will be heading to the ridge soon, and I guess there is no reason to return. Your friend is probably arriving on the noon carriage, and he should be here shortly afterwards. You should be safer then."

"Yes. That is fine, but I was wondering," she paused. "Could I accompany you to the ridge?"

"What?" It sounded like he thought she was insane.

"The reason I was out there yesterday was to study the plant life. There is a very rare little yellow flower that I am interested in. I need to collect a specimen to take back to the university. I figure that with you I will be safer out there."

"A flower." It looked like he didn't understand.

"I am a biologist. It is what I do."

"You put yourself in danger for a flower? I cannot understand that. The answer is no. You cannot accompany me."

She looked down at the table. "In that case, I will go by myself."

"Fine, I cannot make you do anything." Jeff sounded exasperated and took his dishes to the sink.

Amy saw him look back at her and shake his head. She had gotten on her horse shortly after he left and had almost caught up with him. She was not going to ride with him since he didn't want that, but still, they were both going in the same direction.

After following him like that for a while, he stopped. She stopped as well. He turned and shouted, "All right, Amy. You can ride next to me. That way I will not feel like I am being hunted."

She rode up next to him. "Finding this yellow flower is the most important thing of my trip."

"Don't you see that is a strange thing to say?"

"It is the truth."

They continued quietly for a while.

"It may have very valuable medicinal attributes," she added.

"You are quite passionate about your work, aren't you?" he asked.

"Probably as much as you are."

"All right," he nodded in agreement. "Amy, just up ahead, I will head to the east side of the ridge. That is where the entrance to the mine is."

"And I will continue up the western slope as I did yesterday."

"If you like, wait for me there, and we can both return together. It should not take too long to talk to the men there."

"The shouting men."

"Smart men don't usually shout at the sheriff."

Before she reached the top of the ridge, she dismounted and started to walk. She didn't want the horse to trample the flowers that were blooming. It was a colorful carpet and even from a distance, she could see several yellow flowers that could be the corydalis curvisiliqua. She could take several specimens back to the cabin to analyze them further. She had brought a small spade, and she started to look for a healthy plant. Suddenly, she heard men shouting below.

This time she was braver, knowing the sheriff was down there, and she peeked over the ridge. She saw two men standing in front of the opening to a cave. They were looking at Jeff, who was facing them.

"You'd best leave now," said one.

"Answer my question," said Jeff.

"We know nothing," said the same man. "All we know about Jeb was that he was trespassing on private property. He was interfering where he shouldn't have."

"So you killed him?"

"We did not," shouted the second man, who appeared to be more emotional.

"Well, this property is private, but it is not yours, so I could cite you for trespassing," stated Jeff.

"We have a right to be here," said the first man. "Ask Mr. LaForce."

"Why don't we ride into town to clear this up," said Jeff.

"No. We don't want to waste time just as we are about to strike it rich."

"Did you see Jeb here?" asked Jeff.

"Yes," said the first man.

"No," said the other at the same time.

"It's hard to decide which one of the two of you is telling the truth. I think it best you both come with me. Right now," said Jeff forcefully.

"Wait, I don't need to go," said the emotional man.

Jeff had his hand on his gun when suddenly he looked up at her. The spade she was carrying had reflected the sun to his eyes. Almost immediately, the nervous man pulled out his gun and shot.

The scene unfolded in slow motion as she saw the puff the smoke, heard the sound and watched Jeff fall back. She ducked down immediately.

Oh my God, she thought. She was responsible for Jeff being shot. She was sure she had distracted him. What had she done, and how was she going to fix it?

She heard one man calling the other an idiot for what he had done.

"I thought he was getting ready to arrest us," said the other.

"And now you will be arrested for killing a lawman," said the voice that appeared calmer and in charge.

"Wait, wait, he is still alive. He is breathing."

Alive, she thought. She had to get down there. Once the men left, she could help him. She had the latest medicines in the cabin, and then he would be fine. She had to hope for that. She crouched down and started down the hill. It was steep, but she could do it. There were large boulders strewed along the way that would give her cover from below.

The men were continuing their discussion on what do to.

"Maybe we just leave him," said the man who had shot him.

"It looks like you hit his shoulder. He's not going to die from that. He must have hit his head when he fell."

"If we left him and he died, it wouldn't be my fault."

"Right, or he may recover and not agree you. Then he will come after us. You best finish him off."

"You want me to shoot him as he is lying there?"

"Since when have you had difficulties with doing that?"

She had almost reached the ground and she paused.

"Tell you what, let's finish loading the cart and then we check on him. Maybe if we are lucky he will be dead from the brain concussion."

Damn, she thought, it sounded like Jeff was very injured. She needed to get to him. She peeked around the rock and saw that the men had gone back inside the cave. One was telling the other how a cousin had died of a brain concussive thing. Then their voices were drowned out by the noises from their work. Jeff was still lying where he had fallen.

She sat down behind the rock to think. She could see Jeff's horse where he had left him. Luckily, the horse had not run away. If she could bring the horse over to Jeff, she might be able to help him onto his horse, but she needed time. The men would not stay away too long. Then an idea popped into her head. It was not the best idea, but she was running out of options.

She rode up to the cave on the sheriff's horse and shouted a greeting.

Both men immediately came out.

53

"Good morning, gentlemen," she said.

They stared for a moment, and the one in charge answered.

"Good morning, Miss, what brings you here?"

They obviously had not recognized the horse she was on.

"I am sorry to interrupt your work, but can you direct me to Durango? I have lost my way."

They looked at each other, and one glanced towards the sheriff. From where she was she could not see him, and she had done that intentionally.

"I can help you with those directions," said the man in charge. He turned to the other man, "Go on, Bob, finish what you were doing. Why don't you get down, Miss, and I will draw a map for you."

She dismounted and he walked to her.

"You are a beautiful woman to be out here alone," he said when he reached her.

She gave him a big smile. "Thank you, sir."

"My name is Tom. It occurs to me that maybe after I give you directions, we could get to know each other?"

He was a creep. "I think some sort of payment would be appropriate," she said as she took some steps, moving away from the entrance of the cave. "Do you and your friend live in Durango?"

"I do. Were you thinking of paying us a visit there?" he moved closer to her.

His breath was horrid, and all she could do was smile not wanting to inhale. "Why wait until then? I could show appreciation right here."

"Right here?"

They both heard a cough coming from the other side of the entrance. Jeff was coming to. The man glanced in that direction, and she brought out the stun gun and shot. At the close range it was easy, and Tom went down without a sound. Then she pricked him, she had fifteen minutes and counting.

She ran to Jeff and saw he was stirring.

"Jeff, Jeff, can you hear me?"

He mumbled something.

"Can you get up?" She tugged on him. "Please get up." He got on his knees, and she helped pulled him up the rest of the

54

way. He stood, but was wobbly on his legs and she had to hold him while he regained some of his balance.

"My head," he mumbled. "Oh, my shoulder."

There was blood on the backside of his head. She briefly wondered about a concussion, but if they didn't get out of there, that would be the least of their problems. She could hear Bob still working inside the cave.

She helped push Jeff up the horse and climbed behind him. As soon as she was up, she got the horse moving. She picked up her horse on the way back to the cabin.

Gustav arrived several hours later. She had seen him coming and met him on the porch.

"It is good to see a familiar face. I can't believe the stupid machine sent me so far away," he said.

"It is good to see you, too, and I agree about the machine. Come inside."

"Hey, I noticed an extra horse in the barn and... there is a man in the bed!"

"Yes, that is the sheriff; he is sleeping, I gave him a sedative."

"Dr. Holbrook said he was nosing around."

"It is worse than that, Gustav. I am responsible for him being shot." She went on to tell him the story.

"Damn, damn," was all Gustav could say afterwards.

"What are we going to do?"

"Well, he would have died if you left him there and maybe that was not supposed to happen. If you are sure he was shot because of you, he should not die." He shook his head. "We have to call Dr. Holbrook."

"He is going to call us soon." Amy went into the kitchen and prepared tea. She brought Gustav a cup and sat down with him.

"This whole time experiment is failing," said Gustav.

She sipped her tea. "I did find the corydalis curvisiliqua."

"Oh?"

"But I was not able to get a specimen because of what happened."

"Oh." He drank some of his tea. "Maybe I can go and get the specimen after the call."

"As long as those men are gone."

"I can handle two stupid men."

His tone was surprising to her. Anyone would be a bit scared, but he sounded very confident.

He saw her studying him. "Do you think that you were the only one having to deal with problems?"

"No?"

"No. If you remember, I was here before, setting up this cabin and getting the horses. It was easier then because the transport dropped me off close to Durango. This time, I was dropped 270 damn kilometers away."

"I'm sorry."

"It was not your fault, but these trip have affected me. I am not the same man you knew."

He did look different.

"Hello, hello." The ComLink activated.

"Hello, Dr. Holbrook," Amy answered quickly.

"Has Gustav arrived?"

"Yes, Dr. Holbrook, I am here," said Gustav.

"Good, good. Now we can get underway. I want you back today if possible."

"There is a complication," said Gustav. "Why don't you tell them, Amy?"

There was silence from the future as Amy told her story.

The silence continued for a moment after she finished, and then Dr. Holbrook asked, "The sheriff is in the cabin right now?"

"Yes, he is here. What did you find out about his lifeline?" she asked.

"It is a most complicated lifeline. It branches out in many directions, and we cannot tell if that is because of some error in coding or if the machine is malfunctioning."

"What should we do with him?" asked Gustav.

"Nothing for now. We are going to run his lifeline again and, knowing what you have told me, we may have better visibility. Now, give me the name of who you have come into contact with."

"There is Tom and Bob from the mine," said Amy, "but I don't know last names."

Jeff started to cough and Gustav looked at Amy. "Go see if he is awake; I'll finish here."

As Amy walked into the bedroom, she heard Gustav giving the names of the people that he had contact with. She heard Rick LaForce's name and thought that was an interesting coincidence.

Jeff was still asleep. She checked his pulse and it was strong. His fever was down, as well.

When she went back to the kitchen, Gustav was talking softly. "I will take care of it if we have to."

"I don't think you will have to," said Dr. Holbrook.

Then Gustav saw her and a tinge of guilt crossed his face. "Amy is back. So you want us to wait until tomorrow?"

"One more day should allow the sheriff to recover and will give Susan time to arrive," said Dr. Holbrook.

When they disconnected the call, Amy asked about Susan. "I thought she was coming with you."

"I saw her in Grand Junction, but she missed the stagecoach. It left rather early, and I could not afford to wait for her."

"Oh, that's too bad. She will probably catch the next stagecoach and be here tomorrow."

"Yeah, probably," he said without much care. "Amy, the critical issue is we need to leave ASAP, and I would like to make sure we have the specimen before that."

"I can take you where I found it."

"No. You need to stay here," he pointed to the bedroom.

"But," she stopped. He was right. They couldn't leave Jeff alone to wander through the cabin. "All right, I'll draw a map so you can get there faster."

"Thanks."

Gustav was soon on his way, and she returned to the bedroom.

She checked Jeff's bandages and his eyes opened.

"Hello," she said. "How are you feeling?"

"Good," he paused. "Maybe as well as can be. My head is still pounding."

It was a minor concussion, but she had been able to treat it. "When you fell backwards you hit your head on the rocks. Luckily, it is not bad."

"Luckily, I have a hard head," he grinned.

"I feel so bad about what happened. It was all my fault," she told him about the reflecting light and the reason he got shot.

"I think he was going to shoot me regardless of what you did."

"But you could have defended yourself better if you had kept your eyes on them."

"I don't know that. You came to get me. How did you get there?"

"I crawled down the ridge and snuck past them as they worked in the cave. Your horse was still there, and you were just waking up when I arrived."

"I do remember that."

"Let me change your shoulder bandage."

He sat up and she started to remove the old bandages. There had been a lot of blood, but once she had cauterized the wound, the bleeding stopped. She cleaned the wound with an antibacterial solution.

"It doesn't look so bad," he said.

The solution was speeding up the healing.

"I heard Gustav leave," he said.

"Yes."

"He has gone to get the flower you mentioned?"

"Yes."

"I noticed he didn't want you to go and you paid attention to him. It didn't seem to work with me."

She realized he had overheard some of the conversation and wondered how much. "I didn't want to leave you alone." She finished putting the bandage back. "Your wound is clean and it should heal well."

"I am sure it will."

"Jeff, we will most likely leave for San Francisco tomorrow."

"I guess your eight days or less has turned into less."

"We will have the flower today, and Gustav wants to get back soon."

"What about his sister?"

"She was in Grand Junction and should be arriving tomorrow." She turned to leave the room.

"Amy, you saved me."

She looked at him. "I saved you after I almost had you shot."

"No, I don't look at it that way. You saved me after being shot. They were probably going to kill me. A wounded sheriff is like a wounded bear. You have to finish him off or he'll keep coming after you."

She had to laugh at the analogy.

"Good. I prefer a nurse with a brighter disposition."

"All right then. Do you want anything to drink? Gustav brought coffee."

He fell asleep afterwards and she started on the dinner preparation. She had planned on making chicken, but seeing that they were going to sell her a live chicken, she had opted for making eggs with hash browns. She realized she could easily become a vegetarian in this time.

"Hello, hello," said a voice through the ComLink. She quickly muted the voice and peeked in the bedroom. Jeff was still asleep.

"Hello, Dr. Holbrook," she said softly.

"Is the patient awake?"

"He is asleep."

"And Gustav?"

"He went to get the specimen."

"That's good. On our side we have good news and some bad news."

"Go ahead."

"The sheriff should be alive. His lifeline shows he is alive in 1895."

"That is good news."

"The next years are still unclear for the sheriff. The bad news is that one of the two men you mentioned should have been killed."

"Killed? Are you sure?"

"Yes. Bob had no lifeline after this year."

"Oh." She knew that the dates and places were an estimate on the computer. "Bob could still die later this year."

"Yes, he could, but maybe the sheriff should have shot him."

She did not know what she was supposed to do about that. She was not about to chase Bob to kill him. Maybe Gustav would do it. He had changed and might be capable of doing that.

"We will keep an eye on Bob and let you know of changes. Meanwhile, Susan should arrive tomorrow. I want you to wait for her, and then I want all of you here by the evening."

"All right. That is exactly what we were planning."

When she looked into the bedroom, Jeff was sitting up.

"Gustav is back?" he asked.

"No, I..." she realized he might have heard her. "Yes, he did return, but went out again to get more firewood."

"I thought I heard you speak to someone."

"Yes." She did not add any more, wondering what he might have heard.

"I know you are very interested in that yellow flower for medicinal purposes, but did you know that there are other flowers the Indians use?"

"Really?" It would be fascinating to study those. Maybe she could stay a few days to study them. Then she realized there might be another reason prompting her to do so. It would be better to leave and return some other time.

"You might consider staying to study those," he said.

"Our schedule is quite set; I don't think I can change it."

"Of course. Well, I'm thinking it is best I go back into town."

"Now?"

"I am feeling remarkably well, and it will give Gustav and you more privacy tonight."

She knew it was for the best. "Will you come and visit tomorrow?"

"No, I don't think so. There is no reason."

"You don't think Tom and Bob will be back at the mine?"

He looked at her for a moment before answering. "No, they should be long gone. They probably left soon after they discovered I was gone."

She turned to go back to the kitchen. "Well, if you like eggs and hash browns, that is what is for dinner and you are welcome to stay."

"Amy?"

"Yes?"

"How did you know their names?"

She looked at him blankly.

"Tom and Bob?" he prompted.

"You must have told me."

He nodded, but did not look convinced.

Damn, she thought. He had not told her and it had slipped out. She hadn't told him the truth. The story of sneaking past them had seemed like a simpler explanation, and now he had caught her lie.

Gustav returned shortly with the corydalis curvisiliqua. "Isn't she beautiful," he placed it on the kitchen table spilling dirt all over.

She didn't complain because he was right; it was beautiful. "It is an excellent specimen."

"Hello there," Jeff was standing at the door of the bedroom.

Gustav threw her a look and went to greet him.

They introduced themselves and shook hands.

"So that is the famous flower," said Jeff coming closer to the table. "Amy, Miss Waterman, has talked about it. Kind of looks common."

"We hope it will be the cure to several diseases," said Gustav.

"So I hear. Hey, I'm glad you found your sister," said Jeff.

Gustav looked bewildered and Amy jumped in. "Yes, it is wonderful Susan will be here tomorrow, and we can all travel together as planned."

Gustav nodded.

"Well, I will be on my way," said Jeff.

"You are not staying for dinner?" asked Gustav.

"No, I best leave you two with your flower."

"Maybe you should stay. That was a nasty bump on your head." The words were said, but Gustav didn't sound concerned about Jeff's well being.

Amy realized Gustav might be thinking Jeff should not be allowed to leave. "I think the sheriff is well enough to go, Gustav, and my culinary skills could not persuade him otherwise. Meanwhile, I know Dr. Holbrook will be very happy with this specimen when we see him soon."

"Have you noticed she talks a bit differently?" Jeff asked Gustav.

"Well, you know women," said Gustav.

"I'll walk out with you," said Amy as Jeff headed out the door.

She helped him put the saddle back on his horse, but before he climbed on he turned to her. "I know something is going on here. I know you are not a criminal, but there is something strange about you and Gustav."

"We will be gone tomorrow, and then you will not have to worry about us."

"Too bad."

"You want to worry?"

"It is not the worry I am going to miss." He swung up on his horse and left towards town.

She watched him for a while, thinking about that last comment.

Chapter 10
Finally, Susan

Gustav had not brought curtains, so the next morning she was up with the sun again. It was all right; she was getting used to this schedule. She dressed and met Gustav out in the kitchen. They ate breakfast with little conversation.

At dinner he had been more engaging although the several beers might have helped. He had said a couple of surprising things, and maybe this morning he regretted being so open, she reasoned. The bit about being underappreciated at work and having to find a different way to make more money was slightly troubling.

"Not a bad breakfast," he said as he finished.

"Yeah, it's lucky we have the packaged meals. It's so hard to cook anything here."

"You seemed to do all right. The biscuits were good."

"It was a premade mix," she smiled.

He looked at her. "Hey, what is going on with you and the sheriff?"

"The sheriff?"

"I saw how you pampered him."

"He was injured due to me. I probably could not pamper him enough!" she said forcefully.

"Okay, okay. You obviously have feelings for him, otherwise you would not be so defensive."

"And you have a degree in psychology now?"

His face turned dark. "No. I am not a doctor like you, Dr. Waterman. I realize I am in the minority at the lab, and I am reminded of it all the time, but where would all of you be without me?"

She had not realized he was sensitive about that. "I didn't know that you didn't have your doctorate, Gustav, and I don't think it makes a whole heck of a difference out here." He still looked upset.

"I guess you did hit a nerve with me," she conceded. "I may have developed some feelings for him."

"I knew it," he nodded. "Don't you want to stay here with him?"

She looked at him to see if he was joking. He wasn't, but she took it like a joke. "Yeah, right. Can you imagine how Dr. Holbrook would take that news?"

"I think you would do very well here," he said seriously. "Well, let's start packing."

They were taking very little back with them. Most of the packing involved putting away things that would be used for the next visitors. Extra nutrition bars, the perimeter monitoring system, another specimen container and several other items were stored in a canvas bag.

On a previous trip, Gustav and Anthony had built a storage compartment under the floor. The area was accessed through a small trap door that was disguised to look like a floorboard. Gustav showed her the tapping code that would open the door. The area underneath was quite large, and the canvas bag fit easily.

"Should we put the bedding and pillow in here as well?" asked Amy, thinking about animals that may get into the cabin while they were gone.

"No. The next visitors will probably want to sterilize all of it anyway."

"Yeah, that's probably true," said Amy.

"Hey, we are almost finished here, and I was wondering if I could take a ride to see more of this beautiful country," said Gustav. "I didn't get a chance last time."

"Oh yeah, it is beautiful out here, and thanks for the horse by the way. She is really wonderful."

"Both horses are great," he said. "Just think, if you stayed, you could keep yours."

She thought it was a strange comment, but he left soon after that. She finished putting things away and closed the trap door. It fit seamlessly. Now all she had left to do was to wait for Susan to arrive. It might be hours. Amy decided to bake again; it helped pass the time and would make a good lunch.

A couple of hours later, Susan showed up, and she was not alone. She came in a horse and buggy driven by Rick LaForce.

They were laughing and enjoying themselves so much it took them a moment to notice her standing on the porch.

"Oh my, it is Miss Waterman," said Rick. "I did not know you were here as well. How can it be that the two prettiest girls in the county are staying in this run-down cabin?"

"Hello, Mr. LaForce," said Amy. "It is just temporary lodgings, and we will be on our way soon. Hello, Susan."

Rick turned to her. "Susan? I thought you told me your name was Suzanna?"

"She calls me by my plain name," sighed Susan. "I really prefer Suzanna."

"Then, my dear, Suzanna it is," said Rick magnanimously.

They climbed off the buggy, and Amy had a chance to really look at Susan. She had aged in the weeks gone by. She looked thin and her normally clear complexion looked dry and reddish. Her hair had lost its shine and it was cut short, hacked was a better description. Amy wanted Rick to leave so she could talk to her.

"Shall we go inside?" asked Suzanna.

"Of course, Sus... Suzanna, come this way," said Amy. She turned to say good-bye to Rick, "Have a good day, Mr. LaForce, and thank you for bringing ..."

"No. Mr. LaForce should not leave just yet," said Suzanna.

"Your brother Gustav is here," Amy told her.

She laughed. "Gustav? My brother? How amusing that Gustav has deemed to be here."

Amy became nervous that Suzanna was going to say something stupid and added quickly, "We were both worried about you."

"Maybe it is best I go," suggested Rick.

"No. Mr. LaForce, please come into this," she looked at it, "this cabin. Amy do you have something we can drink?"

"Tea and coffee."

She laughed. "That is very much like you, Amy. So no whiskey or gin, or even claret?"

Amy shook her head.

"Come on, Gustav probably has some liquor hidden inside," she went into the cabin, and Rick and Amy followed her.

Gustav had still not returned, and Amy started to wonder how long a ride was he taking.

"Oh, Gustav," shouted Suzanna. "Where are you, my dear brother?"

"He must have gone to get more firewood," said Amy, thinking it was becoming the standard excuse for him.

"I smell something good," said Suzanna.

"I made biscuits. Would you like some?"

"Yes. I am famished," said Suzanna. "How about you, Mr. LaForce?"

"Tea will be fine by me," he said.

"I have lost weight these past weeks," said Suzanna, "notice?"

"Yes, I noticed," nodded Amy. "How did you and Mr. LaForce meet?"

Suzanna laughed. "Probably not the same way you did."

"I met him on the carriage coming to Durango," said Amy.

"I met him in a saloon in Grand Junction."

Amy wondered what that meant.

"He is a good tipper," said Suzanna.

"And you are a most excellent companion," said Mr. LaForce, touching her chin in a familiar manner.

It was too much information, thought Amy. They obviously knew each other quite well.

"I see you are shocked," said Suzanna. "How do you think brother will take it?"

"Not too well, I think," said Amy.

Suzanna laughed. "Or maybe he will be pleased I am paying my own way."

Amy cut large slices of cheese and served them with the biscuits, thinking that would help Susan's disposition.

"Look at you, the domesticated scientist," said Suzanna. "You know she went to college?"

"I studied biology," said Amy wanting to intercept anything she might say. "Suzanna went to college also."

"It did not serve me as much," said Suzanna, munching on the biscuits. "These are quite good. From scratch?"

Mr. LaForce looked puzzled.

"Sure," said Amy. "Have another cup of tea, Mr. LaForce?"

"No. I really must go back. My darling," he turned to Suzanna. "I will visit you tomorrow?"

"Yes. I will stay here tonight, but tomorrow I think it is best I move to a more becoming location."

"I agree. If you stay at the hotel, it will cut down on my travel time."

"And then we will have more time for you know what," smiled Suzanna.

Mr. LaForce winked back. He left soon afterwards.

"So Amy, what is new with you?" asked Suzanna.

"Apparently nothing, compared with you. What happened, Susan?"

"Suzanna. It's Suzanna now and shit happens, that's what happened. When I left the lab I thought I would arrive here. I knew the boxes were being shipped here, and I would have no problem surviving. I would show the people in the lab that I was better than they thought. I could do the mission just as well as any of them could. I had the cash and the equipment from the boxes. I could have done it, easily."

She sounded bitter, thought Amy.

"Of course, things did not turn out as planned. They rarely do for me. I was dropped in some god-forsaken town in eastern Colorado and used most of the money to get to Denver and then Grand Junction. Then I realized the timing was wrong! I had to wait for weeks, and the money ran out. That wasn't even the worst of it. You know what was?"

Amy shook her head.

"The filth and disease. I was so afraid of catching something and dying, or worse, barely surviving. And then, somehow I found strength to make it. I ended selling my hair; notice the haircut?"

Amy nodded.

"I think this haircut suits the new person that is me. You know, I thought you would come looking for me. I really hoped you would."

"We did look for you. We left just hours after you did."

"What? How can that be! I have been here four weeks!" she complained

"Wait a moment. You were the one who snuck away and left in the middle of the night. My project was going to be cancelled and all the resources were directed to finding you. Luckily, Gustav convinced Dr. Holbrook that we could find you and complete the project at the same time. Your escapade almost ruined it for all of us."

Suzanna gave her look, but it was a bit more contrite.

"As to why you were sent elsewhere? Apparently the senso-static controls drifted during the day, and no one was there to check them when you left."

"That is true," she said

"In fact, there is another problem besides the controls drifting. Gustav, who was seated right next to me, did not appear here with me. He was deposited near Grand Junction, and he just arrived yesterday."

"It sounds like our time machine is seriously flawed. I guess we should be thankful we are here in one piece and not strewn across time and space."

"Yeah," said Amy more calmly. "At least the travel back to the lab seems to work well. We will be leaving soon."

"Speaking of which, where is my dearest brother? I did see him in Grand Junction."

"I don't know. He went for a ride and should have been back by now," Amy was getting worried.

Suzanna walked around the little room looking at things. "By the way, have you used the solar shower?"

"Yes," smiled Amy. "That was a wonderful idea. I have stored it away, but I can take it out."

"That would nice. I could shower while we wait for Gustav. It would make me more presentable for my return."

"Sure."

"And do you have shampoo? I am tired of using soap on my hair."

That would explain the dullness, thought Amy. "I brought a small bottle."

While Susan showered, Amy took a look outside for Gustav. It was strange. Why was he taking so long? Dr. Holbrook wanted them back soon, and Gustav knew that.

She walked back into the kitchen and that is when she noticed. The container with the flower was gone. He must have taken it.

She was still staring where the container had been when Suzanna came in toweling her hair. "What's wrong?"

"I can't find Gustav, and he has taken the specimen."

"He probably took it to the future. Maybe he wanted to take the credit for bringing the valuable specimen."

"You think? But we can go now, so it does not gain him much. I will call Dr. Holbrook and let him know we are ready." She opened the cupboard and froze. The communication device had been crushed. Then she looked at Suzanna and ran out the door. She was very much afraid of what she would find.

Suzanna ran after her and almost bumped into her as she stopped abruptly. The stump next to the barn was gone. "The transport marker is gone," said Amy.

"Are you sure?" asked Suzanna.

"Of course, I'm sure," said Amy harshly. "It was right there and now it's not. We cannot transport, and no one will be able to come to get us. The worse part is we can't even talk to the future to let them know what had happened." She turned and slowly headed back to the cabin.

"But why would Gustav take the marker and break the ComLink?" asked Suzanna.

"I don't know why. We will get back eventually, so I don't know what it buys Gustav."

"Everyone will know that he left us here, and he will be in trouble. It makes no sense."

"You don't happen to have a ComLink on you, do you?" asked Amy.

"No. I transported without one. I was afraid the lab would track me down too easily if I brought one, so I didn't. That was a big mistake."

"But, how did Dr. Holbrook know you were in Grand Junction?"

"Like I said, I saw Gustav. He spent the night at the hotel above the saloon where I worked. He came into the saloon and we talked. He must have told them."

"And why didn't you come with him?"

"He left very early. We had planned to come together, but he gave me the wrong time for the stagecoach departure and I missed it."

"So he didn't want you here, and he was anxious about getting the specimen himself," said Amy, thinking about it. "In the right hands, that flower could be quite valuable in the future."

"Of course, that's it. He must have a buyer already lined up," said Suzanna. "That would be the only explanation. Maybe he plans to quit his job and leave the lab before we get back."

Amy looked at Suzanna with despair. "I hope we can find a way back soon. I'm not sure how much longer I can handle this place. I know I put on a brave front, but that was because I knew it was a short time, but now ..."

"I know what you mean, but you just have to be strong. I did it, and I know you are stronger than me."

Amy had been stronger than Susan, but Suzanna might be stronger now. In any case, she was right; they needed a plan. "There is another transport marker in San Francisco."

Suzanna nodded, "I know about that one."

"On the other hand, maybe we should wait here," continued Amy, thinking out loud. "What if they send someone to look for us? We would have better chances of meeting them here. What do you think?"

Suzanne gave a crazy laugh. "You are going through the same thought process I went through. I waited for days, and no one came. I should have started making my way to Durango, but I clung to that hope that someone would show up. I am not doing that again."

"All right then, that decides it; we will go to San Francisco," said Amy decisively.

"Wait a moment, how much money do you have?"

"Oh," said Amy, realizing that was probably the first step. "Let me get my bag."

"We need to figure out how much the transportation, plus lodging and food is going to cost."

"This is all I have," said Amy spilling the contents of her purse. She started to count it.

"I think we might have to get a job," said Suzanna, looking at the amount.

Amy glanced at her and continued counting. She didn't want to talk about the work Suzanna had in mind.

"You know, Amy, I almost starved before I started to work. Hunger makes you do whatever it takes. Luckily, I have some class, or so I'm told, so I attract the higher paying clients."

"Thirty-nine dollars. Is it anywhere close?" It sounded like a trivial amount.

"Well, it's not enough, but it is a good start. I think the rail fare to San Francisco from Denver will cost about $25 for each of us. We can catch the train closer to here and not have to go all the way back to Denver; that will be cheaper."

"We have to add the stagecoach to the train," said Amy.

Suzanna nodded and continued. "To stay at a decent hotel is $1.50 to $2 per night, and we could share a room. Food runs about the same for each of us, so say $6 per day for both of us. Give us four days in San Fran to find the transport marker; that is $24. So all together we need at least, $74. I have four dollars, so together we have more than half."

"Just barely," said Amy.

"Look on the bright side," said Suzanna. "Mr. LaForce's establishment in town is nice, and he is not a bad man. He can give us both jobs. I can teach you how to avoid getting scammed or hurt."

"I don't think I can do it, Suzanna."

"Well, I am not working the streets of San Francisco if we run out of money. I'd rather work for Mr. LaForce here, at a decent place, and earn the money that way."

"I will borrow the money."

"From whom?"

"The sheriff. He is my friend."

"Really? He would give you 30 bucks, knowing he won't get them back? That is quite a bit of money. It would take me, one of the highest paid people, at least three weeks to make that."

"Three weeks?"

"Three weeks at a good, reputable establishment like Mr. LaForce's."

Chapter 11
Borrowing money

The following day Amy walked into the sheriff's office. The deputy was sitting at his desk.

"Good morning," she said, "I was hoping to see the sheriff."

"The sheriff has just stepped out. How can I help you?"

"It is nothing urgent, I just wanted to talk to him."

"Well, he will not be gone long. He likes to walk around the town. You are welcome to wait here for him."

"Thank you, but I will come back."

"Do you want to give him a message?"

"No, thank you." It was too complicated for a verbal message, and she didn't see any paper to write on. Anyway, she didn't want to leave her name on something that might affect the future.

She wondered where he usually walked and decided to take a walk herself. As she went around the corner, she saw him.

A young woman was talking to him just down the street. By the inclination of her body and the fluttering of her eyes, she was interested in the sheriff and he did not seem to mind the attention.

She walked towards them slowly.

The woman was talking rapidly and finally she came to a pause, at which time Amy jumped in. "Good morning, sheriff."

"Good morning, Miss Waterman. Let me introduce you. This is Miss Penn."

The ladies nodded at each other.

"What brings you to town?" asked Jeff.

"I need your opinion on something."

"In that case, why don't we go to my office?"

She nodded.

"Good day, Miss Penn," said Jeff.

"Excuse me, sheriff?" asked Miss Penn. "Mother wanted me to remind you about supper this Sunday."

"Yes, I appreciate the invitation and will attend if I am able. Like I told her, I am on duty that day."

"Of course," said Miss Penn. "I understand that." She put emphasis on 'I,' as if she was the only woman in the world who could understand him.

Amy and Jeff headed back to the office.

"She appears to be an admirer," said Amy.

"I am twenty-nine and single, so it does not hurt to have an admirer."

They entered the office, and Jeff asked the deputy to finish making the rounds. Once the deputy left, Jeff took a seat behind his desk.

She sat down opposite him. "There have been some developments since I last saw you."

"I figured that. Weren't you leaving today?"

"That is one of the things that has changed."

Jeff waited.

"I need money."

"How much?"

"Thirty-one dollars."

He opened his desk drawer and took out a few bills. He went to the coat rack and took out what was in the pockets of his jacket. Then he opened his wallet and emptied it. "This is all I have."

It was all he had, and he was giving it to her. She watched him count the money, amazed at his generosity.

"Amy, I want to know what is going on, but if you do not feel like telling me, I will not interrogate you about it. Here are twenty-two dollars. I am sorry I do not have more. I do have some savings in the bank and..."

She cut him off. "No, I cannot take your savings. It is terrible I have to ask you for the money as it is, but I have no choice. Suzanna and I need to get to San Francisco, and we do not have enough funds for the trip."

"What happened to Gustav?"

"He left. He took the flower and left."

"He took your flower?"

"Yes."

"Not much of a friend."

Amy nodded slowly and stared out the window. Across the street she saw Mr. LaForce talking with Suzanna.

Jeff came over and stood next to her, "Are you thinking of asking him for the additional money?"

"No. I would not do that. The person with him is Susan, or Suzanna, as she now wants to be known."

"Your friend? They know each other?"

"She is hoping to work for him. Apparently she had been doing this type of work for the last weeks."

"Oh. I now see the urgency of leaving."

"Suzanna was desperate. It is hard to know what people will do when faced with hunger."

"I will get you the rest of the money."

"I can't pay you back, ever."

"Never? You will never come back this way?"

"I don't think so."

The door of the office opened, and the deputy walked in. "I finished the rounds sheriff. Everything is in order."

"Thank you, deputy. I am stepping out with Miss Waterman and will return shortly."

They left the office and he steered her towards the bank. "I will take out whatever you need."

She grabbed his hand. "No. I am serious about this. We will find some other way." She let go of his hand before people noticed. "Come with me, I might as well introduce you to Suzanna."

Suzanna and Mr. LaForce were conversing animatedly, but when Rick saw the sheriff he became serious.

"Hello, sheriff, Miss Waterman," he said.

"Hello, Rick," said Jeff.

Amy introduced the sheriff to Suzanna.

"My, what handsome men live in this town, Amy," said Suzanna. "We could stay here forever in such good company."

Amy stared at her friend and could not think what to say. Suzanna was taking her role very earnestly.

"Isn't she delightful," said Rick, but he didn't wait for response, "I will be hiring Miss Ross, and you can also find out how charming she is, sheriff, if you have the time."

Amy's mouth fell open in surprise. "I think this was a mistake. I am going back to the cabin, Suzanna. You can either come with me or not."

"Wait," said Rick. "I do not think that cabin is safe for two young ladies. Especially since the sheriff has not had much luck in finding the killer of that poor miner."

Amy glanced at Jeff wondering how he would take the accusation, but he looked unperturbed.

"I agree with Rick," said Jeff. "It may be best for you to find a room at the hotel for the night."

"Well, since that is settled," said Rick, convinced it was so. "Are you currently employed, Miss Waterman?"

Was the man going to make her a job offer? "I studied biology in college," she replied coolly.

"Ah, the study of the living things," grinned Rick. "The study of a man's body."

Suzanna giggled.

"It's also the study of slugs and worms," answered Amy.

Jeff smiled.

"I think Miss Waterman does not approve of my livelihood, sheriff," said Rick.

"I do," said Suzanna. "Your establishment satisfies a great need for the men of this town and provides good employment for the women."

Rick nodded approvingly.

"Rick, I need a word with you," said the sheriff.

"All right, sheriff. Ladies, why don't you go ahead inside and get a drink on the house. I will be with you immediately."

Suzanna and Amy walked into the saloon. Four men were seated at a table, playing cards and drinking, and another man was sitting on a stool at the bar. Otherwise the place was empty.

"What do you want to drink?" asked Suzanna.

"I don't know. Do they have tea? Suzanna, I don't like this business at all. You could get hurt easily."

"I wear protection, you know."

"It might protect you from getting a venereal disease, but what about a black eye, or a broken bone," she said, looking at the men.

"I am a saloon girl; it is different than a prostitute, Amy."

"Is there a difference, really?" She had not thought there was.

"Yes, and even as a prostitute, I would never 'bed' any of those men. Now the sheriff, he could be a possibility."

"No."

Suzanna smiled. "No? Why would you care?" She looked at her. "Oh, I see. You care for him."

"Yes, I care," said Amy. "So what? He just gave us all the money he had. It is twenty-two dollars, and he didn't ask for anything in return. I even told him we could not pay him back, ever."

"Oh my, it sounds like he cares for you too."

"I don't know, and it doesn't matter. Don't you get it? We need to get out of here as soon as we can."

"So how much money do we have right now?"

"Sixty-five dollars."

"We are almost there! I will only have to work a week, and then we will have plenty to make the trip to San Francisco."

"I don't want you to work a week here."

"This is my way to contribute, Amy. Let me do this. A saloon girl dances with the guys, listens to their stories, helps them buy drinks and the saloon owner keeps the guys in line. It is not bad. I make the money quickly, and I enjoy it. I am also very good at it."

There was nothing she could say to contradict that.

The bartender served them a drink in a champagne glass.

"What is this?" asked Amy

"A champagne flip," said Suzanna. "It is not as damaging to the liver as whiskey or rotgut, and it is the most expensive drink on the menu. Taste it, it isn't bad."

Amy felt like giving up. She sipped the drink. At least the alcohol would kill the bacteria, she reasoned. Mid-afternoon, she was in bar drinking, and she was considering a job as a saloon girl. What had happened?

"Hey ladies, you want to have some fun?" The man sitting on the stool addressed them.

They both turned away from him.

"Okay, there will always be drunks like that," said Suzanna, "but you learn how to deal with them."

Great, thought Amy, looking towards the exit.

Mr. LaForce walked in at that moment and came to them. "I am glad my establishment is treating you well," he said, looking at their drinks. "I am also glad Suzanna knows what to order."

"Of course, Mr. LaForce."

"Now, come to my office, Suzanna. We need to figure out the terms of employment." He started to walk away and then remembered. "Miss Waterman, the sheriff had to leave. You can stay here as long as you like, but don't interfere with the customers, please," he added so politely.

"Thank you, Mr. LaForce," said Amy, and then she whispered to Suzanna. "I am going to get a room at the hotel. I'll come back later to see how you are doing."

"No. Don't come back at night. People will think you are one of us."

Later that afternoon, Amy sat on her bed in the hotel room thinking about their situation. The room was going to cost $1.10 per night, and Susan could share the room. She felt quite hungry, but worried about the expense. Anything she spent would cost Suzanna more hours of work. She had picked up a menu from the restaurant downstairs earlier, and now she analyzed it. She finally decided she could have soup; it would fit the budget.

She went down the stairs and into the adjoining restaurant. It was mostly empty, and she was taken to a table by the window. She could see the saloon from there, and it looked very lively. Nikola Tesla had supplied Durango with an AC power plant, making it one of the first towns in the United States to have electricity. Electric lights lined the street and lighted both the saloon and the hotel.

"Would you like some company?" a voice asked.

She looked up and saw Jeff. "Please. I would love the company."

He sat down. "I am a bit surprised you followed my advice."

"Yes, I was overruled by you and Suzanna."

The waiter brought her soup and asked Jeff what he would like.

"I'll have the soup as well, and what are you having next, Miss Waterman?"

"The soup will be plenty for me."

"I will have the chicken with the roasted potatoes." He looked at her. "Are you sure?"

She nodded and the waiter left with the order.

Amy glanced out the window. "It turns out Suzanna has been working as a saloon girl. I thought she was a prostitute. It is a relief."

"Saloon girls are rarely prostitutes," said Jeff, "The pay is better for saloon girls and usually they are treated better."

Amy knew that now. "She wants to work for a week. Her salary, with what you gave me, will be enough to travel to San Francisco."

"So you will be here for a week?"

"Or less," she said and realized she was always doing that. "Anyway, how was your day? Did you get any closer to finding Tom and Bob?"

"No. Not really. They have disappeared."

"Tom and Bob," she said. "You know I lied to you."

He nodded slightly.

She told him about how after she had come down the ridge, she heard the men say they would finish him off. She had to act fast, so she came up with an idea. "I know it was a crazy idea, but I pretended to be lost and asked Tom and Bob for help. Tom offered to draw a map to Durango. At that point, Bob went back inside the cave and I was able to knock Tom unconscious. That is how I knew their names, and that is how I got you out of there."

"You risked your life for me?"

"A little."

He looked at her with admiration.

The waiter served the chicken and it smelled wonderful.

"Are you sure you will not have a bite?" he asked.

"Well, maybe just a bite."

After a couple of bites of chicken and a few potatoes and a couple glasses of claret, Amy was feeling better. "Thank you for sharing your meal, Jeff. I am wondering how you are going to pay for this? Didn't you give me all your money?"

Jeff smiled. "The restaurant lets me pay on credit."

"If I had known you were going to treat, I would have ordered more food," she laughed, feeling giddy.

They walked to her room and he waited as she opened the door.

"I would very much like to invite you in, but I can't and I can't do anything about it."

"I thought Gustav was the reason."

"Oh no. It is more complicated than that. Look, come over to the desk." She took out a fountain pen and used a piece of paper from the desk. She drew a line. "Say this is your life. When you make one decision over another, it takes you in slightly different directions. Do you see it?" She drew a couple branches off the line. "As you make other decisions, the branching continues."

"Where are you?"

"I am a completely different line."

"Do our lines meet?"

"No. They never cross each other. We have to keep the lines separate."

"But we are both here now."

"You know, you are right," she realized surprised. His statement was true. As soon as you made any contact with someone, there was an intersection, a crossing of the lines. It didn't matter how slight the contact was, they were both in the same place at that time.

"I am right," he said, "and with that thought, I leave you, Miss Waterman. Good night."

"Wait." She leaned over and kissed him on the cheek. "Thank you for dinner."

He smiled and closed the door after himself.

It was close to dawn when Suzanna tiptoed into the room.

"Susan?" asked Amy, half asleep as she crawled into bed.

"Yeah, it's me. I had a hard time getting in the hotel."

"What time is it?"

"Almost two thirty. I can't help how popular I am. I made good money tonight, but I was so busy I had to say no to several customers. Together we could make more, you know."

"Sure, sure," she said not listening. "Good night or morning." And she rolled over.

Chapter 12
Trying to make ends meet

Suzanna was still sleeping in the morning when Amy got out of bed. The pitcher had been filled with water the night before and she used the basin to wash up. She felt invigorated. The hotel was a much better place to stay.

She went into the restaurant and saw there were many people having breakfast. She casually looked for the sheriff, but he was not there. The waiter recognized her and took her to the same table as the previous night.

She ordered toast and tea.

After her meager breakfast, she went up to check on Suzanna. She was waking up so Amy let her know she was heading to the cabin.

"Do you want me to go with you?"

"No, I can go by myself. I am just going to make sure every thing is put away. I'll be back around lunch time."

"I will have lunch at the saloon. As an employee, it is included."

"That is not a bad benefit," said Amy, thinking about her options. She had nutrition bars in the cabin. "I'll try not to spend too much on lunch."

"It's okay. The budget we made covers the food. There is something else."

"What?"

"Rick has asked me to stay the night tonight."

Amy wondered if it was the job or for something else.

"It makes sense you know," continued Suzanna. "The hotel had a problem with my early morning arrival, and this way I can even work longer. It is Saturday night, and that is one of the busiest at any saloon."

Amy nodded. "Rick seems to be a good employer."

"Yes, the saloon girls there are quite happy. It is a much better place than where I worked in Grand Junction."

"I am so sorry for what happened to you."

"What are you talking about? I feel I have finally found something I excel at. I am very appreciated for my listening and dancing skills."

Amy started to be alarmed. "Does that mean you don't want to go back?"

She laughed. "Of course, I want to go back. Everyone here dies young. What is the average live span, thirty? No, I just mean I have found something I am good at, and there could be other things. It has boosted my confidence."

"Which is a good thing," Amy smiled, "and I am sure there are lots of things you are good at."

"Thank you." Suzanna hugged her. "Why don't you join me for lunch; I'm sure Rick won't mind."

The cabin looked the same as when they had left. She walked in and looked at everything critically, ensuring that there were no signs of the future left behind. The cupboard still had some debris from the destroyed communication device and she took those pieces outside and buried them.

Then she tapped out the code, and the floorboard, sprung up. She pulled it open and took out the canvas bag. The nutrition bars were not there. She was disappointed. She thought she had packed a couple of those in the bag. She started to return the bag to its place when she noticed the bed had been slept on. Someone had been there the previous night. She looked around carefully and found another sign. There was water in the pan, and she had been careful to empty it out, since she didn't want it to rust.

Someone had been there, and they knew how to access the trap door. If anyone tried to pry the trap door open without the code, the things inside the storage bag would be instantly incinerated. Destroying the contents was better than having anyone access things from the future.

She went back to check the canvas bag more carefully. The extra stun gun and the perimeter monitoring system were also missing.

What was going on? To get access to the bag, it had to be someone from the future. If it was Gustav, what was he still doing there, and why was he hiding from them? Had the lab given him a different agenda? It made no sense.

Right before she returned to Durango, she checked around the barn to see if somehow the marker had reappeared. It had not.

She walked into the saloon at noon and found Suzanna talking to Rick next to the bar.

"There she is," said Suzanna. "I am glad you came. You will like the lunch here."

"Good afternoon, Miss Waterman," said Rick. "I still have an opening for a saloon girl."

"Thank you Mr. LaForce, but I think I will pass at this time."

"I notice you are warming up to the idea, Miss Waterman, I can see you have talent, even if you can't see it yourself. Meanwhile, enjoy your lunch, ladies."

Amy smiled.

Suzanna took her to a table. "I think he likes you."

"Well, I think he likes you."

"Of course he likes me. I am a valuable employee. I bring money and status to his place. With you, it may be different. He does not give free lunches to everyone."

The bartender placed a couple of plates in front of them, and they started to eat.

Suddenly, a man came running into the saloon. He looked around and, seeing Rick, hurried over to talk to him.

Amy could not tell what they were talking about, but the conversation was quite animated. Shortly afterwards, Rick came to their table. "I have some news that may be of interest to you, Miss Waterman."

"Yes?" She wondered what it could be.

"Apparently there was shooting near my mine this morning. The sheriff and his deputy were there."

"What happened?" Her heart started to sink.

"Well, you know about the miner that was murdered last week?"

"Yes, yes," she said, thinking he should get on with the story.

"Well, we had two men working in the mine, for me and the other investors. Like I told the sheriff, I did not know what they had done. They said there had been an accident and I believed them, but the sheriff wanted them for questioning, so ..."

"Was anyone hurt?" Amy interrupted.

"This morning, one of those men was killed, and the deputy was injured. The sheriff is fine."

"Thank goodness," she sighed with relief. Both Suzanna and Rick looked at her.

"Oh. I am sorry for the miner, and I hope the deputy will be all right," she added.

"Hmm," said Rick and walked away.

"Damn, girl, you are so obvious," whispered Suzanna.

Immediately after finishing her lunch, she crossed the street to the sheriff's office. Jeff was at his desk.

He stood up when she walked in. "Good afternoon, Miss Waterman."

She noticed there was a man occupying the cell behind the bars. It was Tom.

"Good afternoon, sheriff. I heard about what happened this morning. How is the deputy?"

"He is home with his wife, and he will be all right. Can't say the same for Bob."

"There is the bitch that hit me with the rock," shouted Tom from the cell.

"I prevented you from killing a sheriff," she said, "That would be an instant hanging. You should be thanking me."

"I will thank you when hell freezes over."

"And that is probably where you are heading," said the sheriff, moving further away from the cell.

"Can you have dinner with me tonight?" she asked quietly.

"Yes."

"The restaurant at the hotel?"

"It is either that or the saloon."

"All right, the hotel. I have decided to give you my horse."

"I can't take your horse. It is a beautiful creature."

"Yes it is, but I can't take it to San Francisco with me. He is at the stable at the end of the main street. The horse should cover the money you gave me."

"And more. I will hold your horse until you come back."

"We can talk about this tonight."

That night she waited for him in the hotel lobby. When he arrived, they both entered the restaurant, and they were taken to her usual table.

"So, is this an official date?" he asked.

"It could be."

"Normally, I do the asking."

"Oh. Well, we don't have to count this as a date if you like."

"I don't mind being asked."

They both smiled and looked at the menu.

"Well, since I asked, it will be my treat," she said.

"And in that case," he handed her an envelope. "You may need this. It is for the horse. I checked him this afternoon, and I believe this, in addition to what I gave you before, is a fair price."

"I trust you with that, but are you certain you want him? I don't want you to feel obligated you have to take him."

"I figure you need the money, and I will hold him for you."

She bit her lip. She was not coming back. She studied him from behind her menu and felt reckless. It could be their last night together, and she was going to make it the best.

The waiter came around and she ordered an aperitif and an appetizer for both. Then she ordered the trout as the main course.

"You seem to have quite an appetite tonight," said Jeff after the waiter left with their orders.

"Yes. I want tonight to be special."

He looked at her.

"I was worried when I heard about the shoot out," she explained.

"It is part of my job."

"Regardless, it just makes me realize how vulnerable we are and how we have to live in the moment."

"Yes, we are vulnerable," said Jeff thoughtfully.

He was probably thinking she was crazy, thought Amy. "So tell me, how was your day?"

"You know, a lot of people ask that question, but they don't care what I say. It is done to be polite. You are different in that respect, it seems you care."

"I do care what you do and what you say." I am interested in everything about you, she thought.

"Well, there are many things I appreciate about you as well Amy."

Oh no, thought Amy alarmed, it sounded like the beginning of a proposal.

"I just thought I would tell you that," he said.

She laughed with relief. "I was beginning to worry you were warming up to a proposal."

He smiled back, "You will know if I do."

Later, he walked her to her room. He said good night and kissed her on the cheek.

She looked at him and kissed him on the lips. It was a passionate kiss, but then she realized that it was and she pulled away.

"I better go," said Amy. She opened the door to her room. "Good night."

"Good night," answered Jeff, although he looked puzzled.

She closed the door and leaned against it. Oh my goodness, she thought. What had she done? Why couldn't she control herself with this man? But it was her last chance with him. Soon she would be gone, and she would never see him again.

She yanked the door open, and he was standing where she had left him. "You are still here?"

"I didn't hear you walk away from the door," he grinned.

She took his arms and pulled him in the room.

She awoke early and saw he was lying next to her. He was looking at her.

"Good morning," she said.

"It is a most excellent morning." He continued to study her.

"Why are you looking at me like that?"

85

"How tall are you?"

"Five nine." A bit tall for this era, she thought.

"That is perfect, and I like how the your hair has different shades of brown."

"The sun does that; it's called highlights."

"Come let me look at your eyes."

She scooted closer and looked into his eyes. "My eyes are brown, but yours change with the light. They are a darker green right now."

"Yeah, they turn steel grey when I am hunting down criminals."

She laughed. Maybe they could spend all day like this.

"There are a lot of things you are not telling me, but at this moment, I don't seem to care about any of them," he said.

"I wish I could tell you, but it might ruin the future."

"You mean our future?"

"No, I mean everyone's future."

"That is a strange thing to say." He rolled out of bed and starting putting on his clothes. "I have to get going. I have a meeting this morning."

"But it is Sunday."

"Yes, neither the crooks nor the lawmen have a day off. Oh, I forgot," he added.

"What is it?"

"I have a dinner engagement tonight."

"With Miss Penn, isn't it?"

"Yes, it may be difficult to cancel."

Difficult to cancel, or maybe he didn't want to cancel; she inspected him as he dressed. He did have a gorgeous body. He also had to continue to live his life in this town after she left. She couldn't be angry if he accepted other invitations.

She got out of bed, threw on her camisole and went to the basin. She splashed water on her face thinking it would be great to have a bath.

"What are you going to do today?" asked Jeff.

"I went to the cabin yesterday and closed it as well as I could. Now that I don't have a horse, I guess I am limited to the town," she smiled.

"You can borrow your horse back any time you need."

"I don't think I will need the horse. You know, I think someone stayed at cabin the previous night."

"That will happen, especially since you fixed it up. You didn't leave anything of value did you?"

She shook her head. "No. Later today I will meet with Suzanna at the saloon for lunch."

"I was under the impression she was sharing the room with you."

"Yes, she is, but she was too busy at the saloon to come back last night."

"That was convenient."

"I didn't plan it that way. What happened was spur of the moment. The kiss spurred the rest on."

He pulled her next to him. "You drive me crazy. One moment I am angry you are not telling me everything, and the next moment I never want to leave your side."

"I love that."

"That you are driving me crazy?"

"No, that you never want to leave me."

"Remember, it is not me that is leaving."

"And I hate that it is me, but I can't help it."

Chapter 13
The plans go awry

Later that morning, she thought about their conversation. Maybe there was someway she could take him with her. Why not? He had no family in this time. He had told her his parents had passed away. He was an intelligent man, and he could adapt well.

His job here was so dangerous, he had to see the benefits of going with her. She could teach him everything, and he could make a good life in 2066.

She mentioned some of her thoughts to Suzanna when she saw her at lunch.

"You are thinking of asking him to come with us?" asked Suzanna.

"What do you think?'

"Oh my god, you are losing your mind. How is it that I can see that that is stupid idea and you don't see it?"

Amy just blinked.

"Of course we can't take him!" continued Suzanna. "What would happen to his lifeline? It would be all over the place. What if he was supposed to marry here and have children? Nothing of that would happen. I am sorry Amy, but you are not thinking straight."

"I know, I know. You're right, but I have never had such feelings for anyone. I am so miserable right now, I don't know what to do."

"Poor Amy. I think it is best we leave as soon as we can."

"It may be for the best. How much have you made so far?"

"Ten dollars."

"That seems quite good."

"It is. I think tonight will not be as good. Fridays and Saturdays are the busier nights. My ten with the twenty-two from the sheriff and with the original forty-three adds to $75. Technically, we can leave."

"I made some money, as well. I sold the horse."

"Really?" exclaimed Suzanna. "Well, I guess we won't be needing the horse, and we are desperate for money. Who bought it?"

"Wait," she added immediately. "The sheriff."

"Yes, the sheriff."

"You two are so..."

"In love, Suzanna. We are in love."

She ignored that and asked, "So how much is the total?"

"$125 and that is plenty for the trip."

"We will leave on Tuesday morning. I will give Rick my notice today."

"We should leave right now. I can't keep seeing Jeff. It is too hard."

"Look, you don't have to see him. Go back to the hotel, take that bath you wanted, and do whatever it takes to pass the next two days. I will buy the tickets for the early Tuesday morning coach that takes us to the train station."

"All right. Are you coming back to the hotel tonight?" asked Amy.

"I don't know."

"Oh."

"Are you worried about being alone?"

"He spent the night last night."

"You have really lost it Amy," Suzanna said with pity. "Don't let him stay again. It will not help in any way."

Suddenly, the doors of the saloon swung open and Rick looked around. He saw them and immediately walked to them. "I want both of you to accompany me, right now."

"Of course," said Suzanna, standing up. Amy also got up, but noticed Rick had not issued the standard greeting, and he looked upset.

They walked out of the saloon and crossed the street. They were heading to the sheriff's office.

"Are we going to the sheriff's?" asked Suzanna.

"Yes," he said. He banged open the door of the sheriff's office and held it as Suzanna and Amy walked inside.

Jeff was sitting at his desk and rose slowly. "Good afternoon, Rick, ladies."

"This is official business, sheriff," said Rick brusquely. "I have found someone stealing from me, and I want them arrested."

Amy knew she had not taken anything from this man and looked to Suzanna for an explanation. Had she?

Suzanna shook her head indicating she knew nothing.

"Are you accusing these two ladies of stealing?" asked the sheriff.

"Not them, exactly, but someone they know well. I think they should be made responsible," said Rick.

"Who are you accusing?" asked Jeff.

"Suzanna's brother, but I am sure they know all about it."

"Gustav?" asked Amy. "When did you see him?"

"He left two days ago," said Suzanna.

"No, he did not," said Rick. "I saw him near my mine this very morning. It was early, but the sun was up and I clearly recognized him. You see, I met him when he came through town earlier. Well, he had a cart loaded with crates. I thought it strange that he was in the area, but I continued to my mine. As soon as I got there, I saw what he had done. I have been robbed."

This was not good, thought Amy. If they had introduced Gustav as some guy traveling with them, they might have been able to plead innocence, but by making him Suzanna's brother, how could they do that now? And now, if they said they had been lying about the brother thing, they would lose all credibility.

"You have taken advantage of my good disposition," said Rick to Suzanna. "I trusted you. I don't know what stories you might have heard, sheriff, but you cannot believe these con artists."

"Rick, did you check the cabin where they were staying?" asked Jeff.

"I went there immediately and searched for my property, but there was no sign of the cart or of anyone there."

This was going to be hard to explain, thought Amy, racking her brain for a plausible story.

"Do you ladies have anything to say?" asked Jeff.

"I did not know Gustav was going to do anything like this," said Suzanna, "I swear I did not."

"Gustav has been acting very strange lately," said Amy. "We both thought he had abandoned us when he took my flower specimen. That is why I came to you, sheriff, and that is why Suzanna asked for a job with Mr. LaForce."

"This is more serious than stealing a flower," said Jeff harshly.

"Of course it is," shouted Rick. "I don't know anything about stealing flowers, but this is infinitely more valuable."

"What did he steal, Rick?" asked Jeff. "I don't think you would have left crates of silver ore lying around?"

"Of course I would not leave crates lying around. What he stole is the vein of silver. The whole thing."

"What?"

"It is very clear sheriff. My mine has...had a vein of silver. You could see it as plain as day. Well, Tom and Bob were working the mine for me. That was before you had that run-in with them, sheriff." Rick threw a nasty glance at the sheriff as if blaming him for some of his misfortunes. "After that incident, the mine was abandoned, so I went up there to reassess the situation."

"Are you referring to the run-in when the sheriff was shot by your men?" Amy was shocked he could accuse Jeff of anything.

"Well, it could not have been too bad since he seems quite recovered," said Rick.

"Go on with the story," urged the sheriff.

"Well, three days ago, I went and checked things out. Everything was much as I thought. There are other investors in the mine and I reported to them. Well, they asked additional questions, and today I went to find the answers. That is when I found that brother of yours coming from that direction and silver was gone. Completely gone."

"But how can that be?" asked Jeff. "He would have to work day and night and more to remove a vein of silver in that short a time."

"Maybe he had help," he pointed to the girls.

"You know that is not true, Mr. LaForce," said Suzanna. "I was working at your saloon all night."

"How about her?" he pointed to Amy.

"I did not help Gustav," said Amy. "I was at the hotel the entire night."

"Says who?" asked Rick. "Anyone see you?"

"I can vouch for her," said the sheriff quietly.

Rick looked surprised and then changed his attack. "Maybe you know more about this than I thought, sheriff. Maybe you are part of their plan? Even if you are not an active participant, how will your constituents take the news of you mingling with criminals?"

"Please, Rick, stop accusing everyone that crosses your path," said the sheriff. "Why don't we go to the mine, and you can show me what has happened?"

"We can go," said Rick, "but even when you see it, you will find it hard to believe."

Jeff turned to Amy and Suzanna. "I want you ladies to go to the hotel and stay there. I am considering you persons of interest, and you should not leave town."

As the two men left, Amy and Suzanna walked to the hotel.

"What are we going to do?" asked Suzanna.

"I guess we wait until they come back. How could Gustav do this? He has become a thief and worse, he is putting the entire future at risk with his actions. I suspected he was still around, you know," said Amy, telling her about what she had found at the cabin.

"So, he didn't leave?"

"No. He took the flower and now the silver ore."

"He must have used tools from the future to remove that vein of ore so quickly."

"We do have our small lasers, but I don't think that would do it," agreed Amy. "He must have had something bigger."

"So he moved the transport marker from the barn and stayed in this time."

"Yeah. He couldn't very well travel back and forth without the lab noticing."

"I wonder what excuses he is using to stay. Maybe he told the lab that he is looking for us? That we are lost somehow?" asked Suzanna.

"Maybe, but I'm pretty sure he is back home now. He has the silver and he has the flower; there is no reason for him to stay."

"I think someone back in the lab must be helping him, I can't imagine him doing this by himself," said Suzanna.

"You may be right. You know he told me I would do fine in this era. It was almost as if he was preparing to leave us."

"Well, if the sheriff does not believe us and we go to jail, we will be stuck in this era forever," said Suzanna nervously.

Later that afternoon, Amy noticed that the bathroom in the hotel that had a tub was available. She quickly paid for half an hour and took the entire allotted time. She couldn't remember the last time she had felt a bath so luxurious.

That evening, Suzanna and Amy dressed for dinner and went down to the restaurant. They sat at Amy's usual table and watched the saloon down the road as they ate. For a Sunday night, the saloon was still quite lively.

"They probably returned from the mine hours ago, but they did not come by to tell us anything," noted Suzanna.

"Well, maybe they got back late. Anyway, I know Jeff had a previous engagement for supper tonight."

"I think we should leave tomorrow," whispered Suzanna.

Amy considered the suggestion.

"We have enough money," continued Suzanna, "and who knows what else Gustav has done? I don't want be responsible for it, as his sister, I mean."

"I know calling you that was unfortunate, but how else to explain a man traveling with us?"

Suzanna sighed. "I don't know. Wasn't it you who was supposed to be his sister?"

"I guess, but we would still be in trouble."

"I can't believe the lab does not know what he is doing."

"I was thinking that he couldn't have taken the silver with him," said Amy. "He probably hid it somewhere so he could find it in the future."

"Whatever. The only thing I care about is that he has abandoned us here," said Suzanna. She played with the food on her plate for a moment and then said, "I am so bored."

"Why don't you take a bath? It was nice."

"That is your highlight for the day? I can't imagine another day here not doing anything. What do you think about my suggestion to leave Durango?"

"I think we should stick with our plan to leave Tuesday. I don't want it to seem as though we're running away, and in any case, the train to San Francisco is Tuesday evening."

"Fine," said Suzanna, looking out the window. "I'm going to the saloon after dinner."

"Will it be all right with Mr. LaForce? He seemed angry at us."

"If my brother stole from him, do you think I would stick around and work for him? I'm not that dumb and he knows it. He has to know I am innocent."

"All right, at least if he kicks you out, your walk back to the hotel is short."

Suzanna smiled. "Want to come with me?"

"No, I think Mr. LaForce wants to be angry at someone for what has happened, so if it is not you it is probably me."

"No, I think he is blaming the sheriff."

"What is the story with those two? They don't seem to get along."

"I don't know. It could be a male competition thing, seeing that they are both eligible bachelors."

"Yeah, I don't think that's it."

"Thinking about it, now that he knows you two spent the night, it may be best you don't go."

Amy sighed. "I wasn't planning to. There is a book I brought on this trip, and I can start it tonight. At least the electric lights make reading easier."

Before she reached her room, she saw Jeff waiting out in the hallway.

"Good evening, Jeff. I thought you were dining with Miss Penn?"

"Good evening, Miss Waterman. Yes, I did dine there."

The formal use of her name did not bode well, she thought.

"I wanted to talk to you," he said.

Standing outside her room was not good, said a part of her brain. Yeah, right, said another, and she opened her room and told him to come inside.

She sat at the desk chair while he remained standing.

"You saw the mine?" she asked.

"Yes," he sighed. "Rick was right. The silver vein was removed," he looked at her carefully, "almost surgically."

That is the way it would look if a laser had been used. "Oh, how strange," she said.

"Yes, there has been much strangeness ever since you came."

"Are you accusing me of something? I am not a criminal," she stated again.

"You keep saying that."

"I don't know what Gustav did, and I don't know why he did it."

"Why? He did it to get rich," said the sheriff in an obvious manner. "You say you don't know, but yet, you spent a night with him. You could have told him about the mine."

"I did tell him about the mine, in conversation, but I did not expect him to go rob it!"

He looked disappointed.

"I was with you when he went to get the plant specimen. He must have seen the mine then. I probably didn't even have to say anything."

He turned to leave.

"Jeff, I do not have any romantic inclination towards Gustav. My feelings are for someone else." She wanted to see where they stood with each other.

"Well, Miss Waterman, if that someone else is me, I'd rather you keep them to yourself. I cannot afford to be associated with someone like you."

So that was where their relationship was, she acknowledged to herself. She looked away a moment to pull herself together. "Don't worry," she said. "I will not have any feelings for you from now."

"Are you still leaving on Tuesday?"

"I don't think so. I want to return the money you gave me, so it will take us longer to make enough for the trip."

"Keep the money," he said coldly.

She was going to insist, but then realized she would be stuck here in Durango for much longer and she just couldn't, not with him this way. "In that case, we will leave as scheduled. We still have to go to San Francisco."

"I will be accompanying you."

"Am I your prisoner?"

"No, a person of interest, but I will be pursuing Gustav in San Francisco."

"Good, I hope you catch him."

The tears started to flow as soon as he left. Her heart was breaking and she felt worse than ever. She should have never allowed this to happen. She needed to have better control of those stupid feelings.

The next morning when she woke up, she looked in the mirror and saw the results of all those tears. She couldn't go down to breakfast with her eyes so puffy.

Suzanna arrived soon after and was very animated. "I was so busy last night," she said, "it was unbelievable. Several girls took the night off, so of course, Mr. LaForce was happy to see me. All I know is I really need a long nap." She suddenly looked at her. "What is wrong? You look a mess."

Amy told her about Jeff's visit.

"It is for the best. I tell you, you were getting too close. Cut it off and don't see each other. That is the remedy."

"Well, that will be hard to do. He is coming to San Francisco with us to look for Gustav."

"Damn. Gustav messes things up again. Well, avoid the sheriff for at least today."

"That will be easy as I do not plan to leave the room."

"Fine," said Suzanna, getting undressed. "Just let me sleep a bit and then I can keep you company."

Amy nodded and opened her book. After ten minutes of reading and rereading the same page, a thought came to her. Her subconscious had been thinking about Gustav and places he could hide the silver ore, and a solution popped up. The secure compartment under the cabin's floor could provide a perfect place. It was a large area, and in the future they had the exact coordinates of that cabin.

She could go back to the cabin and check it out. If the silver ore was there, she would return it. She hoped it would make things better with the sheriff. She nudged Suzanna to see if she would wake up.

"What," Suzanna barely opened her eyes.

"We have to go to the cabin," said Amy, and she explained her theory.

"Yeah, it is possible, but can we go later?"

"It looks like it's going to rain, so we should go now." She looked at Suzanna, who was falling asleep again. "Never mind, I will go by myself."

"No, no, wait," said Suzanna, trying to wake up.

"I can borrow my horse back from the sheriff, and I will be back soon. It will not take long at all, don't worry."

"Are you sure it's safe?"

"I will take my stun gun just in case."

She checked herself in the mirror and washed again with cold water. The puffiness had gone a bit.

"Good morning, sheriff," she said as she walked into the sheriff's office.

Jeff was at his desk and he greeted her coolly.

"I was hoping I could take the horse out for a ride," said Amy. "It is my last day here."

Jeff studied her briefly and then said, "Of course you can use the horse, but it is going to rain."

"Thank you, I will be back before then."

She hurried to the stable and saddled the horse. Soon she was on her way. Even though the sun was shining, she could feel the weather changing. As she got closer to the cabin, she suddenly veered toward the ridge. She wanted to get a specimen of the corydalis curvisiliqua for herself. It didn't matter if Gustav had taken one, it may be the only chance for her to get one and it was her project.

Getting the flower did not take long and soon she was heading to the cabin. She knew there was an extra specimen container under the floorboard and that would preserve the flower. As she rode up to the cabin, she saw that the door was wide open. She jumped off the horse and approached the cabin carefully. She peeked inside and found the place in shambles. Rick and his men had been very thorough in looking for their missing silver. All the dishes and pots and pans were strewn on the kitchen floor. The cupboard itself had been broken. It was stupid, she thought. You didn't have to break things when you were looking.

In the bedroom, the dresser had all the drawers pulled out and one had also been broken. Luckily, the mattress was in one piece, although it was now propped against the window. She had to clear things out before she could even access the trapdoor.

She started to put away things and then noticed the dark clouds were piling up. She didn't want to get stuck out here alone. That is when she heard a horse approaching. She clenched the stun gun and stepped into the kitchen to look out the window. It was the sheriff.

"Sheriff? What are you doing here?" she asked as she went out onto the porch.

"Miss Waterman, I could ask the same," he seemed angry as he jumped off his horse. "I am not a babysitter, having to follow you to make sure you are all right."

"I didn't ask you to come," she protested.

"You didn't, but Suzanna was worried about you. She told me you were looking for the silver ore and asked me to check on you. Why didn't you tell me you were coming here?"

"What difference would it make if I told you?"

"I would have advised you not to. But if you insisted on coming, it would be on you and I would not have to, ..." he stopped as he walked into the cabin. "What happened here?"

"I think Mr. LaForce was a bit zealous in his search for his silver."

"You still think the silver ore is here, even after he searched like this?"

"Just because you shove and break things, it doesn't mean you have searched thoroughly," she said. "Anyway, I haven't had a chance to search, all I've done so far is clean up."

"Well, I might as well help since I am here." He pointed to the cupboard pieces. "Do you want this out?"

"I guess."

"It could be used for firewood."

She nodded.

"I'm sorry he was so violent in his search."

"These things are not mine, but I still hate to see broken things."

"I see a lot of broken things in my job," said Jeff as he started to pick up the pieces of the cupboard. "Some things

98

you can mend, others you have to replace." He walked out onto to the porch where he stacked the pieces.

Amy wondered if he was referring to their relationship and if he was, theirs was hopefully the first.

Together they worked quickly and soon she could access the trapdoor. She had decided to show Jeff the secret storage compartment. She knew the bag hidden there was canvas and looked the right era. And the last time she had checked, the insta-warm blanket and a specimen container were the only things of any worth inside. Both could pass off as being something belonging to the era.

"Sheriff, there is a secret compartment under the floorboards and I thought Gustav might have hidden the silver there. That is what I wanted to check."

He looked interested.

She went to the corner of the kitchen and tapped the code. The trapdoor sprung open.

Jeff's eyebrows went up.

"German mechanism," said Amy. It was a reasonable explanation, she thought. She was not going to mention the incineration part. That would be too hard to explain with this age's technology.

She opened the trapdoor and grabbed the canvas bag. As soon as she pulled the bag out, she saw it. "There, I was right. There are some rocks down here, but I am not sure if this is what you are looking for."

He came over next to her to look down. "It is silver ore."

"It does not look silvery."

"No. When it comes out of the mine it looks charcoal gray; the shiny deposits you sometimes see in mines are actually zinc and lead."

"So this is the silver, then?" She was hopeful.

"Yes, but that is not all of it. I will take this to Rick, but I don't think it will do much to persuade him to drop charges against Gustav."

"I still don't understand why Gustav would do this," said Amy.

"You know the law does not hold you accountable for things done by friends or relatives."

So the law would not consider her guilty, but Jeff would still not trust her.

They headed back to Durango afterwards. The rain started as they got on their horses and soon it was pouring. They were very soaked as they rode into town. The cold rain mirrored what her soul felt, thought Amy.

"I will take the ore to Rick," said Jeff when they arrived. "You better change out of that wet clothes."

She noted a hint of concern, but maybe it was something she was hoping to hear. "All right."

"Have a good day, Miss Waterman," he said formally.

"Good day to you too, sheriff."

Chapter 14
Traveling day

Early the next morning, Amy and Suzanna were the first to arrive to the stagecoach. They sat patiently inside as they waited the other passengers. Eventually, a middle aged woman arrived with her reluctant teen boy in tow.

"I still cannot believe the sheriff is coming with us," said Suzanna as she watched them load their bags up on top of the stagecoach.

"It's his job," said Amy. "How about Mr. LaForce, was he sad to see you go?" She could see Rick watching the stagecoach from across the street.

"I think he will miss me. He would have been sadder if it wasn't for my brother stealing from him, but he did get some of his silver back. Oh look, there comes the sheriff."

He was carrying a small bag, and he climbed the outside of the stagecoach and sat next to the driver.

"I guess he is going to ride up there," said Suzanna as the stagecoach started to move.

The woman had taken a seat across from Amy, but she kept throwing disturbed glances at Suzanna. Suzanna had put on makeup this morning and looked a bit like the saloon girl she had become. She didn't seem to care about the looks of the woman or the ogling of the boy.

"I think I will take a nap," she said.

"It is probably the best way to pass the hours, " said Amy.

Soon Suzanna was asleep with her head resting on Amy's shoulder.

"You must be a good friend to accompany her," said the woman. A woman such as her was implied.

"We are good friends," said Amy, realizing that it was the truth.

After a few hours, the stagecoach came to a stop. There was not much of a rest stop, but the driver, the sheriff and the teen all got off the coach. Suzanna was still asleep.

"You don't need to use the facility?" asked the woman.

"No, I don't, do you? I could accompany you if you like."

The woman looked to her with gratitude. "I would like that. The outhouse has no door and I feel very much exposed in front of the men."

While Amy disentangled herself from Suzanna, the woman took out a Farmer's Almanac from her bag and proceeded to rip off a few pages. At least she had that for toilet paper, thought Amy. She accompanied her off the carriage and to the lean-to where she stood in front of the doorway, trying to block all views.

"Hurry up, ladies," shouted the coach driver. "This is not a picnic."

"This is not a rest stop, either," shouted Amy back to him. "The door is broken and it is barely usable. You might have someone fix it." She then turned to tell the woman not to worry.

"Thank you, I really appreciate it," said the woman.

"You are welcome," said Amy, thinking again how hard it was to live in this place and time.

They went back to the coach and the sheriff helped them on board. As Amy took his hand, she and Jeff exchanged a brief look and then she was back inside.

Suzanna stirred awake and then went back to sleep. The boy pretended to go back to sleep, but Amy could see tiny slits in his eyes as he studied Suzanna across from him. The woman noticed and shook her head.

"He is in such a difficult age."

Amy smiled. It seemed quite natural to be eyeing a woman.

"I saw you having dinner with the sheriff the other night," said the woman.

"That must have been Saturday night," Amy smiled remembering the nice dinner.

"Yes, that is the day my husband and I go into town," said the woman. "By the way my name is Maribelle Patrick."

Amy introduced herself.

"I mentioned to my husband that you seemed to be enjoying each other's company and that you looked good together," continued Maribelle.

"It is surprising how appearances can be misleading," she said sadly.

"I don't think so. I think men have difficult jobs, and of course the sheriff has one of the hardest jobs. The good comes with the bad in all cases. As women, we have to be strong, and it is up to us to make the relationship work."

What was this lady thinking, wondered Amy. Did she think she could not handle Jeff's job and that was the reason for their 'difficulties'? It was not that at all. He thought she was a liar and he was right to think so. It was not something she could ever fix, because she could never tell him the truth.

The next time the coach stopped, it was in a little town. A few houses and a couple of buildings lined either side the main road, but that is all there was. Still the town did have a saloon and a general store.

"Where are we?" asked Suzanna as she awoke.

"I don't know," said Amy.

"This is the last town before we get to the train station. I suggest we get some food here," said the woman.

"Thirty minutes," shouted the driver as he jumped down and opened the door. He then hurried off.

The sheriff climbed down and helped the ladies out.

"Are you joining us for lunch, sheriff?" asked Mrs. Patrick.

"No, Mrs. Patrick, I will see you later." He nodded to all of them and walked away.

"Where shall we eat?" asked the teen.

Mrs. Patrick looked worried. "I don't see any place that can serve us. The general store may have some bread and hopefully something to go with it."

"There is the saloon," said Suzanna. "They should be able to serve us lunch."

Mrs. Patrick eyes grew large. "We can't go there."

"It is the middle of the afternoon, it should be quite safe," said Suzanna.

"Please, mother, please," said the teen. "I saw the sheriff and the driver go that way."

"It may be the only place to get a real meal," said Amy. "And don't worry, we will be together."

Mrs. Patrick looked around the town once more and agreed.

The saloon was not as nice as Mr. LaForce's, but there were tables and the teen had been correct, the sheriff and the driver were seated at the bar.

"Is the driver drinking?" asked Amy, astonished, and then realized it sounded stupid to say that. It wasn't as if he was going to drive off the dirt road.

Suzanna scolded her with her eyes.

"Those type of men always drink," said Mrs. Patrick.

"Let's sit over there," said Suzanna, picking a table away from the bar.

A girl came and took their order. As they waited for their food, they could see that the sheriff was eating something, but the driver was still on his liquid diet.

"Excuse me, Miss," said the girl to Suzanna as she served them. "Mr. Fergo, the owner, would like a word once you are done eating."

"What could he want?' asked Suzanna.

"I don't know, Miss," said the girl as she retreated.

"Don't go," said Mrs. Patrick. "We will just finish our meal quickly and leave." She started to eat her food a bit faster.

"This place is not bad, mother," said the teen, barely looking at the food and studying the women lounging about the bar. "It is quite interesting."

Amy also studied the girls. They were mostly pretty, and if one looked through the copious amount of makeup, you could see that some were quite young. One of the older ones had a black eye, and she had seen the bruises on the arm of the girl that had served them. She felt sorry for them as they waited for the evening and for customers.

"Amy, I know you are thinking this type of work is kind of degrading," said Suzanna, "but it is a good job if the boss is good."

"We really should be leaving," said Mrs. Patrick, trying to eat faster. "We don't want to miss the coach. Edward, can you please hurry?"

"These girls have minds and they could be using them," said Amy, ignoring Mrs. Patrick. "And how long can they last doing this? As soon as they get old, there is nothing for them. What happens to them?"

"Quite a few marry before then," said Suzanna. "Remember, most are not prostitutes."

With that last word, Mrs. Patrick stood up. "We are done here." She put some money on the table and pulled the teen up. "Let's go, Edward."

"Mother," he protested, but he followed his mother out.

As soon as they left, a man that had been sitting at the end of the bar came to them. "Good afternoon, ladies," he said. "I am the proprietor of this establishment and would like a word."

"Of course," said Suzanna, putting on her charm.

"Well, let me tell you that we rarely have a chance to entertain two such fine looking ladies. I was wondering if you would be staying in our town."

"No," smiled Suzanna. "We are passing through."

The man looked as if he was trying to decide something and then blurted, "This is a good town to live in, and this is a good establishment, as you can see. I also pay a good salary, I don't know if that interests you."

Suzanna smiled again. "It is a pity, but we are leaving..."

Amy interrupted, "And do you keep your employees safe?"

The man turned to her as if he was looking at her for the first time. "Of course I do."

Amy looked at the group of girls.

"Some of the girls have accidents," said Mr. Fergo, "but that is because they are young, inexperienced and frankly a bit dumb."

"Young and dumb?" said Amy harshly. "Is that what you think about your employees..."

"Miss Waterman," the sheriff interrupted. He was standing behind Mr. Fergo. "I am sorry to interrupt, but the stagecoach is about to leave."

"Thank you, sheriff," said Amy and she stood up. "Good day, Mr. Fergo."

"Good day, Mr. Fergo," said Jeff.

"Sheriff," said Mr. Fergo.

"Good bye, Mr. Fergo," said Suzanna as she also got up.

The three left the saloon together.

"I guess I should be glad we have few stops along the way," said Jeff. "You almost got into a fight back there."

"He is allowing the girls to be mistreated," said Amy.

"I think so as well, sheriff," said Suzanna. "I would not work for such a man."

"And at the previous stop, you antagonized the driver, although I admit he was a bit rude with Mrs. Patrick."

"They do need to fix the rest stop," said Amy.

They reached the coach, and the sheriff helped Suzanne in first. He turned to help Amy.

"Frankly I don't care what the driver or anyone else thinks of me. There is only one person's opinion that I care about, and he does not think much of me," said Amy as she took his hand and climbed inside.

Chapter 15
Catching the train

It was early evening when they arrived at the train station. The sun was setting as the train from Denver was pulling into the station.

"Thank goodness we did not miss it," said Mrs. Patrick. "We would have to wait two days if we did. Oh look, this is a vestibuled train," she sounded excited as she climbed out of the coach.

"Vestibuled?" whispered Suzanna to Amy.

"The cars connect through an enclosed passageway or vestibule. It allows the passengers to cross from one car to the next easily. It also means this train will have separate cars for dining and sleeping."

"I thought all trains in this era were set up that way," said Suzanna.

"No. It was a recent invention. Before that, everyone stayed in one car for the entire trip. They ate when the train stopped and had to do it very quickly."

"Well, thank goodness we can walk around. I can't imagine sitting in one place for as long as it will take to get to San Francisco."

They got out of the stagecoach and met with the sheriff. Together they went onto the train platform.

"I think there is no need to follow us so closely once we are on the train, sheriff," said Suzanna. "Where can we go?"

"I don't know, but from what I know of you two, I will be keeping an eye on you."

"How come he doesn't trust us?" asked Suzanna as he bought his ticket to sit close to them. "Everyone else does. Even Mrs. Patrick followed us into the saloon."

"Jeff knows we haven't told him everything, and he has a suspicious nature," said Amy sadly.

The found their seats on the train easily, but once it started moving they decided to visit the various cars. The train not only had a sleeping and dining car, but also a lounge with a bar. They walked to the end of the train and then headed back to their seats. On the way back they stopped at the dining car.

"Let's make reservations for dinner," said Suzanna.

"All right," said Amy.

The sheriff had followed them most of the way and was watching them from the end of the car.

"Better make the reservations for three," said Amy. "He might as well join us."

"Are you sure? I thought you were trying to keep your distance from him. That is why I suggested he leave us alone on the train."

"Thanks for trying, but since he is still here with us ... Make it for seven o'clock."

While Suzanna made reservations, Amy walked to Jeff. "We're having dinner at seven and you might as well join us."

"No, thank you. I'll sit somewhere else."

"Well, good luck then, the maître d' said they are quite busy and will not be able to fit anyone else at that time."

"Really? He really said that?"

"No, he didn't. I just thought it would be better if you sit with us rather than watch us from the distance as if we are criminals."

He nodded slowly. "All right then, dinner at seven."

They both returned to their seats a couple of cars back. He could see her from where he sat. She returned to her book, which was going nowhere.

"Good evening, Miss Waterman." It was Mrs. Patrick.

"Good evening, Mrs. Patrick, have you settled well on the train?"

"Yes, it is marvelous. I was wondering if you have made reservations for dinner. I thought it would be nice to share a table."

"Oh, I am sorry. I have already reserved a table."

Mrs. Patrick looked at the sheriff and he turned away. "With him?'

"With Miss Ross and him," clarified Amy.

"I hope you can resolve whatever your differences are because I think I was right about the both of you," said Mrs. Patrick. "You know he is interested. I have seen that look before."

Yeah, it was the wrong kind of interest, thought Amy.

During dinner, Amy sat next to Suzanna and opposite Jeff. They ordered the meal and a bottle of claret.

"I am so glad we are here and on our way to San Francisco," said Suzanna. "Let's toast to that."

They raised their glasses and toasted. Then they toasted to the city of Durango, to the electricity in Durango, and then to San Francisco and to the good weather they had been enjoying.

With the second bottle, they toasted to the train and the dining car. By then, they had reverted to calling each other by their first names.

"Okay, I have another toast," said Amy. "Let's toast to the wide open spaces, to the blue sky, to the nights with all those stars and...."

"To the red dirt," interrupted Suzanna. "The dirt that gets everywhere."

"Okay, but it is the first time I drink to dirt," said Jeff.

"Shall we order some dessert? I would like to try the cobbler," said Amy.

"Not me, thanks," said Suzanna. "I have a date to play a game of backgammon."

"Really? How did you get a date already?" asked Amy, amazed.

"I met someone who asked," she said.

"In that case, I guess we are done," said Amy, folding her napkin.

"You don't need to go, Amy. Someone needs to finish that bottle of claret, and I'm sure Jeff will help."

"I guess it would be a waste," agreed Amy looking at Jeff. "I'll stay. How about you? It is the best way to keep an eye on me."

"I wanted to try the applesauce cake anyway."

They placed their order and sipped on the rest of the claret as they waited.

"I've been thinking," said Amy.

"I think you do a lot of that," said Jeff.

She glanced at him and continued. "There is a lot of that is right about this moment. They may not be in the future or maybe they were not right before, but they are right now."

"Does this have to do with your line drawings?"

"A bit." She didn't really know, maybe she had had too much to drink.

He took a paper out of his pocket. It looked familiar, she thought, and then she took a closer look.

It was the paper where she had drawn his lifeline with the branches to show the possibilities. She could see another line had been drawn right above it. Jeff had labeled it 'Amy' and both lines joined part of the way to become one.

She looked at him.

"I drew this in a sentimental moment," he said.

"It is one of the nicest drawings I have seen."

He laughed. "You must have not seen many drawings."

"Are you having another sentimental moment?"

He smiled and she smiled back.

"Good evening, Miss Waterman, Sheriff Lindsey," said Mrs. Patrick as she walked by. "Did you enjoy your dinner?"

The woman had an uncanny sense of timing. "Yes, Mrs. Patrick. Did you enjoy your dinner?"

"Very much so. I am happy to be going to the sleeper car where I have reserved a berth."

"And your son?"

"He has found a friend to entertain him. If he comes around to bother either you or Miss Ross, please let me know."

"Good night, Mrs. Patrick," said Amy.

Mrs. Patrick winked at her and continued on her way.

"What was that about?" asked Jeff after she left.

"She thinks I should be more understanding of your work. That if I did, our differences would be resolved."

"So she thinks you are not understanding?"

"If that were our only problem, I think it would be easy."

"Yes, there is the problem that is hanging over us, but you refuse to tell me."

She studied him. "I am going to tell you."

He didn't say anything, but she saw the doubt in his eyes.

"I am going to tell you when we reach San Francisco. Things I have said or done will make sense to you then."

"I just have to wait?"

She nodded.

"What about ruining the future."

"I think the future is already affected."

"All right, hopefully I will understand all of it when you explain it to me."

The waiter served the desserts.

"You know I really care about you. You are the nicest man I have ever met."

"This sounds like a beginning of a proposal to me," joked Jeff.

Amy laughed. "No. It is just a comment."

"You did ask me out on our first date, so I guess it was only natural you would do the proposing."

"Wait, it was you who insisted to accompany me to the cabin that day in Durango. That was kind of a date."

"Was it?"

She sighed. "Jeff, I am torn between my work and my personal feelings. I was not supposed to get involved."

"I suspect your profession is more than a biologist."

"It is."

That evening when Suzanna returned to her seat, Amy was cuddled under a blanket.

"You aren't asleep?"

"No, not yet," said Amy.

"Where did you get the blanket?"

"Jeff lent it to me. I had no idea we had to bring one onboard with us. We can share if you like."

"The sheriff? Well that answers my next question, which was, how did the rest of dinner go?"

"I don't know what I am going to do when it is time to leave."

"You will leave."

Amy looked at her with uncertainty.

"You will leave when the time comes," said Suzanna. "But you can be together while you are here. Why not? I have changed my mind after seeing how you and he are mad for each other, even when you try not to be. If it gives both of you a moment of happiness, go for it."

"You are absolutely right. I was trying so hard not to getting involved and then when he pulled away, I was so miserable. I know we don't have much time, but I am going to try to be happy together." She looked at where he was sitting. He appeared to be asleep. No one was seated opposite him and he had put his legs up on the seat.

She continued to watch him until she too fell asleep.

The next morning the three had breakfast together.

"The train is right on schedule, and we should be arriving at five this evening," said Jeff.

"Five, California time?" asked Suzanna.

They would be on the same time as the lab in 2066, thought Amy.

"Yes," said Jeff.

One more day with him, thought Amy. "Have you taken the train to San Francisco before?"

"Yes, a couple of times. Mostly for work with Wells Fargo Bank."

"You were elected sheriff, were you not?" asked Suzanna.

"Yes, the kind people of La Plata County elected me four years ago."

"La Plata means silver in Spanish," said Suzanna.

"Yes, it does."

The comment about silver cast a damper on the conversation.

"I don't know what Gustav was thinking," said Suzanna, shaking her head.

"Suzanna, I am going to tell Jeff everything when we get to San Francisco," announced Amy.

"Really," said Suzanna. "I don't know what you are thinking. Honestly, I think it is a stupid idea."

"I have made up my mind."

"Should I go?" asked Jeff as he watched the exchange with interest.

Suzanna ignored him. "Then why wait until San Francisco, Amy? Why not tell him right now?"

"We are way off our original plan now," said Amy, "and we need his help."

"Whatever. Do whatever you feel. I have never been able to influence you much; even before we came, you didn't listen."

"I am different from then."

"We both are."

They finished lunch, and Suzanna headed towards the lounge car, while Amy and Jeff returned to their seats.

"She was not happy with your announcement," he said.

"I know. It does affect her, as well."

Soon after, the train made a stop and more passengers got aboard. A woman took the seat in front of Jeff and immediately started a conversation. She went on and on, even when Jeff pretended to doze.

After watching that for a bit, Amy stood up and walked over to him.

"Good afternoon, sheriff," she interrupted the woman. "I am sorry for interrupting ma'am, but the sheriff was going to help me with a problem."

"That is correct, Miss Waterman, I remember the problem," the sheriff stood up. "You will have to excuse me, ma'am."

They went to lounge car and found a table in a quiet corner, away from the bar.

"Thank you for saving me from that woman," said Jeff as he took a seat. "I sometimes run into someone who thinks their nephew or son would make the perfect deputy and I should be grateful to be introduced to him."

"No problem," said Amy. "Jeff, I think Suzanna is right. I am going to tell you everything now. There is no point waiting."

"I think she meant it sarcastically."

"I know." She took a breath. Once she said it, there was no turning back. Their relationship would be changed forever. She just had to do it. She had to be honest with him. "Have your read H.G. Wells?"

"Some of his books," said Jeff. "Any one in particular?"

She suddenly realized that even though *The Time Machine* had been published before the turn of the century it might not be out yet. She asked another question. "Never mind that. When do you think I was born?"

"I was born in 1866 so you were probably born in 1870? Or how about 1875?" he joked.

That would make her twenty years old. "It is much later than that."

He smiled. "I know women always like to say they are younger, but I don't believe you are a teenager."

"2040."

"What is that, the month and date? But what kind of month is twenty?"

"It is the year 2040."

Jeff stared at her as he tried to understand what she was saying.

"I have come from the future."

He took her hands and looked into her eyes. "I don't think you are delusional."

"I'm not. We came to take a specimen, the yellow flower, back to the future for analysis. We think it has medicinal properties, and none of those flowers survived in the future."

"You were born 145 years in the future."

"Yes, and I am twenty-six years old."

"Suzanna and Gustav are from the future as well?"

She nodded.

Jeff sat back and stared at the ceiling. Then he looked back at her and then again at the ceiling. Amy said nothing more. She knew it was quite a shock.

A waiter approached them and asked if they wanted to order anything.

Amy ordered tea.

"A whiskey," said Jeff. "Make it a double."

The waiter returned with the order and Jeff took a gulp of his drink. "*The Chronic Argonauts*," said Jeff. "That is the story you were referring to."

"What do you mean?"

"It is the H.G. Wells short story about a time machine."

She nodded. It must have been written before *The Time Machine,* she thought. "So you read science fiction. I find that interesting."

"It is fiction and even though I enjoyed the book immensely, I don't know if I believe you, Amy."

"I know this is hard to believe, Jeff. I just wanted to be honest with you. I am tired of lying to you."

"And you told Suzanna, you need my help."

He did have a good memory, thought Amy. "I think so."

"And you want me to forget all the lies you have told me?"

"A lot of what I said is true. The story about my family is true, my parents died, my aunt raised me and I did go to school in Berkeley. I work in a lab where I am a kind of biologist."

"And Gustav and Suzanna work in the lab as well?"

"They are coworkers of mine. Gustav and Suzanna are not related. Suzanna, who was known as Susan, was my assistant. And Gustav was one of the first time travelers and now he is a criminal. He stole from this era, abandoned us and destroyed our only way back. There is another time transport in San Francisco, and that is why we are going there."

"But, I saw you arrive in the stagecoach."

"I was sent, or transported, to one of the stagecoach stops, and I picked up the stagecoach there. The transport had a problem, and Gustav was sent somewhere else. Both of us were supposed to arrive together in Durango."

"You kept saying your friends were coming."

She nodded.

"And why was Suzanna not there?"

"She transported before us and had a worse time of it. She ended up east of Denver and it took her a while to get to us. She ran out of money and had to become a saloon girl."

"Are there more of you? People from the future?"

"I don't think so. We were the first project of the company. Gustav and a couple of others had traveled through time to check places and to setup the transport markers, but none had ever stayed for this many days."

"Is there a problem staying long?"

"I don't think so. There may be some side effects from staying long, like forming attachments to people."

"Or forming attachments to things, like the silver Gustav took."

"Yes, I guess that is true."

"Are you telling me I will have to go to the future to recover the rest of the silver?"

"No. I've been thinking about that. Gustav could not transport the silver without the people in the laboratory noticing. He must have hidden it somewhere to retrieve it in the future. It is probably close to the cabin."

"Probably close to some recognizable landmark," said Jeff, then he laughed. "I am talking like I believe you, but part of me is still dubious about your story, Amy. You have to understand that I have survived so far by being wary about what people do or say."

"I understand." She saw Suzanna walk into the lounge, and she saw them. She walked over and then looked at him and then at her. "You told him, didn't you?" She flopped down on a chair near next to Amy.

Amy didn't say anything.

"My god, do you realize what have you done?"

"If everything had gone according to plan, we would not even be here," reminded Amy.

"So what do you think of us, Jeff? Do you think we are like creatures from another world?"

"Have they found creatures in other worlds?" he asked seriously.

"As far as we know, there are no humans in other worlds," said Amy.

"Never mind that, Amy, what is the plan now?" asked Suzanna. "What shall we do when we get to San Francisco?"

She looked at Jeff, who was still staring at her. She knew it would take time for everything to sink in. "Okay, the lab is probably worried we did not show up, and they know something happened to the marker in Durango. They will assume we are heading to San Francisco to the other transport marker. The problem is we do not know where in San Francisco it could be. They have to let us know that somehow."

"They could send someone to tell us," said Suzanna.

"Yes, I think they will, but how would that person find us? The city of San Francisco has close to 300,000 people, so it would be impossible to find a fellow traveler among the crowd."

"I would use the train station," said Jeff. "It is a central location and most people coming into the city pass through there."

"Yeah, that makes sense," said Suzanna.

"What is 'yeah'?" asked Jeff.

"It means yes, and it also means Suzanna is slipping in her speech."

"Well, he is one of us now," said Suzanna. "I thought we could relax a bit."

"No. We can't relax until we get out of this era."

They made plans on how to proceed once the train arrived. Amy noticed that Jeff was taking it all quite well and was going along with their plans. They were just reviewing the plans when Mrs. Patrick came into the lounge. She saw them and walked over.

"How is everyone?" she asked.

"Fine, Mrs. Patrick, how has your trip been?" asked Amy.

"So far it has been quite pleasant. I was in the sleeping car last night and slept like a baby. Have you ever tried it?"

"No, not yet," said Amy.

"Suzanna, can you come with me? I have a question," asked Mrs. Patrick. Suzanna followed her, and they conversed in low voices. They parted ways soon after.

"What is it?" asked Amy as Suzanna returned.

"She suggested I leave you alone to give you a chance to make up."

"I can't believe it," said Amy. "I do not think that lady tires in her matchmaking."

"I have known Mrs. Patrick for many years," said Jeff. "My parents were friends with her. I think she wants to see me settled."

"Oh, now I understand her motivation," said Amy.

"She is encouraging you to pursue me, so she approves to you."

"Just barely, I'm sure."

"I wouldn't say 'barely'."

"Okay, on that note, I will see you later," said Suzanna.

As Suzanna walked away, Amy asked Jeff, "What do you think about all I told you?"

"I will have to think about all this for a while before I give you an answer."

That was fair enough, thought Amy.

Chapter 16
San Francisco

Hours later, the train pulled into the station at Emeryville. From there, one could take the ferry across the bay to San Francisco. They had agreed that the train station was the most probable place to check for a message. There was one train station, and there were many ferries one could take.

They found the main rail office, and Suzanna went inside to check for messages. She came out immediately and was excited. "Yes, there was a message," she said holding a piece of paper in her hand.

"What does it say?" asked Amy.

She opened the note with Amy hanging on her shoulder. The date was three days ago.

"It says we should go to San Francisco and check in at the Palace Hotel. Someone will be looking for us there," said Amy.

Suzanna beamed. "We are getting closer, and the Palace Hotel is supposed to be nice."

Amy glanced at Jeff. She didn't want to leave right away. Of course, she wanted to return to 2066, but not just yet.

They caught the next ferry heading to San Francisco.

Suzanna was quite animated and continued to talk most of the way. "Now that we are so close, I want this to happen right away. It feels I have been gone for ages."

"Is this period in time so bad?" asked Jeff.

"No, it is not," said Suzanna, "but there are some conveniences I just miss terribly, like hotel rooms with their own bathrooms and plumbing, my favorite toothpaste and other things like that. I had really romanticized the past, and the reality was much more stark than I imagined."

"And you, Amy, do you feel the same as Suzanna?" asked Jeff.

"I actually did not romanticize the era at all. I knew the difficulties and expected the worst. It has turned out much better than I had thought," she said.

The Palace Hotel was beautiful. In any age, it would be beautiful. The horse drawn carriage took them inside the hotel to a large courtyard. Walkways on each of the floors over looked the courtyard. The reservation desk was located where the carriage stopped, and they checked in. Reservations had been made for two rooms.

"We have been holding your rooms for several days," said the hotel manager.

Amy noted that the rooms had been paid for; no wonder the manager was not upset.

"Welcome to the Palace Hotel," he said, as he told the bellboy to take them to their rooms.

The bellboy then took them through the lobby and into the 'rising room'.

"Please do not be distressed at the movement you will feel," said the bellboy in a well-rehearsed voice. "It is perfectly normal and safe. This modern convenience saves you time and effort from climbing the stairs, especially since we are going several floors up."

They could feel the movement and then it stopped as they arrived at their floor. It was the top floor.

"We are on the seventh floor," announced the bellboy proudly as he pulled the doors open. "Isn't it wonderful?"

Suzanna and Amy pretended to be impressed, but Jeff actually was. The bellboy then led them to down a hall to their rooms. Suzanna and Amy were staying together, and the bellboy opened their door and started to show them all the features. When he opened a door off the bedroom, Suzanna ignored the rest.

"It has its own bathroom," she sighed, "with plumbing."

The bellboy continued with Jeff further down the hall. Amy watched him go, wondering how all the news of the day was affecting him.

They met in the lobby afterwards and Amy suggested they walk around. Maybe someone would recognize them. Nothing happened during their walk, and they sat down in the lobby to order something to eat.

"Why aren't they here?" asked Suzanna. "Do you think they gave up?"

"No," said Amy. "It has been only three days since they left the note. I am sure they would not give up so easily."

"But what if Gustav does not want you to return?" asked Jeff.

Both looked surprised. "I had not thought about that," said Amy.

"I sometimes suspect the worst in people. Maybe you should consider it," said Jeff. "He stole the flower and the silver and might not want you to return and accuse him. What could he do to prevent you from going back?"

That idea had not crossed her mind, but Jeff could be right, thought Amy. "He is just one person. I don't think he can do too much. The others in the lab would not let him."

"What if he said we were dead? Then, no one would come for us," interrupted Suzanna, looking worried

"No, he couldn't," said Amy. "They would check our lifelines and know we were alive."

"Oh, yeah. Thank goodness," said Suzanna, looking relieved, "Also, you talked to them just before we were supposed to be transported, so they know we were ready to go back."

"Hmm," said Jeff. "So you don't think he will present any problem?"

"I don't know. What could he do? The transport machine in the lab is quite sensitive and has been prone to some problems, but everyone is aware of this now, and I am sure they will be checking and rechecking things before each trip."

"Yes. Too bad they sent me to eastern Colorado instead of Durango before they became aware of it," said Suzanna.

"And it also sent you four weeks earlier than us," said Amy.

"Yeah," said Suzanna.

They sipped on their drinks, each lost in their thoughts.

"How long do you think we should wait for them?" asked Suzanna.

"Definitely more than one day," Amy smiled. "We'll give them a couple, and then we'll look for more reasonable lodgings."

"I could look around for a saloon to work in," said Suzanna, but her voice was filled with dread. When she had offered to work for Mr. LaForce, she had been upbeat. Maybe the thought of remaining in 1895 had changed that.

"No, don't think of that; we will hopefully resolve this before then," said Amy.

"Well, I am going to go back upstairs," said Suzanna.

"I will stay a bit longer here," said Amy.

She smiled at both of them and left.

Amy studied Jeff as he watched her. "I hope you are all right?"

"I can't remember a day that has been filled with so much startling news."

"You believe I am from the future now?"

"You are definitely from somewhere else. You still could have come from another country."

"I see, and the whole conversation about transports and time lines? It was you who suggested Gustav would try to stop us."

"If I were Gustav, I would do the same; there is nothing unusual about that. I think both of you are quite good actresses and have practiced this scene. Right now, I am playing along to see where it leads, but as soon as I see Gustav, I will arrest him."

"I don't think you will ever see him again."

"I will find him," said Jeff. He stood up. "I am going to my room now."

"I'll go up as well," she said.

They both rode the 'rising room' silently.

They stopped in front of her room, and she opened her door and wished him good night. She saw Suzanna was already in bed, but she turned towards the door as Amy came in.

"You're back?"

"Yeah."

"Retiring a bit early."

"Yeah, I guess."

"I would have thought you two would be spending every last minute together."

Amy thought about it.

"It may be your last night," said Suzanna.

She was right; the finality of it struck a chord. She didn't want it to be the last night. "I could go to him."

"Hmm," said Suzanna.

"He still does not believe we are from the future, you know."

"It is a hard thing to understand, even for a college educated guy like him."

"He thinks we are actresses, playing out a scene."

"It is his way of coping."

"Yeah, I should go to talk to him."

"Well, I'm not going to wait up. Just lock the door."

Amy went down the hall and knocked softly on Jeff's door. There was no answer and she knocked a bit louder.

The doors of the hotel were quite thick, so she could not hear anything. She was sure Jeff was inside, and she was ready to knock more forcefully when the door opened a crack.

"Amy?"

"Yes, it's me. I needed to talk to you again. May I come in?"

Jeff paused for a moment, "I was taking a bath."

"Oh. Do you want me to come in or shall I come back later?"

The door opened wider and she went in. He was wearing a towel. He closed the door and he returned to the bathroom, where she heard him step into the tub.

"I can help you wash your back, if you like" she said.

The answer took a moment. "I would like that," he said from the bathroom.

She took off most of her clothes and went into the bathroom. "Hand me the soap and washcloth," she said.

"You are serious about washing my back?"

"Yes" She lathered the soap and worked on his back

"I really hope you are a liar and that you are not from the future," he said.

"That is a strange thing to say."

"That way you would not be leaving."

"Yes, I was thinking about that."

They made love afterwards, and it was different from the first time. Both were gentler with each other.

Chapter 17
Surprise, guess who?

The following morning, Amy met Suzanna in the lobby.

"I checked the front desk and there were no messages for us," said Suzanna. "How much longer is it going to take for them to get us?"

"It is only the second day, Suzanna, pull yourself together."

"I know, I know, but we need to do something or I am going to go crazy waiting."

"You want to go for a walk?"

"I'm not sure."

"We could go to Golden Gate Park."

"Does the Golden Gate Park exist?"

"It is probably not like we know it, but the Conservatory of Flowers was already built. I don't think the windmills were there yet."

"Well, that might be okay, but I really think we need to update our wardrobe. Who knows how many days we are stuck here, and this is a fancy hotel."

Suzanna was right, and Amy agreed to go shopping.

"Where is the sheriff, anyway?"

"He went to talk to the local police, and he said he would be gone awhile. He is still looking for Gustav."

"Stubborn guy. How are things with you two?"

"Good, very good. I started to think we can take him with us again."

Suzanna smiled and shook her head. "Have you even asked him?"

"I actually did this morning."

"And?"

"He thought it was an absurd idea. Even if he believed we came from the future, he said, how could he live in a place that was so foreign to him."

"He's right."

"I could help him."

"He would lose his self esteem if you did that too much, and you would start to look at him as a hindrance."

Amy sighed. "Maybe you should have gone into psychology."

"I did take some psychology courses."

When they returned from their shopping excursion in the early afternoon, Suzanna went directly to the front desk to ask about messages again. The front desk, being familiar with her many previous requests, had something ready for her. She returned to Amy quickly.

"A note has been left for us." Suzanna showed her.

"Open it."

Suzanna tore it open and both of them read.

Be on the rooftop of the hotel at 5:30. It was signed 'Anthony'.

"This is it," said Suzanna, excited. "Finally."

Then they saw Jeff walking towards them.

"Oh," said Suzanna. "You are going to have to tell him."

"I know," sighed Amy. She went to talk to Jeff while Suzanna went to their room.

"So this is the place?" asked Jeff, as he surveyed the rooftop. "Nothing looks out of the ordinary."

She had brought him up there to explain what was going to happen. "I should hope everything looks ordinary. We take great pains to ensure everything looks natural." She looked around. She knew what to look for and yet, she too was finding it hard to find.

"So, how does this work?" asked Jeff.

"The transport marker can only send two people at a time. Both have to be holding onto the marker, and then they are sent to the future. Basically, you tell the lab you are ready to go and the machine in the lab, the Temporal Transporter, does most of the work. The transport marker here helps with the process, and suddenly you are in the lab in 2066." There it is, thought Amy, as she saw the funny looking vent coming out of the rooftop. It had to be that. She walked over to inspect it closer.

"And who is Anthony?" asked Jeff, following her.

"He is another coworker."

"Like Gustav?"

"Yes, he is a time travel setter."

Jeff looked out into the distance. From the rooftop of the hotel one could see most of San Francisco, and he studied it quietly. "So at 5:30, you will disappear forever."

Amy felt her heart break, but there was nothing to be done. Her life was in another time and she could not stay here. "Have you given any more thought to my proposal?"

Jeff smiled sadly. "Of me going with you? As much as I would enjoy the adventure, I don't think I will accept."

She had to accept his decision, she thought as they returned downstairs.

A bit after five, the three returned to the rooftop. The sun was making its way towards the ocean. It was difficult to wait. Amy was torn between her affection for Jeff and going back home, but there was not much to say. They could not promise anything, and writing letters or making calls was out of the question.

They waited about ten minutes, and suddenly they heard two men's voices coming up the stairs.

"I thought Anthony was by himself," said Suzanna.

"I thought so too," said Amy.

As the first man reached the top, Suzanna recognized Anthony. "Hey, Anthony over here."

Anthony waved and headed their way.

The second man followed him up the stairs and froze. It was Gustav.

Before she could say anything, she heard Jeff commanding Gustav to stay put. Jeff had pulled out his gun and was pointing it at Gustav.

"What is going on?" asked Anthony.

"I am arresting Gustav for stealing," said Jeff.

"What?" said Gustav, recovering somewhat, "I didn't steal anything."

"What about the silver ore from LaForce's mine?" asked Suzanna. "And what about her flower?"

Anthony looked at Gustav, "You told us the flower was with her."

"I don't have it," he said, and he sounded honest.

So that was his story, thought Amy. "We know you took the canister with the flower, Gustav. Did you sell it to some pharmaceutical company already?"

"You're crazy, Amy. I think you and Suzanna have been in 1895 too long, and you can't think right. I don't know what they are talking about. Anthony, you have to believe me, buddy."

"I am not here for the flower," said Jeff. "I am the sheriff in Durango, and I am here to arrest Gustav. Here is my badge." He showed the badge with his left hand while his gun remained pointed at Gustav.

Anthony moved towards Jeff to look at the badge. Gustav probably sensed the tide was turning against him, and suddenly he pulled a gun out from his pocket. It was not a stun gun. It looked like something of the period, very similar to the Colt in the sheriff's hand.

"What are you doing, Gustav?" asked Anthony, stepping further away from him. "And where did you get that?"

"Always be ready, Anthony. You don't know when accidents can happen. I really didn't expect all of you would be here, but I can't have you go back. It will ruin everything. Just step away from the marker now." He sounded desperate.

"Come on, Gustav, put your gun down," said Jeff. "Like you said, there are many of us and only one of you. Whom are you going to shoot first?"

"That one is easy, sheriff. There is only one of you with a gun," said Gustav as he swung his gun towards the sheriff. He pulled the trigger.

Amy was slightly in front of the sheriff, and she just had to lean in. She felt the burn of the bullet as it went into her side, and she crumpled on the ground. The pain was shocking. She could barely breathe as she watched a pool of her own blood forming quickly. Then she heard the discharge of a gun nearby and heard Gustav shout out in pain.

"Amy, Amy," said Suzanna, crouching next to her. "Hang on."

Hang on, thought Amy. It usually was not a good thing to hear.

The next moments were a blur. It sounded like Anthony and Jeff were discussing what to do. Jeff wanted her transported to a hospital in the future right away, but Anthony did not think that was a wise idea.

"We need a doctor now," said Suzanna.

Yeah, thought Amy. That was a good idea, though now she was going to sleep.

Chapter 18
Near death can change things

She opened her eyes and noticed she was in still in the Palace Hotel. There was sunlight coming through the window. She tried to sit up, but it was hard and she sunk down again on the pillows.

"Amy?"

It was Jeff, and she smiled. "Jeff, hi. I'm glad you are here."

"Oh my God, Amy," he said, as he sat next to her. "They told me you were going to be fine, but you know I have a problem believing people."

"I can't argue with you there," she smiled, and it hurt. "What happened?"

"Gustav shot you and I shot him. His aim was more damaging than mine, and he managed to limp away. I think I grazed his leg. At that point, I didn't care. You were bleeding so much I was afraid I'd lose you." He took her hand.

"I thought I heard you discussing with Anthony."

"It might have been temporary insanity on my part. Anyway, Anthony called the laboratory, and they sent a doctor right away. The doctor said you will make a full recovery, but it will be a couple of days before you can travel."

A few more days, she thought. "What time is it?"

"It is close to three in the afternoon. You have been out for almost a day."

"Oh. And where is Suzanna?"

"She was here most of the time, but they wanted her in the future. She just left with the doctor. He will be back tomorrow. It is amazing how quickly they fixed you."

"It must be so confusing for you Jeff. Seeing all this."

"It is, but I am glad they could do it fast."

"I wanted to stay longer with you, but I guess I didn't think it would be like this," said Amy.

"Your boss wants you to call as soon as you can. They showed me how to turn on the communication instrument." He stood up to get the ComLink.

"Wait, I want to wait a bit before I talk to them."

"Do you want something to eat? I was going to order something."

"What story did we give the hotel?"

"We. Yes, I guess I am now part of the cover-up."

"I'm sorry to drag you into this."

"Don't worry, I am just glad to see you better." He sat down and took her hand again. "Tell me about the future."

"What do you want to know?"

"How are the cities? How are the people? How bad is the crime? Meeting Gustav, I know that there are still criminals."

"Yes, there is crime, but there are fewer violent crimes because those criminals are found easily. There are also fewer guns of the bullet variety. The cities are much bigger. Remember when you were looking over San Francisco yesterday? Well, the San Francisco of my day is over three times bigger, and the Bay Area has about eleven million people.

"Eleven million? What is the population of the United States?"

"It is over 520 million."

"It is 69 million right now," he said in shock.

"Yeah, there was a big surge in population in the early 1900s, but the growth has slowed down."

"Are there any wilderness, like in Durango? I need to have that."

She realized he was considering accepting her offer. Her heart skipped a beat, but she would be honest with him. She wanted him to make the right decision. "There is open land. Through the 1900s people built without regard to their environment and resources, but now we are more careful about the habitats of animals and plants. Housing is more concentrated, and that allows more open spaces. Durango is still surrounded by open areas, and even the Bay Area has over 1.2 million acres that are preserved as open space."

"Amy, what would I do there? What kind of job could I have? I see the technology you have and cannot even begin to understand how things work. I have used telephones, but they are not common, and I know you cannot call places far away. You are at ease talking to someone without even considering you are talking through time."

"Technology is not a problem. You use it like a tool. Now to your question about what you will do? There are many things you can do."

"I don't think I can be a lawman."

"I don't know, we can look at your skills and match you to a job you would enjoy doing even more than being a lawman. You have a degree in geology, so maybe something along those lines? I would be with you to help you out."

"Won't you tire of having me?"

She shook her head. "No, I can't imagine ever being tired of you."

He looked at her carefully. "Why did you jump in front of me when Gustav shot?"

"I had to protect you."

"It is me who should be protecting you, Amy. Always."

"I love you," she said. The words just came out, and it almost surprised her, but it was true.

"And I love you, too."

She reached out to hug him, but could only reach so far. He moved close to her, but was tentative about touching her. After some awkward holding, they separated.

"We better call," he said.

"Amy, hello, we are glad to hear from you."

"Hello, Dr. Holbrook."

"There are several people here who are eager to hear you."

"Oh, hello everyone."

"Amy, this is George. How are you?"

"Better, George. It hurt a lot, but apparently I was lucky. Nothing important got damaged."

"Hi, Amy, this is Beebe. I am glad you are doing better."

"Thank you, Beebe."

"Yes, Amy, you were lucky," said Dr. Holbrook. "Is the sheriff there?"

"I am here," said Jeff.

"We found where Gustav hid the rest of the silver ore. He had the coordinates in his computer, and Beebe got them. Should I give those to you?"

"That would be fine."

"I'll wait until you get a pen and paper."

"No need for that," said Jeff. "Go ahead and tell me."

"Latitude 37.2456 and longitude -107.85."

"I got them, thanks," said Jeff.

"I believe that it puts it quite close to the cabin, on the south side," said Dr. Holbrook. "Now can you excuse us, sheriff? We have to talk privately with Amy."

"All right," said Jeff. He stood up to leave.

She hung onto to his hand and shook her head. "Stay," she said softly.

"You sure?" he whispered.

She nodded.

"All right then, Amy, is he gone?"

"Go ahead, Dr. Holbrook." She didn't answer his question.

"Susan told us about what happened. We were very upset with Gustav's behavior," said Dr. Holbrook.

"Upset is an understatement," said Amy.

"Yes. We realize that our psych evaluations will have to be more rigorous before we send any more travelers, and that should fix that problem."

She wondered if she would pass the new evaluation. Or would it show that she was also a risk.

"Amy, you told the sheriff all about us."

"Yes, I did." Suzanna had probably told them that.

"Why did you? You know you have caused a big problem."

"A problem bigger than Gustav stealing from the past?" she asked, but went ahead without waiting for a reply. "I did it because we needed his help. After Gustav abandoned us, we would not have reached San Francisco without the sheriff."

"I guess so," sighed Dr. Holbrook. "Susan said something similar, and I guess what is done is done. I just wished there was another way."

"There was no other way that I could not think of."

"Well, we are now trying to decide what to do with him. I am not sure we can wipe all his memory clean."

Would they even consider it, wondered Amy. They must be desperate indeed.

"Amy?" asked George. "Susan mentioned you want him to return with you."

"Only if he wants to," she said, looking at him.

"That is a foolish proposition," said Dr. Holbrook. "We cannot even consider such a thing."

"Have you checked his lifeline?" asked Amy.

"We have," said Dr. Holbrook.

"We still don't have resolution on that," said George. "We have run the variables through the computer several times and cannot determine his lifeline."

"Why do you think that is so?" she asked.

"We don't know," said Dr. Holbrook, and he sounded like he hated that.

"I have thought about this a lot. Have you looked at my lifeline?" asked Amy.

"Well, we can't look at your future, but looking at the previous months, your lifeline is severed in several places. It is probably due to the time travel," said George.

"It looks just like his. Don't you think that maybe he was meant to be a time traveler?"

No one said anything.

"His lifeline does not show he dies this year, so where is he?" she asked.

"Well, we hadn't considered he could be a time traveler," said George.

"Maybe Gustav was supposed to shoot him, and he died," said Dr. Holbrook. "Maybe his body was never found and there was no report of his death."

"Wouldn't there have been a search for his body? He has been in contact with the local police, and I think they would at least look. The newspapers would certainly mention such a thing as a missing sheriff."

"There is no mention of him in the San Francisco news," said George. "I have already looked."

"We will have to give this further thought," said Dr. Holbrook, "and we will consider all options. Dr. Knobby will be heading your way tomorrow."

"All right." said Amy.

"Since you are bedridden, we can call anytime we have a question. Don't worry, we will be in touch," Dr. Holbrook. "By the way, Amy, Susan also told us about your relationship with the sheriff. I hope that is not clouding your professional opinion."

It was clouding it, but her theory about his future was a very plausible explanation. "I need to rest, Dr. Holbrook."

"Some of that was beyond my comprehension," said Jeff, when she disconnected the ComLink.

"It is a lot to understand, but the important part concerning you has to do with your lifeline. You remember the line drawings? Well, when we interact with someone, we can check the past to make sure that we did not affect the person by our presence. That is why we try to keep interactions to a minimum. For example, they knew Bob was supposed to die this year. It was in the records and that did not change. In your case, they could not tell anything from your lifeline."

Jeff smiled, "I am an enigma. Of course, I have had lots of 'interaction' with you."

"Yes, that is true," smiled Amy, "but even before our interactions, they were not able to see your lifeline clearly."

"They checked me out?"

"Yes, from the first time I talked to you."

"So your explanation for it is that I am a time traveler?"

She nodded. "Yes, it would explain a lot."

"What if I decide I don't want to go? Will you erase my memory? Will I remember you?"

"I know Dr. Holbrook said that, but I cannot think they would seriously entertain that option." She debated whether she should tell him about the needle they used with the stun gun. She'd better. She knew that if she found out later about something like this, he would be disappointed or angry, and she didn't want that.

"There is something else you should know. All the time travelers have stun guns. They can incapacitate people without harming them for about fifteen minutes. After we stun the person, we don't want the person to remember about the gun, so we prick them with a needle that erases a couple minutes of memory."

"Do you have this stun gun and needle?"

She nodded.

"Have you used it?"

"I used it on Tom and then made him think I had hit him with a rock."

"Have you used it on me?"

"No. I wouldn't."

"How do I know you haven't?"

"Jeff, I just wouldn't. I only used it on Tom because there were no other options, and I was afraid they would kill you."

"So you erased several minutes of his memory. When do you decide that a loss of couple minutes is acceptable, but not of five minutes, or several hours, or several days?"

"I," she paused, "I don't know."

"You people from the future don't have all this worked out, do you?"

"We don't, and I never said we did. This whole project is just to recover extinct plants so they can be used to make medicines. It is simple!"

"Yet you found it not so simple. Gustav turned out to be a thief, Susan or Suzanna had to become a saloon girl to survive, and you are lying here shot, and you almost died."

Amy bit her lip. It could be the effect of the drugs she was on, but she was going to cry.

He saw it and his tone softened. "Wait, Amy, don't cry. I am just confused and lashed out. I am sorry. I know you are not responsible for all this; it is just hard to understand, and I feel a bit trapped."

She looked at him through her teary eyes.

"Look, I have to think about all these options," said Jeff. "I am going to go out for a walk. Will you be okay?"

"Yes, I will."

"I'll order some food when I get back, and we can have dinner together."

"That will be nice," she said.

It was not nice for him, she thought as he left. He was angry and rightly so. Maybe wiping someone's memory should be revisited, even if it was for a tiny period. Maybe it was not the ethical thing to do, but then how to explain the stun gun? Then she realized she was thinking about work to avoid the bigger issue.

Jeff was considering going with her. What did it mean to their relationship? It was a big step. Would she tire of having to teach him everything, like Suzanna had said? Would Jeff miss his familiar surroundings? Would he want to return, and would that ever be possible? She didn't think so.

An hour later, she received a call from Dr. Holbrook again. Jeff was still out walking.

"We rechecked Jeff's lifeline, and we compared it to several other travelers, including Susan's and yours. It seems Jeff's lifeline is similar," said Dr. Holbrook. "He could be a time traveler."

"Amazing," said Amy. She was surprised her suggestion was true.

"Yes, amazing about covers it," said Dr. Holbrook. "Of course, the decision is his to make. You also have to tell him the decision is irreversible."

"Irreversible. I'll tell him," she said.

"We have also decided to move the transport marker. We don't know where Gustav is, and we don't want him to return without us knowing. In his current state of mind, he could damage things in the lab. We will move it after you return."

It made sense. It wasn't only Gustav knowing the location. There had been many people going up to the roof of the Palace Hotel and different people coming down. Anyone who saw the activity could be suspicious.

When Jeff got back, they ordered room service. Soon afterwards, a waiter rolled in a table set with silverware and even a candle. He plated the meals, lit the candle and left.

They started eating quietly.

"How was your walk?"

"I don't even know where I went," said Jeff. "I just walked and thought about everything."

"There is something else that will affect your decision," said Amy. She told him about the call while he was gone.

"So there is no turning back once I go," said Jeff.

"I know that makes it a harder decision."

"I have been thinking about what I would leave behind. There is no family left. There are some friends I would miss and my horse," he paused.

Of course, his horse would be high on his list, thought Amy.

He didn't continue, and she thought maybe he couldn't. "The decision is not so easy, I'm sorry for that," she smiled gently.

"It is mostly the horses, Amy, and the open land. You told me the land was the same?"

"The city of Durango has grown, but there is a lot that has not changed."

"And what do you think about us? I know I love you now," he paused.

She knew he was thinking about the future. There was no way to know. "For me, I can't imagine our feelings for each other changing."

"I feel the same way, so I have come to a decision."

She looked at him, hoping it would be what she wanted.

"I am going with you," he said.

She was able to breath again.

Chapter 19
Returning home

The following day, the arrangements were finalized, and then Dr. Knobby arrived with Ryan Campbell.

Amy introduced him to Jeff. "He is a time travel setter," she said," just like Gustav."

"Well, not exactly like him," smiled Ryan. "I am better looking and not a criminal."

He was cocky, just like she remembered him in high school. "I was surprised to see you and not Anthony."

"Yeah. Anthony wanted to take some time off. I guess you guys had a rough time the last time he was here."

"I don't know what happened to Gustav."

"They are actually looking into it. It could be a side effect of time travel."

"Is that possible?"

He shrugged.

"How many times have you traveled?" she asked.

"This is my fifth time."

"Do you feel any different?"

He laughed. "Miss Waterman, I have already endured vast questioning in the lab. I am all right and I do not feel any different. I am not going to try to shoot anyone."

"Thank goodness," said Amy. "And you always called me Amy."

"Well, I am glad to see you are doing all right," he paused, "Amy."

"I am better, thank you."

"We were pretty worried."

"It will be good to get back. Are you going to look for Gustav?"

"Not on this trip. Dr. Holbrook wants us all back in the lab. Then he will send a different group to find him. I will move the marker once you leave."

Dr. Knobby checked Amy one last time and decided she was well enough to travel. She did feel better, she thought, and wondered how much of it was due to having Jeff come along. They went up on the rooftop, and the doctor transported first.

Jeff and Amy would be next. Protocol was to wait at least ten minutes before trying another transport. That would give the lab ample time to clear the machine and check the power levels.

"Okay," said Ryan. "It's your time."

Amy and Jeff moved to the vent that was the transport marker.

"I'll see you soon, in the future," said Ryan.

"Remember, do not release the marker until we are in the lab," she told Jeff. "I will tell you when."

Jeff nodded and took a breath.

As the transport started, Amy watched Ryan turn and head down the stairs into the hotel. Then out of the corner of her eye she saw Gustav. He must have been hiding somewhere on the rooftop waiting for an opportunity. He was running straight at them, while dragging his injured leg behind him. She shouted to him to stay away, but she couldn't even hear her own voice. He reached them about the time the Palace Hotel rooftop vanished.

Chapter 20
Richmond

She closed her eyes holding onto the rod tightly. Then she felt all motion stop. She looked around. It was not the lab. She was standing in utter darkness. It should have been about three in the afternoon.

"Ohhh," She heard someone moan in pain.

"Jeff is it you?" she whispered, worried it might be Gustav or someone else.

"It's me," answered Jeff.

"Thank God," she said as she took out her small laser and used it as a flashlight to light the way to him. He was lying on his side on the ground. "Are you all right?"

"My head is pounding, but I'm all right. Did you see Gustav?"

"Yes, it was horrible. I don't know if he made the transport," she looked around. There were no sign of Gustav anywhere. "I don't know where we are."

"It looks like a storage area," said Jeff, standing up. They were in a room filled with very large crates. There were no windows, but she saw a light switch against one wall. She went over and turned on the light. The fluorescent tubes flickered and finally turned on.

"Wow, that's a strong light," commented Jeff.

"Oh, no," she said. "These type of lights are no longer used in 2066. We are in the wrong time."

Amy walked up to one of the crates and read the label. "Ford," she said. "Hmm, this crate contains a 'Jeep'. I don't know what that is." She was not sure of the pronunciation.

"A 'Jeep'?"

"Yeah and from the size of the container, it looks quite big."

One side of the room had a large, roll-up door. There was another door opposite the roll-up, and there was also one next to the roll-up. "I think we should get out of here," said Amy.

"Yes, you might get a better idea of where we are."

They stepped through the door next to the roll-up, and it did not help. They were outside, but it was nighttime. They had stepped outside from one end of a very large building. The building was well lit, but she could not see anything that would give them an idea of where they were. They could see some people working inside.

"This building is bigger than anything I have seen," said Jeff.

"I'm going to call the lab." She turned on the ComLink.

"Amy? Where are you?" asked Dr. Holbrook right away. "We are waiting for you."

"I don't know. It is night, and we are outside a huge building. You can't tell us where we are?"

"No, I am afraid not. What happened?"

Amy told him about Gustav.

"The transport is not supposed to handle three people. Is Gustav with you?"

"No."

"Well, look around and see if you find some sort of indication of where you are."

"We are still in the past." She told them about the lights. Then she told them about the crates labeled 'Ford' and 'Jeep'. "Maybe that will give you a hint to where we are."

"All right then, we'll call back."

She hung up and they walked around to the other side of the building. Then she saw it. "Look at that. It is a car. I have seen similar types of cars in museums, and maybe it can take us where we want to go."

They went to the vehicle and studied it further.

"This looks a bit similar to some of the motor wagons I saw in New York," said Jeff, "but the tires there were thinner and much larger in diameter. The car I saw had a steering tiller like this, but it was set in front of the driver. This one is off to a side and it has numbers on it. And what is that?" He pointed to a metal, circle-looking thing set in front of the left front seat.

"I believe that is a steering wheel, and it replaced the tiller for steering, so I don't know what this stick with numbers does. I never saw one work in the museum," she said, touching the tires. "Well, let's get on and see if it will take us somewhere."

Jeff climbed behind the steering wheel, and she got on next to him. "Take us to the University of California," she said and waited.

Nothing happened.

"Take us to the University of California at Berkley," she said carefully. "I should be more exact," she told Jeff, "there are many campuses, and it may have caused confusion."

Still the car did not move.

"Hmm, maybe it has to recognize my voice," she said.

"Look there is a key inserted here," said Jeff. He turned the key and the car lurched forward. It barely paused and jumped forward another time before Jeff turned the key back to the original position.

They both looked at each other in disbelief.

"I'm not going to do that again," said Jeff.

"And I can't help with this. I don't know how to drive one of these," Amy shook her head. "No one I know owns their own vehicle in 2066; there is no need to. Public transportation is very good, and you can rent a vehicle if you need, but it works off voice commands. Most cars are owned by the wealthy, since they are very expensive to own and operate."

They sat in the car, looking out into the darkness. The sun was on its way and the black sky was starting to lighten.

"What era do you think we are in?" asked Jeff.

"By the car, 1930s or 40s, but I'm not sure."

Her ComLink activated. "Hello, hello."

"Dr. Holbrook, have you figured out where we are?"

"Ford was a car manufacturer, and they made a vehicle called the Jeep for a brief time. It is an open air type of vehicle with four rubber tires..."

"We are sitting in one right now," interrupted Amy.

"Oh? Well, Ford had a plant in Richmond, California. They built Jeeps there, and they put them in crates to transport them to the front lines. You must be there."

Richmond was not far from Berkeley, she thought. "What about the year?"

"Ford built those only during World War II, so you are probably in the early 1940s."

"Oh. I don't know much about living in this era," said Amy.

"It is World War II. It has been going since 1939, but the United States did not enter it officially until 1941. That is when Japanese attacked..."

"I know about the history," she interrupted. "I just don't know about the people and fitting in with them. When can we get back?"

"Once we know your exact location and time, we can send someone with a transport marker. Meanwhile, you have to blend in as much as possible."

"For how long?"

No one said anything, and then Dr. Holbrook said, "It will take some time."

He was vague, but she knew it would take long. The first time they set a marker in San Francisco in 1895, it had taken almost two months. "We don't have any money," she stated.

"There is no marker, so we can't send you anything," said someone.

She knew that, but wanted them to think about it. Maybe there was something they could do to speed up the process.

"Well, you know the skills we have, so maybe you can research what type of work we can do here. We will be needing to find a job soon," said Amy. She knew that being a saloon girl was not an option in this time, and she did not want to think about the other option.

"We'll look into that right away," said Dr. Holbrook.

"Amy, this is George. Do you know how to drive a stick shift?"

"I don't even know what that is," she said.

"It is a car with manual gears, and I know how to drive one," said George sounding very animated. "I can step you through it while the others are finding answers to your questions. Do you see the pedals on the floor of the car?"

"Yeah, I see them," she looked at Jeff, who was looking at them.

"Left to right, the first is the clutch, the next is the brake, and the one on the right is the accelerator. You press the clutch when you want to change gears. You need to be in different gears to attain different speeds or to go in reverse.

143

Look at the gearshift; it is the stick in the middle of the floor. It has a knob on top and may have with numbers on it."

"This is too complicated, George," said Amy. "We can't do this now."

"You should learn to drive," said George. "Public transportation was not great in that era, so most people drove."

"I can do this," said Jeff quietly.

She looked at him to make sure, and he nodded.

"Okay George, go ahead."

"To start the car, it is best to have it in neutral and have the clutch depressed. Why don't you try it? Turn the key. Oh, and you should hold onto the steering wheel and keep it steady while we do all this."

Amy braced herself against the dashboard while Jeff gripped the steering wheel tightly with one hand. He depressed the clutch with his foot and turned the key on.

The engine started and the car did not lurch.

"Yay," said Amy, relieved that worked, but then she noticed they were moving. "The car is moving!"

"You must be on an incline," said George. "Put the brake on."

"With the same foot? I can't reach it with the same foot," shouted Jeff.

"Use the right foot."

He stomped on the brake and the car stopped abruptly. Jeff turned the key off.

"Okay, that was good," said George.

What did he know, thought Amy, he wasn't there with them. "The sun is rising, and I think the people that work here will be arriving soon." She wanted to stop this experiment.

"Let's try again," said George. He explained how to use the different feet on the pedals.

Jeff got the car started again.

"Now, while you have the clutch in, change the gear to number 1. Probably a forward position; look at the drawing on top of the gear shift."

Jeff did that, and the car seemed to do all right.

"Now release the clutch slowly while you press the accelerator at the same time."

The car started to go.

"Turn the steering wheel in the direction you want to turn the car."

Jeff tried it and it seemed to work. He pressed the accelerator more and the car started to go faster.

"Don't go too fast," said Amy.

"How fast are you going?" asked George. "Look at the speedometer."

Amy looked at the dials on the dashboard. They were hard to read compared with digital displays. "I think it's somewhere between 20 to 25. Is that miles per hour?"

"That is fast," said Jeff holding onto the steering wheel more tightly.

She looked at him and didn't say anything. It was really slow, but it did feel fast, sitting out in the open with the wind blowing against them.

"Hear the engine?" asked George. "You need to shift to the next gear, to number 2."

Jeff changed gears successfully and then the engine sounded better. He pressed the accelerator and looked at the dial. "All right, thirty-five miles per hour. This is amazing."

"Okay, we are running out of road," Amy pointed nervously. "We need to stop."

"Wait," said George. "You have to shift down as you slow down."

Jeff did, and the car came to a stop peacefully. They were now a distance from the building and very close to the water. As the sun's rays lit up the sky, they could see parts of San Francisco across the bay.

"What are those lights going across over there?" asked Jeff.

"That is the Bay Bridge," said Amy. "It was built in the late 1930s and runs from Oakland to San Francisco."

"Really? It must be one long bridge. I remember taking the ferry across."

She nodded and looked in the other direction. She could see a vast shipyard. "We better return the car before anyone misses it."

"George, if I want to go backwards, do I start in neutral as well?"

"Yes, but remember that going backwards, you have to be careful how you steer. You might think it is opposite, but it is not."

Jeff turned the car on and started to back up slowly. "Are there gears for going backwards?'

"No. Just one gear," said George.

Amy was impressed. Jeff had figured out how to drive quite well. He backed up close to where they had started, and they both got out.

"Oh, no," said Amy.

"What is it?" asked Dr. Holbrook.

"I am still dressed like 1895."

There was silence from the future. There was nothing they could do. She looked at Jeff, who had the same problem, but being a man, he would be able to get by with his pants and shirt.

"Try to find some clothes," someone stated the obvious.

"We'll call you back when we get some answers to your questions," said Dr. Holbrook.

As soon as they disconnected the ComLink, she suggested to Jeff they go back inside the building. "Maybe we can find something we change into."

They went back in through the storage area where they had arrived and this time took the door into the main building. It led them directly inside a huge room with high ceilings and windows along one side. The open layout reminded Amy of the lab. She could hear people working, although she did not see any. Along one of the walls, there were signs indicating bathrooms. She headed that way and went into the one with a 'Men' sign posted outside. Inside the bathroom, there were lockers.

"Try to open those lockers," pointed Amy, as she started to try to open the ones close to her. "See if we can find any clothing we can use."

Most of the lockers were locked. The few that were open contained nothing inside. Then finally, they found a locker with two sets of overalls. "Perfect," said Amy. One set was larger than the other, and she handed those to Jeff. "Put these over what you are wearing."

In her case, she couldn't fit the overalls over the long 1895 dress. She took off the dress and put it into a locker. Then she put the overalls on.

As they walked out of the bathroom, two big side doors opened and workers started filing in. A whistle sounded, and she could see the big clock on wall showing it was six thirty.

"Just try to stay out of everyone's way and try to not appear too suspicious," she told Jeff. "We should try leave as soon as we can."

He nodded.

As Amy watched the workers go to their lockers, she knew someone would not find their overalls, so she stepped away from the area.

Chapter 21
A job in 1944

"Hey," said a man's voice. "Where are you supposed to be?"

He was talking to her. "I am new; I don't know," she said.

"Damn, we are getting so many new people, I can't keep track."

Great, thought Amy, this could work in her favor.

"Go to resources. It's down that hall. They will assign you." The man turned and said, "And you? Where did you come from?"

The man was looking at Jeff. Amy quickly noticed why the man was astonished at seeing Jeff. Very few of the male workers were Jeff's age. The younger men would be fighting in the war, thought Amy. "He is my cousin, and he is almost deaf. He can barely speak," said Amy. It was the first thing that came to her mind to excuse him from military service.

Jeff looked surprised, but didn't say a word as he looked at them mutely.

"He can't hear or speak? Oh my God, what else are they going to send down here," ranted the man. "How is he supposed to work?"

"He is very good with his hands," she said.

Jeff stifled a smile.

"Well, it may be blessing if he can't hear or talk. He might become one of our better workers, and at least you look strong," said the man looking him over. "Go to the tank assembly section. Over there."

Jeff looked at him and then looked at the direction he was pointing.

"Oh right, you can't hear. I'll take you," said the man.

Amy looked with concern as Jeff was led away.

"Don't worry, Arnold might seem like a gruff foreman, but he is actually very nice," said a woman standing next to Amy.

Amy smiled at her and headed to the resources office. The same woman followed her there and then went around the desk and sat down.

"Hi, again. What is your name?" she asked her.

"Amy Waterman."

"My name is Eleanor Felder." She looked through her paperwork. "Your application has to be here, otherwise they would not have let you through the gate," the woman sighed. "And your cousin?"

"Jeff Lindsey," said Amy, deciding to keep their names.

The woman searched again and looked dejected. "We need to have a better system. We keep losing paperwork."

"Maybe I can help with that?"

"Can you type?"

"Yes," said Amy.

"How fast?"

"I don't know."

The lady looked at her with pity. "Where are you from?"

"Durango, Colorado."

"Huh," said the woman thinking. "I'll give you a typing test. Come over."

The woman told her to sit in front of a big black machine that dominated the desk. The keys on the machine were in the same order as a keyboard she had once seen in high school. The teacher had devised an experiment to test the students to determine how many of them knew how to type. She had done abysmally, but afterwards she had practiced many hours on that keyboard to get better. Of course, she had not used such a thing since then.

The woman fed a sheet of paper in the top of the machine and used the roller to line the page up. Amy paid careful attention.

"Have you used a Royal before?"

"No, I don't think so," said Amy.

"It is the latest typewriter, and you will love it once you know the features. Okay, why don't you try it for a bit before I give you the test? Meanwhile, I will find a new application for you to fill out," said Mrs. Felder.

"Thank you," said Amy, as she set her hands over the keys like she had done with the keyboard. The little finger pressed the letter 'A' and the key barely went down. Nothing showed on the paper. Maybe it had to be turned on. She looked around the machine for such a switch, but did not find anything.

Maybe it was voice command, she thought briefly, and then immediately discarded the idea. It was just wishful thinking.

She hit the 'H' forcefully with her index finger. An 'H' appeared on the white paper. That worked, she thought. She started to peck at the machine, and words started to form.

The keys were hard, and they had to be depressed the whole way. Her fingers quickly started to feel sore. Then she saw a newspaper lying on the desk nearby. She picked up the newspaper and brought it back. The date was May 8th, 1944.

She set the paper next to her and started to copy the main story.

Mrs. Felder came back and watched her for a moment. "You are not very fast, are you?"

"This is not fast?" asked Amy. She thought she was doing quite well.

"Not really. 70 words per minute is fast, and I think you are typing about 30 words per minute."

"Oh."

"The good thing is you are using all your fingers correctly. Some people only use two fingers, and they will never increase their speed. You at least have a possibility of improvement."

Mrs. Felder's kind comment did nothing to improve the feeling that she had failed.

"I have an application form here," said Mrs. Felder. "Let's see, what skills do you have?"

She had no skills, she thought. Reading, analyzing, running experiments and simulations...nothing seemed right. "I graduated from college."

"That's a good one. What was your degree?"

"Biology."

"Biology," Mrs. Felder repeated, sounding disappointed, as she wrote that down.

Amy realized she could not miss this chance to get a job. She would not be able to apply for anything else dressed in overalls. "I am a fast learner. I know Spanish. I am good at organizing and analyzing."

Mrs. Felder smiled. "Those are good skills, although Japanese or German might be more desired." She looked through a listing. "Well, we do have several openings on one of the teams working on the tanks."

Amy nodded.

"Your cousin is working in the area nearby and that way, you can help him if needed."

"Thank you, Mrs. Felder."

"Let me tell you about the schedule. We work 24 hours a day on 3 shifts. Your shift is 6:30 am to 2:30 pm, and that is when most of our employees are here. The night shift is quite light in comparison. We work everyday except Sundays. You get paid on Saturday."

Amy nodded, wondering how they would make it until Saturday.

"Do you have any questions?"

"Well, there is one," said Amy. "Can you give me an advance on the salary?"

"No. We do not do that, and it would be a bad practice to pay employees before they work."

Well, she asked, thought Amy. She didn't know where they were going to sleep tonight, much less what they were going to eat.

She was led to the tank unit and shown what to do. It was manually intensive work, but quite easy, and time passed quickly. A whistle blew at lunchtime, and she went to look for Jeff. There was no one in the area where he had been working. She looked around and finally saw him. A woman was holding his arm and leading him towards the doors labeled 'Cafeteria'.

Amy quickly caught up to them. "Hi," she said.

"Hello," said the woman. "He can't hear you," she pointed to Jeff.

"I know. He is my cousin."

"Oh. He didn't hear the lunch whistle so I was taking him to the cafeteria."

"That is very kind of you, but I think we will have our lunch outside. The day is quite nice." smiled Amy.

"Yes, it is," said the woman. She then turned to Jeff. "See you after lunch," she shouted as she gesticulated.

He nodded and smiled.

"He is a sweetie," said the woman.

Amy smiled her thanks and walked away. "So, a sweetie?" she asked Jeff in a low voice.

"Being mute is making me very attractive," replied Jeff. "I'll have to remember this when we leave here."

"Well, I least I found out what year we are in," said Amy.

"1944", they both said it at once.

"How did you know?" asked Amy.

"I looked at my time sheet," said Jeff. "Apparently it is a sheet that keeps track of the hours one works so you can get paid at the end of the week. May 8th, 1944, is the date. Interesting, right?"

"Yeah," said Amy, thinking that Jeff was taking all this better than she was. "What else did you find out?"

"The company partially subsidizes lunch, so we should try to eat here when we have some money."

Amy nodded. "I found that several of the workers are renting rooms within walking distance from the plant. It will cost about $15 a week, and it includes breakfast, so that might be an alternative. And I agree with you, first we need to get some money."

"I do have four dollars," said Jeff, "But it is not enough."

"Yeah that will not...," she stopped in mid sentence, "Are they coins or bills?"

"Four silver dollars," said Jeff.

"You are a life saver," said Amy, almost hugging him. She refrained and squeezed his hand. "Those silver coins are worth much more than four dollars. In my time, they would be worth hundreds of dollars, but here we will have to find what they are worth. I will ask Mrs. Felder where we can go to sell them."

"You are not eating lunch?" asked Mrs. Felder when they walked in her office.

"No, we are not hungry, but I have a question. Jeff has an old 1895 silver dollar he wants to sell. Who would be the best person to buy such an object?"

Mrs. Felder thought about it and took out a big book. She went through the pages and finally stopped. "You could sell to an antique dealer, but seeing that it is silver, I would go with a coin dealer." She took out a piece of paper and wrote on it. "Here is the address of one. I have dealt with this man, and I know he is fair in his evaluations."

"Thank you, Mrs. Felder. Thank you," said Amy. She took the paper and started to turn.

"Amy?"

"I brought extra apples for lunch; would you like them?'

"Sure, if they are extra."

Mrs. Felder handed her a couple of apples.

Amy gave one to Jeff, who bowed his thanks.

"He is a sweetie, isn't he," said Mrs. Felder.

"Yes, I guess he is," said Amy.

After work, they went into town and sold one of the silver dollars; it was enough, since they were given $57 for it. Jeff had a hard time hiding his surprise. The next thing they did afterwards was to find a place to eat.

"Fifty-seven dollars," said Jeff, still amazed as he took a bite of his grilled ham and cheese sandwich.

"It should help us get through this week," said Amy. She had paid a nickel for a newspaper and was looking over the rent section. Getting an apartment would be the best, she thought, and that way they would save on meals. "I was thinking that we should not rent too close to our work place, since you are supposed to be kind of mute."

"I don't know what you were thinking, making me deaf and mute."

"I saw the way the foreman looked at you. He was wondering why an able young man was not fighting in the war. You are obviously not lame or blind, so it was the first thing I could think of."

"I guess that was reasonable. Did all young men go to war?"

"The majority did. They called it the draft, and if you were between the age of 18 to 37, you could be enlisted in the armed services."

"Who won?"

"We did, if there is winner from war." She explained how the war had started and how the countries around the world had banded into two groups, the Allies and the Axis. Soon the restaurant started to fill with more people and they left. It was best no one heard Jeff speak so close to work.

153

Next, they headed to a clothing store. Amy wanted to get out of her long camisole and into real underwear. The brassiere was another matter. In 2066, there were different bras for different activities, and not all women used them regularly, but in 1944, she could see most of the working girls wore them. You could tell by the way the sweaters looked conically pointed. She tried on a bra and felt it was constricting and pushing her breasts into a strange formation. She couldn't imagine surviving everyday, all day with something like that and didn't buy it.

They had to go to a drug store to find the rest of the items. It seemed that there were different stores depending on the products sold. Finding a shaver took the longest, as Jeff marveled over the new 'injector' razor. She had no idea what would be better, and the pharmacist took his time enumerating the attributes of one razor over the other. Finally, they got what they needed.

It was late in the evening, so they decided to stay in a small hotel for the night. Tomorrow, when they had more time, they would search for apartments. Finally, once settled into their room, they called Dr. Holbrook. He had not called them back earlier, and Amy worried it may be a bad sign.

"Hello, Amy, this is George."

"Where is Dr. Holbrook?" asked Amy.

"He is in a meeting with the GovTime sponsors." He didn't add any details and for George that was odd.

"What is going on, George?"

"Nothing, nothing."

"George?" She asked and waited for George fill the void.

"Okay, Amy. They feel we are making too many mistakes, and they want to shut the lab down," he said.

There it was. She knew she could get the information from George, but it was disturbing. What about her project? What about all the work everyone had done for so long? Would they throw all that out? The potential for good was very high, but George knew this as well as she did. There was no reason to point it out.

"Of course, they will get you back before they do that," he quickly added.

"Would they shut things down while we are here?" she asked, surprised.

"No, no," said George. "That is exactly my point. I know they have already started the process to get to your time, so you shouldn't worry."

She knew how long the process was going to take. Going back to 1895, 171 years, had taken over 100 days of meticulous calculations. And that was considering they had increased the time intervals to regressing three years per day. She had used that faster rate to estimate their return and knew it would take close to two months. "Well, our exact date is Monday, May 8th, 1944," she said.

"Good, I will make sure Dr. Holbrook knows. You said Monday? It is Sunday here."

"Yeah, I noticed the time of day changed during transport. Somehow, we went forward over one day." She knew they liked to keep the days the same to help keep things simple. If you were in the same time zone as the lab, the time was usually the same.

"What is the time there?" asked George.

"Right now it is 9 pm, Monday, how about for you?"

"It is just past 7 am Sunday morning," said George. "We will have to take that one day and 14 hour difference into account when we talk to you."

"Sounds like you are working very early."

"Yeah, we knew you would call. It's a bit crazy here."

"Do you have any idea how long it is going to take to get to us?"

"There is good news about that. We have a transport marker in the year 2000, and we can work off that one."

"They left a marker in 2000?"

"Yes, as you know, they move the marker with each trip, but in this case, someone had requested the year 2000 as a possible destination."

"Thank goodness for that," said Amy. That was only 56 years away. "So that should take about 18 days."

"Yes. By the way, where are you guys staying? I was wondering how you are coping with no cash?"

"Jeff and I got a job," Amy gave him the details on their jobs, and then told him about the silver dollars Jeff had.

"Wow, it was fortunate Jeff had that with him."

"Yeah," said Amy, smiling at Jeff. "He right here with me."

"You seem to be fitting right in with the times, Jeff. Have you had a chance to drive again?'

"No. I checked the price and, sadly, a car would cost $1200. That is quite a bit beyond what Amy and I can make, even at our good salaries of 70 cents an hour."

"Yeah, owning a car was necessary, but still a luxury for many in those times," said George.

"70 cents? I am only making 60 cents," said Amy, surprised. "How are you making more? We have the same skills."

"Maybe the same skills, but I am a man."

George laughed.

"It's not funny, George," said Amy.

"What about Gustav?" Jeff changed the subject. "Any news of him?"

"No. And that is bewildering. He did not appear here, and I guess you guys have not seen him."

"We haven't," said Amy. "I hope he didn't ..." She couldn't finish her thought.

"Disintegrate," said George helpfully. "I don't think so. You would have found the pieces."

With that thought, they said good-bye.

Chapter 22
Laura

After work the following day, they rented a furnished two-bedroom apartment. It was far enough from the factory they would probably not run into any people from work people, but close to the bus line. They had rented the place on a week-by-week basis hoping to be gone before the month was out.

That evening, as they moved in, they met Laura in the lobby. She introduced herself. "It is nice to have new neighbors," she smiled as she looked at Jeff. "So how are you related?"

She went directly to the point, thought Amy.

"We are cousins," said Jeff.

Cousins, thought Amy. Why would he say that?

"Welcome to the building," said Laura. "I'm sure you will like it here."

They both agreed it would be nice, and then left Laura and headed to their apartment on the second floor.

They had purchased a suitcase at the drug store so that it would appear they had more things than they actually did. They did not want to raise undo interest when they moved into the apartment. It did not take much time to unpack and put away their few belongings.

Not long afterwards, there was a knock on their door. Amy went to answer.

"Hello again," Laura smiled.

Amy noticed that she had changed into a flattering dress. "Hello, Laura."

"I thought I would stop by and bring you some pie. I made it this morning and since you just moved, you probably don't have much food."

"That looks and smells wonderful," said Jeff.

Laura breezed into the room. "Here, let me put it in your kitchen."

Amy couldn't stop her, and Laura checked things out as she went.

"Oh," she smiled at Jeff. "So which is your bedroom? Is it the small one? Or the big one?"

It didn't seem she was talking about the bedrooms at all.

"The smaller one, of course," said Jeff. "Ladies always get first choice."

Laura laughed. "You are a true gentleman. It is so hard to find someone like that these days." She turned to Amy, "It does not seem you have many things. Are you waiting to have them delivered? I ask because I could lend you anything you need while you wait. Anything at all."

"That is kind of you," said Amy. "I may need to borrow some pans while ours get delivered. The pans here are awful."

"Yeah, I bought my own. Why doesn't Jeff come down with me now, and I will give him a couple you can use."

"Are you sure?" asked Jeff.

"Of course, what are neighbors for?" she smiled.

"Yeah, thank you," said Amy, noticing he was quite willing to follow her. She made a mental note to get her own pans as soon as possible.

She was left to survey the apartment further. It was not bad. It even had a small balcony that looked onto some trees and a parking lot if you looked down. She made the bed with the sheets provided and started to make a grocery list. She was hoping to go shopping before the stores closed, and she wondered what was taking Jeff so long.

Finally he returned. "It took a bit because I had a cup of coffee. She lent us a frying pan and a pot," he said. "She is very nice."

"Yes, I'm sure. Why did you say we were cousins?"

"What do you mean?"

"You told her we are related," she said.

"That is what we are at work. I wanted to be consistent."

"You are mute at work, but I notice that didn't stop you from talking with her."

"You want me to be mute?" He looked at her incredulously. "I thought that was the point of getting a place away from work, so I didn't have to be mute."

"I don't want you to be mute. I was just taken by surprise on how that woman is going after you and how easily you are following her."

"After me? I don't think so. She is just being neighborly, and I didn't know you were the jealous type, Amy."

"I'm not," said Amy, realizing that maybe she was sounding that way.

"Well, I didn't say anything when you and that Ryan guy were talking in code back in San Francisco."

"What?"

"He was very interested in asking how you were feeling and how 'they' were missing you. It would be hard to be more obvious."

"Ryan is my friend. I have never considered him any other way."

"Okay, then, Laura is my friend."

Maybe she was overreacting. She didn't want to fight with Jeff. "I'm sorry I made that comment Jeff, it just looked like she is too interested in you."

Chapter 23
The Ford plant

In the next couple of days, Amy and Jeff entered a working rhythm. They had their breakfast early in the apartment, took the bus to work, spent the day there and returned to make dinner together.

A couple days later, Amy purchased some pans and was able to return the borrowed ones. She went down to Laura's apartment. Laura seemed to live by herself and didn't seem to work. Amy wondered how she could afford it.

"So you got your own pans?" asked Laura when she opened the door.

"Yes, and I thought you would like yours back. Thank you for lending them to us, Laura."

"You're welcome," she said. "Hey, I have a question, why don't you come in?'

Amy went inside the apartment; it was very neat. The thing that struck her was how impersonal it looked. There were no pictures of people. Even she had pictures of the people dear to her and she was not in her apartment much.

"You live here alone?" asked Amy.

"Temporarily," smiled Laura. "Maybe not for long. I'm hoping to move to a house out of the city. You know, somewhere nice, with good schools."

Right, thought Amy, she had heard this dream from several of the women in the plant.

"Meanwhile, I was wondering about your job," said Laura. "Is it hard to do?"

"No, it's not hard at all."

"I am going to have to find work soon," she sighed. "About how much does it pay?"

"60 cents an hour."

"That seems good, is it?"

"It adds up when you work eight hours a day, six days a week," said Amy. "Are you thinking of applying for a job at the Ford plant?"

"Frankly, I was hoping to get married and to be settled by now," she said. "As you can see, I like keeping a home and am good at it. I have no strings attached, no nasty relatives to deal with, so I would think that makes it desirable for some nice guy."

"You really don't have family?"

"Not really."

Amy nodded as she looked around again.

"I get a feeling you don't approve," said Laura.

"I rather depend on myself to survive," said Amy. "I would like to be married if I find someone I love, but if I don't find the right person, I don't have to get married."

"Yeah, finding the right person can be hard."

"Even when I get married, I will continue to work. Some marriages fail, and I don't want to be a prisoner of the marriage. I can leave anytime things get rough because I can support myself."

"But then you are never fully committed to the relationship. You will leave anytime you hit a bump in the relationship."

"No, relationships always have setbacks, but no one rules over the other. You can be fully committed to each other as equal partners. Anyway why would you leave if you are in love?"

"You are very modern in your outlook, Amy. I just don't agree with you. I want my husband to rule over me; I expect it. Of course, he has to provide the security and the material benefit that come with a marriage."

Laura was very different, realized Amy, and she wasn't going to change her mind. Amy opened the door to leave, "If you are interested in working at the Ford plant, I can talk to human resources to set a meeting for you. Mrs. Felder is very nice, and I think you could do well there."

"Thanks, but maybe not right now, something or someone may still come up." Laura smiled.

Chapter 24
Are the feelings real?

It was Friday when Mrs. Felder asked Amy to stay and work late.

"I am in a bind," she said. "One of the other girls has been sick for several days and the payroll is tomorrow. Is there any chance you can work? I remember you telling me you could do accounting?"

"Yes, Mrs. Felder. I would love to help."

"You will get overtime for this, and I could put in a word for an eventual transfer into my group."

"The overtime is welcomed, but the transfer is not necessary," said Amy.

"My group pays better. Amy."

"Thank you. Mrs. Felder. I appreciate it."

She let Jeff know she would be late, and he offered to wait until she was done. She told him to go ahead and she would meet him at home. "Mrs. Felder says we will be done close to 7:00 or 7:30."

"Five hours of overtime," said Jeff.

"Five hours of time and a half," she said, feeling proud about it. That was funny, she thought; she was getting excited over getting paid 90 cents an hour.

It was close to 7:00 when they finished the payroll.

Mrs. Felder was thankful and praised her ability with numbers.

"I was glad to help. If we didn't finish, no one would get paid tomorrow," said Amy.

"I would have made sure that would not happen, even if I had to stay up all night."

Amy knew she would have. Mrs. Felder was a conscientious person, just like she had been in 2066.

"How is your apartment?"

"It is quite nice. It is fully furnished, and we are making a lot of use of the kitchen."

"Good, you young people should be eating healthier."

"The apples you gave us were healthy," smiled Amy.

162

"But it is not so healthy if it is the only thing you eat," said Mrs. Felder. "Did you sell Jeff's silver dollar?"

"Yes, we got a good price for it. The man didn't remember you."

"My family sold him things through the years, but that was a long time ago," said Mrs. Felder, remembering. "My father gave me several beautiful Spanish silver coins when I was a teen. I think he got them in a trip to Florida. He said it was for my school, and I used them to go to secretarial school."

"That was good."

"Yes, it was. Otherwise, I probably would not have had a career. Anyway, I am glad you two are getting on well. Thank you again for staying."

When Amy got back to the apartment, she heard voices as she opened the door. She could see into the kitchen, and Laura was standing in front of the stove with Jeff right next to her. She was wearing very short shorts and some sort of halter-top. Her hair was up and it looked very nice. Amy knew she looked grungy and tired, and that was exactly how she felt.

"See," said Laura. "Put your hand here and stir this for me." She took his hand and held it for way too long before putting it on the spoon. She giggled and went to get something out of view.

Amy walked in and slammed the door.

"Hello, Amy." Jeff waved from the kitchen. He continued to stir.

"Amy, that is so nice you are here," said Laura. "Jeff was not sure when you were coming. He and I started to make dinner, and we were hoping you would make it in time. I am starved."

"I ..." said Amy.

"You might be wondering why I am dressed this way?" Laura interrupted. "It was too hot in my apartment, so it was either wear these shorts or my pajamas, and I figured this is more decent. My pajamas are quite transparent."

"Thank goodness for the shorts," said Amy. "You know, I am not that hungry. Maybe it is the heat. I am sorry, but I am going to take a shower. You two should go ahead and have dinner."

Jeff raised his eyebrows, but didn't say anything while Laura was already busy with something else.

She went into the bathroom and turned on the shower. It took a while to get the temperature of the water warm enough.

Jeff was not hers, she thought. They had said they loved each other, but that was in 1895, in other circumstances. If this is what he wanted, she had to let him. Really, they had only known each other for less than a month. She stepped into the water and very soon felt better.

The water splashed all around her, and Amy had to admit that this amount of water was a real luxury. The showers in 2066 were a blend of air and much less water. Of course, the shower was surely one of the best inventions. A shower and the electron microscope...it would be hard to decide which invention was more valuable on her list. She shook her head; she was avoiding the big issue again.

She loved Jeff. She was sure about it, and it didn't matter how recently they had met. As soon as she finished her shower, she was going to have dinner with them and make sure they knew what she felt. She was ready to fight for him. She was not going to make it easy for that girl.

Then she heard something at the door and waited. There it was, a knock on her door.

"Yes?"

"It's Jeff, can I come in?"

"Sure."

She saw him looking at her through the frosted shower curtain. "Did your friend leave?"

"Yes, Laura left."

"Hmm."

"I asked her to leave."

"Oh?"

"I think she had the wrong impression about me." He started to take off his clothes.

"What was that?"

"I am in love with a certain woman, and Laura was just supposed to be helping me make dinner for her."

"You told her that?" She smiled.

"Something along those lines."

"How did you explain the cousin thing?"

"I told her we were very distant cousins. She must think we are very strange. Can I join you?"

Amy peeked at him around the shower curtain, "Definitely."

"You know, you can't blame Laura for having good taste," Jeff propped himself on a pillow on the bed later that evening.

"Okay, let's not go overboard on what a good catch you are. I already know that. All we have to do for the next days is not arouse too much suspicion."

"Didn't you say it was about three weeks to get to us?"

"Three week or less," she smiled. "They can go back three years in one day, so from the year 2000, it should take a bit over 18 days, and we have already been here five."

"Thirteen more days," said Jeff. "You know, I am kind of enjoying myself here."

"I noticed."

"I'm serious. At work, I feel I am making a contribution to something important, and I enjoy being at home with you. I knew the sex part was good, but we are also good in the day-to-day stuff."

"You are so romantic."

Suddenly, the ComLink became active.

"Hello, hello." They heard Dr. Holbrook.

"This is quite late for a call; I wonder what it could mean?" asked Amy, getting out of bed to answer. "Hello, Dr. Holbrook."

"We have found Gustav, and he is with you."

"You mean in Richmond?"

"Yes. He should have arrived quite close to your location. The transport back to the lab works perfectly for two people. We had never tried with three, and so we ran some simulations here. It seems to work fine with three people as long as their total weight is below 600 pounds and they are all holding onto the marker. Both of you with Gustav did not exceed the limit."

"But Gustav was not in the storage area with us," said Amy.

"He was not holding onto the transport marker," said Dr. Holbrook.

"That is true. He was running towards us when we made the jump," said Amy.

"We have found that if you are not holding the marker, you do not arrive in the same location as the others. There is a displacement that occurs. We ran the scenario and found that Gustav was probably just outside the storage area you were in. No more than five hundred feet away."

"We arrived before dawn," said Amy. "He might have been there, and we just didn't see him."

"You might want to start to make some inquiries. Quietly, of course."

Did Dr. Holbrook ever listen to himself, wondered Amy. How could you make quiet inquiries? She disconnected the ComLink after that.

"Do you run tests with real people?" asked Jeff.

She realized that Jeff would have that conclusion listening to their conversation. "No, we don't. When we run tests, which we call simulations, we also use simulated people."

"Simulated?"

"It is a copy. It has all the attributes of a real human, but it is not real. It is like going to a movie. You can see and hear the person, but they are not actually there. Have you ever been to a movies?"

"No, and it is something I would like to see. There were no cinemas in Durango."

"Well, cinemas have improved quite a bit since 1895. I think it would be a fun thing to do on our day off. I think *Casablanca* is playing in the theater nearby."

"There you go again, asking me for a date. I accept, of course."

Chapter 25
Fitting in

Saturday morning, Mrs. Felder came into the work area looking for Jeff. She handed him a note and he nodded. Then they both passed near where Amy was working.

"Mrs. Felder, good morning," said Amy, wondering where they were going.

"Good morning, Amy. I am borrowing your cousin to drive me into town. I need to pick up some things from the hardware store."

"Oh," she said, worried.

"Don't worry, I will have him back before lunch. I know you like to spend that time together."

"No, it's not that." She took Mrs. Felder aside. "He does not have too much experience driving in a town."

"The way there is easy and there is very little traffic. Don't worry, I'll keep an eye on him."

Amy did worry the entire time they were gone. She kept her eye on the door and finally they came back. They were both smiling.

"Your cousin is a very good driver. We had no problems," said Mrs. Felder.

Amy looked at Jeff with admiration; he was adapting so well to this time.

At lunchtime, Jeff struggled trying to remain mute. Finally, he found some paper.

'It was fantastic' he wrote. 'Her car was great. I hate having to write this and not tell you.'

"What kind of car was it?" she asked.

'A 1942 Ford Super Deluxe.' he wrote. 'I wish you had been there with me.'

"Me too," said Amy.

That afternoon they were paid in cash. Jeff was paid $28 and Amy received $28.50 with the overtime. She was quick to point it out.

"You are quite competitive, aren't you?" said Jeff.

"A bit. Okay," she relented, "so it may be quite a bit. Most scientists have to be competitive, since we are always battling for resources. It might be ingrained in me."

The following day, the weather was perfect. They had a late breakfast, did grocery shopping and then went to see the movie. Their life in 1944 was becoming very normal. When they returned to the apartment, they were still discussing the movie.

"Ingrid Bergman was wonderful in the movie," said Jeff. "What a beautiful woman."

"I had heard that *Casablanca* was a great movie, although I had not seen it. I wish it could have ended differently," said Amy. "I wanted them to be together."

"Maybe it is more realistic this way," said Jeff, unlocking the door to their apartment.

"No, I don't want to believe that," said Amy. "Do you want some coffee or tea while we wait for Dr. Holbrook's call?"

"Sure, whatever you are having."

"Life doesn't always have a happy ending, and that is why I want my movies to have happy endings."

"Thank you for suggesting this movie. I noticed that next week they are showing a musical, *Meet Me in Saint Louis*. Maybe we can go again?"

"All right, it's a date," laughed Amy, "and remember you asked this time."

She heard Dr. Holbrook calling and quickly went to answer.

"We have good news," he said. "We have been able to increase the regression rate to 4 years per day. That means you only have seven more days to wait."

"A week," said Amy.

"Have you heard anything about Gustav?"

"No. I started to look through the newspapers for the past week to see if there was a mention of a body, assuming the worst case. There was nothing there, so I checked some of the hospitals. I know his leg was injured, so maybe he was admitted into one. There are three in the area and got to two."

Chapter 26
A visit from the police

The beginning of the week started very much the same as the previous days had gone. Their routine was comforting in that way, and Amy looked at the calendar with mixed feelings. There were a few days left in 1944, and she was enjoying the time with Jeff. It would not be the same in the future.

On Monday, they visited the third hospital in the area, but there was no sign of Gustav. The following day, as they were preparing dinner and talking about work there was a knock on the door. Amy went to answer and found a policeman at her door.

"Good evening, are you Amy Waterman?"

"Good evening, officer. Yes, I am Amy."

"I am Officer Lawrence." He extended his hand and shook hers. His grip was strong for a man in his sixties.

Then he signaled to another policeman who was waiting down the hallway. She had not noticed him standing there. The second policeman was a bit younger, and he turned and talked to someone behind him. Then the person came around; it was Gustav.

As soon as Gustav saw her, he didn't need any prodding. "Sister, sister," he limped as he ran to her. He fell against her in a tight hug, and she ended flat against the wall. Jeff immediately appeared and pulled Gustav off.

"You!" shouted Gustav looking at Jeff. "What are you doing here? Why aren't you back in Durango?"

"I am here to make sure you don't hurt Amy."

"This is your brother, isn't it?" asked Officer Lawrence.

"Yes, he is." She started to think of some sort of fictitious story that would be accepted by the police.

"I wouldn't hurt Amy. Why would I?" asked Gustav.

"Except for when you shot her," said Jeff.

"I did not..." Gustav started to shout and then stopped as Amy lifted the edge of her blouse to show the bullet wound on her side.

"You did," she said softly.

"I don't remember doing that," he said, and it sounded truthful. "How could this be?" He looked at the floor.

"Well, Miss," said Officer Lawrence. "Seeing what he did, I think the best place for him will be back in the psychiatric ward."

"Is that where he was?" asked Amy.

"Yes. He was found in the bay near the Ford Assembly plant. We don't know how long he was in the water, and he was very confused. His leg was also badly injured."

She looked at Gustav's leg and noticed the splints on either side.

The policeman continued, "At first, he was at the hospital and then he was moved to the psych ward just this weekend."

"I have not seen him in a while," said Amy.

"We think maybe he jumped from the bridge or fell off a boat. He can't tell us because he doesn't remember," said the younger policeman.

"So, where were you when he shot you?" asked Officer Lawrence.

He was going to look for the records, thought Amy. "It is kind of a long story; can you come inside?" she asked. Gustav was already inside.

"This is Jeff Lindsey, my fiancé."

They all shook hands.

"Please sit down. Would you like some coffee or tea?" asked Amy, still formulating her story.

"No, thank you," said Officer Lawrence, cutting off the younger officer who was going to accept.

"All three of us lived in Durango," started Amy. "That is where he shot me, and it was an accident. He didn't mean to shoot me." She had changed the location to Durango. San Francisco was too close, so it would be easy to check records there and find nothing to validate her story.

"After that happened, he disappeared from Durango," said Amy. "We discovered he had come to the Bay Area, so I came to look for him. I knew he had not meant to hurt me, and I knew he was very confused. Jeff, who was a deputy in Durango, decided to accompany me." Saying he was sheriff would be too prominent, she had decided. If they checked,

170

they would find a sheriff 49 years ago with his name and then wonder why he looked so young.

Officer Lawrence nodded, as the younger officer was taking notes. They seemed to accept the story. "What are your plans now?'

"Well, Jeff and I took jobs at the Ford Assembly plant. We needed to make money while we looked for Gustav. Now, we will probably give our notice and return to Durango in the next week. We have to talk about it," said Amy, looking at Jeff.

"This man needs medical help," said Officer Lawrence. "He was talking about the future, drugs, cowboys and all sorts of strange things."

"I will talk to his doctor when we get to Durango," said Amy.

"He is in a good facility here," said Officer Lawrence. "He was scheduled for shock therapy, and that may set him right."

"Shock therapy?" repeated Amy, amazed they would use such archaic methods.

"Yes, I hear it is a new type of therapy."

"Please, Amy, don't let them do that," pleaded Gustav, looking scared. "I can't go back there."

"I have heard bad things about that therapy," said Amy, understanding Gustav's distress.

"What is the alternative? How are you going to keep him here?" asked Officer Lawrence. "Both of you work, and he could be a menace to others. He obviously is a menace to himself. They found a bullet in his broken leg."

"A bullet," said Amy.

"A bullet similar to the one you have on your side," said Officer Lawrence. "It does not mean it is the same, but it could be."

"He might have tried to shoot himself when he jumped off the bridge," offered the other policeman.

Amy nodded. "I will quit my job to look after him."

"No, Amy. I don't trust him alone with you," said Jeff.

It was looking like the only solution was to send him back to the facility, thought Amy.

"Please, I promise I will not cause any problems," said Gustav, obviously worried about that option.

"Crazy people tend to promise anything," said the younger policeman. "You can't believe them."

"Well, officers," said Jeff. "We will have to resolve this issue ourselves. We do not want to take any more of your time."

"You are right, Jeff. Thank you very much for finding him," said Amy as they stood up.

"I'll come by in a couple of days to see how you are doing," said Officer Lawrence.

"That would very considerate of you," said Amy as she led them to the door. As she closed the door, she heard the officers' comment on the 'wild west' and how people often shot themselves there. Then she heard someone calling them.

"Officers, officers."

It was Laura's voice. Amy kept the door ajar.

"Yes, Miss?" asked Officer Lawrence.

"What was happening there?"

"It is not your business," said Officer Lawrence.

"Have you noticed that the man that lives there is not in the military service?"

Amy couldn't believe Laura would stoop so low as to accuse Jeff of being a draft dodger.

"That is not our concern, and it should not be yours."

"How do you explain it?" asked Laura vehemently.

"He could be a Quaker or he could have flat feet. It is not my department, Miss. What did you say your name was?"

"Never mind that," said Laura, and Amy heard a door slam shut.

Amy also closed the door and looked at Jeff and Gustav seated at the kitchen table. What a mess, she thought. "Let's finish making dinner, Jeff. Are you hungry Gustav?"

"Very much so," said Gustav. "The facility had decent meals, but I was afraid of what they could be putting in the food."

"Wait a moment," said Jeff. "Before we do anything, I want to know what you are doing here, Gustav."

"You mean this time and place? I came with you."

"I know you did, but why? Why did you put yourself and us in danger by running through when we were transporting."

It was a good question, thought Amy.

"I don't know why. I just had to. I couldn't be left in 1895 forever." He looked at them with wide eyes. "You don't have to let me stay. I am injured and don't have money, but I'll manage somehow, out there."

He wasn't whining, but he sounded pitiful, and Amy knew it would be bad for him. He might even starve, and she couldn't do that to someone who had worked with her. He had shot her, but she was sure he hadn't meant to.

"You tried to kill me, and you shot Amy," said Jeff, reading her mind.

"I don't know." Gustav slapped his forehead with his hands. "I am trying to remember that, but I can't."

Jeff threw a glance at Amy. He wasn't buying Gustav's act, she could tell.

"Look, we are just about to have dinner. Why doesn't he stay for that, and we will make a decision later," said Amy.

Jeff nodded.

She turned on the oven and put the seasoned piece of beef in a pan, while Jeff finished washing and peeling the potatoes and carrots. He then grabbed a couple of beers from the refrigerator and gave Gustav one.

Gustav took a big swig and drained most of the beer. Suddenly, he took a deep breath and sat up straighter. "You two look very domestic." His voice sounded different.

Amy turned to look him.

"I had no choice," he sounded calm.

"No choice? About what?" asked Jeff.

"About catching the transport with you," he said.

"I knew you were lying about not remembering," said Jeff.

"The transport marker was going to be moved. Dr. Holbrook had reminded me of that rule many times. The marker is supposed to be moved after it is used a couple of times, and this marker had been used a lot," said Gustav.

"How could you be so ..." Amy looked for the correct adjective. "Stupid, selfish, greedy, inconsiderate," she stopped listing the possibilities.

"I told you at the cabin that I was underpaid and underappreciated," said Gustav. "I told you."

"You put everything at risk. They are talking about closing down the project," said Amy.

"Well, what do you care? You got what you wanted."

"What?" asked Amy.

"You got your flower, didn't you? And you got him," Gustav pointed to Jeff.

"Jeff's lifeline showed he could be a time traveler. And that flower may help people with depression and maybe even more," she said. "Anyway, don't you remember? You took the flower. What did you do with it? Did you sell it to the highest bidder?"

"No, I didn't sell it," he said forcefully. "I gave it to someone."

He didn't sound as sure about that, noticed Amy. Amazing, she thought, he had stolen the specimen, put his job on the line and was not receiving anything for it.

Gustav looked at the table. "I don't know what is happening to me. I really don't remember shooting either of you. I can't believe I would do that."

"Do you remember arriving in the bay?"

"No. I remember I was in the water and it was cold. I seemed to have lost pieces of memory." He looked away, and she almost felt sorry for him. "They were about to put me in shock therapy when I remembered your name. Thank God. I told the nurses, and they called the police. It took the police a couple of days to find you. I think it was through your work."

That would be the only way, thought Amy. No one else in 1944 knew them.

"I was fortunate the nurses were kind, and they cared for me. Who knows how much I would have lost in shock therapy."

"So shock therapy does not work?" asked Jeff.

"Not the kind they were using in this year and not for a long time afterwards," said Amy.

"I just want to go back to our time, Amy. I don't care if they will put me in jail. At least it will be a jail in 2066 and not a hospital here."

Soon after, Amy called Dr. Holbrook to tell him that Gustav had been found. "Actually, he found us," she said.

"How is he?"

174

"You can ask him yourself," she said. "He is right here with us."

"Gustav?"

"I have a broken leg, and they removed a bullet from the leg, but it could have been worse," said Gustav.

There was silence from the other side. "I guess we should be thankful they found you, and that you are all right," said Dr. Holbrook. "The only question is why, Gustav? Why did you do it?"

"It was an opportunity, and I was not planning to harm anyone. That guy, LaForce, was moving out of town soon, I checked his lifeline, and so stealing a bit of silver from him was not going to affect him. And who was going to know? Some mines have silver, and then they dry up."

"And what about shooting Amy?" asked Dr. Holbrook.

"Like I told these guys, I don't remember doing that. Are you sure it was me and not someone else?"

Amy was surprised at his suggestion. "We saw you Gustav. That is why Jeff shot your leg."

"So you were the one who shot me," Gustav turned to study at Jeff. "I guess I should be grateful you just got my leg and not something more vital."

"Gustav is not remembering things," explained Amy. "How much longer is the wait?" She didn't have to say what she was talking about, everyone knew.

"Five days, Amy, we can't go any faster," said Dr. Holbrook.

"What are we going to do with him?" she asked, looking at Gustav.

"Gustav," said Dr. Holbrook. "You need to stay with Amy and Jeff and wait for us. We'll bring you back and find out what is going on with you."

"Sure, Dr. Holbrook, whatever you say."

Amy knew Jeff would not be pleased, but what could they do? She looked at Gustav looking so pitiful, and then she saw a slight change come over him. He smiled, but the smile did not reach his eyes. He no longer looked confused. The way he looked right now reminded her of the unfeeling Gustav she had talked to in the cabin, before he abandoned them. She suddenly felt scared.

"We can use the handcuffs," said Jeff when they discussed what to do with him.

"You brought a pair with you?" asked Amy.

He nodded.

"I didn't take you for the kinky type, Jeff," said Gustav.

Jeff looked at him briefly and turned away.

After the call, Gustav had become more belligerent. "You should be glad we have handcuffs," said Amy, "Otherwise, we would have to tie you up and you couldn't move at all."

"As long as you did the tying, it would be all right," he winked.

"Don't worry, Amy, I will deal with him," said Jeff.

"You really don't have to do this, Jeff. Where will I go? I have no money, and I can barely walk," protested Gustav.

"I will cuff him to the bed rail; that should allow him to sleep," said Jeff, ignoring him.

Amy agreed.

Jeff helped Gustav onto the bed in the smaller bedroom and securely attached the handcuffs to the bed rail. Amy watched and once he was done, she went to prop the pillows around Gustav. She put an extra pillow under his leg. It looked swollen. "Does it hurt?"

"Not any more. You know what would make it feel better?"

She was afraid to ask.

"I think you should stay and help me. You could keep an eye and anything else you want on me."

That was it, thought Amy, stepping to the door. Something was very wrong with Gustav. "Good night, Gustav."

"You and Jeff better not keep me up with your wild..."

She closed the door, but had an idea of what word he had shouted.

"It is strange," she said to Jeff, who was in the living room. "Gustav can be so normal and then he becomes that," she pointed to the room.

"He is a dangerous man," said Jeff. "He will do anything to get his way, remember that."

"What shall we do tomorrow?"

"You will go to work, and I stay here."

"It is too bad I have to go to work at all."

"We still have to live here four days. What if the transport is delayed? It could be more days, and then we would be without money."

"You're right, Jeff." She realized she had been saying that a lot lately.

"Now come over and explain to me how I became your fiancé?"

"Fiancé?"

"You told Officer Lawrence I was your fiancé, but I think you forgot to tell me. Did I miss the proposal?"

Chapter 27
Hanging out with Gustav

In the morning, Jeff went to check on Gustav. He accompanied him to the bathroom and then both came to breakfast.

"It smells wonderful, Amy," said Gustav. "I am quite hungry."

"How did you sleep?" she asked.

"Not bad, even with that handcuff attached to my arm."

He was sounding normal again, thought Amy. Maybe a good night sleep was what he needed. She served Jeff a cup of coffee and asked Gustav if he wanted any.

"Yes, please, with a little cream and sugar."

They sat down to eat the scrambled eggs and muffins she had made.

"I have to get going," said Amy, "otherwise I'll miss the bus."

"Hey, I just wanted to thank both of you for helping me," said Gustav. "I just wanted to tell you I really appreciate it. I didn't want to go back to the loony bin."

Both Jeff and Amy looked at him.

"I'm just saying thank you," said Gustav.

It was nice, thought Amy, but was it too nice? Gustav in the future had been polite, but maybe not so appreciative. She kissed Jeff on the cheek as she left and warned him about Gustav.

"You know I am distrustful to start with," said Jeff. "I will keep an eye on him."

She hated leaving.

The hours at work passed interminably slow. Without Jeff there, the idea of lunch did not provide much of a break, and it just made her wonder how Jeff was doing. There was no way to communicate with him. They had allowed a dangerous person stay with them, and she hoped he was all right.

When she got home that evening, she found Jeff and Gustav playing chess on the kitchen table. Everything looked peaceful. Jeff had already made dinner and they ate soon after.

"I quit for you today," said Amy as she washed the dishes.

"I think that is the only choice we had," said Jeff, looking disappointed.

"Mrs. Felder was not pleased. I couldn't blame her, but it was going to happen soon anyway."

"That is true, we don't have many days left in this time."

"How did he do today?" she asked softly. Gustav was reading a newspaper in the living room.

"He was as you see him now, calm and friendly. We played chess multiple times, and I read the newspaper in its entirety. It was a very quiet day." He emphasized 'quiet' and she could feel his irritation.

"Why don't you go out to the store? We need milk for the morning and it will give you a chance to get out of the apartment."

Jeff glanced at Gustav. "When he is like this, I have no qualms leaving him with you, but just in case, keep the stun gun nearby."

"Okay, go then. Pick up something that will entertain you guys tomorrow. Maybe some books, a puzzle or even a radio. It's just three more days."

The following evening, they had just sat down for dinner when there was a knock on the door.

Amy went to answer the door. She opened it to find Officer Lawrence waiting.

"I told you I would check on you," he said, "and here I am."

"Yes. Thank you for that. Are you hungry? We were just about to eat," she asked.

He didn't reply right away, and she knew he was thinking about it.

"We made lasagna, and you know how easy that is to share. Come on," she urged.

"Maybe just a small piece," he said. He walked to the kitchen table and greeted everyone.

"You were the policeman who found me," said Gustav.

"Not exactly," said the officer, "but I was the one who brought you here."

"I do remember that."

"So did you quit your job?" Officer Lawrence asked Amy.

"No, I didn't, Jeff did. He feels he can manage Gustav better. I gave my notice though. We will be leaving early next week."

"You know, San Francisco has a facility that specializes in mental illness. It may be the best place for him," said Officer Lawrence.

"I have already made arrangements with his doctor in Durango. Of course, if we do not see an improvement in his condition, we could be back," said Amy.

Gustav did not say much during dinner, and as they finished their dinner, he went into the living room to work on a puzzle. Amy started washing the dishes while Jeff and Officer Lawrence followed her to the kitchen.

"Would you like a cup of coffee?" asked Jeff.

"I'll have a cup, if you are making it," said Officer Lawrence.

"You know, when he is like this, he is no problem whatsoever," said Jeff softly as they all turned to watch Gustav work on the puzzle. "I took him out to the park today, and he was very pleasant. He seemed very interested in everything."

"Maybe he was, but this is not the Gustav I knew. This guy is too passive; he is like a little boy."

"So, Gustav is normally more aggressive?" asked Officer Lawrence

"Not like last night, but more normal. He was a confident, self-assured man. A bit aggressive, but I guess you men are like that," she said.

"Some more than others," said Officer Lawrence, "and then there are women that are a bit aggressive. That reminds me, I wanted to warn you about your neighbor."

"Our neighbor?" asked Amy.

"The young lady down the hall."

"Laura," said Jeff.

"She wanted me to look into why you were not in the military service. I know it is not her business, but it did make me curious." He didn't add anything, but he wanted to know.

Amy had been worried that might come up after hearing Laura in the hallway, so she had done some research.

A 4-F was the classification given to people who were unfit for the military service due to mental or physical defect. Jeff had decided it would be a best option. He could hardly be a conscientious objector, based on religious reasons, since he had been a deputy before. He was also too old to be a student. It was funny, but as a worker in the "support of war production," he might have received an exemption, but that was now and would not explain why he had not been drafted before.

"I have a problem with my feet, so I got a 4-F," said Jeff. "It didn't bother me when I was deputy, since I mostly got around on horseback."

"You were a deputy in Durango, right?"

"Yes."

"Do you miss it?"

Jeff smiled and started to describe his duties as deputy. As they drank their coffee, both men described their jobs and compared one with another. Soon they were telling stories, and Amy was glad that Jeff was having some distraction after watching Gustav all day.

She looked at the living room just in time to see Gustav going to the bathroom. She was going to interrupt Jeff's conversation to ask him to go check on him, but it seemed overly cautious. Gustav was accepting his situation and like he had said himself, he did not have options in the outside world. She finished the dishes and thought she would check on him. It had not been long.

She knocked on the door softly, "Gustav, are you all right?"

There was no response.

Jeff immediately was next to her. "He went to the bathroom?"

"Yes, but just minutes ago."

"Open the door, Gustav," said Jeff sternly.

There still no sound and now Officer Lawrence joined them at the door. "Is there another way out of there?"

"A window," said Jeff, "but we are on the second floor."

'You don't have a key to this door?"

181

"No," said Amy.

"Okay, step back," said Officer Lawrence. "I'll break it open."

"Wait, Larry, I can do this," said Jeff.

Larry Lawrence, thought Amy a bit amused before the door splintered. There was nothing amusing about what they found.

There was no one inside, and the window was wide open.

"Damn," said Jeff. He looked out the window briefly, turned around and ran out the front door. Larry followed him.

Amy peered out of the window. There was a wide ledge that circled the building, but no one was on it as far as she could see. She climbed out the window and stepped onto the ledge.

If he were in a hurry, which way would he go, she wondered? Directly below was the alley, and to the left was the back of the building with the parking lot and small garden. To the right was the street, and that is where she would go. She edged her way along the outside of the building. When she reached the corner, she saw a fire escape. It had been lowered already, and she quickly went down to the ground. That is when she saw the taxi pull away, and in the back seat she could see the profile of a man who looked a lot like Gustav.

Jeff and Larry joined her then.

"There is no one out in back, or in the alley," said Jeff. "Did you see anything?"

"No, I followed the ledge and came down the fire escape. I think he was in that taxi," said Amy, pointing at the car that was now down the street.

"Did he have any money with him?" asked Larry.

"He must have taken some from us," said Amy.

"That is a city taxi," said Larry. "They keep track of where they take their customers. Let's go to the patrol car, I have a two-way radio there."

Amy nodded, while Jeff looked a bit baffled.

Larry noticed. "You probably have not seen two-way radios; they are quite new to our department," he said as he hurried to the police car. "We had one-way radios for several years. That was how headquarters could inform us quickly about stolen vehicles, missing children and such." They reached the car and he unlocked it. "They had to play music in between announcements to be licensed as a radio station and that was not bad either."

He sat down in the front passenger seat and took a large microphone-looking thing. He pressed a button on the side and talked. "Charlie 101 to dispatch," he waited.

"It is like a movable telephone," whispered Jeff to Amy.

"Yeah, except only one person can speak at a time. You have to press the button on the side to transmit," she said.

They heard crackling, and then a voice came through, "Go ahead, Charlie 101."

Larry asked for assistance in locating a taxi's destination. He gave the street address where the taxi had picked up a passenger.

"I don't know if the taxi has a radio," said the voice.

Before Larry could respond, the voice said, "I'll check and get back to you."

Larry put the microphone away and looked up at them. "It may take a while."

There was nothing else to do.

"You went on the ledge and came down the fire escape?" asked Larry. He seemed amused she had opted for that path.

"I just followed the way he took. I thought I might catch up to him."

"Well, you better go up and lock the apartment before someone robs you," said Larry.

She didn't want to leave. What if they got the call and left? "There's not that much to rob."

"I think she wants to come with us," said Jeff.

So now it is 'us', she thought. "I do want to go with you."

Larry shook his head. "No."

"He is my brother. I may be able to reason with him."

"Talking does not seem work. I know you two have been making an effort to keep him with you, but you can't control him twenty-four hours a day. It is too much to ask from ordinary people. When we find him, I will take him to the psychiatric hospital in San Francisco. It's the best hospital around."

Amy bit her lip. Larry was being very nice, but she couldn't let him take Gustav. Once again, Gustav was creating problems.

"Why don't you go upstairs," suggested Jeff. "I will accompany Officer Lawrence if he likes."

"Officer Lawrence?" asked Amy, wondering why he had become formal with him.

"This is work," explained Jeff. "I believe it is better to be formal in work situations."

"That is exactly the way I feel," Larry nodded. "If you stay in the area, Jeff, you might think about applying for a job as a policeman."

This was sounding like a mutual admiration society, thought Amy.

"Have you ever driven one of these patrol cars?" asked Larry.

"No, but it looks like it would be a good ride," said Jeff.

"Come over and sit in the front seat," offered Larry.

"I learned to drive on a Jeep," said Jeff.

He learned about a week ago, thought Amy, looking at him incredulous. Jeff disregarded her look and went around to sit in the car behind the steering wheel.

"It figures you would learn in a Jeep, living in Durango," said Larry. "Do they have many Jeeps on the Durango force?"

"A few, we still use horses quite a bit."

"The stick in the middle looks different," said Amy, looking from outside.

"A stick," Larry smiled at her condescendingly. "That is the gear shift."

"You better go and make sure the door is closed," said Jeff to her.

She had to, with Laura or anyone else lurking around, she just had to. She turned and ran into the building. She got to the apartment to find the door wide open. Jeff had been right to send her. She ran into the bedroom and checked the most valuable thing they had, the ComLink, and found it was still there. She ran out again, grabbing the keys on the way. She locked the door and ran downstairs.

Larry's car was still parked. As she walked over, she heard them talking about cars.

"You are back?" said Larry. "I thought you were going to…"

Suddenly, the radio interrupted him. "Dispatch to Charlie 101."

Larry quickly answered, "Go ahead, dispatch.'

"You are in luck. The taxi did have a radio, and he just dropped off his passenger at the ferry station."

"Ferry station, copy that. No assistance is required."

He hung up the microphone and turned to Jeff, "Let's go. Start her up, Deputy Lindsey."

Jeff had been studying the controls, and he turned the engine on.

Amy opened the back door and jumped in.

"What are you doing?" shouted Larry.

"Please, let me come. You won't even know I am here."

Jeff looked at Larry. "It will take longer to get her out."

"All right," sighed Larry. "Just stay back there and not a peep."

Jeff pressed the accelerator and the car picked up speed quickly. The ride was much smoother than the Jeep had been. She was pushed back into leather seat. The seat had a lot more spring than the Jeep's seat had, and she bounced along.

"Turn left at the next corner," said Larry as he started the siren. "Just slow down a bit if you see traffic, but everyone should pull out of the way."

Jeff down shifted, braked slightly and made the corner nicely.

"Don't go too fast," said Amy, worried about his driving skills.

"You're doing fine," said Larry, and he turned to glare at her. "You just have to hang on. Remember, you were the one who wanted to come along."

There was not much to hang onto, thought Amy as she slid across the back seat. She grabbed the seat in front as Jeff turned another corner. She could see the ferry building up ahead. If Gustav got on a ferry, it would be hard to find him. "A ferry is already there," she said as she saw one near the dock.

"It's the one to San Francisco," said Larry.

They pulled up to the curb, and Larry and Jeff jumped out. "You stay in the car, Miss," commanded Larry as Amy opened her door. "No arguments."

"Okay," she said meekly. She could tell he was not changing his mind on this, and someone should stay with the car anyway, she thought.

Jeff and Larry ran into the building. Shortly afterwards, she heard the ferry toot its horn, and it started pulling away from the dock. It was too soon, and she didn't think neither Jeff nor Larry had reached it in time. San Francisco, with a population of 300,000 in 1895, would have even more now. Finding Gustav would be impossible.

The ride back to the apartment was very quiet. Larry drove. He parked near their apartment.

"I am going to go back to the station, and we will put out an alert," said Larry.

"What do you think the chances are of finding him?" asked Jeff.

"San Francisco has over 600,000 people. You do the math."

Amy leaned back into the seat and sighed.

"If he behaves, we will probably not find him," said Larry, looking at her in the rear mirror. "But that is a good thing, isn't it? He was living on his own before and maybe he is well enough to do so now."

Amy looked back at him and shook her head.

Jeff opened his door and stepped out. "Thank you for your help, Officer Lawrence."

"I'm sorry we didn't catch him," said Larry to Amy.

"Losing him was my fault," said Amy, "not yours. You have helped us beyond anything I could have imagined. Thank you, Larry."

"Come on, Amy," said Jeff as he opened her door.

She slid out, and they both watched Larry drive away.

"How does this affect us?" asked Jeff.

She studied him. Jeff fit so well in this era, he even had multiple job offers. Maybe they should stay in this time? Maybe she could adapt to this time? Was it even an option? "Let's call Dr. Holbrook and see if he has any ideas."

They went back to their apartment and placed the call. There was no response from the other side.

"He wasn't expecting a call tonight," she said. "He will see that we tried and will call back soon."

"Maybe I should go to the city to look for Gustav tomorrow," said Jeff.

"That's really a long shot."

"At least it will be a useful way to pass the time," said Jeff.

"It was just a few more days, and we would have returned." She was sure they had lost him.

"It wasn't our fault; he is a grown man, Amy."

"A grown man, but I worry he is not capable of making good decisions. In the state his mind is in, who knows what he will do or what he will say. I want Dr. Holbrook to run his lifeline. He might as well run mine as well."

"Gustav knows where we live and when we are leaving. If he wants to go back home, he will be here Sunday."

"I guess you are right."

"Your lab didn't run your lifeline before you traveled?"

"I had to travel so suddenly I don't think they had a chance."

"Hello, hello, Amy," said a voice from the bedroom. Dr. Holbrook was on the ComLink.

She ran into the bedroom. "Hello, Dr. Holbrook, thanks for calling back so quickly I have some bad news." She told him about Gustav. Dr. Holbrook didn't say anything.

"Have you run his lifeline?" she asked.

"We can only run your lifelines to this moment. We cannot tell what happens in the future," he said.

"Of course, I forgot," she said.

"In this case, it is even more complicated since your lifeline is spread through several periods in time."

"So, you can't tell anything about him?"

"He is not going to die in 1944. That is about all we know right now," Dr. Holbrook paused. "Amy, there is another problem."

Amy sat on the bed wondering what more could go wrong.

"Anthony is displaying psychological problems. He had to take time off for severe depression, and he is under medical supervision. Last time we talked, you mentioned Gustav was also having some mental issues. Having two of our top time travelers suffering from similar symptoms has made us consider that maybe the Temporal Transporter is responsible for the those issues," said Dr. Holbrook.

"What about Ryan Campbell and the others?" All of them had made multiple trips to set the transport markers.

"No one has transported as much as Gustav and Anthony. Gustav had logged eighteen trips and Anthony fifteen."

"Dr. Holbrook, for Gustav, it is more than depression. He is displaying multiple personalities."

"You mean like bipolar disorder?"

"No, I think like several distinct persons."

"So, you think he has DID, or dissociative identity disorder?" asked Dr. Holbrook.

"I'm not a hundred percent sure, but one moment he was very aggressive and then a couple of hours later he was very submissive. I don't remember Gustav displaying either of those traits so distinctly."

"Only one to three percent of the population has DID, and in some people it may never really manifests itself. If it is DID, Gustav probably had this condition before, and it has nothing to do with time travel."

"I don't know much about this disease. What is the cure, and what can I do here?"

"Once it manifests itself, it is rare that a person can totally integrated in one identity. Even in 2066."

"So, even if I brought him back there is no cure?"

"There are things we can try," said Dr. Holbrook. "I will check on it, but this is all for nothing, isn't it? Gustav is gone."

"And it is going to be nearly impossible to find him. Jeff and I are going to San Francisco to see if we run into him by chance. In any case, Gustav knows we plan to leave on Sunday, and hopefully he will decide to join us."

"He only has two more days to change his mind."

"By the way, who is coming with the marker?" she asked.

"Don't worry I'll let you know tomorrow."

She could imagine no one wanting to come now that there were health risks associated with the transport. She wondered if she too had been affected somehow. Would she be able to tell? Was she feeling depressed or different?

Jeff was looking at her from the doorway. "Amy?"

"Did you hear?"

"Most of it. It sounds like the travel machine is making people sick."

"Well, the people that have traveled many times are displaying some issues. You have only traveled once and I have traveled twice. We should be fine," she said with more confidence than she felt.

Chapter 28
Final details

Just a couple of days more, thought Amy, arriving at work. She had not wanted to come, but Jeff was insistent. Maybe he didn't think that they would transport in three days. She was certain that they would and that Dr. Holbrook would not fail them.

She watched as Mrs. Felder came towards her. Dr. Holbrook was so different from Mrs. Felder, but she could trust both to do the right thing.

"Amy, I have found a young lady who will take your job," said Mrs. Felder. "I was hoping you could show her what you do?"

"Sure, I would love to."

"Good, you can leave afterwards."

Amy nodded; it would her get home sooner.

She spent the next hours working with her replacement. At the end, she wrote out the instructions. It was not difficult work, but you just had to do things in sequence and this girl was finding it hard.

"If you make a mistake, it is fixable. Don't worry," Amy told her.

Mrs. Felder came by several times to see the progress.

When the lunchtime bell sounded, Mrs. Felder came over to them. She then told the girl to get her lunch and that Amy could leave.

"Thank you for helping her get started," said Mrs. Felder as they watched her go. "I was thinking about what you said about your brother, and I think he might have multiple personality disorder."

That was the old name for DID. "I think you are right, Mrs. Felder, and I have talked to his doctor about it already."

"You should go and take care of your brother. Give my best wishes to your cousin, Jeff. I have included his pay for the days he worked."

"Thank you, Mrs. Felder. I appreciate your help."

"Amy, someone once helped my father in Florida and that also helped me. I have always been fortunate, so I try to help others. Good luck wherever you go."

It was good that both had gotten paid because when she arrived home, Jeff informed her that Gustav had taken most of their money. They had kept most of it in a drawer by the bed, and when Jeff went to retrieve it, it was gone.

As they took the ferry into the city that afternoon, Jeff was still thinking about it. "Talk about biting the hand that feeds you. How much were we paid?"

"Mrs. Felder gave me my pay and yours for the two days you worked."

"So, $35 all together?"

"I think she made a mistake; she put $40 in the envelope."

They looked at each other and realized the explanation. "She is a very sweet lady. It was fortunate we fell into that job," said Jeff.

They watched as the city of San Francisco grew in front of them. "Where do you want to start looking?" she asked.

"The docks. I always find people when I look on the docks."

"Isn't that because you're always looking for criminal types?"

"Maybe."

"Doesn't that make a it a bit dangerous?"

Jeff looked at her. "Yes, especially for you. A pretty woman comes to the docks, I may spend most of my time fighting the men off."

She smiled envisioning that picture. "You know, I can take care of myself. I have taken self defense courses."

"Self defense?"

"They are techniques that can help me defend myself from an attack. They work for women and for men. Maybe I'll show you next time we are in the bedroom."

"Yeah," Jeff smiled, "that sounds interesting."

"I have a picture of Gustav," she said opening her purse. "We can show it around and see if anyone recognizes him." She gave Jeff the picture.

"You carry a picture of Gustav with you?" He sounded disappointed.

"It was given to me in case I needed to find him in 1895. It was taken at work in 2066 and then aged to look old. I would love to have a picture of you. Maybe we will see a photo studio in our search for Gustav."

The photo studio was much easier to find than any sign of Gustav. They talked to many at the docks, but no one had seen anything. She suspected that even if they had seen him, they were not talking. The people there seemed very suspicious of anyone asking questions.

"Maybe if we had brought Larry with us, they would cooperate more," commented Jeff afterwards.

"I don't know if it would make a difference to those type of people," said Amy as she read the sign outside the photo studio. "Oh, too bad. I don't think we can have our picture taken. We would have to come back in five days to pick up the developed picture."

"Ah yes, I forgot about the time it takes to develop the photograph," said Jeff. "I have only had my picture taken a few times."

"I also forgot about the development time," said Amy. She was used to taking a picture and seeing it instantly. If you wanted a professional printed copy, it may take a day, but most people printed their own pictures. "I guess we will have to wait until we get to 2066."

They wandered a bit more through the city and caught the evening ferry back to Richmond.

"I will be seeing you in two days," said Dr. Holbrook when he called that evening.

Of course he would, thought Amy. They would see him in the lab when they got back. "Okay, Dr. Holbrook," she said. "I was just wondering who is coming with the transport marker?"

"Me. I am going to be the traveler."

Amy didn't know what to say. Dr. Holbrook had no previous experience, and she was not sure how well he would adapt if things went wrong. Was it a wise thing to do?

"I can't ask my team to do anything that I would not do myself," he said.

"I see," said Amy. It probably meant no one else wanted to make the trip.

"I think it is a great opportunity for me to experience how the transport works. The best part is that I will be gone for very little time, since I will just be picking you up."

She could not argue with her boss. She knew that once he was set on an idea it was hard to change his mind.

"Okay," he said. "The plan is for me to arrive in the morning. Hopefully, it will not take too long to get to you. I will take a taxi to your place." He read the address out to her and she confirmed it was correct.

"Take the stairs up, and we are the second apartment on the right," she told him.

"Good," he said. "How much do you think the taxi will cost?"

"Well, it depends where the marker is," she said. "Are you bringing enough money?"

"About $100 dollars and change."

"That is more than sufficient. To give you an idea, I worked a week and got paid $24."

Dr. Holbrook laughed. "Unbelievable for a biochemist with a doctor's degree."

Jeff, who was listening from the doorway, looked surprised.

"Where was the marker in the year 2000?" asked Amy.

"It was at the university. Every time we have gone back from then, we kept it close to the university, so that is where I should arrive."

"There is no one accompanying you?"

"There is no need."

Something was going on, she thought. She had kind of bought into the idea of him coming, but to come alone was unusual for him. He was the type that preferred an entourage.

"Even though the transport can handle three people, it is best to go two at a time. You and I will transport, and Jeff will follow."

"Wait a moment. Jeff should come with me," said Amy. "If something goes wrong, he would not know how to proceed. You can go first, Dr. Holbrook, and Jeff and I can follow."

"Details, details. We will figure it out once I get there. Don't worry, this part is easy."

Yeah, thought Amy. Her first trip was supposed to be easy as well. She disconnected the ComLink.

"When were you going to tell me you are a doctor?" asked Jeff.

"Oh, it's not a real doctor, it is just the degree after a master's."

"I know that," he said slowly. "Maybe you assume I know too little. I know you are not a medical doctor, I was just surprised you had studied beyond a master's degree."

Amy knew he was right. She kept thinking he was from 1895 and that he would not understand things. "I am sorry, Jeff."

"And why were you pushing for us to transport together? Wouldn't I just follow where you went?"

"The transport has to be set for each trip. I am not as confident as Dr. Holbrook about it. If you are sent somewhere else, then you would be alone in a time you know nothing about. Even if you don't need me, like you don't need me in 1944, I would like to be there with you."

"You don't think I need you here?"

"You are so much better adapted to this time than I am."

"I have adapted well because you are here with me."

Amy smiled. He said such nice things. "Thank you, Jeff; those ladies at the factory were right. You are a sweetie."

"I know," he said seriously, and then he smiled.

"Actually, there shouldn't be any problem getting to the lab," said Amy. "There haven't been problems going in that direction, but there is something he said that bothered me." She explained about Dr. Holbrook's personality and how unusual it was he was traveling and even more unusual that he was coming alone.

"Maybe there really is no one else who will do it," suggested Jeff.

"Maybe, but then he wanted to transport with me and leave you to follow. I find that very odd."

"Maybe they don't want me to go with you," said Jeff.

"Why would you think that?" asked Amy.

"Well, it makes sense to me. Your boss is coming, and you can't argue with his decision when they send me somewhere else."

"But they agreed I could bring you back to 2066. Your lifeline showed you to be a time traveler."

"Maybe a time traveler, but not in your time."

"I will not let that happen. I am going with you. I love you, Jeff. It has been over forty years since I said it, but my feelings have not changed."

"Forty-nine years since we said it," he grinned, "and I agree, my feelings have not changed either. I love you as much as I did back then." He came over and kissed her.

Chapter 29
Worries about the future

She could see Mrs. Felder was sitting in the living room. Amy heard her talking to someone and when she walked into the room, she saw it was Officer Lawrence. How strange, she thought; she didn't know they knew each other.

"Hello, Amy," said Mrs. Felder. "I'm happy you are finally here."

"Hello, Mrs. Felder, Officer Lawrence," she said.

"We are glad you are staying here with us."

She was surprised at this statement. "Really, I am staying with you?"

"Of course. Dr. Holbrook has decided you will be living with Mrs. Felder and me," said Officer Lawrence.

"I didn't know you lived together."

"We have been together for a long time," they both smiled. "Forty-nine years."

"Oh," said Amy. "Where is Jeff?"

Mrs. Felder and Officer Lawrence exchanged worried glances.

"Where is Jeff?" asked Amy more loudly.

"Jeff has left," said Mrs. Felder. "He is gone."

Amy felt despair. "Where is he?"

"He was transported to the future. They decided they wanted him, and they couldn't take both of you."

"No," she shouted. "We should be together."

Officer Lawrence moved towards her. He had handcuffs in his hand.

She woke up in a sweat and turned to look at Jeff. He was sleeping peacefully next to her. She touched his arm to ensure he was real. He was, and he moved closer to her.

She didn't think it could have happened, but he had become a part of her life. She wasn't sure how she would survive without him.

That morning during breakfast, they made plans for their final day in 1944.

"We could go back to the city today and look for Gustav in another district," suggested Amy.

"We could, but I think it would be a waste of time," said Jeff. "Is there anything else we need to do to get ready?"

She was feeling a bit anxious about Dr. Holbrook's arrival. Maybe Jeff was correct, and they didn't want him to go to the future. One thing was certain; they could not sit in the apartment and wait the entire day.

"There is nothing to prepare. Let's go to Berkley. I want you to see the university."

"A visit to your alma mater. I would like that."

They splurged on a taxi and were dropped off just in front of the Doe Library.

"I love this place," said Amy as they walked through the campus. Some of the buildings were still there in the future and some were not there yet, but the feeling of the university was the same.

"There is the Lawrence Berkeley Lab. I bet Dr. Lawrence is working inside," she said wistfully, "But of course, I can't meet him. It still is best we don't interact too much with the locals."

They found a spot with a pretty view of the Campanile and the bay, and Amy commented how beautiful it looked.

"Almost as nice as the flatirons in Boulder," said Jeff.

"Oh, that is right," smiled Amy. "You went to University of Colorado in Boulder, didn't you?"

"Yep."

"Okay, I agree that campus is nice as well."

"It is. Have you been there?"

"Yes, there was a conference I attended there about a year ago, I mean in 2065."

"I wonder if the campus you saw was similar to the one when I went."

"Well, I can tell you this campus is different in 2066. There are more buildings and newer buildings replaced some of these. The Memorial Stadium is now quite different," she pointed at it. "I think they've rebuilt it several times since 1944." They continued to walk and came upon a building that she knew was not there in 2066. The sign outside indicted that it was Bacon Hall, and it housed the Geology Department.

"Do you want to go inside?" asked Amy. "There may be things you didn't have at your university."

"Excuse me, but Colorado had a very good geology department."

"I see. I didn't mean to stir up your inter-school rivalry. I meant they might have things in 1944 that they didn't in 1895."

"Geology is the study of earth and in forty-nine years, I doubt anything has changed. Rocks are rocks."

"Was that the cheer of the geology department?" teased Amy.

He laughed, but then he agreed to go inside. Once inside, Amy was amazed to see the number of books and the easy access to them.

"Are there no books in the future?" asked Jeff as she marveled about that fact.

"You can go to libraries, but you can't touch most books. You can read them on a screen, and they are protected from the environment."

"A screen?"

"Like the one we saw in the movies, but much smaller."

"What about your biology building?" asked Jeff.

"That's off on the northwest corner of campus, and I don't think there is anything there in 1944."

Later as they left the building, she saw a tree and realized it was still there in 2066. "This tree is still here in the future. Isn't it funny how it works? All these building are different and the tree is the same."

Jeff didn't say anything.

"The campus is too big," she said with disappointment. "I was hoping to get an idea of where Dr. Holbrook would be arriving tomorrow, but I don't have any idea."

"So, this wasn't just a nostalgia outing?"

"No."

"What were you going to do?"

"I just wanted to know where the transport marker is. Just in case Dr. Holbrook..." She couldn't finish her sentence. The dream had made her think of the worst scenario.

Chapter 30
Dr. Holbrook

The following morning, Amy made pancakes. She wanted to use up some of the remaining ingredients, but more importantly, she wanted to pass the time and she had found cooking to be soothing. Dr. Holbrook would be arriving soon, and later today, she would be in her apartment in the year 2066, with Jeff. How many days had she been gone? She had left on a Saturday and had been gone twenty-seven days. In any case, she would have to get groceries right away, she thought.

She was feeling nervous, and it looked as though Jeff was feeling some apprehension as well.

Dr. Holbrook arrived a bit past ten in the morning. He shook her hand heartily and remarked how well she looked. It was nice and she let him in, thinking how it was strange seeing him in her apartment. She introduced him to Jeff.

"So, you are the man who has stolen Amy's heart."

"I don't think I had to steal it," said Jeff.

"Well, it was bound to happen sometime," said Dr. Holbrook as he started to look around the apartment. "So, this has been your home."

"Yes," said Amy, "but we are ready to go."

"Do I smell pancakes?"

She nodded.

He walked into the kitchen and she followed.

"Look at his stovetop. Remarkable. And the refrigerator, what a collector's item."

He did not seem to be in a hurry. "Would you like some pancakes?" she asked.

"I would love some if it is not a bother. I can't remember the last time I ate some freshly made pancakes."

"Sure, I still have some batter." She poured some batter on the pan that was still warm and waited as the pancakes formed.

He opened the fridge and looked inside.

"Are you leaving a transport marker here?" she asked.

"We might." He walked over to look out the window.

"Don't you have to? I mean to return to find Gustav."

"Hmm," he said.

"Are you thinking of leaving Gustav in 1944?" wondered Amy.

"Yes, for now we are."

It seemed kind of ruthless. What about not leaving anyone from the future behind? What about his influence on history? She stared at him, shocked.

"We are not going to abandon him, Amy. Time travelers have a chip implanted in them, and we can find him anytime we want," he said.

"A chip?" She didn't have one.

"Yes, that way we can track anyone who gets lost, injured or dead. You left before we had a chance to put the device in you, but everyone else has one."

"But, why didn't you know Gustav was here in 1944 right away?"

"The chip was damaged. Maybe Jeff's bullet had something to do with it."

"But now you know where Gustav is?"

"Soon. We will be able to tell very soon. We are reprogramming the damaged circuits."

"Okay, that's good," said Amy, still digesting the news about implanted chips.

"Amy, there have been many things that have happened in the last month. Things that you don't know about," said Dr. Holbrook. "I have been under a lot of pressure."

"What happened?" asked Amy.

"Some of our partners have been less than thrilled about our progress."

"You mean GovTime? Aren't they one of our major partners?"

"They are partners, but it's not only them. Susan's escapade didn't help at all, but they are more concerned about Gustav and you."

"I can understand Gustav's personality disorder is concerning, but me?"

"Yes. You fell in love with that guy," he pointed to the other room where Jeff was, "and you are bringing him back."

"But Dr. Holbrook, you agreed that he is a time traveler and he could come back."

"I did not agree one hundred percent. You were injured at the time and maybe I let you convince me."

"So now you don't want Jeff in 2066?"

"It's not only me," he lifted his shoulders. "Some decisions are not mine to make."

She was not buying the act. "Jeff is supposed to be a time traveler; you saw his lifeline."

"We are still reviewing his lifeline."

"You are never going to accept it, are you? He suspected you had changed your mind."

"Please, Amy, don't make a big deal out of this. I know you and Jeff are in love and that is a wonderful thing most of the time, but in this case, it is not going to work. Everyone has had to make some sacrifices."

She looked at him, wondering what sacrifices he had made.

"Some of our colleagues had to leave BioTime. Francine is no longer there."

"I'm sorry," she said.

He looked at her. "It was for the best. I had gotten too close to her, and we can't have such relationships at work."

Wow, thought Amy, and he was saying that after his second work related affair. Worse, how could he compare his casual fling with her relationship; it was not the same.

"I have had to take on more responsibility for all the projects," said Dr. Holbrook. "That is one of the reasons I took this trip. I need to see what exactly are the problems one encounters. I have not seen any problems yet."

"You have been fortunate," she said, thinking he should have been responsible for all projects from the beginning. "I guess you didn't travel with anyone or else you would run into the problem of arriving in different locations."

"That problem has been fixed. It was due to currents and waves that occur in time. I don't fully understand it, but now we can use them to guide us correctly. GovTime fixed this problem in their machine just recently, and they helped us fix ours."

"They just ran into this problem? I thought they have been running their machine for some time?"

"Yes, but mostly transporting one person at a time. They do not have many transport markers, so they have not set them in all the places we have. They have been using some of our transport markers. It saves them time."

"You let them use our transport markers?"

"Of course. They helped us with our problem, and we can help them. It is a good thing to collaborate."

"Yes, but what exactly are they using their Temporal Transporter for?"

He looked at her briefly and then away, "I don't know."

He knew, but he didn't want to tell her. "Do you want some maple syrup?" she asked.

"Please. I wanted to sit here with you and explain things. I know you are a logical person and I can appeal to you."

"What's going to happen with Jeff?"

"We'll send him back to San Francisco 1895."

"With his current knowledge?"

"No." He shook his head. "Think about it, Amy. If we allowed him to keep all this knowledge and it slips out, what a mess it would make for the timeline. In addition, they may think he is crazy and put him in an insane asylum. It is better he forgets."

"So you are going to erase his memory. How far back will you go? Will he remember me?"

"I don't know."

"Are you going to erase my memories as well?"

"No, Amy. We wouldn't do that."

"I don't believe you, Dr. Holbrook."

"I give you my promise. There is no other option, Amy. We are not taking both of you to the future."

It was just like her dream. "Well then, I am not going."

"You would stay here?" he asked, amazed. "This era is filled with diseases and crime. The life expectancy is 66 for women. You really want that? You would probably die twenty years earlier than in 2066."

"Hum," Jeff cleared his throat. He was standing in kitchen doorway. "Excuse me. Can I talk with you, Amy?"

"Jeff, did you hear what we were talking about?" asked Dr. Holbrook.

Jeff nodded. "Some of it."

"Well if you heard the last part, please try to make her see the reason. You know I am right. She should come back to 2066, and you should return to your time."

She shook her head in disagreement.

"Go ahead, discuss it. I have time while I enjoy these pancakes," said Dr. Holbrook.

She followed Jeff to the bedroom and closed the door.

"You should go," said Jeff. "Your work and your home are in the future. I will go back to mine. I think you were expecting this."

"No. It is unacceptable. He comes and changes things that have been promised. You are better than any of these other time travelers."

"But he is your boss, and you have to go along with what he says."

"No. I know you may think a boss is infallible in 1944, but in the future, we don't always agree with the boss."

Jeff thought about it. "That must cause a lot of chaos."

"Sometimes there is, but better decisions are made when you ask questions and stand your ground for what you believe in."

"Okay then, what should we do?"

"Well, I am glad you are thinking of we again, instead of just me."

Jeff smiled and looked towards the door. "We can't stay in here forever."

"We will go to Berkeley, and I will pretend to go along with Dr. Holbrook, then..."

"You want me to come running when the transport starts, like Gustav?" interrupted Jeff.

"No. No, that is too dangerous. Right before the transport starts, I will step away from it."

"Why even go with him to Berkley?"

"We need to know where the transport marker is."

They joined Dr. Holbrook back in the kitchen. He was reading the newspaper and looked up at them waiting for a response.

"It seems Jeff agrees with you, Dr. Holbrook."

"Of course he should. Now, was he able to convince you?"

"Yes, he did," said Amy sadly.

"It is the for the best."

"It doesn't seem you are anxious to get back, Dr. Holbrook. Did you want to visit anything special in this era? Go anywhere before we go back?" asked Amy.

"I don't get out of the lab too much," he smiled. "I may ask to take the long way back to the university. I love seeing the cars. I saw several beauties on the way here. They are so solid and classic looking."

"Jeff learned to drive stick shift," said Amy, still trying to sell him on Jeff's skills.

"Was it hard?" asked Dr. Holbrook. "I would like to learn some day. Oh, by the way, I forgot to mention I have a colleague with me. He is waiting just downstairs."

Amy didn't like that Dr. Holbrook was just mentioning him now. It was going to be harder to implement her plan. "I thought you said you were coming alone?"

"You must have misunderstood me."

"Who is it?"

"You don't know him," said Dr. Holbrook. "Suffice it to say, he was sent to ensure you did the right thing, Amy, and I am glad you came to that decision yourself."

"You were going to force me to go with you?"

"Well, let's not talk about maybes. I don't know if it would have come to that."

She threw him a dirty look.

"Please, Amy, you don't know how things have changed."

"You allowed this to happen," said Amy.

"Amy," Jeff interrupted, "Since you will be leaving soon, I was wondering if you could give me something to remember you by?"

"Yes, I'll see what I can find," she said bravely and headed to the bedroom. He followed.

"There isn't a back door out of the bedroom, is there?" winked Dr. Holbrook.

"No, Dr. Holbrook," said Amy.

"I'm not worried about you escaping, just keep that door open. You mind if I make some coffee?" asked Dr. Holbrook. "I want to try my hand at this old fashioned gadget."

"Go ahead," said Amy.

"Plans have changed," whispered Jeff once they were in the bedroom. "I think your boss has a different agenda. We know that ledge goes around the building."

"Yeah, we could make a run for it," said Amy.

"Oops, maybe not," said Jeff, looking out the bedroom window. "See that guy over there? By the way he is looking at the building, I'll bet he is Dr. Holbrook's companion."

"I am going to give you my stun gun," she took it out of her purse. "And here is all the money we have. If I am forced to go, I want you to run."

"But, won't it be better I go back to 1895?"

"They plan to wipe your memory, and I am afraid of the harmful effects you could have from that. They have never erased so much of a person's memory."

"They would erase you from me."

"Yeah, and you would be left in San Francisco, not knowing how you got there."

"That wouldn't matter as much as losing you."

"Oh Jeff," she wrapped her arms around him.

"I wondered if that was what was going on," said Dr. Holbrook watching from the doorway. "Well go ahead, don't mind me."

Amy turned to Jeff and kissed him passionately. She heard Dr. Holbrook walk away. "Maybe we should stun him and make a run for it out the front door?" she whispered.

"I like it. The direct route."

"We will be fugitives, just like Gustav."

He nodded.

Dr. Holbrook was just pouring his coffee when she stunned him. Jeff helped him down to the floor quietly. Then Amy pricked him with the needle. He would obviously know what had happened to him, but she wanted him to suffer the outrage of minutes of lost memory. For a man like Dr. Holbrook, it was a big thing.

They then disguised themselves as much as they could. Jeff would go first, hail a taxi and then she would follow. Dr.

Holbrook's companion was outside in the back of the apartment complex, but they didn't want to take any chances.

Amy watched from the building lobby as Jeff walked out. That is when she saw the other man. How many had come with Dr. Holbrook? It was no wonder he was not worried they would try to escape.

The man studied Jeff and moved a bit closer, probably wondering if he was the right person. No one in the future, except Suzanna, knew how Jeff looked.

Then Amy heard someone coming down the stairs and stepped away, wondering whom it could be. It was too soon for it to be Dr. Holbrook and the steps sounded lighter. As the person rounded the corner she saw it was Laura and she got an idea.

"Hello, Laura," she said.

"Hello," said Laura coolly.

"I was wondering if you could use some extra groceries?" She looked at her suspiciously.

"Jeff and I have decided to go back to Durango. We are leaving today, and I noticed I have quite a bit of foodstuff in the apartment."

"Do you have sugar and flour?"

"Yes, and coffee and noodles. You are welcome to all of it. Were you heading out?" Amy was next to the door.

"Yes," said Laura more civilly.

Amy opened the door and stepped out with her. A taxi was just pulling up to Jeff.

"Why don't I give you the key to the apartment now," said Amy, walking with Laura like they were best of friends.

The man looked at them and then walked away. He talked into the lapel of his jacket. They were probably starting to wonder why Dr. Holbrook was taking so long.

"So you don't need your key anymore?" asked Laura.

"No, we are leaving right now. Hey, I'm sorry we didn't have time to get to know each other better.

"Yes, you should have been more honest about your feelings for your cousin."

"Yeah, I know that now," she was almost at the taxi. She gave Laura the key. "I left the apartment open, but I wouldn't go now. There is an older man checking the place. I think he wants to rent it."

"Too bad, another old man," said Laura. "Well, have a good trip."

Amy opened the taxi door and joined Jeff inside.

"Where do we go?" asked Jeff.

"To the University of California in Berkley," she told the taxi driver.

The taxi driver nodded and the taxi pulled away.

That is when the man, talking to his lapel, realized a man and a woman had gotten into the taxi. Amy saw him start to run after the taxi waving, but he had no jurisdiction in this time and place and could not do anything more.

The taxi driver asked, "Do you mind the music?"

They did not. It would allow them to speak with privacy.

The driver turned up the volume on the radio and his head started swaying to a big band song.

"Did you see that man?" Amy asked Jeff.

"Yes, it appears Dr. Holbrook was accompanied by more than one."

"Definitely looked like military."

"And you still want to go the university?"

"I wanted to see where they have the marker. Maybe we can see it when they transport back."

"The university is big, and it could be anywhere. I don't think it is a good idea."

She really wanted to know where the marker was and if they would leave it. It was their only way back.

Jeff studied her. "We should be thinking of where we are going to live and how we are going to pay for things."

"That is our second choice. First, I want to see if we both can get to 2066."

"You want to go back, even if they press charges against you?"

"What kind of charges would they press? Refusal to go along with a hair brained scheme of the boss, or refusal to have my mind wiped clean, which, by the way, is illegal in the future."

"Well, I am glad to hear that is illegal."

"I think Dr. Holbrook is functioning out of the realm of ethical and legal rules right now, and he does not even seem to realize it."

"I don't think there would be a need to erase my memory. No one would believe me if they heard my story."

"Are you having regrets over the decision we made?" she asked. "Do you want to go back to 1895?"

"No. I made that decision before and it remains the same. I am with you and together we make this work."

"Thank you," said Amy sincerely. "And you are right. Let's not go to the university. I brought the ComLink and we can talk to them any time we want; that is, if we want."

"That's a good decision. There could be more men waiting at the transport."

"Okay, so where do you suggest we go?"

"San Francisco. It is easier to hide there, as Gustav has proven."

"And we are already well acquainted with the district by the docks," laughed Amy.

"Yes, though I don't recommend we stay the night there."

Chapter 31
The streets of San Francisco

Shortly afterwards they were on the ferry heading to the city.

"I don't think we can work at the Ford assembly plant anymore," said Amy. "BioTime knew we were working there, and it may be the first place they check."

"I agree, but it is too bad. I was getting quite good at tank assembly."

"Right, but I know the real reason. You just wanted to drive Mrs. Felder's car some more."

"There may be some truth to that," he smiled. "The job was okay, the driving was fantastic. I even enjoyed driving the Jeep. So there are no cars in the future?"

"It's considered a luxury, even more than now. With so many people in the Bay area, mass transit is the most convenient and fastest method of transport. The train I take home from the lab takes me less than ten minutes, and I am over twenty miles away."

"Ten minutes?" asked Jeff, he thought about it for a moment. "That is over 100 miles per hour!"

"And the Bay commuter is not the fastest. For longer distances, we use the Hyperloop, which is a train inside a tunnel that moves about 800 miles per hour on a cushion of air. We also have airplane commuters and for very long distances, we take the high-speed civil transport, which goes over 1500 miles per hour, almost double the speed of sound."

"The speed of sound," said Jeff. "I remember that from physics. How can you see anything along the way?"

"You don't. The plane flies at a very high altitude, and it can only go that fast when it is over the ocean because of the sonic boom created at that speed. Of course, the fastest form of transport in 2066 is the space plane."

"Space?" smiled Jeff, as if she were joking.

"Really, a space plane. You can go visit the moon if you like, and that will take you a bit over three days. But there is not much to do or see when you are out there. They are still trying to develop it."

"Huh, I guess you want to get to your destination quickly, and you don't care about how you get there. I like seeing the sights along the way."

It struck her again about how smart Jeff was. "Yeah. No one I know travels for the sake of travel. Everyone wants to get there as quickly as possible. Maybe they are missing out."

"I think so," he said, as they both watched the city approach slowly.

When they debarked, they bought a newspaper and headed to a café to review the ads.

"If you went back, where would you work?" asked Jeff, sipping his coffee as he looked over the newspaper.

"BioTime is just one company," said Amy, munching on a sourdough sandwich. "After what I did, I probably will not work there anymore, but there are other companies in the Bay Area that will gladly hire me. That wouldn't be a problem."

"What about me? Who would hire me, an ancient sheriff?"

"You would be surprised how many skills you have, once you start to list them. You have also an excellent mind, so you can do anything."

"I am glad you have so much confidence in me."

"Yes, even though you are an ancient sheriff."

He smiled and showed her an ad. "What about this place?"

"The price is right," said Amy. "I wonder about the area. I think San Francisco had some dicey areas in 1944, and it doesn't say if the rent is by the month or week to week."

"San Francisco has no bad areas in 2066?"

"Not really. The city has become quite gentrified. My aunt lives off Mission in a fabulous old place. The area was unsafe before, but now it isn't, and the weather is better on that side of the city. The fog is always a factor in San Francisco, but that has not changed since the city was founded."

After lunch, they walked up and down the hills of the city, making notes of possible places to stay. The place mentioned in the ad proved to be in a very dicey part of town, and the building itself was run-down, so it was quickly discarded.

Amy wanted to have an apartment where they could cook their meals, but Jeff pointed out that most of what was available, especially in their price range, were rooms in boarding houses.

"And as soon as we find somewhere to live, we will have to look for work," he said.

He was already planning ahead, but she was still finding it hard to accept that they were stuck in 1944. As they wandered around looking at properties, she felt she was running out of energy. This morning everything was going to be resolved and now suddenly, they were again worrying about money and trying to find a place to live.

Maybe it was part of a bad dream, and she would awake with Jeff in 2066. Even if not a dream, Dr. Holbrook had to realize he couldn't leave her here, she thought. What about her aunt, or her friends; would they be able to find her?

"What do you think of the last place?" asked Jeff.

"I don't know, and at this point I barely care. I just want to find something."

Jeff studied her. "I think we will stay at a hotel for tonight. We will continue to look again tomorrow."

"Good, I'm feeling very tired."

"Don't worry, Amy, there is a lot out there, and we shouldn't give up."

After they checked into their room, Amy took out the few belongings they had brought from Richmond. One was the ComLink.

"Should I connect it?" asked Amy, looking at it.

"Do you really want to talk to them?"

"I am curious as to what they have to say. Maybe they have changed their mind."

"They can't find us through that, can they?"

"No," she said, and then realized she was not sure. "Maybe I'll wait until the morning, just in case."

"I don't see any harm in waiting."

In the morning, she connected the device and immediately heard Dr. Holbrook.

"Hello, Amy." His voice was subdued.

"Hello, Dr. Holbrook."

"You shot me with the stun gun."

"Yes. There was no other way to stop you. You were not listening, and you broke your promise."

"Not listening? Me? It is you that needs to listen. My solution was the best for Jeff."

"That is your opinion, Dr. Holbrook, and I don't know what you have based that on. Shouldn't it be his choice? Jeff is here with me right now, if you want to ask."

"No, it is not his choice. He would not do well here in the future."

"I am right here, Dr. Holbrook. You can talk to me directly," said Jeff.

"It is not your choice alone, Jeff. We don't know what happens to the time continuum when someone leaves their time for an extended period. It is best not to do it."

"What do you consider an extended period?" asked Amy. "It seems that these squishy parameters are causing problems."

"Squishy parameters?"

"The extended period you talk about…is that one week, or one month, or one year? How do you decide that? For example, Suzanna was in 1895 for four weeks. And what about the couple of minutes you lost of memory? Was that too much or just right, Dr. Holbrook? Who decides?"

"It was too much. I now realize any memory loss is too much." He sounded honest about that. "As for the extended period, this is time travel, Amy. I don't have all the answers. I just know that we have to keep things under control as much…"

"Miss Waterhouse, if I may interrupt," a new voice came on, "my name is Peter Corse. I am from GovTime and am here to advise Dr. Holbrook and to help provide security."

"Security for the lab employees or security for Dr. Holbrook?"

"For both, of course," said Peter. "In any case, I just want to know when and where we can pick you up."

He didn't even phrase it like a question, and that bothered her. "I assume nothing has changed in regards to Jeff?"

"You are correct; Jeff's situation is the same," said Dr. Holbrook.

"In that case, both of you may have to wait some time," said Amy.

"We will find you," said Peter in a careful, measured manner.

"Dr. Holbrook, you would spend time and energy looking for us instead of advancing other projects?" asked Amy, ignoring Peter. "Instead of discovering possible cures to serious diseases?"

"We decide what is of importance, Amy."

"Well, Dr. Holbrook, along that line of thinking, I still have a specimen of the corydalis curvisiliqua. I don't know if you are planning to get a new specimen, so I wanted you to know before you spend time doing that."

"Thank you for telling me. I don't know what happened to the specimen that Gustav brought, and we can't get a new specimen easily. The marker is gone from Durango. Somehow, Gustav destroyed it or hid it before he left."

"Oh, that is too bad," said Amy.

"Amy, please come back. As you say yourself, you have much important work to do. It could mean the cure for thousands. Doesn't that mean anything to you?" Dr. Holbrook pleaded.

"Dr. Holbrook, you know I am pretty dedicated to my job. The years you have known me, you have been able to count on me and that is why you should trust me. I firmly believe Jeff is a time traveler and going to the future is the solution."

Her speech must have had some effect, as there was no reply for a moment.

"By the way," she added, "you advocate a balance at work and he happens to be the something that balances my life."

"We will talk later, Dr. Waterhouse," said Peter, and the link was disconnected.

"So, I am the something you have been missing?" asked Jeff.

"Yeah, you are the something," smiled Amy as she put away the ComLink. "Let's get out of here and find a place to live." She felt much better about her decision.

Chapter 32
A boarding house in Noe Valley

After another day of searching for housing, they spent the night in another small hotel, but this one was in Noe Valley.

"I like this area," said Jeff, "and I noticed several help wanted signs in the shop windows."

"I saw those as well. Tomorrow we can try for a job," she said, as she got into bed feeling more positive.

"I was thinking about what Dr. Holbrook said about our life span. Was he right? Has it changed so much?"

"Yes, the life expectancy in 2066 is 88 for both men and women. Now in 1944, it is 66 for women and slightly lower for men; a twenty year difference."

"What was it in 1895?"

"About 52."

"Wow, that is quite different as well. What changed?"

"Better medicine, better diet, jobs that are less dangerous, probably a lot of things."

"Amy, you can't give that up. You have to return."

"Jeff, what is the point of living to an old age if you are going to do it alone and be unhappy?"

The following day, they pooled their money and counted it again, as if the amount would somehow magically grow. It hadn't.

"We can't stay here tonight," said Amy. "It's too expensive."

"Yes, and I think we better start looking for work while continuing our housing search. There's a newspaper delivery position open. I'll inquire about it."

That night, they settled in a boarding house. Jeff was quiet about the details of the job interview. Amy didn't want to pry and let it go.

"I think we should call again," said Amy, trying to convince Jeff. "Dr. Holbrook was sounding more reasonable at the end of our last conversation. Maybe he has changed his mind."

"You think that is possible?" He looked at her. "I am a bit concerned you are so anxious to go back to 2066 that you are not putting as much effort into living in 1944."

She had no response; he was right. She would go back in an instant if Jeff were allowed to come with her. She was still hoping things would get resolved like she wanted.

He sighed. "Well, go ahead and call, but let's make sure it is away from the boarding house. I worry they can find us through that device and I don't want to move again."

They ended up in the library, several blocks from the boarding house. There were a couple of meeting rooms that could be scheduled for free. Jeff decided to stay outside the building to keep an eye out for anyone that may be from the future. He was convinced they could trace her call.

She didn't have to wait long before someone answered. "Amy?"

It didn't sound like Dr. Holbrook. "Yes?" she answered.

"It's me, George."

"Great to hear you, George; why are you whispering?"

"They don't know I am talking to you."

"What is going on, George? And who is Peter Corse?"

"They brought him over after the Susan incident. He is ex-military and works at GovTime. He is just on loan, says Beebe, and he won't last long. Apparently she's heard him argue with Dr. Holbrook. And speaking of Susan, have you heard?"

"No. I didn't want to talk to Dr. Holbrook about her."

"They were about to put her in jail, but they couldn't figure out how to make the charges. Instead, they laid her off, but it was fine by her. She's going to start a new company in the service industry, I think."

I bet it has to do with being a companion, thought Amy. Susan had really enjoyed being a saloon girl in 1895. "Dr. Holbrook said a lot of people are gone."

"The core group is still here. All the scientists are here, but Francine is gone."

"Hmm."

"GovTime people have been visiting us more often, as well."

"Apparently, they helped us fix our time travel location discrepancy."

"Yes, but they have been using our transport markers quite a bit in return. I don't like it. Why don't they tell us what they are doing?"

"Well, if it is government and military, they are usually not informative."

George didn't respond, and Amy knew they were skirting the real issue. "I'm never going to get back, am I?" she asked quietly.

"No Amy, don't think that. I think there's less opposition to the idea of having Jeff come with you. I put in a good word for him, telling them how valuable he would be for our projects. I also mentioned how there is nothing for him in 1895 and how his lifeline already appeared like a time traveler."

"Yeah, that is what I said."

"You should know we have lost some of our time travel setters, and Jeff would be a perfect candidate."

"More than Gustav?"

"Anthony is not coming back to work. He got very spooked when you were shot. In addition, the remaining time setters were tested with stricter psychological parameters, and four did not pass. Out of the remaining, several are close to the travel limit."

"They put a limit on the travel?"

"Yes, the limit is twelve, and that is way below the eighteen trips of Gustav and the fifteen trips that Anthony took.

"Is Ryan still there?" He was the one who had come to get her in San Francisco.

"Yes, he is still cleared to travel. They are training another group of time setters, but there are fewer people interested in that job. You know the list of twenty-eight scientists and researchers who wanted to time travel? Less than half of the names are still there. I took my name off."

"I thought you really wanted to go?"

"I like my current life too much to risk it. It is no longer a glamorous adventure. From what we are seeing, it is dangerous, unreliable and causes psychological problems."

"So that is the reason Dr. Holbrook came to get me himself."

"I think so. He was quite angry when he returned. I heard you stunned him and erased his memory," he chuckled.

"A bit of his own medicine. Jeff pointed out that erasing someone's memory, even a little, is not ethical and I agree."

"Did you do that to Jeff?"

"No, but I had to do it to someone else."

"See, I don't think I could do it. It just makes me more certain removing my name from the list was the right decision. Hey, I have to go, but can we talk again?"

"Yeah. George, I was wondering, is there any way they can trace my call?"

"Not that I know of. But I'll find out for sure. Take care, Amy."

"Thanks. Thanks for everything, George."

As they walked back to the boarding house, Amy told Jeff what had happened.

"You can trust George?" asked Jeff.

"Yeah, he has always been a good friend."

"When are you talking to him again?"

"Tomorrow. George said he is trying to convince the others that you would make a good time traveler. He noticed they are less opposed to the idea."

"After hearing all the problems time travelers are having, I am not sure I want to become one. In any case, I do not think that a future job will pay for our food right now. We really need to find work now," said Jeff.

Amy noticed that he sounded stressed. "Did you see anything in the want ads that interested you?"

"Since I supposedly have flat feet, I cannot take a job that makes me stand for long periods. It has limited my options."

That must have been the problem with applying for the newspaper delivery job, she thought. "I saw a job opening in the library, and that is something I could do easily. I am going to apply tomorrow."

"How much does it pay?"

"I think it is minimum wage, which is 40 cents per hour."

"That is $16 per week. We were doing better at the Ford plant."

"There is no point thinking about that. Anyway, I hope this situation is temporary."

That night they told the boarding house owner they wanted to rent for one week. The owner had a small apartment on the top floor and offered that. It had a small kitchen and living room. Amy loved the idea, and they put down the money for the week.

The following morning, Jeff accompanied Amy to the library for her interview. She did well with the interview, and they said they would call her with the decision, but that it looked like she had the job.

The library was located close to a large park, and afterwards Jeff and Amy went for a walk there. Suddenly, they heard the galloping of horses and a couple of park rangers rushed by on their horses.

Jeff eyes lit up.

"I think you have found your job," smiled Amy.

"Getting paid to ride a horse through the park? There has to be more to this job."

"There probably is, but you just saw the fun part. Look, there is the park office. You can inquire if they have an opening."

Suddenly, Jeff looked worried, "Do I tell them about being a sheriff? Do I tell them I worked at the Ford Assembly plant? Or do I pretend I was a deputy with flat feet? What can I say?"

"I'm sorry it is confusing. You just have to choose the role you want to play. It is like being an actor. For my interview, I told them I had gone to college and knew a lot about library systems, both being true. In your case, maybe tell them you were a deputy and that we are here in San Francisco looking for my brother. Try to keep the story simple so you don't get mixed up."

"You know, I'd rather tell them the whole truth. It is easier."

"Which truth? Are you going to tell them the part of time travel? You know they will not believe that."

"I know. I know. And if I say I have flat feet and they test me, they will find I lied, and that will not work either."

He was right.

218

"I don't think this job is the right one," said Jeff as he turned away.

That night, Amy and Jeff were at the library again connecting the ComLink.

"Hello, Amy," said George.

"Hi, George. Jeff is with me tonight."

"Hello, George," said Jeff.

"Well, I checked if anyone can trace your call and the answer is no, so at least you should feel easier about that."

"Thanks, George," said Amy.

"How is your money situation? I worry about you guys."

"I interviewed for a librarian job and there are good chances I will get it. They will let me know tomorrow."

"What about you Jeff? You should find a driving job," suggested George.

"Actually, that is a good idea," said Jeff, more animated than she had seen in the past days. "I really enjoyed driving."

Then they heard other voices. They sounded muffled, but above them they could hear George protesting. Then heard him clearly say, "Shut it down, Amy. Disconnect."

She was just about to when another voice came through, "No, please, don't."

It was Dr. Holbrook. "Please, there is something I need to tell you."

She paused. He couldn't trace her, so there was no risk in hearing him out. "Go ahead, Dr. Holbrook."

"We have been able to find Gustav. Since he is not well, it is imperative we get him back. I can trust you to not change the past, but we cannot trust him for anything."

That was true, thought Amy.

"Anyway," said Dr. Holbrook. "We know he is in San Francisco. We are going to send Ryan to pick him up."

"He is not going to go easily," said Amy. "Remember how he escaped before? He pretended to go along, but he had another agenda."

"I know. Ryan is going to carry the transport marker with him, so when he meets Gustav he doesn't have to take him anywhere. Of course, he also has the stun gun. The plan is to stun him, then tie his hand to the marker. Ryan will have fifteen minutes to transport him."

"Ryan is coming by himself?

"We are short on time travelers right now. We only have six time setters, and two are close to the limit of twelve trips."

"But, isn't the transport marker heavy?"

"We have devised an old-fashion two-wheeler that he can pull behind him. Ryan is confident he can do this by himself."

Of course, Ryan would say that, thought Amy.

"I just wanted to let you know, in case Ryan needs some help."

"All right," she said. Dr. Holbrook was sounding quite reasonable and nice.

"Good. That is all I wanted to hear. Thank you."

"If that will be all then, good-bye," she said.

"Wait, there is something else."

"Here it comes," she whispered to Jeff.

"Ryan is going tomorrow, and he will be taking the ferry across from Berkeley in the morning."

"Why are you telling us this?"

"Just in case you want to return with him."

"I have not changed my mind, Dr. Holbrook."

Chapter 33
Ryan arrives

Ryan would be arriving this morning. It was the first thought she had when she woke up. Jeff was still asleep next to her. She had already checked the ferry schedule from Berkeley, and there was a ferry every hour on the hour starting at seven until noon; six ferries to check. She wanted to see him. It wasn't that she had any feelings for Ryan, like Jeff has suggested, but he was someone she could trust to get information.

She wondered if she should tell Jeff about it.

"This morning I am going to apply for a position in a restaurant. It is a place closer to downtown," said Jeff as they had breakfast.

"A restaurant?" It could be all right, thought Amy, but she hated to have him disappointed again. "What kind of position?"

"A dishwasher. Not much skills required," said Jeff with a smirk. "What about you?"

"I have no plans except," she paused. "What do you think about going to the ferry building?"

"You want to see Ryan?"

"I want to talk to him about home. I'm also thinking of sending a message for my aunt. She is probably worried about me, since it has been over four weeks. I had told her I would be gone for a couple weeks."

Jeff nodded. "And you probably don't mind seeing Ryan?"

"It's not that, Jeff. You can come with me. I'm pretty sure I will get the librarian job, so you don't need to find a job right away."

"I don't want to become a helpless charge, Amy. You go to the ferry building and wait for Ryan, I will go look for a job."

She arrived at the ferry building as the ferry arrived and watched it unload the passengers. She recognized no one. It was the same with the next ferry.

She had felt a bit upset that Jeff didn't want to accompany her, but could understand his reasoning. He had been so independent and confident, and now he had nothing. She had noticed some despair as he babysat Gustav, trapped all day at home. Women coped with those feelings better than men, she thought.

The 9:00 ferry came in, and she didn't have to wait long. Two burly men were helping Ryan off the ferry while a third man dragged a case. She immediately ran to him to find out what happened.

"Amy, thank goodness," said Ryan as the two men propped him up on a bench. He grimaced. "I was really hoping you would be here."

"What happened?" asked Amy.

"I injured my leg getting on the ferry."

"That heavy case got caught on the ramp and when he pulled it, the wheel ripped off. The case rammed his leg against the scaffolding and cut it," said one of the men.

"Oh no," said Amy looking at his leg. It looked painful. Someone had wrapped it in some sort of discolored cloth.

"I don't know what happened next," said Ryan. "I think I passed out."

She looked at the injury closer but didn't want to touch it.

"Don't worry about the pain," said the man. "We've given him something that eases that."

"Whiskey?" she asked.

The men laughed. "No, although that never hurts. We gave him morphine."

"Hey, no wonder I don't feel bad," said Ryan, smiling.

"I'll take you home right away," said Amy.

"Well, we have to get back on the ferry," said the man. "Do you need help taking him to a taxi?"

"No, that will be all right, thank you," said a voice. It was Jeff. "We can take care of it."

"Yes, thank you," said Amy, looking at Jeff with gratitude. She noticed the men were waiting. It must be for a tip, she looked in her purse and found three dollars. It was the last dollars she had. She gave each of the men a dollar.

"Thank you, Miss," said the man, and the others repeated the thanks as they returned to the ferry.

"Thank you for coming," said Amy to Jeff.

"I should have been here earlier."

"You were just in time."

Jeff helped Ryan up and together they hobbled to the taxi stand. Amy dragged the case along.

"Thank goodness we rented this bigger place," said Amy, looking at Ryan sleeping on the couch.

"It seems we are always picking up time traveling strays," said Jeff. "I don't know if I want to belong to that group, even if they ask."

"Oh yeah? What about the fringe benefit of having me around?"

"Okay," he smiled. "That counts for something."

They smiled at each other for a moment.

"I almost got the dish washing job this morning," he said.

"Oh?"

"Then I realized I should have gone with you."

"I was very happy to see you."

He nodded. "What are we going to do about him?"

"Well, I cleaned out his injury as best I could. It was a nasty cut, but what they did on the ferry stopped the bleeding, so I think he will be all right. In any case, we have the transport marker, so we could get the doctor here if we need him."

"Wait," said Jeff. "That means they can transport anyone here?'

"Oh yeah, that could be a problem," said Amy, looking around. "We can lock the marker in the closet or the bathroom."

"The closet is better," said Jeff, "I would hate to be surprised by a visitor in the bathroom." He pushed the case into the closet and locked the door.

"We should call Dr. Holbrook to tell him what has happened," said Amy.

"I am sure he will be thrilled," said Jeff.

Dr. Holbrook was not thrilled.

"Why can't we have one mission go according to plan?" he asked no one in particular.

"Ryan is resting right now," said Amy. "Do you want him to call you when he wakes up?"

"Please. Thank you, Amy, for helping."

"Of course, but Jeff is the one who helped us."

"Thank you, Jeff," said Dr. Holbrook a bit reluctantly.

"You're welcome," said Jeff.

Amy disconnected the link.

"The 'thank you' was a bit forced, don't you think?" asked Jeff.

"I think he is warming up to you," said Amy.

Ryan woke up soon afterwards. Amy opened a canned soup and made grilled cheese sandwiches. The kitchen had no oven, and with the small two-burner stovetop, making anything more complicated would stress the facility. They ate in the living room sitting around the coffee table.

"So this is where you are living," Ryan said as he looked around.

"For this week," said Jeff.

She liked that Jeff was cautious like that.

Ryan also smiled at the comment. "It's good to be careful."

"So, what are you going to do, Ryan?" she asked.

"Well, I was not planning to stay the night in 1944, but seeing that is mid afternoon already, I may have to. Can I stay with you?"

"For tonight?" she looked at Jeff, who nodded. "You can stay, but I meant what are your plans to get Gustav?"

"I have a tracking device," said Ryan. He tried to get up off the sofa and quickly put out his hand back on the sofa, to steady himself. "Whoa, I feel a bit woozy. I wonder what they gave me on the ferry?" He sat down again.

"They gave you morphine, but you might be dehydrated. I'll get you some water," said Amy.

"I vaguely remember them giving me an injection. Anyway, the plan was to track Gustav, stun him and then transport him. Simple right?"

"And you would do this while pulling that heavy case?" asked Amy as she filled a glass with water. She handed him the glass.

"That was the idea. You drink the water from the tap?"

"Yeah, it's all right," said Amy.

He took a gulp. "I need your help, especially now."

"I don't know if I can help you, I'm supposed to go for another interview tomorrow," said Amy. The library had sent a message.

"Interview?"

"For a job. How do you think we are living here?"

"Oh. That reminds me, George sent you something." Ryan looked around the room. "Where is the case?"

"In the closet," said Amy.

"Smart," smiled Ryan. "You never know who will appear. Well, there is an envelope addressed to you in there."

Amy opened the case and found it. She opened the envelope and pulled out a small stack of newly printed, nicely aged ten-dollar bills.

"Wow," she said.

"I know George was busy with the printer," said Ryan.

"It's over two hundred dollars," said Amy, counting it out. "That should cover expenses for a while."

"So you can help me then?" asked Ryan.

"Maybe I can help you," said Jeff, who had been mostly listening.

"I would really appreciate it, Jeff. Maybe we can start after I regain some of my balance."

Jeff nodded. "We'll see."

"Let me show you how the tracker works," said Ryan.

"Are you feeling well enough?" asked Amy.

"Yeah, I need to do this." He pulled out a compass-looking device from his jacket. "It's quite simple. Come sit next to me," he said to Jeff.

Amy stood behind them to watch as well.

"See, right now Gustav is west and slightly north from this apartment," said Ryan. "You can read the distance here. One and half miles west and about the same north."

"That would be about the Golden Gate Park," said Jeff.

"How do you know that?" asked Ryan.

"Jeff has a good sense of direction," said Amy.

"Well, that will make my work easier," said Ryan. "Here is the map they gave me."

They checked the distance, and Jeff had been correct.

"There is a problem, Ryan," said Amy. "There is not much public transportation in the park."

"Hmm," said Ryan. "I guess we were not expecting Gustav to be in some remote location."

"Maybe you can rent a car?" asked Amy.

"I don't know how to drive," said Ryan.

"I do."

"Okay," Ryan looked at Jeff. "I am beginning to see Amy's point for bringing you on."

"I know," smiled Amy.

Dr. Holbrook was pleased with the solution. "Thank goodness we can proceed. I wonder why Gustav is in the park?"

"He stole the money we had in the apartment, but it was not a lot. He might be camping in the park to save what he has," said Amy.

"He is probably not alone. How are you going to transport him?" wondered Dr. Holbrook.

"Jeff and I were discussing that possibility, Dr. Holbrook, and I think we can take care of it," said Ryan.

"And how is your leg, Ryan?"

"It is fine."

"Make sure Amy also goes with you," said Dr. Holbrook. "She did well in the self defense class."

"That is good to know," said Ryan, looking at her.

"Jeff and I are a bit concerned about driving in San Francisco," said Amy, changing the subject. "There are many hills around here. Is George around?"

"I'll send for him," said Dr. Holbrook. "There is something else. We had a meeting, and we have come to a decision. The option to come to 2066 is now available to both of you. What do you think?"

Amy and Jeff looked at each other. Yes, thought Amy without hesitation, but she wanted to make sure Jeff felt the same. He might have changed his mind after what had happened. "Can we answer later?" she asked.

"Sure. Is Jeff there? We want him to know that we could really use him here. We would like to offer him a job as a time travel setter."

"I need to discuss this with Amy," said Jeff.

"Fine, fine, there is no hurry on the decision. Here is George."

Jeff told George about his concerns about driving on hills.

"Yes Jeff, it is tricky. You just have to practice to get used to it. You have to release the clutch and at the same time, press the accelerator. Doing it smoothly is what takes practice."

"I noticed the taxi drivers do it well," said Jeff.

"Yes, they do get a lot of practice. Something else to watch out for is when you stop on an incline I suggest you keep the car slightly revved up with the foot on the clutch. In the worse case, you can use the hand brake to hold your position on a steep hill. Also, remember that to park the car you should turn your wheels so that the vehicle tires will hit against the sidewalk if the car moves.

"That would be to the right going downhill and left going uphill?" asked Jeff.

"Correct," said George.

The last part made total sense to Amy, but she was glad she was not the one to be driving.

"Thank you, George, for your help," said Jeff. "Amy and I are going to rent a car now."

"I envy you guys," said George.

"George, you should have mentioned your desire to be here before I left," said Ryan. "I would have let you come instead of me."

George laughed.

"Thanks for the cash you sent, George," said Amy. "I was going to go for another interview tomorrow, and now I can go play in the park with the boys."

They made light of it, but they all knew it would not be playing in the park. Gustav had many faces, and it really depended on which one he was wearing when they found him.

They left Ryan resting in the apartment that afternoon when they went to rent the car. Then they went for a drive. Right away, they arrived at their first hill. There was a traffic light on the top of the hill and it changed to red just as they pulled up to it.

Jeff stopped. The car was almost at the top of the hill, and Amy could visualize the car's front tires hanging onto the top of the hill.

"Okay, put it in first, clutch down, brake," said Jeff, talking to himself.

Amy tightened her hold on the door handle, but tried to appear casual, so as not to make Jeff any more nervous.

The light changed, and Jeff pressed the accelerator and released the clutch. The car jumped forward, but it was relief they did not slip backwards down the hill.

"Nicely done," said Amy.

"That one was easy," said Jeff, "wait until I have traffic behind me and we are stopped in the middle of hill."

"I hope that never happens."

"So I have you worried?"

"It's not you, it's the uncertainty of how cars work."

"Don't worry, I have this. How about we get a cup of coffee somewhere? We might as well have a destination if we are practicing driving around."

"All right. We do have money now, so why don't we go to Ghirardelli Square?"

"Just direct me."

It was surprising how easy that was. The major streets had retained their names in the future, and Ghirardelli Square was in the same location as in 2066. Parking proved to be a relief, as the area close to the square was not on hilly terrain. They got out of the car and walked across the street. She took his hand and noticed it was damp.

"Okay, I might have been clutching the steering wheel a bit tightly," he admitted.

"Thank goodness. I was thinking that maybe you had nerves of steel."

"I thought a man of steel is what you wanted," he smiled.

"No, that would be uncomfortable to sleep with. Anyway, I am very impressed with your driving."

"I just hope it is good enough for what we have to do tomorrow."

"Have you given any thought to Dr. Holbrook's latest offer about going to 2066?'

"I told you I don't know if I can join a group that is constantly getting into trouble, like the time travel setters do," he joked.

"More important than a job offer, they are saying that you can go to 2066. I think that being a time setter may suit you, and you definitely have more experience in this area, but you can get any other job."

"You want to go, don't you?"

She sighed. "I do."

"Well then, we go."

"Wait. We both have to agree to this choice. It is too important. Back in 1895, I know that you had agreed to come with me, but now you have adapted so well in 1944, I thought you wanted to stay."

"Maybe I had to adapt. Remember, they didn't want me in the future."

"I know, but they have changed their mind."

"And what prevents them from changing it again?"

"I think they have realized how valuable you can be to the project."

"Amy, for a worldly girl such as yourself, you are quite naïve. You trust everyone."

"Is that so bad?"

"No and I love that about you, but I think the truth is sometimes hard for you to see."

She didn't say anything. She didn't want to argue right now, so close to making a major decision. Maybe she did see the best in people, but he always suspected the worst. Who was right?

Chapter 34
Finding Gustav

The following morning Amy walked into the living room to find Ryan walking around in his boxers. He smiled. "The leg appears to be much better."

"Thank goodness," said Amy.

"I will still need your help, of course," said Ryan.

"Yeah, I'm pretty sure Jeff is totally on-board with that."

"It is fortunate he knows how to drive; I can't imagine catching taxis and having to explain to the driver where to go."

Jeff walked in, glanced at Ryan's attire and continued to the kitchen to get some breakfast.

She had to remember to tell him it didn't mean anything to see someone in his underwear. People in the future were quite comfortable with their bodies.

Soon they were on their way to the Golden Gate Park. At the entrance, Jeff pulled the car to one side of the street.

"Where should I go?" he asked Ryan.

Ryan stared at his directional device and shook his head with dismay. "I don't know, it is not giving me any direction."

"Do you think he moved last night and is no longer here?" asked Amy.

"No. I checked right before we left the apartment and it showed he was still in the area," said Ryan.

"Maybe something is blocking the signal," suggested Amy.

"I can start following the road that circles the park," said Jeff. "Maybe your device will show him again."

Ryan nodded.

Amy hoped Jeff was right; the park was quite large and they could easily take all day looking. For the next couple of hours, Amy kept searching out the window while Ryan kept an eye on his device and Jeff concentrated on staying on the road and keeping with the flow of traffic.

"I think the car is running low on gasoline," said Jeff as they finished the perimeter and started on the internal grid of roads.

"Already?" Ryan seemed disappointed. "We have not searched that long."

"It's all right, there is a gas station," said Jeff, seeing one ahead. He pulled the car next to the gasoline dispenser that indicated 'full-service'. "I'm not sure how to fill this car," he said as he got out of the car.

A gas attendant was already on his way to their car. He greeted Jeff and quickly started to work on the car. He pulled out a hose on the side of the gasoline dispenser and plugged it into the car. He then started cleaning the windows.

"I'm going to get a better map of the area," said Amy as she opened the car door. When she returned, she saw that the hood of the car was opened. Jeff was conversing with the attendant while he checked something in the engine.

She got back in and opened the detailed map of the park. "Look at all the roads," she said, handing the map to Ryan.

"I had forgotten how big this park is," said Ryan. "What are they doing out there?"

"I don't know. They are looking at the engine."

"I don't know anything about these vehicles," said Ryan, handing the map back to her.

Amy took a pen out and drew their path on the map. "This is where we have gone so far. We have covered most of the major roads, but there are many roads too small for a car to go on and some places are not close to any roads."

"So we might not see any signs of people living in the park," said Ryan.

Jeff got back into the car.

"How is the car?" she asked.

"Fine. He was checking the oil and said it was fine. The moving parts of the engine use oil for lubrication."

"Oh." She didn't know that.

"The attendant told me he has seen tents near the large windmill," said Jeff. "It is illegal to camp there, but some homeless people do."

"That is on the west side of the park," said Amy. "We can take this road and it will take us close to there."

"Yes, but we will have to walk to the camping area. He said you can't see the tents from the road," said Jeff, starting the car. "Can you manage that, Ryan?"

"Yeah, I'll manage."

They parked near the windmill and after a short walk through a lovely meadow dotted with tulips, they could see a forest with young redwoods. Tents and lean-tos were sprinkled throughout. They stopped at the outskirt of the forest to study the campground from a distance.

"Is this the right place?" asked Amy.

Ryan fiddled with the tracker and nodded. "Yes, he is somewhere in that direction, but that is all I can tell you right now." He looked up. "There is a lot more people here than I expected."

"You don't have homeless people in 2066?" asked Jeff.

"No, we don't," said Ryan. "There are special apartments given to them until they can find jobs, or in the case of the mentally ill, they are taken to sanatoriums that see to their needs."

"How are we going to find Gustav?" asked Amy.

"I think we will have to go in there and search for him," said Ryan.

"I'm not sure the people that live there will like us tromping through. Maybe if I go alone," suggested Amy.

"No, I don't think that is a good idea," said Jeff. "As soon as he sees you, he will wonder why you are here and he might run."

"Well, even if we somehow grab him right now, we left the transport marker in the car," said Ryan. "I cannot imagine us hauling him back to the car without someone noticing."

"I have an idea," said Amy. "Why don't Jeff and I appear to be strolling through the park? We will walk through the campsite and pretend not to look for him. Knowing him, he will come to us."

"You think he will?" asked Ryan.

"It kind of depends on which of the persons he is. The aggressive Gustav will come to confront us, the normal Gustav might be curious, but the timid Gustav, we might not even see."

"Two out of three is sounding good right now," said Ryan.

They made plans of how to set things up, and then Jeff and Ryan went to get the case with the transport marker.

Without the wheel, it was best to carry the case over the grass. They were going to set it close to where they were watching the campground.

Amy stayed to keep an eye on the area. She hoped she would catch a glimpse of Gustav. The trees provided quite a bit of shade, and the shadows made it hard to see. There was a group of the people gathered in one of the small clearings, and she concentrated her vision there. There were a few children running around. Some clothes were hung on lines between the trees to dry. It seemed like a family campground, not a homeless enclave.

"Boo," said a voice close to her ear.

She jumped and immediately recognized the voice. "Gustav, hello." She made herself sound calm.

"Scare you?" he smiled.

"A bit. How are you?" She smiled trying to figure out which Gustav this was.

"What are you doing here?"

"I was looking at those homeless people. I was thinking how sad it is not have a home. I guess it is one thing we have improved in 2066."

"It is not so bad when the weather is good. But what are you doing in the park? I thought you went back?"

It sounded like the normal Gustav.

"They didn't want Jeff to come with me, so I stayed with him."

"Where is he?" It sounded like a demand.

"He went back to the car to get my jacket," said Amy.

"Yeah, he is a regular gentleman," said Gustav. "So you have a car here?"

She no longer thought he was the normal Gustav. His eyes and voice sounded like the aggressive one. She needed to keep him there until the guys showed up. "We rented a car to come to the park. You know, a day off work to spend in the park?"

"Of course. Both of you work and you have money. You can have a 'fun' day. I don't have that luxury." He moved closer to her.

"Well, why don't you work?"

He seemed to think about the response for a bit and then he said, "I don't want to. Why don't you give me your purse?"

"Take it," she said, but didn't hand it over.

He put out his hand. "Well, give it to me."

She grabbed the purse with both hands. "Take it." She really hoped Ryan and Jeff were getting close.

"What is wrong with you? You want me to hurt you over a stupid purse?"

"No. I know Gustav, my friend, would not hurt me." She looked at him, but he avoided making eye contact. She was not connecting with him, and she was afraid he would attack her if made desperate. She opened her purse and took out several dollars. She threw them on the ground. "Take them."

His eyes lit up, and he got down on his hands and knees to pick up the dollars.

It gave her a chance to look around for the guys. She didn't see them and then Gustav was up again, in front of her.

"I bet you have more money in there," he said.

"Let me look," she said.

He quickly reached out and grabbed the purse. He tried to pull it away, but she did not let go. With one hand on her purse, he swung his other hand at her face. She ducked and shoved the purse to him. Off balance, he fell to the ground. She hoped he would stay there for a while; she didn't want to hurt him.

"Oh," he complained as he rolled to one side. He propped himself partially off the ground. The purse had fallen slightly beyond him. "Amy, I think you have hurt me. It is my injured leg. The one your boyfriend shot. Help me get up."

Part of her wanted to help him, but she knew she shouldn't. Which Gustav was he? She didn't get any closer as she watched him and waited.

Suddenly, he leaped up on his feet and lunged at her.

It almost took her by surprise, but she was able to take a step to the side while pushing him in the direction he was going.

He stumbled a bit, but this time he did not fall down. He spun around and went to grab her, but suddenly, he grabbed his shoulder as he looked beyond her. He slowly fell backwards. She turned to find Ryan pointing the stun gun.

"I guess I should have left the stun gun with you," said Ryan.

"Are you all right?" asked Jeff.

"Yeah," she nodded, breathing again.

"So this is the self defense you wanted to practice in the bedroom?" asked Jeff.

She smiled.

Ryan raised his eyebrows but didn't comment as he tied Gustav. Together, they dragged him to the transport marker. This particular marker looked like a stump of a tree, similar to the one that had been in Durango.

"Is it secure?" asked Amy.

"Yes, the stump is well planted," joked Ryan. "That is what took us some time. Well, I am going to activate it. I don't want to risk Gustav waking up before we get back. Will you guys follow?"

"We have to talk to Dr. Holbrook first," said Amy.

"In case you stay, here is some more money. It is what I was given for my mission, and you can use it better than I can," said Ryan. He handed some bills to her. "I hope it helps you here."

"Thanks, Ryan."

"You should come home, Amy. And, Jeff, it has been a pleasure working with you here. I hope to see you soon."

"Thanks. I'll consider it," said Jeff.

Minutes later, Gustav and Ryan were gone. Amy felt homesick as they returned to the car.

Chapter 35
The decision

"We need to make a decision," said Jeff the following day. She was afraid that the time had come to do so.

"I know you want to return," continued Jeff, "and I am warming up to the idea. Frankly, living here is a bit hard."

"You're finding it hard to live here? I thought you were quite content."

"Since I am not in the military service, people look at me oddly wherever I go. I can imagine what bad things they think of me. Usually I have a thick skin, so that does not bother me much, but it does affect my chances of getting a job."

She had noticed some of the looks. "Oh, I had not realized how bad it was."

"Yeah, you should have heard the comments when I applied for the newspaper delivery job. How much longer does this war go on?" asked Jeff.

"Not too much longer. I believe there were some major battles in June of this year, but it will still take over a year to end."

"That is a long time. There is something else, Amy. Dr. Holbrook said you would die twenty years earlier if you stayed here, and I just cannot let that happen. I don't want you to die earlier just because I have some qualms about living in the future."

"It is life expectancies. It does not apply to me particularly. That should not be the reason to go. Maybe we could move somewhere where the presence of the military is not so obvious. San Francisco was the staging area for a lot of the war."

He didn't look convinced.

"As to a job, you know you can also get a dispensation if you work in an industry critical to the country, like at the Ford assembly plant. We can find some other company like that."

"Now I am confused. You want to stay here?"

"I want us to be happy. I don't care where we are."

"And you can be happy here?"

"I think so."

"Can you be happy in 2066?"

"Yes."

"Then we will go. I think I can be equally happy in 2066 as here."

That evening, they called Dr. Holbrook to give him the news. He seemed more relaxed now that Gustav was back.

"Is there a cure for him?" asked Amy.

"There is some new medication they are going to try. It has been successful in some cases like his."

"Good, I hope it works," said Amy. "Meanwhile, Jeff and I have made a decision."

"Yes?"

"We both want to go to 2066."

"Wonderful. When can we expect you?"

"How about tomorrow?"

"Tomorrow is good," said Dr. Holbrook. "Remember it will be Saturday here."

"All right then."

"It will be nice to have you back, Amy."

The following day, they went to the park and used the transport marker. The trip was uneventful. Few people were gathered around the transport when they arrived, and Amy wondered if it was because it was Saturday, or maybe Dr. Holbrook had not told many of their arrival.

She could understand it. She had gone against his wishes several times and she had stunned him. She really should look for work elsewhere.

Dr. Holbrook looked very glad to see them. He shook Jeff's hand vigorously and quickly led them right his office; there was no chance to talk to anyone on the way.

She managed to see George waving and she waved back.

"Obviously, we cannot debrief in a couple of hours," said Dr. Holbrook as he asked them to sit down. "It will take many days to cover the time you were away, Amy."

She had expected this.

"I have asked Dr. Knobby to give you a quick look to ensure you both are physically fit. You look fine to me, but you know it may be best to get a professional opinion."

237

"Sure," said Amy.

"Jeff, I believe he will be giving you some vaccinations today, and later he may want to run some additional testing."

Jeff nodded slowly.

"It's really nothing, but you are the first person from the past," he smiled as if he just realized this.

Amy could almost see his mind measuring this fact to gain some political or financial advantage.

"I know you are probably anxious to get home," he continued. "So go get your physical, and then come in Monday morning. We can wait for debriefing then."

"Thank you, Dr. Holbrook." Amy thought that was quite considerate of him.

"Do you have any questions, Jeff?"

"Not at this time."

"So I will see you Monday as well?" asked Dr. Holbrook.

Jeff looked at him, and Amy realized Jeff had not thought he had a choice.

"Like I said, I would like you to join our team," continued Dr. Holbrook. "I know you said you wanted to think about it, and I am hoping to sway you. I think we can offer you a good job package."

Jeff nodded. "I'll come in and we can talk."

"Good. Here is some material I have put together to present to investors. It gives you an idea of what we do. It is very important work," said Dr. Holbrook as he handed him a folder. "And Amy can always tell you more about that."

They left the office and went to see Dr. Knobby.

"This is a huge place, isn't it?" said Jeff as they walked over.

Amy explained the layout of the lab. "My lab is across the way, over there."

He glanced in that direction and gave a sigh.

Dr. Knobby was waiting anxiously.

"How are you feeling?" he asked Jeff.

"All right," said Jeff. "My head pounds a bit every time I transport, but it is quite minor."

"All right. I will start with Amy and get back to you right away. Do you want separate scans?"

"What is that?" asked Jeff.

Amy explained it was a quick way to check your physical health. "Go ahead, Dr. Knobby, scan me first so he can see how it works."

The doctor did. "You are fine. The bullet wound has healed very well. Do you want me to get rid of the scar? It will take a few minutes."

"No. I want to keep the scar for now."

"You also lost a couple of kilos, but otherwise your vitals match your baseline."

"That's it?" asked Jeff.

"It is the first step. If I find something out of normal, there are further tests to do. Those take longer. In your case, I am doing a baseline scan, so it will take a bit longer."

"Fine, go ahead."

The doctor looked at Amy.

"She can stay," said Jeff.

It did take long, and it was late afternoon when they left the lab. She was in a daze. She couldn't believe she was home again and that Jeff was with her. They took the train to the apartment, and she realized they had to pick up some food. After all they had been through, it seemed so mundane, picking up groceries after traveling through time.

Jeff was quiet the way there.

"This shouldn't take too long," she told Jeff. "What kind of food do you like to eat?"

"Anything is all right by me," he said, not being helpful.

They walked into the store, and she put on a headband with a small screen attached. She gave one to Jeff. "Here, put this on. It gives the nutrition information on the foods you pick and gives you ideas of recipes and other things that may go with what you buy."

He took the headband and put it on. "Wow," he said. "Are we seeing the same things?"

"No, what you see on the display depends on where you look."

They walked to the breakfast section and she asked what he would like for breakfast. "I could make Irish steel cut oats or we could try this Swedish Muesli."

"Irish? Swedish? Sounds like food comes from all over the world." Jeff studied the labels.

She put both things in the basket that was quietly following her. The counter attached to the basket immediately registered the products and added the prices. The headband display showed a couple of advertisements. One suggested she accompany her muesli with blueberries found in aisle 5. The other ad asked if she 'Got Milk'.

Yes, she would need both, she thought.

"This store is quite different from the ones in 1944," remarked Jeff, looking around the large warehouse store.

"In a way, it is more similar to the General Store in 1895," said Amy. "They sell almost everything here. They have found that it is more convenient to have food and clothing at the same place. It takes less time to shop."

Jeff smiled, "And that is what I like."

"You don't even have to come to a store. A lot of people order groceries on a computer and have them delivered, but you have to be organized to do that," she said. "I kind of like to wander through the store to get ideas for meals. I also have my domestic aide organize some of the meals."

"Domestic aide?"

"Yes, he is a mechanical device that looks like a human. He helps with cooking and cleaning. You will meet him soon."

"Like a servant?"

"I guess so," she said as she picked up fish and chicken. Both were packaged and ready to cook. She then headed to the vegetable section. Everything sold here was organic, so she didn't have to worry about how it was grown. This was another similarity to 1895, she pointed out.

Jeff picked up an apple and smelled it. "It doesn't smell like an apple."

"That is true. To have apples throughout the year, they are stored in an airtight room that is low in oxygen. I think that is why they lose some of their smell. My aunt only buys seasonal things to avoid that."

"Your aunt that raised you. Am I going to meet her soon?"

"I would love that. I'll call her when we get home." She had never asked too much about his family and now wondered if it was a good time. It probably wasn't, she decided.

She made one of her better meals that evening and they went to bed early. In the middle of the night she woke up and saw Jeff staring out the window.

"Is everything all right?" she asked.

"I didn't wake you, did I?"

"No," she got up and stood next to him.

"I was just looking out at the hills. I am glad you don't live in the middle of the city. It seemed so big and so crowded. I couldn't tell where one city ended and the other began."

"Yeah, I like to live up here, a bit removed from the bustle of the city. Believe it or not, my apartment is large for this time. You must find it small." It was 700 square feet.

"No. Actually your rooms seem large."

She had forgotten Victorian rooms were tiny. Everything must feel so strange and different for him. The transport, the doctor, the store, it was a lot to take in in one day. She worried about Jeff's reaction to all of this change.

"I can see frost out there, but I don't feel cold," he said.

"The temperature in the room is set to what we want," said Amy. "It takes into account our skin temperature and the room temperature outside and adjusts it accordingly. We are standing here next to the window, so the heat will come on soon. If we go to the bed, the temperature will go down a bit. Nice, huh?"

"It's a bit complicated. If I were hot, I could open the window, if I were cold; I would close it and put on a blanket. That seemed to always work."

She noted a note of despair. "Jeff, let's go to bed. I know it is a lot to absorb in one day. We can do it slowly. You know you don't have to go into work Monday if you don't want to."

"What would I do here besides staring out a window? I'd rather go with you. I might as well see what my life will be like for the next," he paused, "56 more years, if I live to the average life expectancy."

It sounded very morose she thought, as she convinced him back to bed.

"I wonder if Dr. Holbrook is offering me a job just to make you happy?" he asked.

"No," said Amy emphatically. "Dr. Holbrook doesn't care about employee happiness. He just cares if the projects are successful and that he gets the recognition he thinks he deserves. He must be seeing how you would help him achieve that."

They were both awake for a while longer, although neither had anything more to add. What was there to say? There was no turning back now.

Chapter 36
A job in 2066

It was her first day back at work and Amy made a large breakfast, hoping some of Jeff's misgivings had vanished. The previous day, they had gone back to the store and purchased clothes for him. He went reluctantly, since he didn't want her to spend money on him. Finally, she was able to convince him that it was necessary if he wanted to fit in. Still he had purchased the minimum.

"What time do you usually head to work?" asked Jeff. He was dressed and had been ready to go quite early.

"Between nine and ten," she said.

"That is late isn't it?"

"It depends how long you work, and I tend to work until seven or eight at night."

Jeff's eyes grew large. "That could be eleven hours! Do you get overtime?"

Amy laughed. "No. I am a salaried employee." She continued dressing as she explained the difference. "I wonder if I'll need a jacket today?"

"When I checked outside, the temperature was in the sixties. I think you might need your jacket."

"Oh, thanks," she said. He had gone outside. Later she would show him how to get the information from the display in the kitchen.

She also had to get Nix, her domestic aide, back.

They reached the lab close to nine twenty.

As she walked in, she was greeted by many of her coworkers. The greetings were warm, but she knew that most wanted to see the man from the past. She worried a bit about Jeff's reaction to all this attention. She moved quickly through the building, greeting and nodding, and then George stopped her.

"Running away from me?" he asked.

"Oh George, it is so nice to see you; this is Jeff," she introduced them and they shook hands.

"I am delighted to meet you in person," said George, "and I am happy to have you back, Amy."

"Thanks, George, I owe you," said Amy. "You can't imagine how helpful you were to us. Not only instructing Jeff how to drive, but keeping me informed of things happening here, and we really appreciated the money."

"Aw, that was nothing," said George. "It was the least I could do for a friend. Speaking of friends, Suzanna wants you to call her, if you can."

"Of course I can. You are keeping in touch with her?" Amy had not known them to be friends.

"We are both of friends of you and that kind of brought us together. Now that she no longer employed here, she is a much more interesting person to know." He turned to Jeff. "And you, Jeff, you are a star here. Ryan came back with high praise, and that is unusual for him. I think that was what finally swayed Dr. Holbrook to accept you."

Jeff didn't say anything and looked uncomfortable.

"Dr. Holbrook has offered Jeff a job," said Amy. "As a time travel setter."

"I knew he was going to do that, but make sure he pays you well," said George. "I heard they are paying those guys a pretty good bonus for each trip."

"Thanks, I'll make sure that is included," said Amy.

"Well, there is a limit to the times they can go," said George.

"Pay is only one of the considerations for a job," said Jeff.

"I have told him, he doesn't have to accept the offer," said Amy.

"Of course. Don't feel you have to accept anything that makes you uncomfortable."

They left George and headed to Dr. Holbrook's office. Beebe Chavez was glad to see Amy and was introduced to Jeff. She shook his hand and seemed very interested. "How fortunate to have someone like you working with us, Jeff. Amy, we have to get together sometime so I can hear more about your adventures."

"Sure," Amy agreed, realizing she knew so little about Beebe. Here was someone she saw almost daily but knew very little about because she was so engrossed with her work. Well, that was going to change; one didn't spend a month in the past without some realizations.

"Have you been busy?" she asked as Beebe led them into the office.

"Yes, it has been quite busy. I am thinking of taking a vacation soon."

"That sounds great," said Amy.

"Well, Dr. Holbrook had to step out," she said, "but he will be back soon. Do you want something to drink while you wait?"

They both declined, and Beebe closed the door after herself.

"So here we are again. I didn't pay too much attention when we were here Saturday," said Jeff, walking around the office. He stopped in front of the BioTime Travel Rules and read them. "I see you broke one these rules."

She joined him and read them. He probably meant rule #4 about minimizing contact with locals.

"I wonder what it will be like to travel through time. I noticed that most of the travel would be to places further back in time than 1895. To the people in those times will be like gods with our technology."

"So, you are thinking about taking the job?"

"I don't know if there is anything else for me."

"Wait, there are other options," Amy turned Jeff to her. "I want you promise me you will not take the job today. Let's hear his offer and then we will go home and talk about it. Please?"

Jeff did not seem too convinced, but agreed to wait.

Dr. Holbrook came in shortly afterwards. "Good morning, good morning. It is wonderful to have one of my leading scientists back, and we are thrilled to have you here as well, Jeff."

Amy had seen this side of Dr. Holbrook. This was the enthusiastic recruiter that had hired her. He would promise heaven and earth. In her case, she had actually received a lot of what had been promised. She loved the job, so the rest just followed.

"So, did you have a chance to read the information in the folder?"

"Yes," said Jeff.

"Let me explain the benefit package that would go with the work," said Dr. Holbrook as he explained the terms of the offer. "What do you think? Any questions?"

"When would my first trip be?"

"As soon as you pass the psychological and physical testing. You will probably pass those easily, so it could be as early as two weeks."

"Good," said Jeff.

Amy glanced at him. Maybe it would be a good if Jeff got busy right away.

"I might have mentioned the bonus we pay per trip is set at fifteen thousand," said Dr. Holbrook. "I think you will agree that is a good amount."

"Fifteen thousand," said Jeff not appearing affected by the large amount.

Amy kept thinking about their meager wages of the past month. Of course fifteen thousand didn't have the same buying power in 2066.

"I will need to discuss this with Amy and will get back to you."

"Great, absolutely great. Do you know when you can give me a response?"

"Tomorrow," said Jeff.

"Wonderful," said Dr. Holbrook.

Afterwards, Amy told him he could have taken a few days to make the decision.

"There is no need to delay a decision," he said. "I either go for it or I don't. The facts are all there and those won't change."

She didn't say anything.

She took him to her lab.

"Here it is, my home away from home," she joked. She was going to show him how important that little yellow flower was going to be.

He looked around the place as she brought up the projection with the chemical analysis.

"This is the analysis I was doing right before I transported," she started.

"So you work here alone?" asked Jeff.

"Now I do. Suzanna worked with me before." She smiled wistfully, thinking about her and how empty the place felt without her.

"I find it hard to breathe in here," said Jeff. "There are no windows, and all this artificial lighting, I feel it is claustrophobic."

"Windows would have been nice," she agreed, "but we have to keep a controlled environment in the lab to run the chemical tests. When I start testing the yellow flower, I will have to be even more careful and wear protective clothing."

"I don't think I could do your job."

She felt badly. She thought he would be thrilled with what she did. "Do you want to go?"

"If you don't mind."

She shook her head, "No, I don't mind." She started turning things off.

"Hey, you are leaving already?" asked a voice from the doorway. It was Ryan.

"Hi, Ryan. I was just showing Jeff what I do."

"Hi, Jeff. So what do you think? Did she blow your mind away?"

Jeff barely cracked a smile.

"Yeah, I can barely understand her when she gets going," said Ryan. "I was wondering if you two would like to go out for a drink afterwards?'

It would be good for Jeff to make some friends, thought Amy. "I think that would be nice, Ryan."

"I'll send you directions for a place that serves amazing beers. See you at six?"

"Yeah, thanks," said Amy.

"See you around, Jeff," said Ryan, and Jeff nodded good-bye.

"Drinks after work. You go out often with Ryan?"

They had just arrived to her apartment. "No. I thought it would be nice for you to have a friend."

"I like how you determine things for me," he said.

"What is wrong with you? You have been somewhere else all day."

"Sometime else maybe."

247

"Are you angry at me?"

He didn't say anything.

"You don't have to come for drinks if you don't want."

"I want," he said thinking about it. "There is not much I can do about what I want."

"Tell me. What do you want?"

"I want to be a useful, well-regarded member of society. I want people to know me for who I am, not for being the sheriff from the past or the guy with Amy. I don't want to depend on you for everything."

"It takes time for people to know you," she said softly.

"Time?" he laughed. "You have an answer for everything. Well, I think I will stay here tonight in your apartment. You go ahead and have fun with your friend." He stressed the 'your' both times.

He was in a terrible mood, thought Amy, and maybe it was best to leave him alone for a bit. They had been together every moment of the last days, and maybe some separation would help. She got dressed to go out and took the train into the city.

The bar was a modern place serving micro-brewed beer from around the world and appetizers to match. It was full of people, and the conversation buzz and lively music made her feel good. She found Ryan easily.

"Hi, Amy, where is Jeff?"

"He decided to stay home. I think he's having a rough time."

"Yeah, I totally understand."

She looked at him.

"Think about it, Amy. He was a sheriff, so he used to rule the land, and being an old fashioned man, he probably was used to ruling over women. What can he rule here? Are you going to let him rule you?"

She shook her head. "No, but I told him what would happen when he came. He wants to be independent, and today Dr. Holbrook offered him a job. It pays well and he would be independent."

"It's not the same, Amy. In 1895, you depended on him. In 1944, you both depended on each other equally and I think he lived with that. Here, he depends on you completely. The roles have reversed."

"He says I make too many decisions for him."

"You probably do. You have to let him make his own."

"But, he doesn't know everything here. I can help him..."

Ryan raised his hand, "Stop. Hear yourself. He will make mistakes, but they will be his."

"But why must I let him make mistakes? A lot of things we take for granted are so alien to him."

"He is a grown man, Amy. And remember, you learn from mistakes."

"Okay, you have a point. Maybe you are right," she conceded.

"Say thank you, Ryan, for you sage advice," he teased.

She smiled.

"Hey, so tell me about that self defense you practice in the bedroom?"

She laughed, and they talked about other things.

When she got home, Jeff was already asleep. She snuck into bed and promised herself to be less "motherly," as Ryan had put it. She had had a good time and wondered why she had never dated Ryan. Here was someone that she had not even noticed because of her dedication to her work.

Well, now she had Jeff, she thought as she watched him sleep.

Chapter 37
Jeff

"I am going to take the offer," said Jeff as he sipped his coffee.

She knew he would, even though there had not been much conversation about the job or anything else since they had woken up. He hadn't even asked about her outing with Ryan.

"If you want this type of job," said Amy, "you should take it. I just want to say that, even if you take this job, it does not mean you are stuck with it. You can change jobs quite easily in this era; it is not for life."

There, she said it and would not say anything more about it, she reminded herself. Don't mention the other jobs, or retraining, or anything else.

"I'm taking it," he said.

She glanced at him looking so determined. "Did you still want to meet Aunt Betty for dinner tomorrow?"

"Yes."

"Good. I think she's planning a special meal for us. She is very curious about you. I told her we met in Durango during my business trip, and you've moved to the Bay Area."

"At least that is partially true," said Jeff.

When they arrived at the lab, he went to meet with Dr. Holbrook. She wanted to ask if he wanted her to come along, but she refrained. She went back to her empty, 'claustrophobic' lab. Luckily, she was soon immersed in her work.

"Amy, knock, knock," said Dr. Holbrook from the doorway. "As you know, Jeff has accepted my offer and I am thrilled. I am showing him around."

Jeff was standing next to him.

"Well, Jeff," said Dr. Holbrook, acting like a tour guide, "here we have one of our leading scientists working on one of our most promising experiments."

She forced a smile. "By the way, Dr. Holbrook, which is the next project that is scheduled for the time transport?"

"I don't know. There are a couple projects in the running. One is your friend George's."

"The 1750s."

"Correct. I hope Jeff is fully ready by then, and he can be the one to go. Why don't we go see what George is up to?" suggested Dr. Holbrook as he stepped away.

She gave Jeff a little smile as he followed Dr. Holbrook, and he barely acknowledged it.

She had to fix this thing between Jeff and her. They had been so happy before. It took her a while to get back into the work mindset, but then she started to see progress in her calculations and got busy again.

"Do you ever break for lunch?" asked a voice.

It was Ryan, and he had Jeff with him.

"Are you going to lunch?" she asked.

"We were just there," said Ryan. "Dr. Holbrook suggested I take Jeff to lunch and introduce him to the other time travel setters. There are not many of us left."

"I heard about that. When do you take the tests, Jeff?" She could have waited to talk to him at home, but she wanted to interact with him.

"I start tomorrow," said Jeff.

"Hey, I suggested to Jeff that he goes out with us tonight. A group of time setters are going to a place nearby. What do you think?" asked Ryan.

She wondered how to reply. She wanted to convey some enthusiasm for his meeting new friends, but she didn't want to sound motherly. "It's a great idea."

"Yeah, he can meet the others," said Ryan, "right, Jeff?"

"Right," said Jeff, not too enthusiastically.

"I was going to work late anyway, so I'll see you at home."

"Yeah," said Jeff and they both left.

Again, it took her a while to get back to work. Her feelings were all over the place. Her relationship with Jeff was bothering her, but her work was getting exciting. She had just discovered something.

The little yellow flower was definitely a cure for depression, as expected, but in higher doses tied with a small bit of lithium, it might be a cure for bipolar disorder. That would be fantastic, she thought. It was beyond any expectations. She set up the experiments. Then her stomach growled and she looked up at the time. It was seven. Where had the time gone? She looked around at the quiet lab. She needed to go home. In the morning, she would talk to Dr. Holbrook about getting some help.

She got home and Jeff was not there. She was a bit surprised that he had not called, but then she remembered, he did not have his own personal productive device or PPD. Tomorrow they would get one for him. He also needed to get some more clothing. He couldn't wear the same things all week; she caught herself being 'motherly' again.

Okay, food, she thought, hungry. They had purchased the old-fashioned pasta and she would have to wait for it to boil, but it wouldn't take long. In the meantime, she called Suzanna. She realized she would now always call her that.

"Hello?"

"Suzanna, it's me, Amy."

"Oh my God, are you here in 2066?"

"Yes," smiled Amy, thinking how strange that would sound to others. "Here in 2066 and here in the Bay Area."

"We have to meet. I am busy tonight, but what about tomorrow?"

"I'm taking Jeff to meet my aunt."

"Jeff is here?" Suzanna almost squealed.

"Yes, he is."

"Let me talk to him."

"He has gone out with the other time setters."

"Oh. Do be careful, some of those guys are not the best influence."

"Oh?" Amy asked, wondering how she would know.

"I see a few of them professionally, if you are wondering."

"What are you doing professionally, anyway?"

"I started my own company. The name is The Berkley Geisha."

"Geisha?"

"You know, geishas are quite similar to the saloon girls of 1895. I was so good at it so I thought, why not?"

"Wow," said Amy, not sure what else to say. "George told me you had started your own business. Do you have other employees?"

"Yes, there are three of us working at Berkeley Geisha. George is a sweetie, and he helped me get started."

"Really," said Amy and suddenly realized, "He hasn't used your services has he?"

"No, my company doesn't cater to gay men yet."

"Wait, I thought he was quite happy with his partner."

"Hey, you can be happy with a partner and still need something more. Maybe you need someone who will listen a little more, or someone to go out with when your partner is tired, or someone to dance with if your partner hates dancing."

Amy smiled. "You sound like an advertisement."

"Our ads do run along those lines. How about Thursday night? Let's get together for dinner. Are you still working at the lab?"

"Yeah, and I miss you."

"Hah, I knew you would, but I am never going back there."

"Thursday is fine with me, and I'll ask Jeff if he is available."

It must have been the way she said it, because Suzanna paused a moment. "Is something wrong with you guys?"

"No, no," said Amy. "We just got back here. It takes a while to adjust, you know."

"Yeah, and in his case, it may take longer since he has to adjust over 170 years."

They selected a place to meet, and then Amy said, "I notice you are still using the name Suzanna."

"Of course. I registered my company under that name, so I guess it will stick."

She finished dinner, and there was still no sign of Jeff. She got ready for bed and selected some entertainment while she waited. She had started to doze when suddenly there was a knock on the door. If it was Jeff, he should know the combination to the door, she thought as she went to answer.

It was Ryan and Jeff. And Jeff was hanging onto the doorway for support. He looked intoxicated.

"Greetings, fair maiden," said Ryan. "I am practicing my 1750s English, if you wonder."

"Yes, come in," said Amy.

"You look ravenous, my lady. No, maybe ravishing?" said Jeff as he shuffled in. "Maybe delicious?"

"Fine," said Amy as she led Jeff to the couch.

"Ryan," she turned ready to admonish him. He was supposed to take care of Jeff, but then she noticed he was in as bad a shape as Jeff. He was sliding down the wall, smiling goofily.

"If you put him on the couch, I guess I get the bed," he grinned. "Thank you."

"Wonderful," said Amy. There were two to take care of. She pulled Jeff up on his feet and led him to bed. She then had Ryan sit down while she flipped her desk to become a single bed.

"Ah, the guest bed" said Ryan, disappointed. "I guess I get that, but let me tell you something, Amy. I helped him home tonight because I know you love him. I knew that would make you happy."

"Yes, Ryan," she said as she put the sheets on and fluffed up a pillow.

"You know, we made it to your apartment because we came together," said Ryan. "We trust one another and took care of one another. We are true partners."

"You obviously don't take care enough," said Amy. "You should not have gotten to this point of intoxication. Ryan, just get some rest, we'll talk tomorrow."

"Aren't you going to tuck me in?" asked Ryan.

"Good night, Ryan," she said as she headed to the bedroom. Jeff was already fast asleep, fully clothed. She pulled off his shoes and then she pushed him to one side to give her just enough room so she could get into bed. Then she lay down.

Maybe it was good that Jeff and Ryan had gotten along so well, she thought. She had wanted Jeff to find a friend. Hopefully, getting drunk would be an occasional thing. That was the last thought she had before she fell asleep.

She woke up in the morning and realized Jeff was already up. He was in the bathroom. She went in and he looked at her apologetically. "Good morning, Amy, so sorry about last night."

He didn't look bad and it struck Amy that maybe he was used to drinking.

"Let's just get some breakfast," he said.

They decided on scrambled eggs and French toast. Ryan woke up soon after, and he was not fine. They could hear him cursing and moaning, and finally he came into the kitchen.

"Amy, Amy, do you have something for my head? It feels like it's going to explode."

"Yeah, let me get you something.

"How can you look so normal, Jeff?"

"I'm from the old West, I have a tough constitution."

"That is a bit scary," said Amy, returning with a vial.

"Oh good, give me that. In fifteen minutes, I will be fine again," said Ryan.

"Have some eggs and orange juice," suggested Jeff.

"I don't know how you can eat anything right now," said Ryan, looking at him.

"It is probably better than that medicine," said Jeff. "This is an ancient remedy, trust me."

"I trust my drugs," said Ryan as went to the bathroom.

"We went to the lab last night hoping to find you," said Jeff to Amy.

"What time was that?"

"Eight thirty."

"I came home before that. I was tired and wanted to eat something."

"I'll make sure to get you today for lunch."

"That would be nice. I lose track of time sometimes," she smiled at the time reference.

"Hey, Jeff, can I borrow some clothes?" Ryan shouted from the bathroom. "Otherwise, I will be very late to work."

"Excuse me, Amy," said Jeff, getting up. "I'll see what 1944 clothes will fit him."

Chapter 38
Meeting Aunt Betty

They rode the train into work, and Amy tried not to look at Ryan. Every time she did, she would start smiling, but it wasn't her fault. He looked like something from the past as he stood there stoically holding onto the handrail wearing cuffed, baggy pants, cut high on the waist and a formal dress shirt. It was a different look for Ryan.

"Amy, stop looking at him or I will get jealous," said Jeff, next to her.

"I can't help it."

"Please. I still think he should have worn the buckskin jacket."

"I'm glad you seem to be better."

"I don't know what was wrong with me. This place is not so different from 1895. The guys I went out with last night proved it. Deep down, people are the same."

She smiled at him. "You are back to being the wise man I met."

"Ah, you never told me you thought I was wise."

"Oops, I wasn't supposed to. I was afraid it might inflate your ego."

"It's too late for that, don't you think?"

"Guys, this is our stop," interrupted the man dressed in 1944 clothing.

As they walked to work, they talked about the plans for the day.

"I'm looking forward to having dinner with your aunt," said Jeff.

"We should leave a bit early to get there on time," said Amy.

"Personally, I'm glad we aren't going out tonight," said Ryan. "I am going to need at least one night to recover."

"See you at lunch, Amy," said Jeff as he and Ryan headed to their side of the building.

Amy watched them and heard the woof whistles as Ryan passed his fellow coworkers. She felt good again and tackled the experiments with renewed vigor. Later that morning, she realized there was too much to do by herself and went to talk to Dr. Holbrook.

She found him in his office and got right to the point. "Good morning, Dr. Holbrook. I need to talk to you about getting some help."

"Ah, good morning, Amy. Come in and sit down."

She did.

"Well, we have to see if we have a budget for that," he said.

"But I had help before," said Amy, not wanting to use Suzanna's name.

"I know, but that was ages ago, in financial terms," he grinned. "Right now, our efforts are in setting up the next mission."

"You mean George's project for finding a cure to lung cancer?"

"It is one of the stronger contenders. His simulations are showing very positive results."

"Are any of the projects trying to cure DID?"

"No. There is nothing we are currently testing that will help Gustav," said Dr. Holbrook, understanding whom she was talking about. "Have you visited him?"

"No. Can I?" She was not a relative.

"Yes, they let me see him. He seemed so normal; it was terrible seeing him locked up in that facility. Of course, I just had to remember how agitated he was when he arrived from 1944 to know that it is the best place for him."

He was avoiding her request. "So, it sounds like I will not be getting any help?"

"I'm sorry, but I really can't promise anything. Can we talk about this later? I have a meeting down the hall."

She could have told him about her latest findings, but they were too preliminary.

"Amy, why don't you come to this meeting," said Dr. Holbrook.

Going to meetings was the furthest from her mind. "Does it concern me?"

"More than you think," said Dr. Holbrook as he stood up and walked out the door.

Why hadn't she been invited to the meeting if it concerned her, she wondered as she followed Dr. Holbrook down the hall and into the conference room. Ryan, Jeff, George and several others were already in the conference room when she walked in.

"I invited Amy to see if she has any ideas on this subject," said Dr. Holbrook, sitting down.

What subject, she wondered, and then she saw the first page of the presentation. It was titled, 'A *different time, same results*' She took a seat, but was still puzzled.

"Okay," said George. "As you all know, my target plant was plentiful in the 1750s in England. All our efforts had been focused to then and there, but just this week, I found that podophyllum peltatum was also grown in the mid-1800s in Florida by the Seminole Indians."

She immediately was interested. This would be better for the time setters and Jeff, if he were selected to go.

"Obviously, this is a much easier time to get to," continued George. "We still have the marker in San Francisco 1895, and trains are available to cross the continent. There are ships, as well, although the trek through the Panama Canal is not recommended."

"What about all the studying we have done for the 1750s?" asked one of the time setters.

"Yes, that is a problem, but we have several time travelers with experience in 1895, and we have someone from that era with us," said George.

Everyone looked at Jeff.

"Are you familiar with Florida?" asked Dr. Holbrook.

"I have been to Florida, but did not travel much there," said Jeff. "I believe the Seminole Indians do not have a great appreciation for the white man."

"That is an understatement," said George. "When Spain ceded Florida to the United States in the early 1800s, some Seminoles left for the Bahamas and Cuba. They were afraid of becoming slaves. In fact, some slaves had been integrated into the tribe and were known as the Black Seminoles. The United States also fought three wars with the Seminoles, trying to convince them to move west."

"Did they ever leave?" asked Ryan.

"Eventually, most were convinced, but there were still some Seminoles living in Florida in 1895."

"So, the Spanish introduced the plant to Florida?" asked Amy, wondering how it had appeared in the United States from Europe.

"Yes. The Spanish were aware of some medicinal value of the podophyllum peltatum, or Mayapple, as it is also known. It was being used for snakebites, syphilis and certain tumors. They taught the Seminoles to cultivate it, but then it almost disappeared. Apparently, it did not do well with the subtropical weather. With the removal of the Seminoles from the area, the medicinal knowledge vanished."

"But you are sure the podophyllum peltatum is there in 1895?" asked Dr. Holbrook.

"Yes, near St. Augustine. I have the records," said George, looking through his files.

He was one of those old fashioned scientists who still liked paper, thought Amy. There was nothing wrong with that if you were organized, and George was. He found what he was looking for and passed the paper over to Dr. Holbrook.

"What do you think?" asked George.

"I like it," said Dr. Holbrook. "It accelerates your project. I will talk to the board and we will review the plans, but I think it should be the next one. I'll give you a decision by Friday."

"Excellent," said George.

"Should we stop learning about the 1750s?" asked Ryan.

"No, continue to do so," said Dr. Holbrook. "There are other projects in that time period and this one might still be one of them."

At lunchtime, Jeff came to get her and they ate lunch together in the cafeteria.

"Isn't this amazing," said Jeff. "Just like in 1944; you and me in a cafeteria. It's like I told you, a lot of things are the same."

"Yes, they are."

"I am a bit nervous about tonight. Your aunt is your closest relative. What if she doesn't like me?"

"I don't think she will like you," Amy shook her head. "She will love you."

He smiled. "You are so sure about things. In this case, I really hope you are right."

Aunt Betty was ecstatic to see them. "My dear, you have been away for so long." She hugged Amy tightly. She made it sound like it had been years. "Your nice friends, George and Ryan, called to tell me you were all right, but they couldn't tell me when you were coming back."

"I wasn't sure when I was coming back myself," said Amy.

"Of course now I see what was holding your interest in Durango," Aunt Betty, looking at Jeff.

They went inside and saw that dinner was ready.

"Jeff, please sit next to me," she said. As she served, she started the questions. "So, Jeff, what did you do for a living in Durango?"

"I was a sheriff, Ms. Waterman," he said.

They had decided that they would tell Aunt Betty the truth. Jeff was relieved with the decision, as he didn't have to worry about keeping all those stories straight. Amy had also decided to tell her exactly what she did for a living.

"You can call me Aunt Betty. All of Amy's friends do. Please, let's start to eat."

"You made asparagus risotto, Aunt Betty," said Amy. "I love this dish."

"I know you like it," said Aunt Betty and turned back to Jeff. "A sheriff? And you left that interesting job to come to the Bay Area?"

He smiled mysteriously.

"I see, maybe something other than a job brought you here?"

"You are right," he said.

Aunt Betty smiled. "So tell me, how did you meet?"

"I had to go to a cabin a ways out of town, and Jeff accompanied me," said Amy.

"Was it dangerous? Is that why he came with you?"

"No, Aunt Betty. It was not dangerous. He was just going my way."

"I have heard that excuse before. When I younger," started Aunt Betty and continued for a while, reliving some of her experiences.

Soon, they finished their meal and Aunt Betty started to gather the dishes. Jeff took them from her. "Let me do that, Aunt Betty."

"Oh, I couldn't," said Aunt Betty.

"Please, Aunt Betty, let him. I need to tell you something," said Amy.

Aunt Betty sank down on her chair immediately. She looked worried. Amy could imagine all the thoughts crossing her mind.

"First, I am not pregnant, and second, both Jeff and I are in good health."

Aunt Betty took a breath, "I was worried about your health. A pregnancy, on the other hand, would have been good news. I am getting older, you know."

"Okay, I am not going there. This has to do with work."

"Oh, are you thinking of changing jobs? I know some places that are hiring scientists such as yourself."

"No, please, just... You know how I am testing a yellow flower to see if it can cure depression?"

"Yes, I know that."

"Well, I got the flower in Durango in 1895."

She looked confused. "1895? Is that a store?"

"No, it is a year. I traveled through time. There are no such flowers left in Durango in 2066. I had to go back in time."

"You traveled through time? You shouldn't."

"I was not the first to do it. My company has been doing it for a while."

"BioTime," she nodded, "I get it now. Is that where you were for a month?"

"Yes."

Then it hit her. "Is he from then?"

"Yes, he is."

She looked at the kitchen, concerned, and then turned back to her. "You have fallen in love with a man that is over one hundred seventy years old?"

"He is twenty-nine," said Amy.

"No, oh my goodness, no." She got up and touched her. "You are all right?"

"Yes. The trip took a bit longer than I had expected, but I am all right."

"Are you going to do this again?"

"I don't think so."

"Good." She looked toward the kitchen again. "What about him? Is he going back?"

"No. He is going to work at BioTime and be one of the travelers."

"Oh, Amy. I am sorry you have fallen in love with a time traveler. It just cannot end well."

"Besides the job, do you like him?"

"Well a job does influence the person, but besides the job? Yes. I think he is wonderful. He is smart and charming, and I can see the attraction. But a time traveler?"

"It is just a job, Aunt Betty. He will do this for a bit and then do something else."

Chapter 39
Dinner with new Susan

"It would be a feat if your plant is a cure for bipolar," said Ryan. "When will you know?"

Ryan, Jeff and Amy were having lunch together in the company cafeteria.

"I don't know," said Amy. "I've asked for a new assistant, but Dr. Holbrook said there was no money for that. Well, I would still have to train the assistant, so that would take more time."

"Yes, but eventually the assistant would be able to help out," said Jeff. "I had the same problem training deputies."

"Did you have to train deputies often?" asked Ryan.

"Yes, some found other employment and then there were a couple who were killed."

Both Amy and Ryan looked at Jeff and didn't comment.

"Well, at least I know why Dr. Holbrook keeps me around," said Amy.

"Actually, I didn't think he would be as forgiving with the rest of us," said Ryan. "When I heard you had stunned him and wiped his memory, I thought you were out of here."

"Yeah, maybe I shouldn't have done it. But I wanted him to know how it felt to lose minutes of time. Jeff brought it to my attention."

"I didn't know I affected your thinking," smiled Jeff.

"You do, and you were absolutely right," she gazed back at him.

"Guys, let's focus, okay?" asked Ryan. "Are either of you busy tonight?"

"Yeah, we're meeting with Suzanna," said Amy.

"Suzanna," Ryan smiled. "Good ole Susan. I have heard of her new company."

"Really? So what do you think?" asked Amy.

"It sounds very interesting to me," said Ryan.

"Why don't you come with us?" asked Jeff.

Amy threw a questioning glance at Jeff. Did he really want Ryan there?

"I might go," decided Ryan.

"We're not going to her place of work, if you were thinking of meeting the other girls, Ryan," said Amy. "We are going out to dinner at Mansur's."

"Still, it may be interesting to see her again. I didn't see her when she returned from 1895. They were very quick to get her out. And Mansur's is a good place."

"We're meeting at 7:30," said Amy, resigned.

"Thanks, I'll see you then," said Ryan, leaving them.

"You don't think I should have invited him?" asked Jeff.

"It's fine. It actually may work better. You guys can talk while I catch up with Suzanna."

"That is what I thought."

"You are so right so often," she looked into his eyes.

"In a way, it is too bad we are going out tonight," he grinned.

Jeff and Amy were the first ones at the restaurant and sat at the bar to wait. The place was a mixture of South American foods with Indian overtones. Amy ordered a Pisco Sour while they studied the menu.

"I told you they would already be here." They heard Suzanna as she found them. Ryan was with her.

"Hello, hello," she said. She kissed each of them on the cheek.

"That's new," said Amy.

"It is my new way of greeting; it's Latin."

"Yeah, I kind of like that," said Ryan.

"Did you know Ryan before?" asked Amy.

"We met at BioTime. Are we ready to sit?"

"Yeah," said Amy. She noticed that Suzanna's confidence had come with her from 1895. She told the waiter they were ready

The waiter led them down a hallway that had walls of glass. Outside was a thick bamboo forest. They finally arrived at a table.

"This is fine," Suzanna told the waiter as they sat down. "It is one of the better tables," she told the others.

The glass walls surrounded three sides of the table, and Amy could see tall native California grasses and a California

Aster on the other side of the glass; there were no other tables in sight. The gurgling of water could be heard somewhere.

"Wow," said Amy, looking at the Aster next to her. "Do you come here often?" Business must be going very well for you to afford this place.

"It is one of the places that my clients prefer."

"I can see why." Ryan looked around the room.

She turned to him. "I have many well-to-do clients, and this place fits their requirements. I do get a frequent customer discount. Well, what should we order?"

"I'm not sure," said Jeff, looking at the menu.

"Let me order? Please?" asked Suzanna

"That is fine with me," said Amy.

"And I would love to see what you order," said Ryan, sitting back and studying her.

"I love a challenge," said Suzanna. "Amy, why don't you take care of the wine?"

"Sure," said Amy. She looked at the wine list while Suzanna ordered the meal. She asked for the meal to be served family style, so they could all taste the different things.

Then the plates started to arrive. They were small servings, just enough to give everyone a taste.

"Oh, this is delicious," said Amy, taking a bite of a round curried potato stuffed with avocado.

"I like your wine choice, as well," said Suzanna.

"I think I will order something more spicy for the next bottle," said Amy. "What do you think, Jeff?"

"I think I am a lucky guy," he said, staring at her.

"I think the food and wine are affecting you," said Amy.

Jeff shook his head. "I don't think that is it."

"How much do your services cost?" asked Ryan.

Amy looked at him; surprised he would ask such a thing in such a moment.

"Don't be shocked, Amy," said Suzanna. "How do you think I get more clients? It depends on what services you want, Ryan. It also depends on the level of services. For example, a companion for dinner at somewhere casual costs you less than dinner here, where your companion is expected to know the food and the wine choices. A night with dancing may actually be cheaper than dinner here. It depends. You tell us what you want, and we put together a pricing menu."

"What about sex?" asked Ryan.

"That is not a service we offer, but we can refer you to places that do."

Ryan smiled.

"You are probably already acquainted with those places," said Suzanna.

"Maybe," said Ryan.

"So they still have brothels here?" asked Jeff.

"Of course, do you want to go?" asked Ryan.

"No, I have as much as I can handle right now," said Jeff.

Amy blushed and was glad the conversation moved to other things.

Chapter 40
Jeff travels

She was back at work, but her mind was distracted. She knew that there was a meeting where they would discuss what project would be next. Jeff would be there, but she was not invited this time.

Maybe she would start writing some of the conclusions of her tests. It would change the pace of things and she had to do it anyways.

She brought up a keyboard and smiled. The letters were in the same place as that typewriter she had used, but it was so much easier now; there was no strain from pressing down the keys. And all the mistakes were corrected instantly. After the first few sentences, her mind started wandering again and she stopped. She missed Suzanna, someone with whom she could bounce ideas.

It was a bit past eleven when she could not stand it anymore and went for a walk down the hall near the conference room.

The meeting was still in progress. She could see most of the attendants through the small window next to the door. There were a couple of people she did not recognize and was wondering who they might be. Suddenly, some of the people stood up. The door swung open and people started to come out. She had nowhere to hide and froze.

"Hello. Amy," said Ryan as he passed her. "Were you snooping?"

"No, I was just passing by."

He looked at her amused.

"Okay, I was wondering how it was going," she admitted.

"We're on," he said just as George rushed by and gave her the thumbs up.

"Who..." she started to ask, but Ryan interrupted.

"Ask him yourself," he said as Jeff walked out.

She looked at Jeff, but by his smile, she knew he was one of the selected. She felt happy and worried at the same time.

"Want to go for an early lunch?" asked Jeff.

Amy nodded. There was no way she would be able to work without knowing.

"Did Ryan tell you?" he asked as they sat down with their lunch trays.

"No, but I suspect, from the way you look, that you were selected."

"Yeah. It's me and Ryan."

"The two amigos."

Jeff smiled. "That's right. I know enough Spanish to make me valuable for this mission. It is spoken in St. Augustine, you know."

"And the fact you come from that era," she added. Then, another thought came to her. "What about rule #2? The one that says you can't travel to a time when you were alive?"

"They discussed it. There is no chance I will run into myself. Younger me was living in Colorado in 1872; we will be in Florida."

She nodded, but they were breaking the rules again. "1872? Did I hear right?"

"Dr. Holbrook said that the plant had better chances of being there in 1872."

"Oh, you were six years old then."

"This part is very confusing to me," continued Jeff. "It is strange that I can exist in two places at the same time. Like Ryan says, it 'blows' my mind. Well, I don't think I will really understand how it works, but I am willing to go along with it. We leave next Friday."

He was so brave, she thought, trying not to be emotional about it.

"So? Any comments?" asked Jeff.

"I wish I could hug you," she said. "Instead, I have to be professional and just shake your hand."

"I'll take a rain check for the hug."

"Rain check? How do you know about that?"

"Ryan uses that idiom often."

"So you leave in six days? That will come very quickly," she said.

"Six days, and there is a lot to do to get ready," he smiled.

"George's project has a high probability of success. The fact that you are not going to 1750 is also a positive," she said, trying to bring up the good points.

"Will you miss me?"

"You cannot imagine how much."

Chapter 41
Taking a break

Jeff was going to go back to his time. The thought entered her consciousness and it worried her a bit. He was adapting to 2066 quickly, but once in while he seemed to miss the past times. What if he decided to stay, her mind asked, and she quickly quashed that idea.

She had to make this time a more desirable place. She knew Jeff loved the outdoors, so they took Saturday off, and she showed him a list of things they could do. Jeff picked Mount Tamalpais State Park and they took a picnic lunch. They caught the train there and then hiked. The mount is 2,500 feet, nothing in comparison to the mountains in Colorado, but it was a good hike, and she could see how it invigorated him. He was in his element.

They ended talking about his parents.

"They died within months of each other," he said. "Dad caught dysentery, and then the next month, my Mom was killed."

"Oh." She didn't know what she could say that would make that less painful than it sounded. "I am sorry."

"It's not harder than your case. At least I was able to say good-bye to them."

"What happened?"

"Dad's dysentery hit him hard and he did not last long. Mother then was left alone. One day a man came into the house to rob it. He was not expecting anyone there, and when she surprised him, he shot her. I returned from college and found her. She had lost too much blood, and there was not much I could do. It did make me change my goals in life. I became a lawman to go after men like that thief."

An experience like that would make anyone change, she thought. She wondered if he had ever found the thief.

They did spend quite a bit of time together, but it was mostly studying Florida in the 1870s. It was easier to study together. Also that weekend, her domestic assistant was finally delivered.

"In a way, it does look human," said Jeff as he studied it from all sides. It was the first time he was seeing Nix. "A smaller, rounder, metal human."

"The people that make these robots ran tests that showed if the robots looked human they were more accepted."

"Why did you name it Nix?"

"When you give it instructions, you use his name and I wanted something short. I usually refer to it as a him, it seems nicer."

She turned Nix on and introduced Jeff. She then gave Nix instructions to bring some coffee.

"It feels like having someone else with us," said Jeff.

"You'll get used to him. He is very helpful."

Nix brought out two cups of coffee. Hers was just as she liked, his was black, but Nix had brought the sugar and cream.

"You should tell Nix how you like your coffee," said Amy.

"Nix," said Jeff, "I like my coffee black."

"Yes, Jeff," said Nix in smooth voice.

Jeff smiled. "Pretty smart."

"Nix, please straighten up the kitchen," said Amy, and Nix rolled away. "George has invited us to dinner on Tuesday."

"Yes, he mentioned it to me as well. I enjoy working with him."

"Yeah, George is one of my favorite coworkers and it will be good to see Scott. I haven't seen him in a while."

"Scott is George's partner?"

"Yes. What do you think about that?"

He looked at her as if it was test.

"I just wondered, since I didn't hear much about gay people in 1895," she added.

"There were gay people, but it was illegal and punishable with jail time in Colorado. In some states, they could put you to death for sodomy, so people just didn't talk about it. In fact, a lot of gay men married women to ensure no one thought they were gay," he shook his head. "I saw many cases where those marriages harmed both partners. I think it is better to have it in the open."

"I agree. When two people love each other, why shouldn't they spend their lives together? George and Scott have been together over twelve years, I think."

"That is long; it doesn't beat the 171 years we have known each other, but it is still good."

Nix came out of the kitchen then and picked up her coffee cup. He turned to Jeff.

"I am not finished with my coffee yet," said Jeff, but as he set the cup on the table, Nix took it. Jeff managed to grab it. "Nix, no, leave the cup."

Finally, Amy convinced Nix to start the dishwasher without Jeff's cup.

"I thought he was supposed to listen to our commands," said Jeff after Nix left.

"Yeah, he is supposed to."

Chapter 42
The next mission

Jeff started his intensive training alongside Ryan, and he passed all the physical and mental tests easily. They trained in weapons of the time and reviewed their Spanish, and then they started to learn the details of their target time, including the culture and customs. That was easier for Jeff, having lived closer to that time.

During the week, Amy joined them whenever they could break for lunch.

"I'm jealous. It took me weeks to learn what Jeff already knows," said Ryan.

"I think that may be the only benefit of having been born in the 1866," said Jeff as he munched on his turkey and cheese on dark rye. It had become his favorite sandwich, thought Amy.

"Well, I am coming to the limit on trips I can take," said Ryan. "I will just be allowed five more. I don't know if I will stay at BioTime if I can't travel. I'm not a scientist."

That's right, she suddenly realized. She had been so busy with her yellow flower; she had not followed up on finding the reason why time travel was making the travelers ill.

Days were going by, and she had done nothing about it. She needed to, especially now that Jeff was going. Someone should have been looking into it, and she wondered why she had not heard anything about it. Dr. Holbrook should have been on it.

"Amy, you are miles away," said Jeff.

"Miles maybe, but in the same time zone," she smiled, and they laughed. There was no point in making them worried; they had enough on their plate.

She looked for Dr. Holbrook after lunch, and Beebe directed her to a conference room. "You might catch him before the meeting starts," she said as she looked at the clock.

Amy hurried and entered the conference room. Dr. Holbrook was alone. She went in and sat down next to him.

"Amy? I don't think you were invited to this meeting," he said. "Did I miss something?"

"No, Dr. Holbrook. I wanted to catch you before your meeting," she said.

"Can't it wait?"

"No. I don't think so."

"Go ahead then."

"Has anyone been looking into the personality disorders that the time travel setters have been experiencing?"

"Yes, and there is no link. Anthony was just over-tired, and Gustav has been diagnosed with DID, just like you thought."

"Couldn't the stress of time travel have brought some of this on?"

"No. I don't think so."

"So nothing is being done to test the other travelers?"

"Two people do not make a statistically valid sample, Amy. You should know that."

"And, you didn't want to run simulations to verify this?"

"I don't have the manpower for this. Amy, please. I know why you are asking. You are concerned about Jeff and that is very sweet, but you should be concentrate on the new, exciting work you are doing."

"I am concentrating on that, but someone should be looking into this," she said forcefully. She wasn't being 'sweet' and kind of resented being called that.

A couple of other scientists were about to enter the room and paused, wondering if they should continue in.

"Well, you have traveled through time," said Dr. Holbrook. "Do you feel different?"

"No. But could I tell if I have changed?"

Dr. Holbrook looked at her. "Actually, you have changed. You have become more aggressive. Maybe you were always that way, but the Amy I knew would not barge in here and make demands. I also don't think she would have shot me."

"I am sorry about that." She knew that incident would come up.

"You know why I keep you here?"

She glanced at him and shook her head slightly. She had wondered.

"You are a good worker. You are smart and you work hard. That is what keeps you here. I don't think that has changed. Now please, I have to start this meeting."

And she was 'sweet,' she thought, as he told everyone to come in and take a seat.

Chapter 43
Dinner with George

"Welcome, welcome," said George as he opened the door. "It is nice to see both of you."

They stepped into his large apartment. It was located not far from hers, and they had walked over.

"It looks like you have redecorated," said Amy.

"Not too recently. Maybe it has been some time since you were here?" asked George.

"It has been a couple of months. I guess you didn't invite me," smiled Amy.

"I told him that," said Scott, emerging from the kitchen. Introductions were made, and Amy followed Scott back into the kitchen.

"Something smells wonderful," she said. "Of course, I would expect nothing else, Scott."

"Thank you, Amy, and what a handsome man you've found," he said as he started putting the food on several platters. "George forgot to mention that. No wonder they have been working late."

She looked at Scott.

"Kidding, just kidding."

He better be, thought Amy. "What are you making?" she asked. Scott was a chef at a San Francisco restaurant.

"Something South American with Indian accents."

"Amazing," said Amy. She told him about the Mansur's menu.

"I have not been there in a while. That must be their new menu."

"They serve a selection of dishes, which we were able to share. Everything ranged from good to very delicious."

"They are doing a small plate sharing option? They stole that from us. Have you been to La Crema Malai recently?"

"No. My budget does not usually allow me to go to places like La Crema Malai or Mansur's."

"I am going to give you a gift certificate right now," he said as he went to the desk. "I want you to check my place out. If you like it, spread the word."

"I have a friend who may want to take her clients there."

"Clients?"

"Are you talking about Suzanna?" asked George, joining them in the kitchen.

"Yes," said Amy.

"We can continue our conversation at the table," said Scott. "The food is ready."

Amy loved coming to visit these guys. One could tell that they had been around each other for many years. They sometimes finished each other's thoughts, and they helped each other without even using words. The food was also very good.

She sat down and Scott placed a dish in front of her.

"This looks beautiful. I feel so spoiled," she said.

"That is our goal. To make you feel like a queen and a king in medieval times," said George. "Even if we are not going there anymore."

Jeff had been placed opposite her, and he smiled at her.

"Well, let's have a toast," said Scott. "To my wonderful husband and to the best project in the world, which will become a reality soon. No offense, Amy."

She smiled, "None taken."

"So, we are extremely fortunate to have you came onboard, Jeff," said George. "There is nothing like having an expert of the era with us, and your knowledge of Florida is impressive."

"A lot of that knowledge is from studying the material you gave me. I also have to give credit to Amy, since we have been studying together."

"How modest you are, Jeff. But, studying together does bring you closer to each other," said Scott.

"Is that how you two met?" asked Jeff.

"No," said Scott. "He came to the restaurant with some other guy. I caught his eye and saw there was mutual interest. Then I served him something special, and the rest is history."

"I had no chance," admitted George.

"Well, if what you served was anything like this, I can understand," said Amy.

Scott beamed with the compliments and asked, "So, Jeff, you are leaving Friday. Are you ready?"

"Yes, we will be ready," said Jeff.

Amy didn't say anything, but she was thinking that Friday was coming too fast.

"Don't worry, Amy. We are becoming old hands at this time travel," said George.

"I guess you're right, George, although I do have a question," said Amy. "Why did you change the date to 1872?"

"That is a good question, but I don't know the answer," said George. "I didn't make the change. Dr. Holbrook sprang that on me."

"It just doesn't make sense to me. Someone has to take the transport marker twenty-three years back. It adds about eight days of three-year regressions. Why would he want that additional work if the plant was available in 1895?"

"Five trips in five days. Dr. Holbrook says they can speed up the process, and now we can go back five years in one day. But, you are right, I am sure the Mayapple would have been there in 1895."

As they walked home that evening, Jeff commented on the conversation. "It seems you were quite interested in the year change. Is there something bothering you?"

"I worry about everything, especially anything concerning you," said Amy. "Of course, 1872 is not 1750, and I am relieved with that, but it would be nice to find out why Dr. Holbrook changed the target date."

"I was kind of looking forward to the 1750. I had started weapon training with swords and was getting good at it."

She shook her head. "That's not going to help you in 1872. Just remember your stun gun."

Chapter 44
The mental illness

The couple of days before the trip flew by. Jeff was busy with his training, and Amy returned to her project, but her conversation with Dr. Holbrook was still bothering her. She took some time off during the week to visit Gustav.

"Are you his sister?" asked the woman in reception when she arrived at the sanatorium.

"No, just a friend."

"Oh, when he was first admitted, he mentioned a sister and it sounded like someone like you."

She had been his sister in 1944, and that might have confused him. "I also worked with him."

"Well, any visitor is probably welcome for him. Another of his coworkers was coming, but I have not seen her lately."

She briefly wondered who that might have been, but then they entered a large room and she saw Gustav facing the window. Most of the other patients were busy with some task or another, but he was immobile as he stared out into the garden.

She felt sorry for him. Maybe she shouldn't have come, she thought, but it was too late. The woman was already announcing her to him.

"Hello, Gustav," she smiled.

He turned and smiled back. "Amy. I am so glad to see you. Have you come to take me home?"

"No, I, ah, just came to visit."

The disappointment changed him. "Well, now that you have seen me, you can go."

"Do you want me to leave?"

He thought about it for a while. She could almost see the struggle happening inside him. It was terrible.

"No, I don't," he said in a calm voice. "I appreciate you coming, but one of the others doesn't want you here."

He was aware of the others, she thought. That had to be progress. "How are you doing? Are you feeling better?"

"I never felt sick. I don't know why they brought me here." He looked at her and then whispered, "I am perfectly fine."

"This place seems quite nice, very relaxing."

"It's a place for crazy people, Amy"

"No," she said, much too quickly. "It's a place where people can get better. Have you made any friends?"

He smirked. "I don't want to make friends here. What is the point? I will be out soon."

She didn't want to contradict him.

"Tell me," he asked. "How is work? Do they miss me?"

"Yes, a lot of people do miss you," she nodded, and started telling him general things about work. She didn't tell him anything about the limits on travel or how Jeff was one of the time setters. There was no point.

After a while he seemed to lose interest, and she felt it was time to go.

"Thank you for coming," said Gustav. "Will you come again?"

"Yes, I will. Do you need anything?"

"I want my freedom." He looked into her eyes.

She looked back, and he seemed perfectly rational. "I'm sure it will be soon."

"Promise me you will come to visit again," he held onto her hand.

"Of course, Gustav."

"Beebe also promised, but she has not come back. I trusted her and look what happened," he said and let her hands go.

As she walked out, she felt drained. It had been hard to see Gustav like that, but she continued with the next planned visit; which was to see Anthony. This visit was bit trickier, since she had to go to his home. She knocked on the door and waited.

A woman opened the door. "Yes?"

Amy introduced herself. "I worked with Anthony and I was wondering if I could visit him."

"I don't think he wants to talk to anyone from work. I think it brings bad memories."

"Oh," she said. She couldn't very well barge in and ask questions.

"Amy, is that you?" asked a voice from inside.

"Yes, Anthony it is me."

"Come in, girl."

The woman let her in.

Anthony introduced his sister, and she went back to the kitchen. "Hey, I'm glad to see you. I didn't know you made it back."

She glanced in the direction of his sister, wondering how much she knew.

"She knows everything," said Anthony. "I had to tell her so she could help me recover."

"I heard you were ill. What happened?"

"I don't know. One day I was fine and the next, I just couldn't face another minute at work."

"Is it because I got shot?"

"No. As traumatic as that was to you, I have seen violence before during my travels. No, I just couldn't face time traveling anymore. I couldn't sleep," he added softly.

"Lack of sleep can cause anxiety," said Amy.

"I didn't know if I was here or there. I didn't know what was real. What if I woke up and everything I thought was real was just in another time, or a dream? That also causes the anxiety."

She nodded. She could understand that.

"In any case, I was slowing down. Somehow, the travel affected me more than the others, except for Gustav, of course, poor guy."

"He was diagnosed with dissociative identity disorder, and they say he must have had it for some time."

"Yeah, but I still think it strange how it suddenly flared up. Look at me, I was not one to be afraid before and now I worry about sleeping. I am convinced that traveling through time does something to you."

She had the same suspicion, but without facts, she didn't know what to tell him.

"Hey, did your boyfriend come over with you?"

She smiled. "My boyfriend?"

"Okay, so the term is old fashioned, but did he?"

"Yes, he did. He got a job with BioTime. He has become a time travel setter."

Anthony's face turned dark. "Make sure he is careful. I heard that they are limiting the trips to twelve times. Has anyone reached that number of trips?"

"A couple of the guys are very close."

"I tell you, it sneaks up on you."

"I am worried about it. So, there were no telltale signs?"

"No. I was the same."

"I don't agree," said his sister. She was standing by the door. "He did become more irritable, and he was waking up at night a lot more."

"I already told her about sleep," grumbled Anthony.

"Well, thanks a lot for your help," said Amy as she stood up.

"So you came to visit me because you're worried about your boyfriend?" asked Anthony as he also stood up. "I guess that is nice, but what are you going to do?"

"If the time travel machine is hurting people, it should be fixed. That works for my boyfriend and anyone else traveling through time."

"Hmm," said Anthony. "It's too late for me."

The evening before the trip, Jeff brought Ryan for dinner. Amy wanted to treat them to something they would not get on their trip, so she made Chinese stir-fry.

When they sat down for dinner, Jeff toasted to a successful trip.

"Good wine, Amy," said Ryan. "It is just as good as the one we had at Mansur's."

"Thanks. It comes from a small winery not far from here. I like how they blended three types of grapes."

"With your knowledge, you could join Suzanna's company, you know."

"Are you suggesting I leave my job at BioTime?" asked Amy.

"Suzanna pays better, and the perks seem nice. You get to eat in places like Mansur's. I think you would fit right in with the other 'geishas'," said Ryan.

Jeff's eyebrows raised, but he did not say anything.

"You are wrong, Ryan. I am not much for making trivial conversation. In any case, I think the work I am doing is very important."

"Just kidding, of course," said Ryan. "I heard Dr. Holbrook came to visit you yesterday."

"News does get around," said Amy. "He was disappointed in my progress, or lack thereof. I took the afternoon off."

"Why don't you tell Ryan where you went," suggested Jeff.

She nodded. "I visited Gustav and Anthony. I'm trying to determine if the Temporal Transporter is causing mental problems."

"You think it is?" Ryan looked concerned.

"I don't know, and like Dr. Holbrook mentions often, two people does not make a valid sample."

"So he's going to wait around until someone else gets ill?" asked Ryan.

"He might, but I'm not going to wait. I started running simulations to see if there is any problem. I am doing it in my spare time, Dr. Holbrook doesn't know about this."

"I am concerned about that," said Jeff. "Do you think Amy might get fired for that?"

"She didn't get fired for stunning her boss, I don't think she will for this," Ryan smiled. "I propose a toast to Amy, who will be here in 2066 watching out for us."

Jeff lifted his glass, "To Amy."

"And I toast to both of you. I hope you keep each other safe and come back successful." And still healthy, she added quietly.

Chapter 45
The GovTime partners

The day of their departure, Jeff and Ryan were busy with final preparations while she stayed in her lab pretending to work. She was too distracted to think of new experiments or to test out new theories. Once they were gone, she would have time, she reasoned. Thirteen days was plenty of time.

The marker in San Francisco had already been moved back to 1892 and the plan was to take the cross continental train to Washington DC, and then take another train down to Florida. Not too much before 1892, the railway system was not as extensive, and then it would take longer to get to their destination. It was best to arrive in Florida in 1892 and from there, proceed back in time the twenty additional years. That would take another four days at the new rate of five years back per day.

Those additional jumps would bring Ryan to his twelfth trip, and he would be done as far as his time setter job.

They were carrying a transport marker to leave in Florida, and they would use that to get back. In fact, Dr. Holbrook was quite adamant they should leave the marker in St. Augustine.

Amy thought that was a bad idea. The range of the marker was 800 kilometers and most of that would cover areas out in the ocean. That would make it not too usable, but no one mentioned it, and she wasn't going to bring it up now, since Dr. Holbrook was not too pleased with her.

She looked out the window of her lab and saw Dr. Holbrook receiving a couple of guests near the entrance. It was a man and a woman. Amy remembered seeing them in the conference room at the meeting when George's project was chosen.

It was soon afterwards that Dr. Holbrook brought them by her lab to introduce them. "Amy, this is Jack Chase and Linde Dunne. They work for the GovTime, the government agency that has their own Temporal Transporter."

She shook both their hands.

"I was just telling them of the wonderful research you have done with the corydalis curvisiliqua," said Dr. Holbrook.

"You were gone for about a month, right?" asked Jack.

"Yes," said Amy, thinking that had nothing to do with her research.

"You didn't notice any unusual effects when you came back?"

"No, I didn't," she said, wondering if maybe she should have.

"That's good," said Linde.

Amy thought it a strange comment. Was it strange to feel all right? Were they seeing something else in their machine? "How often are you sending people to the past?"

"Oh, that is confidential, but I can tell you, we are running it more often than BioTime is," said Linde.

"Do you have the same time travelers making the trips?" she asked.

"We have a group of fifteen, and we cycle through them," said Jack looking at her carefully.

"Amy is concerned that the Temporal Transporter might have some negative effect on our time travelers," said Dr. Holbrook.

"Hmm," said Jack thoughtfully. "Have you seen a connection?"

"No, of course she hasn't," said Dr. Holbrook, answering for her. "You know about the two cases where our travelers had to be removed from projects, and it had nothing to do with the Temporal Transporter."

She wasn't going to say anything in front of his guests. Technically, he was correct, they had not made a connection yet.

"But you think otherwise?" asked Jack.

She didn't want to get in more trouble with her boss. "As Dr. Holbrook says, two people do not make a statistically valid sample."

"And that is absolutely right," said Linde.

"So you have not noticed anything unusual with your time travelers?" she just had to ask.

"You know, everything carries risk with it," replied Linde. "Even your commute to work has an element of risk in it. We just can't let it stop us from moving forward or else you could have paralysis by analysis."

"And that is true," beamed Dr. Holbrook. "Well, we best be on our way. We'll see you at the launch, Amy."

"Good luck with your flower," said Jack as they walked away.

Interesting, she thought; they had not answered her question.

The following day, she was missing Jeff already and found herself going into work. She knew that Dr. Holbrook would be talking to the guys over the ComLink and wanted to hear their voices. She had heard that both had arrived in San Francisco, but that was all. Today, she was hoping there would be more details.

The departure had gone well, and there had been many spectators watching them leave. It was only the second project, after all. There was an air of celebration as the other scientists could see progress being made and that it could translate into their project being the next one selected.

Right before Jeff left, she had managed to sneak him into a conference room to get some alone time.

Jeff was looking forward to the transport. "You know I will not be gone long. Just think of me as riding out to the plains on assignment. I used to be gone two weeks quite often as a sheriff, just me and my horse."

"Yes, but this time, instead of a horse, you will be with Ryan."

He laughed.

She loved to hear him laugh. "Just be careful all right?"

"I always am, Amy. You don't live in 1895 very long if you aren't."

"Yeah, sorry. I worry."

"It's all right, I like that someone worries."

They hugged for a while until Beebe, who had been sent to find them, found them.

"I'm glad to see you at work, Amy," said Dr. Holbrook when she got to work.

"Good morning, Dr. Holbrook."

"I already talked to Jeff and Ryan."

"Already?" she was disappointed she had missed the call.

"They were in a hurry to catch the train."

"That would be the California Zephyr to Chicago," she said.

"Yes, that's right." He looked at her, "They sounded fine."

"Good."

"They will call when they get to Washington DC. They have several hours while they change trains there, but that will be in four days. I'll let you know if you like."

He was being nice again. "Thank you, Dr. Holbrook, I would like that."

"Amy, I know you are concerned about this whole issue of sickness from time travel, but I want to let you know that I would be all over it if I saw any evidence in that regard. I look at the bottom line, but people are always first for me. You understand?'

"Yes, Dr. Holbrook." She hoped that was true.

"So are we all right?"

"Of course."

"How is your experiment going?"

"I have finished testing the corydalis curvisiliqua and it is as predicted, and even better. Some of side effects we were worried about are not there when synthesizing the medicine from the actual plant."

"Wonderful. That is wonderful. Have you started on the report?"

"I am working on that."

"This is very exciting," said Dr. Holbrook. "I will schedule the clinicians to start running their tests next... Does Thursday sound all right?"

"Yes." She would have plenty of time now that Jeff was not there.

"That means that in as soon as six months, we could start human pilot trials," said Dr. Holbrook, eyes lit up as he envisioned the path the drug would take to finally reach the market. "By 2069, your drug will be in the hands of consumers."

Amy knew that with the use of simulations, animal testing was no longer required, and the old phase I of clinical trials that tested the drug for human safety was no longer needed. In addition, due to advances in pharmacological testing tools, the time that an experimental drug took to go from lab to patient had been shortened to three years from the usual fifteen in the 2010s.

Dr. Holbrook came over and shook her hand. He was obviously filled with emotion and she liked him then. "Thank you, Amy."

He left the lab. She had not told him about the other things she had found. She had decided that the possible good news, of the drug possibly working on other diseases, might wait a bit. Maybe she would need that news when he found she was doing her own testing.

Chapter 46
Jack confesses

It was five days since Jeff had left, and she looked forward to talking to him. Dr. Holbrook had told her the call was scheduled around ten, but she wanted to make sure she was there and went to work earlier than usual.

Work was progressing well and she would be finished with her report in time, even with the surreptitious simulations she was running. So far, she had found nothing to indicate why the travelers were getting sick. Maybe Dr. Holbrook was right and there was nothing there.

She arrived at Dr. Holbrook office a bit after nine. She wasn't sure if the call would be from his office or if he had reserved a conference room.

"Hi, Beebe, is he in?"

"He is, but he is busy."

Through opaque glass Amy could see the forms of several people seated. "Do you know if he is making the call from here or a conference room?"

"Sorry, I don't know that. You can ask him. His guests should be leaving soon."

"Guests?"

"Those people from the government."

"Jack Chase and Linde Dunne?"

"Yep. I don't trust them one bit," said Beebe softly. "I don't know why they come so often."

"That is a good question," she said. She had thought of returning to her lab, but now decided to stay.

"Hey, Amy, what do you think about the mental illness from time traveling?"

"I don't know, Beebe. I think we are getting closer to figuring it out."

"Really? I didn't realize anyone was working on that," she said.

"I am sure it is just a matter of time before we figure it out," said Amy, wondering if she should tell her about her secret experiments.

"Oh, that's good news," said Beebe, but she looked worried.

Maybe she was worried about Gustav, thought Amy. "I went to visit Gustav and he seems to be better. I also saw that you went to visit him..." The door to the office swung opened and she stopped speaking.

Beebe had become pale. Amy hadn't meant it as a bad thing, but before she could say anything more, Dr. Holbrook saw her. "Hello, Amy," he said as Jack and Linde followed him out.

"Hello, Dr. Holbrook, I was wondering about the call. Where do you want to do it?"

"We can do it from my office," he said.

Jack and Linde said hello to her and then Jack asked, "Any news on the flower front?"

"I am writing the report right now," said Amy.

"Good, I hope we can see it soon," said Linde. "You know, as one of the partners, we get access to all of it."

She had an air of entitlement that rubbed Amy the wrong way. "I am sure Dr. Holbrook will give it to you," she said as she decided to fill the report with technical lingo.

"I'll walk out with you," said Dr. Holbrook, and Linde went with him. Jack lagged behind and when they were out the door he asked, "Can I talk to you?"

"Sure, go ahead," said Amy.

Jack looked at Beebe, "In private, please."

"Use Dr. Holbrook's office," said Beebe.

They went inside and he closed the door.

"What are you hiding, Amy?"

"What are you talking about?"

"We know you went to visit Gustav at the sanatorium."

"Of course I went to visit him. We worked together and he is ill. He does not have family here."

"I need you to tell me if you have found anything that might affect the travelers."

"I have not, have you?" she went on the offensive. "I think you are hiding something from us. You said GovTime is making more trips than us. What have you found?"

He didn't answer.

290

"Look, Jack, all I have are suspicions right now, but I have no proof. Together, we might have better chances of figuring this thing out. Why don't you want to?"

"Those are the same words Dr. Holbrook used when he needed our help with the time current issue; the one that was making two travelers end up in different places."

"And what did Dr. Holbrook give you in return?"

He smiled. "That is classified."

"You know what? I think it will be impossible to work with you. I'm leaving."

"Okay, wait." He studied her for a long moment. "We have seen a problem."

She waited quietly, barely breathing, so as not to discourage him.

"One of our travelers is suffering from bipolar disorder."

"Interesting," said Amy. "Both bipolar and depression can be caused by the brain's chemical imbalance."

"I know."

"Are you using the same psych tests we are to vet out the travelers?"

"Yes, the newer, more rigid ones."

"How many trips did he have before he got ill?"

"Eight."

"Shit."

"Yeah, only eight."

"Ryan is on his seventh trip," she said worried. "When they go back twenty years and come back home, it will be twelve trips all together."

"That is not good. We have to find a solution for this. We can't spend all the time and money training a person for only eight trips."

All she could think of was having Ryan affected by the time travel. Which mental disease would he get? How could they prevent it? Through the door she saw the form of Dr. Holbrook waiting outside.

"I have to tell him," she said.

Jack sighed. "Yeah, I thought you would."

"We can't have more people getting ill. By the way, I am running simulations to see if the brain is affected by time travel," she confided. "He doesn't know, but I'll let you know if I find something."

"I knew you were up to something. Telling you this has probably cost me my job, but I too am worried about the guys traveling."

What could she say? He was doing the right thing.

"Well, I hope you can find the solution," he said as he opened the door and walked by Dr. Holbrook.

"What was that about?" asked Dr. Holbrook, coming into his office.

"One of the time travelers in the GovTime machine has a mental illness," said Amy, and she told him the details.

"Interesting," said Dr. Holbrook. "Those illnesses are related."

"Yeah, I said the same. Bad thing is, Ryan is on his seventh trip."

"They will be calling soon. Let's not tell them right away. It will not help, and Ryan has to make the trip back."

It was one of the few times she actually agreed with Dr. Holbrook. "But how about traveling back to 1872?"

The ComLink started up and they heard Ryan talking. Dr. Holbrook did not answer her.

"Hey, is anyone out there?" asked Ryan.

"Hello, Ryan, this is Dr. Holbrook, and I have Amy with me."

"Good, I will tell my mopey companion."

"Mopey?" asked Dr. Holbrook. "Why is that? Is Jeff all right?"

"Nothing to worry about. I think he's missing Amy."

They heard some rustling and then Jeff was on the line. "Amy?"

"Jeff, hello."

"How are you doing?"

"I miss you," she said, thinking this was the most personal she could be with Dr. Holbrook standing next to her.

"I miss you too, but the good thing is that the trip is half over," said Jeff.

"Great way to look at it," said Dr. Holbrook butting in. "Any problems?"

"No, the train ride went well, and we're supposed to catch the next train to Florida this evening," said Ryan. "We'll be getting into St Augustine late tomorrow. Then we will start jumping back."

"No, don't do that," said Dr. Holbrook.

"What? I don't think I heard you correctly," said Ryan.

"Go to St. Augustine, but do not jump back, Ryan."

"Why not? Has there been a change?" asked Ryan.

"I do not think it is necessary for you to go back to 1872. George has convinced me you will be able to find a good specimen in 1892. You have the parameters of the plant, don't you?"

"Well, yes, we do," said Ryan, clearly confused by this change in plans.

"You should be pleased. This will cut the days you will be gone," said Dr. Holbrook.

When they disconnected the ComLink, Amy turned to Dr. Holbrook. "Did George really convince you?"

"He has been trying to convince me," said Dr. Holbrook.

"But you're worried about the extra time travel for Ryan, aren't you?"

Dr. Holbrook nodded.

"If you don't mind me asking, why did you want to go back to 1872?"

He shook his head and didn't answer.

Chapter 47
A new assistant

The following day, Amy almost bumped into Jack and Linde as they rushed into the building. Linde barely registered her, but Jack eyes acknowledged her. They headed straight to Dr. Holbrook's office. Amy waited a moment and then followed, wondering what the great hurry was about.

"I just can't believe you would change the plans," she heard Linde say as she walked by Dr. Holbrook's office.

"It had to be done," said Dr. Holbrook. "For our project, there is no need to go further back. We can still get the plant and..." The door closed and Amy was not able to hear the rest.

Looks like trouble in paradise, thought Amy as she went back to her lab. She wasn't there long before Dr. Holbrook called her. When she walked into his office, she noticed that Linde was gone, but Jack was still there.

"Dr. Holbrook?"

"Sit down, Amy. Apparently you two have caused some problems," said Dr. Holbrook, looking at Jack and her.

She glanced at Jack, but he was busy looking elsewhere.

"He lost his job," said Dr. Holbrook.

"I am sorry, Jack. I can't believe they would rather put people at risk. I think you did the right thing."

"I think so, but Linde said I had betrayed our mission and her trust. She was doing nothing to address the problem."

"Linde also indicated some of our funding may be cut," said Dr. Holbrook.

"Sir, I know that was already in the works," said Jack. "They feel our Temporal Transporter is running well and there is no need to partner with yours."

"Well, I was worried this was coming," said Dr. Holbrook. He looked at Amy. "Jack told me you have been running simulations to find the reason for the illnesses."

"Yes," she said. Maybe Jack did talk too much, she thought.

"What have you found?"

"Nothing yet. I have not been able to dedicate much time to it."

"Are you finished with the corydalis curvisiliqua analysis?"

"I should be finished with the report today."

"Then you'll have time to work on that."

She nodded. It sounded like he was sanctioning her work.

"Jack can help you."

It caught both of them by surprise.

"Sir?" asked Jack.

"You need a job, and she has been asking for an assistant," said Dr. Holbrook. "I believe your background is in biology analysis, so you could help her. What do you think, Amy?"

"I do need the help."

"So, when can you start, Jack?"

"I need to go back to the office and clear my things out. I could start tomorrow?"

"That would be fine," said Dr. Holbrook.

"Thank you, sir," said Jack.

"By the way, everyone here calls me Dr. Holbrook."

She finished her report before lunch, ate at her desk and then started running the simulations to find how the Temporal Transporter was causing mental instability.

"Hello, Amy." Dr. Holbrook was standing at the door of her lab. "How are things?

He usually never came to visit unless it was a tour, but she felt things had changed between them. Maybe stunning him with her gun had made him a better person.

"I just sent you the report," she said.

"So you are working on the illness simulation now?"

She nodded as she tried to get back to her work.

"Maybe we should find a better name for this project."

"That is a good idea," she said, knowing he was good at such things.

"I sometime wish I was down here working on actual experiments instead of managing them."

Oh no, she thought. Was he going to try to help her? It would probably add more time to the project.

"Of course, someone has to overlook everything and it might as well be me."

"Yes. Without a manager to oversee all the projects, it would be chaos," said Amy a bit too enthusiastically.

295

"I hope Jack will work out. I do think he will be a good fit, don't you?"

He had never asked her opinion before. With Suzanna, he had let her interview her, but it seemed she had already been picked as her new assistant. "It was nice of you to hire him." She stopped working to look at him.

"I don't make decisions to be nice," he said. "You should know that."

She wasn't sure how to answer.

"You needed help, and he is qualified to help you."

"Yes, Dr. Holbrook."

"I won't take any more of your time, but it was nice to have this chat."

By the end of the day, he had come up with a name for her project. It would be referred to as TTR - Temporal Transporter Refinement. There was nothing negative about it.

It was fine with Amy, who was too busy to care.

Chapter 48
Problems in Florida

It had been almost six days since Ryan and Jeff had left. Late the previous evening, they had arrived in St. Augustine. They called from their room in the boarding house the following morning.

Amy was in Dr. Holbrook's office waiting to hear from them. Jeff sounded great, but Ryan sounded tired.

Ryan said he needed to do something before they headed out to search for the Mayapple and left the call.

Then, Dr. Holbrook found that he had to go talk to Beebe about something and that left Amy alone with Jeff.

"So are you really okay?" she asked.

"Yes, I am, but there is something bothering me. I didn't want to say anything in front of Dr. Holbrook, but maybe you can check it out. When the train arrived in St. Augustine, there were a couple of well-dressed men waiting. I thought they were expecting someone from the train, but after they saw Ryan and me, they left. I didn't think about it much, but later I went out for a walk, and there they were, across the street from the boarding house."

"Did you talk to them?"

"Actually, I did. I pretended to be a tourist and asked some questions. They knew their stuff, but you remember how I teased you about speaking differently when we first met? Well, these guy sounded different to me; they talked like you."

"That is strange. Only the people from BioTime know you are in St. Augustine. Why would anyone else care?" asked Amy, wondering if Jeff was being too paranoid.

"I agree, but you know my suspicious nature has saved me before, and these men were not from around here."

"I'll try to check it out, but it is probably nothing. In any case, you should have George's plant tomorrow and then return."

"Yeah. How are things going with you? Did you finish your report?"

"It's all done." She wasn't going to tell him what she was working on yet. "I have a new assistant."

"Great. I'm glad you got someone to help you out."

"I think you met him before. He worked at GovTime and his name is Jack."

There was silence on the other end, and then Jeff said, "That's interesting, why would he come work with us?"

"I'll tell you later," she looked out the office door as Dr. Holbrook headed back into his office. "Dr. Holbrook is back."

"Jeff, there is nothing more, but give us a call after you get the plant," said Dr. Holbrook.

They disconnected the link.

"I better get back to the Temporal Transporter Refinement project," Amy had to grin at the mouthful.

Dr. Holbrook stopped by her lab that evening.

"Amy, you are still here. How did Jack work out today?" asked Dr. Holbrook.

"Good, he's also still here. He just went to get some coffee."

"Nice to see he's so dedicated."

"Dr. Holbrook, I'm glad you stopped by, something Jeff said has me concerned." She told him about the two men. "Jeff is suspicious about things, so he might be overreacting, don't you think?" Amy smiled.

Dr. Holbrook didn't smile; in fact, he looked alarmed.

"But, no one knows they are there," said Amy.

"You are wrong, some do know," he said softly.

"You mean GovTime? But why would they care about George's plant?"

Dr. Holbrook thought for a while. "It's not the plant, it is the transport marker."

"I don't understand."

"You know I have allowed them to use our transport markers, right?"

She nodded. She had heard about it, although not from Dr. Holbrook.

"While you were gone in 1944, they used our facilities to send people back several times, even though their own facility was functioning. They wanted to use our transport markers, since ours go back many years. For example, the marker in San Francisco in 1895 has been used several times by them.

And I believe the new marker, the one in 1892, was used by them just days before Jeff and Ryan traveled."

"Why?"

"They don't tell me everything. I am not that kind of partner, and lately I have even less informed about their decisions."

His breakup with Francine might also have influenced that. "And it won't be any better now that you hired Jack."

"Yeah. Anyway, it was they who wanted the transport marker placed in 1872. It was easy for us to do, so I decided, why not win some good will with them?"

"You were combining George's mission with theirs," said Amy.

He nodded. "Of course, when I found about the travel illness, I could not allow Ryan to make any more trips. For our mission to succeed, we can do it from 1892. They will have to get to 1872 on their own."

"But they are already in 1892 in Florida. It should be easy for them to go back from there."

"They don't have a transport marker. In fact, the one Jeff and Ryan took is the last one available for a while. The manufacturer of them has had some problem supplying them."

"So that's why they want ours," said Amy, understanding. "Wait." She had a terrible thought. "If they take ours, Jeff and Ryan won't be able to come back."

"Right. I mean, eventually they will. We will get more transport markers made, and we still can get to San Francisco and work our way to Florida just as they did, but it will take a while."

"We have to warn Jeff and Ryan right away," she said.

"That is what I'm thinking; let's give them a call," he looked at the time. "They should be back from looking for the plant."

Amy followed him to his office.

He started up the ComLink, but no one answered.

"That's unusual, let's wait a moment," said Dr. Holbrook, sitting in his chair.

Amy took a seat opposite him. She realized they never discussed things other than work and there was nothing to say as they waited.

"Might as well try again," he said after a few minutes.

"Good idea," she said, thinking that anything would be better than the awkward silence.

Jeff answered.

"Hello, Jeff," said Dr. Holbrook.

"This is not a good time," said Jeff.

"What's happening," said Amy, worried that they had already lost the marker.

"Ryan is very ill. I think it is dysentery."

Jeff would know that, since his father had died from it, thought Amy.

"I hate to add to your problems," said Dr. Holbrook, "but you were right to be suspicious about those men you saw. They could be military from 2066. They want to take your transport marker."

There was silence from the other side as Jeff digested the information then he asked, "Why?"

"They want to get to 1872, and GovTime does not have a marker of their own," said Dr. Holbrook.

They heard someone coughing violently in the background.

"Is there a hospital nearby?" asked Amy.

"No, but I did see a convent on the way in. Sometimes nuns will take in the sick. I am hoping to take him there in the morning."

"I'll call our doctor. We might be able to get Ryan back tonight," said Dr. Holbrook.

"It's a good idea," said Jeff. "He is not looking well."

"But, then Jeff will be alone," whispered Amy to Dr. Holbrook.

"Can you complete the mission on your own?" asked Dr. Holbrook.

"Of course. I am familiar with the Mayapple."

"I'll call the doctor now," Dr. Holbrook stepping away from the ComLink.

"Jeff, make sure to wash your hands often; every time you touch him. It is a way to prevent dysentery from spreading.

Ryan needs to be drinking lots of fluids, preferably boiled water." Amy had read about dysentery after finding out about Jeff's Dad.

"I'll try, but there is no water in the room."

She had forgotten about that. Suddenly, she heard a loud knocking.

"There is someone at the door, wait a moment," said Jeff. "I'm hiding the communicator."

Take your stun gun, thought Amy. She heard several loud voices, but she could not tell what they were talking about.

"What is going on?" asked Dr. Holbrook, coming back to the office.

She told him quickly and then asked, "Any luck with the doctor?"

Dr. Holbrook shook his head.

Then they heard a bang as the door was shut.

"I have to take Ryan to the convent right now," said Jeff. "A couple of guests complained to the boarding house owner that they are afraid of what Ryan has. The owner wants Ryan out of here tonight. I have a good idea about who the concerned guests were. What about the doctor?"

"He is not available," said Dr. Holbrook. "I'll have Beebe look for another doctor, but it will take some time."

"That means I have a problem," said Jeff evenly. "I have to take Ryan, but cannot leave the transport marker here."

"Ryan can't go himself?" asked Dr. Holbrook.

"He can barely walk."

Dr. Holbrook looked at Amy just as she was making a decision. "I can go," she said. "I can take Ryan to the convent while Jeff stays with the marker."

"You are the best one to go," said Dr. Holbrook. "George is on his way and should be here in twenty minutes, but you are more qualified, having traveled before. Thank you, Amy."

She nodded. "The convent also has Spanish-speaking nuns."

"Right," said Dr. Holbrook.

"Excuse me, what was that?" asked Jeff. "I missed some of your conversation."

"Amy is going to join you."

"I don't think..." Jeff started to argue.

Dr. Holbrook cut him off. "Jeff, there are not many people in the lab at this time of the evening and even if everyone were here, very few people can help you out like she can. She knows both of you, she knows the era and she knows Spanish, which will help with communicating with the nuns in the convent."

Jeff took a moment to respond and he sounded resigned, "You will have to send her nearby. There is no public transportation this late."

"Just tell us where."

"Make it a thousand feet directly south of the marker. There is a park there, and the trees will help hide her. I'll send you the coordinates."

"Thank you, Jeff. Amy, go get dressed appropriately and meet me at the transport."

She hurried out of the office and went to get the 1890s clothing. No one was around to help her, but she knew the clothing would not be too different from the ones she had worn in 1895. She also used the rest room and took several toilet paper rolls. Those might be helpful for Ryan. She hurried as fast as she could back to the transport area. Fifteen minutes had passed.

George and Dr. Holbrook were waiting when she arrived.

"Oh, Amy, I am so glad you can do this," said George.

"I'm glad I was here."

"Remember, Amy, keep this simple," said Dr. Holbrook. "Take Ryan to the nuns; make sure he has good care and return. I will work on getting a doctor over there, but you don't have to wait. You also don't have to wait for Jeff. He should take the transport marker with him as he looks for the podophyllum peltatum tomorrow. Everyone is on their own, you got that?"

"Yes, Dr. Holbrook."

"Also, I know you know self-defense, but these guys are ex-military, so be careful."

She nodded and stepped into the transport.

"Wait," said George. "Take this ComLink."

"She probably doesn't need that," said Dr. Holbrook.

"I want it," said Amy, remembering the problems the first time. She took it and the transport started.

Chapter 49
St. Augustine

She opened her eyes, but she could not see anything. She knew it was night, but there was no moon, no stars, or anything. Panic started to build, then a breeze blew in and leaves rustled around her, allowing some of the moonlight to filter through. She took a breath as she realized that tall leafy trees surrounded her.

She made her way through the trees, and the heat and humidity struck her. It was evening and it was still very warm. Finally, she found a path and followed it north. The town of St. Augustine was somewhere in that direction. As the trees cleared, she could see the lights of the Ponce de Leon Hotel. Amazing, she thought. Just like Tesla had supplied electricity to Durango, Thomas Edison had built the D.C. generators for this hotel, but it was still early for electricity. In fact, the hotel was one of the few-lighted structures in the city of over 4,500.

She found the boarding house easily and waited outside. She debated about knocking on the door at this hour of the night. She stepped back and studied the house. Several rooms were lit by candlelight, but there was no way to tell in which room Ryan and Jeff were.

She knocked and waited a few minutes. Then she knocked again.

"Hold on," said a gruff voice through the door. She heard the door unlock and then the door was opened. "What is the meaning of knocking the door so late? Who are you?"

"I am the sister of one of your guests. I came because he is very ill."

He stared at her.

"Apparently you want him out of his room tonight." She looked at him critically.

"Oh-h," he said, remembering. "Mr. Campbell in room 202."

"I will take him tonight, like you requested."

He nodded and opened the door further, letting her in. "You have to understand that other guests are worried about him. Some of these diseases float through the air, and I can't have my other guests getting ill."

"I know. That is why I am here."

"Follow me," he led her to the second floor and knocked on a door.

Jeff opened.

"Good evening, Mr. Lindsey, how is my brother?" she asked. She was very happy to see Jeff, but had to remain in character. "I am glad you contacted me."

"Good evening, Miss Waterman, I'm afraid he is not well," said Jeff.

She stepped into the room and immediately was struck by the smell. Then she saw Ryan's face. His eyes were glassy and his face was very pale.

"Have you been giving him water?" she asked Jeff.

"Yes, it's boiled. I'm trying to get him to drink."

"Why do you think this is dysentery?" There were many diseases that could involve diarrhea and vomiting.

"He has stomach cramps, and his stool has blood in it, like my father's"

The boarding house owner was watching and listening from the doorway.

"Ryan," she approached him. "Hello, dear brother. I have come to take you to a place where you will be cured."

Ryan barely nodded.

"Can you stand?" asked Amy.

He focused on her and tried. Jeff had to help him the rest of the way.

"How are you going to take him to the convent?" asked Jeff.

"I was going to ask him to get me a carriage," Amy pointed to the owner.

"There is nothing available at this time of the night," said the owner.

"Do you have a carriage or cart we can use?" asked Jeff.

"A cart..." he started to say and then stopped.

"If we don't have a way to take him, we stay," said Jeff. "We will stay until the morning when we find transportation."

"No. No, you can't stay here. I'll lend you my cart."

"You better wash all this bedding with very hot water," said Amy to him, "and make sure to wash your hands as well. This disease does not go through the air, it is transmitted through contact."

He looked concerned. "I will get the cart ready," he said, as he left in a hurry.

Amy and Jeff started down the stairs supporting Ryan, and when they arrived at the entrance, they took a break. Amy wondered how she was going to manage by herself.

"I am going with you," said Jeff, reading her mind.

"What about..." she left it unsaid, as the boarding house owner appeared.

"I'll take it with us," answered Jeff.

Soon they were on the cart heading to the convent. Luckily, it was not far.

"What time is it here?" asked Amy.

"A bit past three in the morning. We are three hours ahead of California."

Amy looked back at Ryan and the transport marker in the back of the cart.

"Why didn't the doctor come with you?" asked Jeff.

"I don't know. Dr. Holbrook called him, but maybe he didn't reach him."

"I hope the nuns can help him. There is the convent," said Jeff.

Amy got off the cart and knocked on the massive door. It took quite a while, but finally someone answered. It was a small woman dressed in nun garments.

"Me disculpan por llamar tan tarde," Amy apologized for the late call, "pero mi hermano está muy grave y no nos dejaron quedar en el hotel."

"Oh dear," said the nun, looking over her shoulder and at the cart. "I speak English. What does he have?"

"I think it is dysentery."

The nun nodded, but she did not show anxiety and did not close the door.

"Do you think you can help him?" asked Amy.

"God willing. It will depend on many things, my dear. His age, how sick he is and whether it is his time to go."

"I don't think it is his time to go," said Amy, not wanting to encourage that option.

The nun looked at her for a moment probably thinking she had no way of knowing that. "Bring him inside."

Jeff helped Ryan inside and the nun directed him to a sofa that was near the door.

"This is nice," said Ryan as he laid down.

It was nice, thought Amy. It was cool inside the adobe building, and the air was fresher than outside.

The nun smiled at Ryan while another nun appeared with water.

"Is it boiled?" asked Amy.

"Of course," said the nun. "It is water with a pinch of salt and sugar."

Amy looked at Ryan with concern as the nun made him drink.

"Go. We will take care of him," said the first nun. "My name is Sister Flora."

"Sister, my name is Amy, and he is Ryan Campbell. I have asked for our family doctor to come, and I think he will be here tomorrow."

"If it is dysentery, it will run its course. It may take a week, and that is usual. Most doctors cannot do much to change that."

"His father died from dysentery," she looked at Jeff.

"Sometimes that happens."

"So there is no cure?" she asked, wondering if there was something in this era that would help.

"Well, we have used the bark of the kapok tree and that sometimes works wonders. We will try that on him, but it may just take some days. You can come visit him tomorrow, but your friend will not be allowed into the convent."

She nodded and walked back to Jeff, who was much more than a friend.

Once back on the cart, Jeff did not go back into town. The sky was lightening up.

"Does this remind you of something?" asked Amy as she snuggled close to him.

"1944,"Jeff smiled. "Although I liked the Jeep a bit more than this cart. I am going to set the transport marker out here. It will be harder for those men to find it in this forest."

"But this is far from town. How will you get here afterwards?"

"Don't worry, I will."

"Why don't I wait until you get the Mayapple, and then we return together?"

"I can't leave Ryan. What if those men find the marker and take it? Ryan will be sick and stranded in this time for who knows how long?"

"That would be bad," agreed Amy. "On the other hand, the nuns are not going to let you visit him. I might as well stay to see how he is doing."

"It may be safer you go and come back later."

"I would rather not."

"Okay, Amy, what aren't you telling me?"

Amy explained about the mental illness that the GovTime transporter had seen after just eight trips.

"Eight! That is not much at all! What about Ryan? How many trips has he done?"

"Seven."

"You just found this out?"

"Yeah, Jack told us. That's why he lost his job. I am on my fourth trip, but I don't want to make too many unnecessary trips back and forth."

Jeff shook his head "For being so advanced, you are so..." He didn't finish his sentence, but the meaning was clear to Amy. They were so ignorant.

They watched the sun rise as they placed the marker in the ground. Then they made their way back to town. In the daylight, Amy was surprised to see so many buildings. She told Jeff so.

"Yes, there are a couple high-end hotels here," said Jeff. "Apparently, someone is trying to make this place a vacation land for the rich during the winter."

"Oh. Where were you are going to look for the plant today?"

"Ryan and I had discussed it. Yesterday, we looked in the park where you arrived and found nothing. Today, we had planned to look in the old part of town, near the Ponce de Leon Fountain. It was already there during the Spanish time."

"The fountain of youth," smiled Amy. "Really?"

"Why not? Next to the fountain is a garden with many different plants."

Jeff directed the cart towards the north side of town. They suddenly heard Amy's bag making noises.

""Damn," said Jeff. "I just remembered I left my ComLink back in the room."

"We'll go and get it right after. It should be alright," she said, hoping that was true.

"You better answer, it's Dr. Holbrook wondering where you are," said Jeff.

"I know, that's why I don't want to answer," she said, but she grabbed the case and established the link as Jeff pulled the cart to a more secluded location. It was very early in the morning, but they didn't want to startle anyone if they heard disembodied voices.

"Amy, are you there?"

"Yes, Dr. Holbrook."

"Why are you still there?"

"Jeff and I dropped Ryan at the convent. The nuns seem quite nice and told me I could visit."

"And?"

"They're not going to let Jeff in."

"So?"

"So, when is the doctor coming?"

"I wasn't going to tell you right now, but Beebe quit. She quit yesterday, and Dr. Knobby is no longer working with us, I..." he paused.

Amy looked at Jeff with concern She had never heard her boss so lost.

"I'm working on finding another doctor," he continued. "If the nuns are taking care of him, you don't have to visit him again. There is nothing you can do, so come back."

"Dr. Holbrook, Jeff is on his way to get the specimen. I thought I would accompany him, then visit Ryan one last time before leaving."

"Jeff, you have the transport marker with you?"

"It is secure, Dr. Holbrook," answered Jeff.

"Okay," Dr. Holbrook took a breath. "Okay. Here's the new plan. Get the plant, then you both can come back with it."

"I can't leave until Ryan is ready to go," said Jeff.

"Dr. Holbrook swore and then asked, "Who's in charge here?"

They didn't answer.

"Okay, I can see why you need to wait," sighed Dr. Holbrook sighed. "And when will Ryan be ready to travel?"

"When you get the doctor here," said Jeff.

"Dr. Holbrook," said Amy. "It could be bacillary dysentery, and he could be well in just a few days, but it could be something more serious and that would take much longer to cure. We can't tell, and the nuns can't either."

"Right, I'll make that my priority today. Shall I just send the doctor to the marker?"

"No. I'll send you the coordinates, but it is about 5,000 feet east of the marker," suggested Jeff.

"That's almost a mile away?"

"That puts him close to the convent."

"Call me when you get the plant," said Dr. Holbrook as he signed off.

"You know, Dr. Holbrook has improved in my estimation," said Amy. "I used to think he was purely focused on the financial and getting publicity, but he stopped Ryan from traveling anymore when he heard about the danger."

"One would hope the boss would be that way."

"Not all bosses are."

Chapter 50
Running out of time travelers

Hours later, they had not found any plant that was even similar to what they were looking for.

"I was so sure it would be here," said Jeff, sounding disappointed, as they got back on the cart.

"Maybe we need to get some help from George on where to look," said Amy.

"Yeah, and meanwhile we might as well pick up my ComLink."

They decided to keep the cart longer. Although they could rent horses, her 1892 women's clothing would make it hard to ride horseback.

As they pulled up the boarding house, Amy realized she had not slept in a long time. "It would be so nice to get a couple of hours of sleep, don't you think?"

"I agree, but I don't think we want to stay in my room. It is probably infected."

"Yeah, I doubt they have cleaned it. Maybe we can get another room?'

"Why don't you check on that while I get my things from the room."

She went to the front desk while he did that. It was nine in the morning, she noted as she waited for the proprietor of the boarding house. His name was Mr. Crawford, she saw from the little plaque on the desk. They had not been properly introduced the night before.

Two well-dressed gentlemen passed behind her on their way to breakfast.

"I can't wait to finish this," said one.

"Yeah, I don't know how they got past us. I really didn't think they would move so late at night."

"We lost a good opportunity. It would have been easy with one of them sick."

"The other one will be back. He couldn't move the marker as well as the sick guy so he probably hid it nearby."

"Yeah, and now he will be alone. It will be easy."

"Please come this way," said the proprietor of the boarding house, showing the men to a table in the breakfast room.

Amy immediately knew who they were and what they were talking about. She hoped Jeff would not come down the stairs any time soon.

"Yes, may I help you?" asked the proprietor, returning to the desk. Then he realized who she was. "Did you bring back my cart?" he whispered.

"Yes. Did you clean the sheets and pillows like I suggested?" she asked equally softly.

"Not yet."

"I need a place to sleep for a couple hours; do you have a room?"

"We rent by the day."

"That is fine. I'll rent a room for the day."

"I don't know if I have a room," he said without looking at the ledger.

"What about room 31?" She had noticed the key was hanging on the wall. "Mr. Crawford, it would be so nice to rest before I leave St. Augustine. I know my brother probably caught this disease somewhere else. It is not a reflection on your hotel," she said, implying it was.

"He did not catch that here." He looked down at the ledger. "Let me see, that room is available, but it is on the third floor and is quite small."

"That is all I need. I appreciate it Mr. Crawford."

"Now, where is my cart? I need it today."

"Oh, about that," she had to lie. "Dysentery affects objects, and it lives for many hours, so your cart has been infected. We are going to wash your cart down with a special cleanser that will get rid of the dysentery, but we have not done it yet."

He looked concerned. "My cart?"

"Yes. Mr. Lindsey will do it after he rests. After he cleans it, the cart will be safe for use."

"Mr. Lindsey is with you?"

"He has gone to his room."

Mr. Crawford nodded, but still looked worried. "You know a lot about this disease."

"I have seen it many times, but in most cases, the person has recovered fully."

"It's good to hear. Miss Campbell, I'll show you to your room."

He had assumed she had the same last name as her 'brother,' and she wasn't going to correct him. On the way up, she stopped at room 202 to let Jeff know where she was going and then continued up.

It was the only room up on the third floor and even though it was small, the bed looked very inviting.

"Do you have any bags? I can bring them up," he asked.

"No, that's all right," said Amy. She closed the door and immediately undressed. She climbed into bed, and moments later she saw Jeff. She barely registered as he lay down beside her and then she fell into a deep sleep.

"Wow," she woke up suddenly and noticed the change in light. Jeff was already awake. "What time is it?"

"A bit past one in the afternoon."

"I think I slept too much."

"It looked like you needed it."

"Did you sleep?"

"A bit."

She had a feeling he didn't sleep much anytime. Even in 2066, he was a light sleeper. She told him about the conversation she had overheard.

"I knew it. I saw signs that someone had gone through our stuff in the room."

"Did they get your ComLink?"

"No, they didn't look in the bedpan."

"Ooo, that's pretty gross," said Amy, wondering how the electronics would deal with that.

"It was the clean bedpan, Amy. I didn't put it in the dirty one, which by the way, was still there."

"Ugh," said Amy.

"Yeah, it is getting quite smelly in that room."

"Let's call Dr. Holbrook."

They established the link, and Dr. Holbrook answered right away. "Did you get the specimen?" he asked, forgoing the greetings.

"No," said Jeff.

"So now we have to decide where else to look, but Amy should come back."

"Dr. Holbrook, have you had a chance to get a doctor?" asked Amy.

"The doctor will be going with Don Gillespie in the next hour. Don is also on his seventh trip, so once he goes and comes back, that's it for him. There are not many time travelers still available." Dr. Holbrook sounded very worried.

"We can meet them at the convent. That way, I can bring the doctor inside when he arrives," she said.

"Good. Then you come back with the doctor. Don will stay with Jeff to continue the search."

They checked out of the boarding house, much to the relief of Mr. Crawford. His last words were about returning his cart, but it sounded like he was starting to give that up, worried about it being 'infected'. "I hope the horses will be all right," he said.

"The horses and the cart will be fine," said Amy, assuring him.

Once Amy climbed on the cart with Jeff, he asked, "I thought this type of dysentery bacteria only lives in tainted food and water?"

"Yes, you are right, but we needed the cart for another day."

He glanced at her, and she wondered what he thought about her dishonesty.

When they arrived at the convent, Amy went inside.

"I am glad to see you back," said Sister Flora.

"Thank you, sister, how is he?"

"Much better. The bark of the kapok tree has done its work."

"The doctor should also be arriving soon," said Amy.

"Like I told you, it was not necessary to bring him," said Sister Flora, bringing her to a room where Ryan was.

"Amy, beautiful sister of mine," said Ryan. "Come over here and give me a hug." He opened up his arms to hug her.

She stepped into his hug and he hugged her tightly. "Don't take advantage of this," whispered Amy. "It is good to see you so well, brother," she said aloud as she stepped away.

"The sisters have been wonderful to me. Have you heard of the bark they gave me? It really works! The bark of a tree!"

Amy looked with concern, at his exuberance. Was he being affected by the time travel sickness, or was he acting normal?

Another patient nearby started to cough violently, and Sister Flora excused herself.

"I am so glad to be better," said Ryan, smiling. "I thought the dysentery vaccine was supposed to prevent this."

"It should have," agreed Amy. "Maybe it helped in making it a milder case. You look well enough to come home with me."

"Yeah."

"Let me find Sister Flora to tell her we're leaving," said Amy. She went into the hall and heard voices. Several nuns were conferring at the end of the hall, and one was Sister Flora. She walked up to them and saw an older man in the room next to them. He looked very ill.

"Does he also have dysentery?" asked Amy.

"No, Mr. Felder has bronchitis," said Sister Flora sadly. "Usually that can be cured, but he has had it for quite a while, and he is getting weaker. He has two young children, and his wife died recently."

She saw two little girls playing in the corner of the room. "What will happen with the children?"

"We will take care of them temporarily until they can be adopted, but we do not have a facility to offer long term care for children."

One little girl stood up and went over to her father.

"Eleanor, please remember not to get close," warned the nun.

Eleanor Felder? Amy couldn't believe it. The name was not that common and this girl could be the Mrs. Felder of 1944. "Do they live here is St. Augustine?"

"No, they were visiting from Richmond, California."

"Excuse me, Sister Flora?" asked another nun that had just joined the group.

"Yes?"

"There is man outside that says he is the doctor of Mr. Campbell."

"Oh," said Amy, trying to assimilate what she had just discovered. "I am glad the doctor has come."

Sister Flora went with her to let him in.

"Sister Flora, is it all right if he sees the man with bronchitis?"

"Of course, my dear. Any help is appreciated, but that man has no money."

"Don't worry about that." Pay was the least of the worries. Changing the future was more serious. Maybe there was a way to make this work, she thought. As she arrived at the door, she saw that it wasn't Dr. Knobby.

"I think you were expecting Dr. Knobby, but he was not available," said the man seeing her surprise. "I am Dr. Mitchel, and I am familiar with Mr. Campbell. Where is the patient?"

"This way," said Sister Flora, letting him in.

"Ryan is doing much better," Amy told him as they walked down the hall

"He has recovered from dysentery so quickly?" he asked.

"All due to the care of the nuns and a special bark," said Amy.

"Miss Campbell, maybe you can take the doctor the rest of the way, I need to check on the other patients," said Sister Flora.

"Yes, Sister Flora, thank you," said Amy as they continued.

"I have a question, doctor. If someone gets bronchitis, what can one do?"

"Ryan has bronchitis?"

"No, another patient here has it."

"Well, you know I can't do anything about that."

"I know you can't give him 21st century medicine, but maybe there was something that could be done with the medicine of this time?"

"Usually rest and plenty of fluids will solve bronchitis."

"Apparently they have tried that," said Amy.

"Let me check Ryan, and I will see what I can do," said the doctor.

"Dr. Mitchel," said Ryan when he saw him. "Glad you could come."

"Yes, Dr. Knobby has retired."

"Really?" said Amy.

Dr. Mitchel's look told her that was not the entire story, but he didn't elaborate. He went ahead and checked Ryan. "You are perfectly fine to travel. You are not dehydrated, and it looks like your dysentery is mild. It can be further treated when you get home. Are you ready to go?"

"Yes, I am," said Ryan, getting off the bed. He seemed a bit weak, and Amy quickly went to hold him. Once he started walking, he was more stable. They made their way to the entrance of the convent.

"Tell me about the other patient, Amy."

"What other patient, Amy?" asked Ryan. "Are you causing problems trying to cure someone in the past?"

"Bronchitis is normally a very curable disease, and all I'm asking..." she started then stopped. "He has two young children and no one to leave them with. Not even the nuns can take the children."

Ryan shook his head. "You are definitely not cut out for time travel. You have to be tougher."

"Well, maybe you are right, but right now it's just a question for the doctor."

"I'll go see the man," said Dr. Mitchel.

Sister Flora appeared to say goodbye, and Amy asked her to take Dr. Mitchel to the man with bronchitis.

"Come on, Ryan," said Amy, opening the door. "Jeff is waiting outside."

"Ah, the gallant Jeff," said Ryan.

"That he is," smiled Amy. "Don Gillespie should be with him, as well. He has come to replace you."

"Yeah, too bad. I could try and stay. I am doing better," protested Ryan, but it was half-hearted.

As soon as they walked out the door, Jeff turned to them. He was smiling broadly.

"Are you happy to see me or is it something else that is making you look so happy?" asked Ryan.

"I am glad to see you better, but I am smiling about something else."

"You shouldn't call Amy something else," joked Ryan.

Jeff shook his head and showed him a plant in the back of the cart. "Look. What does this look like to you?"

Ryan got closer to study it. "The leaves look right; the color and shape looks good. The flower looks right, as well. Were there any fruits?"

"No, none, but it might not be the season."

"Well, it looks like the Mayapple to me. Where did you find it?"

Jeff pointed at the far wall of the convent. "It is growing wild along that wall. I picked the largest plant I could find. Don and I were taking a walk while we waited and there it was. Right in front of us."

"Amazing," said Amy. "So it is fortunate you got sick, Ryan. I don't think we would have looked here."

"Thank goodness my suffering was helpful," said Ryan.

"Are we ready to go?" asked Don. "Where is the doctor?"

"He will be here soon," said Amy. "Hey, Don, why didn't Dr. Knobby come with you?"

"I don't know," said Don changing the subject to remark about the weather.

"What is going on, Don?" asked Ryan. "You're starting to worry me."

"Well, I guess you'll find out soon enough. Have you heard of the problems with some of the travelers for the GovTime?"

"No," said Ryan.

"Apparently, the twelve limit on time travel is too much. They have had two people get sick with fewer trips than that."

"Wait, two people?" asked Amy. "How do you know?"

"Your new assistant has some friends left in his old job," said Don, looking at her.

"Does Dr. Holbrook, know about this?"

"Yes, when Dr. Holbrook explained Dr. Knobby's reluctance to travel. This would have been his sixth trip, so he was not on the limit, but Dr. Knobby does not want anything to do with time travel anymore."

"What is the new limit on travel?" asked Ryan.

"Eight," said Don.

Ryan's eyes grew large. "I can't go back," whispered Ryan. "The trip here was my eighth."

They all looked at him with concern.

"Are you sure?" asked Amy "I thought you said seven?"

"You think I don't keep track of such things? One of my first trips was very short. I went back a few months, so I wasn't counting it, but it is definitely eight. Now what am I going to do?" he asked, looking at her. "I don't want to stay here, but I don't want to have my mind fried." He turned away, shaking his head.

"Ryan, maybe they have it wrong. Gustav and Anthony went on a lot more than eight trips before…" Don didn't finish.

"Maybe they did, but I'm not going to risk insanity. Would you?" asked Ryan.

Don shook his head.

Dr. Mitchel joined them and was told the news. "So what are we going to do?" he asked.

"Amy, weren't you looking into out why the brain is affected by time travel?" asked Jeff.

She nodded.

"You need to go back and continue that work. I will stay with Ryan in this time."

"I can't ask you to stay, buddy," said Ryan.

"You're not asking me. I have to make sure those GovTime guys don't take the transport marker or else you and I will be spending a lot more time together here."

"I think it is our only option," said Don. "How many trips have you done, Amy?"

"This will be five. And you?"

"The trip back will be my eighth," said Don. "I knew it when I came."

They piled onto the cart, and Jeff took them to where the marker was planted. Amy kissed and hugged Jeff tightly and then joined Don and Dr. Mitchel at the marker. She looked at Jeff and Ryan standing in the grove of trees, and then they were gone.

Chapter 51
Back in Berkeley

Dr. Holbrook was there to greet them and lead them to his office for the usual debrief.

Amy waved him away. "The others will talk to you. I have too much work to do," she said as she started towards the lab.

Then Dr. Holbrook noticed the transport was not starting up again. "Where are the others?"

"Come along, Dr. Holbrook," said Dr. Mitchel. "We will tell you what has happened."

Amy noticed the graphs as soon as she walked into her lab. She would have to tell Jack to turn the projectors off when he left for the day. She had left Jack instructions so he would have something to do while she was gone, and it looked like he had gotten right into the work. Of course, it had only been one day. A very long day, she noted.

She moved closer to the projection. It looked like Jack was testing something.

"Hello, Dr. Waterman," said a voice behind her.

"Jack? What are you doing here so late?"

"I know that finding the solution to this problem is critical, so I was hoping to continue your work while you were gone. Did you just get back?"

"Yeah, minutes ago."

"Did anyone tell you about the other guy at GovTime?"

"I heard. What disease did he get?"

"He had anxiety attacks."

"Why are they all different? Why did one of our guys get DID, the other depression and the other GovTime guy become bipolar?"

"They all have to do with the mind and chemicals."

"Yeah, I know, but still, could each person be so different that something affects them so differently?" Amy was thinking out loud. "What have you here?"

"I was playing around with some of the chemical elements used in the transport."

"Yeah, I started doing the same." She brought up the graphs she had created the previous days. "See, I was checking if there was any buildup of chemicals in the body."

"The buildup has to be quite fast," said Jack. "By the eighth trip, they are having problems."

"Yes and no," said Amy. "Gustav was normal in trip eight. In fact, he was still all right all the way up to trip eighteen."

"Well, that makes no sense," said Jack.

"I know. Yet, Anthony was already showing some stress in trip fifteen."

"He was the one with depression, right? That can be caused by other things."

"But nothing changed in his personal life or at work. I checked."

They both sat back to look at the graphs to see if they would reveal something new. "Let's review what we know about the time travel machine," said Amy. "The Temporal Transporter, or TT, generates an electro-magnetic pulse. That pulse provides the power for the trip. It also ignites the gases that encapsulate the traveler in a bubble, protecting the traveler as he goes through time. The TT in the lab does all the work by pushing the traveler through time from 2066 and pulling him back. Pushing always takes more energy than pulling. If there is a transport marker on the other end, the pushing is easy, but the first time the traveler goes there, there is no marker and much more energy is needed."

Jack nodded his head as she explained it. "Also, more energy would be needed for the push of three years versus the push of one year."

"Exactly right. More energy and more gasses are needed. Did I miss something?"

"I don't think so," said Jack.

"Okay, I think it's time to go home. A good night's rest will help, and tomorrow we look at this again."

"Are you sure, Dr. Waterman?"

"Yes, Jack, I am sure, and I'm also sure you should call me Amy. Only Dr. Holbrook goes by a title around here."

It was soon after Jack left that that certain Dr. was at her door. "Knock, knock. I'm glad to see you are still here."

"Yes, Dr. Holbrook. I think I'm going to need a cot," said Amy.

"I think you need to go home, Amy. Wearing yourself out is not going to help you find a solution."

She didn't argue; going home was sounding good. Of course, once she got home, she would be thinking of the two men she cared about the most. She realized she had included Ryan in her thoughts, and she had to admit he had become a good friend.

"I told you Beebe quit, didn't I?" Dr. Holbrook sat down on a stool.

It looked like he needed to talk. "You mentioned it," said Amy. "What happened?"

"She quit very suddenly. We were in the middle of trying to find another doctor when she told me," said Dr. Holbrook. "She said an aunt left her some money, and she didn't need to work anymore. I think there was something else going on."

"She was concerned about the mental illness," said Amy, remembering her talk with her. "She went to visit Gustav; that was nice."

"No, I think you are wrong. She told me she couldn't face seeing what had become of Gustav," said Dr. Holbrook.

But Gustav had mentioned seeing her, and Amy had seen her name on the log. Why would Beebe lie about something so insignificant?

"Amy?" asked Dr. Holbrook. "Where are you thinking?"

"She was there, Dr. Holbrook. And I was trying to figure out why would she lie about it."

He shook his head slowly.

"Dr. Holbrook, there is something else; you need to get another transport marker. Jeff stayed to make sure the marker is not moved, but if they lose that one, they will be stuck there for a long time."

"I know. I am already working on that. The transport marker we set in the year 2000 is being brought back."

"Why don't we have more markers?"

"There is a problem with the availability of one of the inert gases that it used."

Since Jack and her had just been looking into inert gases, her ears perked up. "Which one?"

"I think they said it was an argon compound."

She had not tested argon yet, she thought, excited. She started to set up the experiment and forgot Dr. Holbrook was still there.

"That's a good way to do it," he said at one point.

"Oh, I didn't realize you were still here."

"Yes, although I was just getting ready to go. It is close to eleven."

"No wonder I am feeling tired."

"I am going home and will see you in the morning."

She continued to simulate the compound used in the encapsulant. When she repeated an error for the third time, she realized she was too tired. She decided to head home, and she did so dressed in 1892 garb.

Chapter 52
A particular gas

The next morning, she was back at work early.

Jack was already there before her, running simulations on the various gases. She asked him if he had looked at the argon compound. "That compound is holding up the manufacture of more transport markers."

"I'll start on that one right away," said Jack.

"I started last night, but did not get far," said Amy, showing him her work. As he set up the testing, Dr. Holbrook joined them.

"Good morning, Dr. Holbrook," said Amy, still surprised at seeing Dr. Holbrook so often in her lab. He pulled up a stool and sat down.

"Looks like you made it home after all," he said.

She was no longer wearing her 1890s dress. "Yes, all I needed was a few hours in my own bed. I feel much better today."

"Good," he said. "Any results on testing the argon compound?"

"Nothing yet," she said. "When are you planning to call Jeff and Ryan?"

"Later this morning. Hopefully, we will have some news for them."

She was not sure that they would have anything.

After several hours, she was right. They had tested the argon compound on all parts of the brain and there had been no effect.

"Darn," said Amy, looking at the results. "I was sure this was it."

"Maybe it is in the way the marker works. Could each marker be different?" asked Jack.

"They are all the same," said Amy.

"But who verifies this?"

"We do. Our lab verifies each marker when we receive it."

"But how about the changes we made with the jumps. Originally, we were going back one year per day, but then we changed to three years and recently five years per day. The transport had to be different."

Amy's eyes lit up. "We did make changes. More inert gases were needed, we needed a larger ignition, and more power was needed."

She brought up the argon compound and tested it with a much larger electrical charge, like the one used for the five-year trips. The argon compound started to fall apart.

"Wow," said Jack as he looked. "What is that?"

One of the elements of the compound was affecting the model of the brain. The serotonin levels had dropped to a dangerous level.

"Wow," said Amy, staring at the results. "Jack, I want you to find out what trips Gustav and Anthony were on. I want to know how many one-year, three-year and five-year trips they went on."

Jack gazed at the argon compound breaking apart for a few moments more before going to gather the information needed. It didn't take him long, and he returned with the data Amy needed.

She took a glance and said, "Come with me." She rushed out the lab and headed to Dr. Holbrook's office. She got there in record time, with Jack following close behind. The door was open and she barged into his office, "Dr. Holbrook."

"Amy. I was just going to look for you. I was getting ready to talk to Jeff and Ryan."

"Not yet," she said as she put the paper with the data in front of him.

"What is this?"

"This is how we are making our travelers ill. You can see that at the beginning, when we went back one year per day, things were all right. The travelers could do this indefinitely without any bad side effects. Gustav made ten of these trips, and Anthony made nine. Then we increased the pushback time to three years. This is when the problem started. Gustav made eight of these three-year trips, and Anthony made six."

"But, why would that affect anything?" asked Dr. Holbrook.

"These multi-year trips need higher energy, and it breaks the argon compound down. The brain then absorbs one of the elements. All those diseases we are seeing are the effect of that element attacking different parts of the human brain."

"And it only affects the travelers when we first establish the markers?"

"Yes. Once the marker is set, you can travel back there as much as you like. Not as much energy is needed to go back and forth, and not as much argon gas is needed either."

"What about Ryan? Have you figured out the trips he took?"

"Yes, as a time setter, he has done five one-year trips and one three-year and a very short one at the beginning. The current trip does not count, since the marker was already there," said Jack.

"So, according to your theory, he should be safe to come back?" asked Dr. Holbrook.

"I would say yes, but I want more data," said Amy. "I want to find out about the GovTime travelers. What was the length of their trips?"

"I know that both of them had mental illness after eight trips, but I don't know what kind of trips those were. I will ask Linde about it," said Dr. Holbrook.

"Is she going to share that with us?" she asked.

"Well, they shut down their whole operation when the second person got ill. She is probably anxious to get this fixed. I'll call her right away," said Dr. Holbrook as he picked up his phone. He turned away from Amy and Jack.

"What is GovTime doing with their Temporal Transporter, anyway?" Amy asked Jack.

"Oh, you don't know?"

"I guess they've kept me off the communication loop."

"They have identified some events that occurred in history that were pivotal to the what the USA is now. They think that changing these will make the USA stronger in 2066."

"Really? Is that a good idea to be playing around with the past?"

"I know. I have had some concerns about that too."

"I know we try to be careful about making changes, and some get made anyway. I do wonder what will come of that. Do you know what GovTime was doing in Florida in 1892?"

"I know the target was Florida in 1872, but I don't know why."

"I think you better come down here." Dr. Holbrook after he finished talking. He turned back to Amy and Jack.

"So?" asked Amy. "How many trips and how long?"

"Both travelers had eight trips, and all their trips were three-year ones," said Dr. Holbrook.

"Good, that matches what we think. I will run some more simulations to verify this, and I think that tomorrow Ryan should be able to come back," said Amy. She stood up.

"Linde just informed me about another problem at GovTime. She is on her way here, and she will explain things better," said Dr. Holbrook.

"Did a third person get sick?" asked Jack.

"She wouldn't tell me," he paused. "Jake, why don't you go back to the lab; I need to talk to Amy."

It sounded serious, but she couldn't think of anything she had done wrong recently.

"I found out that Beebe did go visit Gustav," said Dr. Holbrook.

"That's not a surprise; even if Gustav was mistaken, I saw her name on the log."

"Yeah, but what you don't know is that Gustav is doing much better since she stopped her visits."

"What? Why?"

"She was drugging him. He already had bipolar disorder, probably caused by the time travel, but she augmented his condition with drugs, and that caused his multiple personalities. Once she stopped visiting, he has improved."

"That is horrible, but why? Why would she do that?"

Dr. Holbrook sighed. He knew, but he was taking his time. "Your specimen went on sale this morning; I mean the specimen that Gustav brought. That is how we found out."

Amy waited, still confused.

"As far as we can tell, Gustav brought it back, gave it to Beebe and returned to 1895 to get the silver. She helped him hide the specimen in the lab and she also must have drugged him then. It was enough chemicals to push him over the edge, and Beebe probably thought he was never coming back."

"So, when he shot me, his mind was unstable."

"Yes, and then Ryan brought him back. It must have been a surprise to her, and she realized she had to do something. Gustav did not remember much and every time she went to visit, she gave him something to keep him in that state."

"Beebe seemed like a nice person."

"She was, most of the time, but she had a little too much greed and not too much ethics."

"The specimen went on sale today?"

"Yes, but I had warned the pharmacological board, and the police and they contacted me. She was arrested."

"And Gustav, how is he now? "

"His multiple personalities are reintegrating and with the correct medication, he might be all right."

She sighed. "This is good news. And it is very good news for Gustav."

Dr. Holbrook nodded.

Linde arrived within the hour, which kind of indicated the severity of the situation, and Amy was called back to Dr. Holbrook's office.

Linde nodded to her as she walked in and sat down.

"Like I was saying, I am trying to bring them back," Linde continued talking, "but Keith will not come back. He thinks that the mission is everything now. He even knocked out his partner, and disappeared."

"What is the mission?" asked Amy, fearing the answer.

"The mission was in Cuba, in 1872. They were supposed to convince the mayor of Havana and the governor that being purchased by the USA was a good thing. President Grant was going to make an offer in the next few months," said Linde.

"Really?" asked Amy. She was not up to date with the history of the time.

"Yes. President Grant was the third president to try to buy Cuba from the Spanish, but the deals always fell through. President McKinley also made an attempt later, but by then the Cuban Revolutionary Party was already formed, and sentiment against outsiders had grown. It was too late to change minds then."

Amy realized her mouth had dropped open. She was amazed they would try something that would change history so much.

"I know what you're thinking," said Linde. "But you should think of the problems that would have never existed if Cuba was an American territory. Most of Latin America would be a willing partner, without Cuba to incite distrust. All the cold war tactics in the 1960s would be averted, and the list goes on and on. It was a good mission."

"Did our government know what you were doing?" asked Dr. Holbrook.

Linde didn't say.

"You took this on yourself?" Dr. Holbrook was incredulous.

"It was for the best. Sometimes you have to stick your neck out for what you believe," said Linde.

Dr. Holbrook glanced at Amy. Was he thinking she was like Linde Dunne? She wouldn't try to change history. "So what happened to Keith?" asked Amy.

"Keith was on his eighth transport trip. He was acting erratic already. He changed the records to show he was on his sixth trip, just so he could go on this one. We didn't catch it until he was already there, and when we asked him to return, he went AWOL."

"What can we do?" asked Dr. Holbrook.

"I am sure he will go after that transport marker. I guess you have two of your people there? They should be warned."

"One of our people had dysentery and we are bringing both back tomorrow. Amy is running some tests to ensure his mind will stay healthy, since this will be his ninth trip. She can tell you herself."

"Have you figured out why the Temporal Transporter is causing mental illness?" Linde turned to her.

"I think so. Jack is helping me." Yes, the Jack you fired, she added silently.

"So, why are they getting sick?" asked Linde.

Amy explained the whole thing. She told her that the problem was in going back more than one year to set transport markers. "And in the case of GovTime, all the trips affect the travelers, since all of them were traveling back more than one year, and they were all setting transport markers."

"You mean if we had just gone back to where there were existing transport markers, we wouldn't have had a problem?"

"That's right," said Amy. "Jack is running the final tests to ensure our theory is correct."

"I might have overreacted," admitted Linde. "I shouldn't have fired him, but it is hard when it seems everyone is working against you."

There might be a reason why everyone is against you, thought Amy. It may be because you're wrong. She didn't say anything.

"Is Keith's partner still in 1892 in Florida?" asked Dr. Holbrook.

"Yes, Peter Corse is still there."

Amy remembered the name and it was not fondly. This was the man who had hinted he would hunt her down when she was in 1944.

"I think it's best that your guys work with Peter to stop Keith from taking the transport marker. All of them can transport together back here. In the best case, they bring Keith back."

And what was the worst case, wondered Amy.

"I'll talk to Jeff," said Dr. Holbrook.

"Jeff. That was the guy from the 1890s, wasn't he?" asked Linde.

"Yes," said Dr. Holbrook.

"I hope he understand the urgency of my request."

Dr. Holbrook looked at her coldly. "Linde, you went on your little quest and now you want us to fix things. We will do what we can, but the safety of my people is first. Hopefully, we can bring both Peter and Keith back, but we are not going to complete your mission."

Linde didn't look happy, but Amy was kind of proud of her boss. She totally agreed with what he said.

"Now I am going make the call and let you know afterwards what we can do," said Dr. Holbrook.

"You want me to go?" asked Linde, surprised.

"I would like that, yes," said Dr. Holbrook.

After Linde left, Dr. Holbrook connected the ComLink.

Jeff answered right away.

"Hello, guys," said Dr. Holbrook. "Linde was just here. One of GovTime's travelers has gone AWOL. Apparently his mission has become paramount in his mind, and he will try to complete it regardless of the method. You have to watch that transport marker carefully."

"It's too late," said Jeff. "I was afraid something like this might happen, so I hid the transport marker in the swamplands near the convent. Well, he must have followed us when Amy and the others transported yesterday, because I went to check and the transport marker is now gone. I don't know where it is."

Dr. Holbrook exchanged a look with Amy. "This is bad, but I thought this might happen, so luckily we just got a transport marker here in the lab. It is one we had placed in the year 2000."

"That's great," said Ryan, "but I still can't leave here."

"You might be able to," said Amy. She explained what she had found.

"But it's just a theory, Amy," said Ryan, not convinced. "I really don't want to become insane."

"Ryan, the data looks pretty good," said Dr. Holbrook. "Jack is finishing up some additional testing, but I agree with Amy's findings."

"Damn, I really want to get back, but," said Ryan as he struggled with his choices. "Amy, are you really, really sure?"

"Quite sure, Ryan," she said.

"And who are you sending with the new transport marker?" asked Jeff.

"We are looking into that right now," said Dr. Holbrook.

"You have no one, do you?" asked Ryan.

From Dr. Holbrook's expression, Amy could see that Ryan was correct.

"No, it's not that." Dr. Holbrook lied smoothly. "We just want to make sure that none of our travelers are close to the limit in trips."

"How are you going to send someone when we don't know where the transport marker is?" asked Jeff.

"That is a good point, and there are two options. One, we send someone to San Francisco in 1892 and they travel like you did, but as you know, that will take five days. The other option is to have a person bring a transport marker to the location where the previous marker was. Since the person will be carrying the transport marker where there is none, it will count as a time setting job."

"You can do that?" asked Ryan.

"Yes, we can. This can only work since we have the exact coordinates of the previous marker and know it to be a safe location," said Dr. Holbrook.

"And this trip will count towards the maximum eight trips," said Jeff.

"Yes," said Dr. Holbrook before saying good-bye.

Amy had decided before the call was over. "I can go."

"I hate to do this to you, but the same reasons I sent you before apply here, and frankly there is no one else."

"No one else?"

"The others are over eight trips. We had started training a few new time setters, but with the possibility of going insane, several quit and none is as experienced with the time and area."

"I'll take the marker, Dr. Holbrook. I really want Ryan and Jeff to get back."

"Ryan, Jeff and Peter and possibly Keith."

"No. Peter maybe, but we are not spending time searching the area for someone who may be quite dangerous. We don't know much of Keith except that he is ex-military and maybe insane. He is the problem of GovTime."

"Okay. I just hope he is not affecting our present too much," said Dr. Holbrook.

She knew he was playing the guilt card, and she didn't respond.

"Well, get rest tonight, Amy, and tomorrow we send you."

She returned to her lab, where Jack had good news.

"I just finished, and your theory still holds," he smiled.

"Good, at least this is working," she said. "Hey, Jack, are you enjoying working here?"

"Yeah."

"Do you miss GovTime?"

"Not really. Things were too intense over there. The pressure to succeed was very high, and although I can work under pressure, it gets to you after a while."

She nodded. "Do you know Peter Corse?"

"A bit. I think he and Keith were sent to Florida."

"Yeah, apparently Keith has a problem." She explained what had happened.

"I knew it. Keith was really tightly wound. He really believed that might makes right and that he could muscle his way through anything."

"Okay, that is good to know."

"And if you thought Peter was tough? Keith is much tougher. I doubt your stun gun will even work on him," Jack joked.

Amy didn't laugh. It just made her more anxious.

"I'm sorry. I didn't mean to worry you," said Jack.

"Just tell me more about these two guys."

"Linde should give you their bios."

"Yeah, but what I want to know won't be in there. Tell me what kind of people they are. What do they love and what do they hate?"

"I didn't hang out with them much."

"Please, what do you know about them?"

"They both love their work. They really believe in the mission and will do all they can to make it succeed. They are like supermen when it comes to that. On the personal side, I never saw any pictures of their family and I don't think they had anyone. I would see Keith with pretty girls, but they were never the same. Peter? He was at work all the time and I never saw him with anyone. That's about it."

With that information she said good-bye and headed home. She had to get ready to travel again.

Chapter 53
St. Augustine, again

It was Sunday, and she was sitting in the Temporal Transporter again. This was her sixth trip; she was keeping track carefully, just in case her theory was not correct. Linde, Dr. Holbrook and Jack were there to watch her go.

"Remember, this one will feel a bit different," Dr. Holbrook had warned her. "You will feel more pressure, and you might have a headache and be disoriented when you arrive."

She could do this, she kept thinking.

Linde had argued the whole morning about helping her guys complete their mission, but Dr. Holbrook was not budging. Amy's opinion of Dr. Holbrook had improved greatly.

She closed her eyes just as the transport started. It was more violent than the previous ones. When the movement stopped, she opened her eyes and found herself among the trees in the park. It was the same place as before, but it was not dark. In fact, it was bright and sunny.

She heard children playing nearby and quickly looked around, concerned someone had seen her. Luckily, the trees were dense enough and no one had. She dragged the heavy transport marker to one side and managed to shove it under some palm fronds. This transport marker looked like a small boulder, and she patted some dirt around it, making it look like it had been there a long time. Then she got up, dusted herself off and walked out into the sun.

Jeff saw her before she saw him.

"Miss Waterman, you look lovely as ever," he said as he walked up her. He took her hand and kissed it.

"Thank you. Mr. Lindsey, isn't it?" They both smiled, and she took his arm as they started to stroll. She dropped the formality. "Where is Ryan?"

"He is waiting on the other side of the park. We weren't sure which way you would come."

"And have you seen Peter Corse?"

"Not yet. We are meeting him later. We can't really transport with all these people around," Jeff looked around the park.

There were a lot of people around. They walked to the other side of the park and met Ryan.

"My dearest sister," said Ryan as he kissed her cheek.

"Ryan, thank goodness you seem to be quite recovered from dysentery."

"Yes, and how are you feeling? You have become a regular time traveler, haven't you?"

"My head is pounding. I don't remember that when I traveled before."

"You weren't a time setter," said Ryan.

"My head always hurts," said Jeff.

"That's because of your delicate nature," joked Ryan.

Amy felt Jeff's arm tense, but his face was unperturbed; she found that interesting. "Let's find a place to sit," she said. "I need to tell you about these military guys."

They found a café and ordered something to drink. After Amy took a pill for her head, she started to feel better. "You need to have these with you when you travel," she told Jeff as she gave him a couple.

"So, tell us about those two?" asked Ryan.

Amy told them about their mission and about what had happened.

"So it is similar to what happened with Gustav," said Jeff.

"Yes, in that Keith has gone AWOL, but he is a much more dangerous guy."

"I think he has left 1892. He took that transport marker two days ago," said Ryan.

"Yeah, but I also worry about the other guy, Peter. He is supposed to accompany us back home, but what if he decides to go after Keith? These guys are like that."

"As long as we go home first," said Ryan.

"But," said Jeff, looking at Amy. "Why don't you finish your thought?"

"Dr. Holbrook is worried about how they might affect the future; the time when we live in," she said.

"Has Dr. Holbrook asked us to stop them?" asked Ryan.

"No. He just wants us to return. Linde wanted us to help with their mission, but I think she has also resigned herself to just having Peter back."

"What about Keith?" asked Jeff.

"Yeah, good question. I don't know what they are going to do with an insane military guy from the future running though Cuba."

"Well, I think the three of us will go together, and Peter can do what he wants," said Ryan. "It's not our problem. It is the problem of GovTime."

"That is what I told Dr. Holbrook," said Amy.

They finished their drinks in silence.

Afterwards, they headed to the boarding house. It wasn't the same boarding house as before, and Amy could understand the reason for the change. Peter was waiting for them when they arrived, and they introduced each other.

Amy noticed that Peter did not recognize her from a couple of days before, when he and Keith had walked near her on their way to breakfast.

"I appreciate you guys helping us out," Peter said. "When can we leave?"

"Tonight," said Ryan. "Around seven."

"Good. I need to finish up some things, so I'll come back and join you. Where is the marker so we can meet there?"

Amy tried not to smile at the obvious ploy.

"Let's meet here at 6:30 and then we can go to the marker together," said Ryan.

"Have you heard from Keith at all?" asked Amy.

Peter looked at her as if for the first time. "No. He knocked me out, and I have not seen him since."

"Do you think Keith has gone to 1872?" asked Jeff.

"Yes, absolutely yes. He was talking about the mission all the time. I would have gone with him, but he sounded a bit erratic."

"Peter, there is something you should know," said Amy. He should know about the mental illness if he traveled anymore.

Peter turned to her; ready to dismiss anything she might say.

"How many trips have you done to place transport markers?"

"Four."

"Good. You are aware of the mental illness affecting several travelers?"

He kind of shrugged like it wouldn't happen to him.

"You know it happens after eight trips?"

She could see him calculating it out. He was at four, and it would take another four trips to get back to 1872. He would not be able to go home afterwards without causing mental damage.

"Are you sure it is only eight?" he asked. "I thought some of BioTime guys traveled more than that. Didn't Gustav travel twenty times?"

"Eighteen times, but only eight of those were as a time setter. If you go to a place that already has a transport marker, there is no effect, or if you set a marker only one year back, there is no effect. I checked the data for all the travelers that were affected, including the GovTime employees."

"Why haven't I heard about this before?" He was not buying her story.

"We just figured it out. Talk to Linde; she will confirm what I just said."

"It doesn't matter. It has nothing to do with me anyway, since I am returning with you."

"Good answer," said Ryan smiling.

Peter left them soon after.

"Why did you tell him seven o'clock? It makes us wait a long time," said Amy.

"It was the first time that popped in my mind," said Ryan.

"I would have said five. At least we would have sunlight," said Amy.

"Yeah, and there would be people still in the park."

Amy had to agree he had a point.

"I am curious to know what stuff he has to finish before he comes with us," asked Jeff.

"Yeah, why don't we go and help him?" suggested Ryan.

Amy wasn't sure about the 'helping' idea, but she was curious as well.

They left their boarding house and walked across the park. Peter was still staying at the previous boarding house.

"I hope he doesn't get too pissed off when he sees us," said Ryan.

"I can tell him we changed the time of departure and came to let him know," said Amy.

"That's a good story, Amy," said Ryan.

"Yeah, it is amazing how she comes up with stuff like this," said Jeff.

Amy hoped he meant it as a compliment and not that she was pathological liar. Maybe she had to start to watch herself.

They arrived at the boarding house and the owner, Mr. Crawford, recognized them immediately. "We have no vacancies. I can recommend another boarding house not far from here," he said very helpfully.

"No, we have not come to stay. We are visiting someone who is staying here," said Jeff. "Mr. Peter Corse."

"You know Mr. Corse?" asked Mr. Crawford.

"Yes."

"I am surprised. He was the one who complained about your friend's illness," he said.

"I thought that might have been the case," said Jeff.

"I don't think he will see you, and I don't want any trouble," said Mr. Crawford.

Jeff took out his sheriff's star and put on the desk. "I think he will see us."

"You are a sheriff? I did not know," said Mr. Crawford, suddenly looking more attentive. "It is room 205. I will take you."

"There is no need; we will find it ourselves," said Jeff.

"By the way, sir, I do not usually send sick people out in the night. Luckily, I can see that Mr. Campbell has recovered," said Mr. Crawford.

"Yes, luckily," said Amy.

"I don't think all of you will be comfortable visiting in that room," continued Mr. Crawford. "He has a small room, and there are many boxes; also, his partner just came back."

All of them looked at the Mr. Crawford. "His partner, Mr. Sully?" asked Jeff carefully.

"Yes. The gentleman left for a couple of days and just returned."

Jeff turned to them, "We need another plan." He studied them, and Amy knew what he was thinking. How were they, a woman, a sickly man and him, going to take on two ex-military men?

"Are you thinking of capturing Keith?" she had to ask.

Jeff gave her a small smile, "If we can, we should."

"It would be nice to know where Peter stands in all this," said Ryan. "I wonder if he has changed his mind about returning. I detected some regret about not finishing the mission, and now that Keith is back, he can complete it."

"There is no way of knowing," said Amy. "Who knows how Keith will react when he sees us."

"Sees us?" said Jeff. "You mean sees Ryan and me. He doesn't know you, Amy. You were never in the meetings with us, and he doesn't know you are here from the future."

"Yeah," said Ryan thoughtfully. "Maybe we can use that to our advantage."

They mulled options for a moment and finally came up with a plan. It seemed a reasonable plan, but they had to count on Mr. Crawford for the first part. That part was easy.

They all followed Mr. Crawford up the stairs and stayed out of sight while he knocked on room 205. Someone opened the door.

"Excuse me, Mr. Corse? There is a young lady to see you downstairs."

"What?" They heard Peter from inside the room. He sounded surprised.

"You have a girl, Peter?" asked Keith.

"There must be a mistake," said Peter. "I don't have any lady."

"She was most insistent in seeing you," said Mr. Crawford.

"Did she give you a card?" asked Keith.

"No, but she said her name is Amy..."

"I know Amy," said Peter interrupting.

"You old dog. I leave for a couple days and you hook up with someone?" asked Keith.

"Tell Amy this is not a good time and that she should go," said Peter.

Mr. Crawford turned away.

"Wait, Mr. Crawford. Are you sure, Peter? Our task can wait while you 'meet' with her," suggested Keith. "When will you have another chance? It's not like women follow you around."

"Thank you, Keith, but no. I have no desire to see her again," said Peter. "You can go, Mr. Crawford."

Mr. Crawford left, but as planned, the door to room 205 was left cracked open, and they could plainly hear the conversation between Peter and Keith.

"Is it you don't want to see her, or are you afraid I might take the stuff and disappear?" asked Keith.

"You mean, like you did before?" said Peter.

"I didn't take the stuff. I was checking things out and I returned, didn't I?"

"I'm not sure you returned for me or for the stuff."

"Okay, so it may be a bit of both. You do want to come with me, don't you?"

"Of course I do, but maybe we should go back to the lab first. We leave the transport marker here and come back whenever we are ready."

"What are you talking about? We are ready now. I have been ready since we first arrived in Florida. What is wrong with you?"

"I don't think we are quite ready. Don't you believe what I told you about the mental illness caused by the many trips?"

"I don't feel bad. Shouldn't I be getting ill? I have traveled more than eight times and I feel fine, physically and mentally. Maybe there is something wrong you." Keith shouted the last part. Then it got quiet.

Amy decided it was time for her entrance and the next part of the plan. She walked past Jeff and knocked. The door. opened up further. "Hello?" she said, looking into the room.

"Amy," said Peter.

"Oh," said Amy as she realized she had stepped into something dangerous.

Keith had Peter pressed against the far wall. One hand was holding him down while the other held a gun dangerously close to Peter's face.

Keith didn't turn to look at her. "Amy, come on in."

"I don't think I will," she said.

Keith almost turned, but he caught himself. "If you don't come in, I will kill him."

"And if I do come in, you will shoot him and then me," she said. From the corner of her eye, she could see Jeff and Ryan. They had been moving closer to the door, but after what she said, they froze.

Keith released Peter and took a couple of steps away, still aiming at his head. He quickly threw a glance at her. "Well then, what do you want?"

"I came to get Peter. We were going to have a date and I don't like waiting." It was a silly thing to say while the man had a gun on Peter's face, but that had been the original plan, and Keith was crazy anyway. Who knows what he would do.

"I told you to go see her," said Keith to Peter. "I told you and you didn't listen. Now look at what has happened." He was shouting and waving the gun now. "I'm sorry Peter, but I'm going to have to kill your girlfriend. She has seen too much."

Keith swung the gun at her and the next thing she knew, she was lying on her side in the hallway. Jeff was on top of her, but quickly rolled off. "You okay?"

She nodded and they both stood up.

Jeff quickly went into the room, and she could see Ryan was already inside. Peter and Keith were wrestling over the gun.

"Just shoot the stun gun," shouted Peter.

Ryan shot. It was a good shot, and it hit Keith in the back, but he continued to fight Peter for the gun. Then Jeff shot, and it hit Keith again. Keith barely flinched. The stun guns didn't seem to be working.

A shot from the other gun rang out, and the bullet went into the ceiling, making the plaster fall. That gun was working fine.

"Shoot him in the neck," shouted Peter. "He's wearing a shield."

Jeff and Ryan shot several times and finally, both Peter and Keith sank to the ground.

"Wow," said Ryan. "That took more than I would have thought."

"A shield? Why haven't I heard of that before?" asked Jeff.

"Are you all right?" asked Amy, entering the room.

"Yeah, and you?" asked Jeff.

"Fine," said Amy. "We need to tie him up very well," she pointed to Keith. "He's absolutely out of control. I see you got Peter, too."

"We just wanted to make sure to get Keith; he was like a wild man. Did you bring your cuffs?" asked Ryan.

"No, not this time," said Jeff.

"But you at least brought your badge," said Ryan.

"One never knows when it will come in handy," said Jeff matter-of-factly. "Amy, go get some rope from Mr. Crawford. Ryan, help me with these guys." He went over to pull them apart.

As Amy ran downstairs, she heard Ryan suggesting they take the shield off Keith.

"What is happening up there? I heard shots," said Mr. Crawford

"The sheriff has things under control, but he has asked me to get some rope."

Mr. Crawford was happy to give it to her. "Who's going to pay damages?"

The ceiling did have a hole in it, thought Amy. "Let me take the rope to the sheriff, we'll talk about it afterwards.."

She went back up, and they had separated the guys. They were both lying on the floor on one side of the bed. On the other side of the bed, Ryan was looking into one of the boxes. She gave the rope to Jeff, and he immediately tied Keith. Neither of them was going to wake up soon.

"What's in the boxes?" she asked.

"Take a look for yourself," said Ryan.

She walked over and opened up the flap. "Books?"

"Yeah, but open one," suggested Ryan.

She smiled. "This book is hollow, and there is money inside! Are all the books like this?"

"No. Not all, but it is still a lot of money." He opened the smaller crate that was at the end. "Wow. And this one has silver coins."

Jeff finished with Keith and went over to see. "Spanish silver coins."

"They were probably going to use them when they went to Cuba," said Amy.

"Oh-h-h," said a voice from the other side of the bed.

Peter was waking up. "Damn guys, you didn't have to stun me. Did you get Keith?"

"Yeah, he's still out," said Ryan. "Sorry about that, but Keith was not going down.

"We have to get him back," said Peter. "He would have never pointed a gun at me. He has to get some help and then you will see he is not a bad guy."

Amy hoped that Keith's mind would recover and that it was not too far gone.

"What are we going to do with all of this stuff?" asked Ryan, pointing at the several boxes.

"We do have to pay Mr. Crawford for the damages, so that will take care of some it," said Jeff. "Did you guys print all this money?"

"Yes, but not the silver coins. Those are another story, and we should return them to 2066," said Peter.

"Should we carry Keith down like this?" asked Ryan, "or should we wait until he wakes up?"

"Good question," said Peter. "Like this, he is hard to carry down, but if he wakes up and fights us, it will be harder."

Peter and Jeff carried Keith down the stairs, while Amy paid for damages. She also 'rented' the cart again from Mr. Crawford. They were definitely going to have to run that man's lifeline and see how the interactions with the time travelers had affected him.

When they arrived to the park, the sun had set. There was still enough ambient light to make their way to the grove of trees. Keith started to wake up, but seemed quite confused, and they were able to tie his hands to the transport marker. Peter and Keith went first.

"I don't know about this," said Ryan, as they waited their turn.

"Trust me, Ryan," said Amy. "We have run many simulations. You will be fine."

"Are you coming with me?" he asked.

"All three of us can go together," she said.

"And we are leaving the transport marker here?" asked Jeff.

"Yeah," said Amy as each took a position around the marker. She looked at the two guys in front of her, and closed her eyes.

When she opened them, she was in the lab.

"You know you don't have to close your eyes," said Ryan.

"I prefer to," she said. "I think positive thoughts and go to my happy place."

"I hope I am in that happy place," said Jeff.

"You are," she smiled. Dr. Holbrook and Dr. Mitchel were waiting, and she knew they were going to be taken for checkups and debriefing. A crowd of fellow coworkers was watching from below the platform, and she saw Jack among them. He waved and she waved back.

"How are you feeling, Ryan?" she asked as they got off the platform.

"I was just thinking that I feel fine. Maybe your theory worked," he looked relieved. "How do I look?"

"Fine, except for that growth on your back," said Jeff.

"Where, what do you see?" He twisted in vain, trying to look at his back.

There was nothing there, thought Amy and then she saw Jeff smiling.

Ryan saw it too. "Damn Jeff, you scared me."

"A little payback," said Jeff.

Suddenly, George was standing in front of her and he gave her a big hug. "Thank goodness you guys made it back."

"Nice to see you too, George, and I'm as relieved as you are."

"Come on, George, you know the protocol," said Dr. Holbrook. "I get the travellers first."

"Remember to call your aunt," said George. "I told her you were traveling again, and I think she actually knows what I meant."

She would call. She would also connect with Suzanna and maybe even some other friends of old. She glanced at Jeff next to her and knew she could balance her life.

And it was nice to be home. No matter where or when she went, 2066 would be her home, and she was happy to be back.

She felt good. She had helped fix one of the time travel problems and now things at work were going to get very exciting. More trips would be scheduled and more diseases would be cured. The future was looking very promising.

Temporal Transporter Travel Rules and Processes v 2.0
–BIOTIME LABS – **revised**

1. The Temporal Transporter, or TT, can only be used to go back in time, for time regression.
2. The lab set all the target dates to pre-2000. This will ensure that travelers will not have contact with themselves. There is no need to use any target dates after the year 2000 to meet their goals.
3. Time travel process –
   a. Time and space are carefully calculated to ensure the traveler arrives to a good location in the past.
   b. The TT pushes travelers to the past and pulls them back to the present. It is the main driver.
   c. The transport markers help with the return. The transport marker provides additional energy and also encapsulates the traveler for safety during transport.
   d. Once the transport marker is set in a location and time, it can be used immediately to transport the traveler back to the lab.
   e. If further regression is required, the time setter returns to the marker, retrieves it and goes back another year from there. This can be done as many times as needed.
   f. Transport markers are not set in every year. They are currently limited in number and their reuse allows further time regression.
   g. Initially transport markers are moved back one year each day. (See Notes). Regressions of a year in one day have been confirmed to have no ill effects on the time traveler.
   h. To return to 2066 and the lab, you must be in physical contact with the transport marker. Two people can travel together. **As many as three people can make the trip back together, as long as their combined weight is less than 600 pounds.**
4. Influencing the present with actions while in the past is illegal. The Time Travel Committee will determine the

gravity of the infraction and the appropriate punishment will be applied.

5. Keep contact with the locals to a minimum. The lab will check the people's lifeline to see if any changes have occurred once the traveler has contact with them. Not knowing whom you will encounter ahead of time, the first meeting might have some influence, but from then on it is monitored.

6. Lifelines are the plot of a person's life and can only be plotted for the past.

7. Hours in the past match the hours in the present.
   a. If the location is the same, i.e. Pacific Time for both the lab and the travelers, the time of day is the same.
   b. This lab will also match the day of the week to simplify things, especially in communicating with one another.

8. The transport marker provides a transport radius of 800 kilometers. Arrival location can be anywhere within that radius. Since local transportation can be an issue, it may be necessary to place several transport markers in the same target year, but at different locations. Placing each of these markers is considered a travel setting trip.

9. The transport marker should be moved from a location after a certain number of uses (to be determined on a case by case basis).

10. All time ~~travel setters~~ **travelers** will have a location chip implanted subdermally to help in locating them if lost or injured.

Notes: The calculations take almost a day to complete, but larger regressions are being considered. Currently regressions of three years in one day are the norm and up to five year regressions are being considered. **Three-year regressions have caused accumulation of chemicals, which are damaging to the brain.**

www.ingramcontent.com/pod-product-compliance
Lightning Source LLC
Chambersburg PA
CBHW030014180626
46810CB00001B/27